D0625599

About *Y Fro Dywyll*, the Welsh-language original version of this novel:

A powerful, alarming and very timely novel.

William Owen Roberts

Jerry Hunter is a boundary tester par excellence... a well-researched and accomplished novel with a strong narrative which delivers on many levels.

Mair Rees, *Planet* magazine

A good historical novel also asks questions about today, and this novel definitely does that. The story of Rhisiart Dafydd will linger in the memory – his physical and his spiritual journeys, and the sadness that history insists on repeating itself.

Janet Roberts, Gwales

The work of a master. Jerry Hunter has created nothing less than a classic.

Jon Gower, *Barn* magazine

DARK TERRITORY

Jerry Hunter

TRANSLATED BY
PATRICK K FORD

For my brother, David C Hunter

First impression: 2017

Cover design: Sion Ilar
Cover photo: iStockphoto / Mimadeo

ISBN: 978 1 78461 455 3

The publishers wish to acknowledge the support of Cyngor Llyfrau Cymru

Published and printed in Wales
on paper from well-maintained forests by
Y Lolfa Cyf., Talybont, Ceredigion SY24 5HE
e-mail ylolfa@ylolfa.com
website www.ylolfa.com
tel 01970 832 304
fax 832 782

Preface

With this translation, Jerry Hunter's masterful novel *Y Fro Dywyll* can now be shared with a wider readership. The devastating horror of the English Civil Wars and the attendant sectarian violence are carefully and passionately described here. But there is much, much more: the play of light and dark in the life of Rhisiart Dafydd, the protagonist, is evident from page 1, coloring the love and affection he bears the women in his life. The story moved me deeply from the very first read and it's safe to say that this translation was indeed a labor of love.

I am grateful to Y Lolfa and the Welsh Books Council for their support of this work.

Patrick K Ford
October 2017

About the translator

Patrick K Ford was born in Lansing, Michigan, USA. He received his doctorate from Harvard in 1969, teaching at Stanford and the University of California, Los Angeles before returning to Harvard in 1991, where he is the Margaret Brooks Robinson Professor Emeritus of Celtic Languages and Literatures. He is also an honorary Research Fellow in the Centre for Advanced Welsh and Celtic Studies at the University of Wales. His publications include an acclaimed translation of the Mabinogi, *The Mabinogi and Other Medieval Welsh Tales* (never out of print since its publication in 1977), and other translations can be found in *The Penguin Book of Irish Poetry*.

His passion for Welsh literature and his long friendship with Jerry Hunter meant that Professor Ford felt passionately that this powerful novel should be brought to a wider audience.

About the author

Jerry Hunter was born in Cincinnati, Ohio, USA. He has had a distinguished academic career, and is now a Professor of Welsh and Pro Vice-Chancellor at Bangor University in Wales. He learnt Welsh as an adult and is an enthusiastic advocate of the language and its literature. He has published five academic works and four novels for adults, the latter all in Welsh, as well as some children's fiction. He was the recipient of the extremely prestigious Arts Council of Wales Book of the Year Award in 2004 and the 2010 National Eisteddfod Prose Medal. *Dark Territory* is his first novel for adults to be translated into English.

Fe roes i ti gannwyll ynot i ddangos y ffordd.
Yn gyntaf, gwrando ar dy gydwybod oddi fewn.
Pa beth y mae hi yn ei geisio ddwedyd wrthyt?
Pwy bynnag wyt, mae cloch yn canu o'r tu fewn i ti.
Oni wrandewi ar y llais sydd ynot dy hunan, pa fodd y gwrandewi di ar gynghorion oddi allan?

He placed a candle within you to show the way.
First of all, listen to your conscience inside.
What is it trying to say to you?
Whoever you are, a bell is ringing inside you.
If you will not listen to the voice which is inside of yourself, how will you listen to external counsel?

Morgan Llwyd,
Gwaedd yng Nghymru yn Wyneb Pob Cydwybod

There was nothing either above or below him... He had kicked himself loose of the earth.

Joseph Conrad, *Heart of Darkness.*

I
Reaching the Shore

Deffro, deffro, deffro, a rhodia fel plentyn y dydd.

Awake, awake, awake, and walk as a child of the day.

Morgan Llwyd

—I—

The water is cold, the waves are huge, and the night is dark.

But he can swim.

Cold water. It sucks the heat from his body, threatening to suck life itself from him.

Huge waves. They're smashing down on him, violently. He knows that there are jagged rocks close at hand, stony blades ready to carve up his body. His heart leaps into his mouth every time a wave tosses him, awaiting the impact, awaiting the power of the blow that will tear the life out of him.

The dark. It's a moonless night, clouds hiding the stars. As he struggles in the grip of the waves, the water blurring his vision, the place where the black of the air and the dark of the water meet is unclear and always changing. He could dive beneath the waves on purpose and swim under the water when the sea surges. It would be a way of lessening its ability to toss him about like a toy at the mercy of the elements. But he doesn't want to go down into that black water again of his own free will.

He had plunged deep when he jumped from the side of the foundering ship. He hit no rocks but leapt into a peril of a different sort – his body going down and down. The water black, and the combination of disorientation and dizziness confounded him, making it difficult to see which way was up and which way down. All of it black and cold, as if he had vanished into a pool of oblivion. This is the portal of hell, he thought. Not a hot, fiery pit, but a cold, dark hole, sucking you down and down, away from the land and the realm of the living.

But up he came, in the end, like a human cork.

And he can swim.

He's lashing out, kicking, striking out with all his might. He knows that the waves are rushing to the shore, and so he too is moving in that direction. He's trying to speed between waves, hoping to reach the rocks and cling to them before the waves toss him onto them and grind him into tiny chunks of flesh. He's pulling through the water with his arms, kicking with his legs, thrusting with his entire body. Swimming. Moving towards the shore he cannot see.

–ΔΩ–

Let us move to the past. Not too far, only a couple of months. We begin at the end of summer, 1656. We begin in London.

Busy, noisy, filthy streets.

A myriad of sounds reach his ears. Merchants crying out to potential buyers, occasionally a customer crying out to be served. Drivers shouting to clear the road in front of their coaches, the whinnying of their horses drowning out human voices at times. Acquaintances greeting one another, friends calling out to each other across a street or square. Sometimes an argument, angry voices contending with one another about a deal, or religion, or politics, or a command to clear the way. A preacher chanting a psalm or verse, trying to gather a flock from the crowd that pushes on past him. Children laughing. Dogs barking.

A medley of smells too, but the unhealthy ones are stronger by far and overpower the others. The bitter fumes from the tanning house chimneys had lessened since he crossed the river, but there are still plenty of wretched odours here. The stench of animal and human excrement is the most prominent element in the entire mix. Smoke assails his nostrils now and then, billowing out of a house or tavern or smithy – something to be grateful for since it masks the other smells for a while.

And the bustle. It is at its worst on the bridge. Rhisiart has come up from the south through Southwark and on across the bridge – the most congested, laborious and slow to travel of all the streets. He thinks of it as one whole small city uprooted by some crazed giant and pressed into a row along the sides of the bridge: dwellings and shops and workhouses squashed into tall buildings, sometimes containing as many as seven floors, leaning boldly over the river on one side and shadowing the narrow street on the bridge on the other, looming over the swarms of people that filled it. Travellers seeking to cross on foot or on horseback or in coaches, merchants doing business, the poor seeking alms – a microcosm of London's population squeezed into this confined route. He has to dismount and lead his horse through the crowd. It takes him nearly an hour to elbow his way through this mass of humanity to the other side of the bridge.

Although he is in a hurry, Rhisiart pauses in front of the gatehouse on the south side before stepping through the gate and starting to cross. He pauses and looks up, surveying the heads rotting away on pikes. *Memento mori*. Remember that death is near. He had destroyed engravings of the sort in English churches during the wars, skeletal shapes on tombs carved in olden times to remind the viewer that death lurks beneath the living flesh. A reminder of the end that will come to everyone of every sect and religion, but which seemed too much like papist images to the soldiers who believed they were doing God's work, purifying the churches and cleansing the land.

Of course, the motive behind these sobering signs is different: remember that this is the end to be expected by traitors. But Rhisiart sees every head on a pike as a perfect *memento mori*, better than any carved in marble that he has ever seen. The skull gradually appearing from under the rotting flesh, mouth twisted ugly, lips torn to ribbons by birds, some without lips at all. All of them without eyes, the first delicacies to go to the beaks of the gulls and ravens that croak and hop and half-fly from head to head, fighting for that last little bit of flesh.

He has seen their like many times before. His own hands have been instrumental in producing a number of them. On the battlefields at Edgehill, Newbury, and Naseby. And he has seen the heads adorning the pikes of this gatehouse before. He and his friends used to try to identify them. That must be Lord Burnet over there, with the raven boring into his nose. And there's James Parker, I swear: easy to recognize his face – only the day before yesterday that his head was cut off, and there's plenty of it left to see. This time the death tokens stay with him as he makes his way through the crowd on his difficult passage across the bridge. A face catches his eye for a moment as some other traveller pushes past him or some merchant tries to get his attention and he sees the *memento mori* there before his eyes. Take care, brother: death is at hand. Buying and selling worldly things is not important, sister – your death is upon you. The skull presses close behind the face of every one of us. That's what you will be tomorrow, or the day after, or the day after that, sooner or later. A bunch of corpses, an assembly of skulls.

But he has crossed the bridge now, and although the streets are still busy, he's able to move faster. He hasn't remounted yet. He pushed his horse hard on the way up from Southampton, and he wants to give the animal a chance to recover. He's walking as swiftly as possible, leading his horse, not slowing to look at anything or anybody. All the wonders, all the wealth, all the wretched humanity woven together on the streets of London. He's not lost the way, knows precisely which streets to follow to his destination, though a few corners or squares have changed a bit since the last time he was here. Here and there a building has been torn down and a new one put up in its place, but the pattern of the streets has not changed. The feel of the place hasn't changed either.

Since the last time. Nine years ago. 1647. The year of the Little Plague. That's what some call it. It claimed just under 4,000 people in London that year. More had died in other places at other times, and sometimes very many more, and so some called it the Little Plague. But he can't think of it that way. It took too much from him, took too much out of him. So he has avoided setting foot in the city ever since. Nine years. Has used every influence he has to deflect any orders that would take him to London, reminded those above him of debts and favours they owe him, reminded them of what he knows and what he's done and chosen not to do for their sake. Everything, anything, to make sure that he would not have to visit the city again. But now here he is, returning of his own free will after receiving the letter from Colonel Powel.

He leads his horse along Cheapside, past the stalls of meat merchants. The morning is slowly yielding to afternoon and it's beginning to turn hot. Swarms of flies are everywhere, rising up from one stall and alighting on another, and the smell is assaulting his nose. It's that smell which announces blood drying and flesh rotting in the heat of the sun. He can hear the insects sometimes, despite all the noise – the voices of buyers and sellers, live chickens clucking, the clamour of carts clicking across stones or sloshing through mud and muck, and then the gluttonous buzz of the flies every now and then rising in a crescendo of buzzing. The path opens out a bit and Rhisiart moves faster, his horse following close behind. Onward, past the site of the Cross.

He was here that day. Witnessed the last moments of the Great Cross, the end of the Cheapside Cross. There were plenty of foot soldiers and cavalry there to keep the crowd away from the workmen, but Colonel Powel himself had ordered them to go as well. In case. One of the foot soldiers told him that he had been there the winter before by order of Parliament, guarding the

Cross from violent townspeople who wanted to pull it down. But Parliament had changed its mind by spring, and now that same soldier was stationed there as part of a troop making certain that the Cross was destroyed. A memorial some ten yards tall, a great mass of stone and lead presiding over the bustle of the street, all of it colourfully decorated. Images of saints and angels. A large, beautiful cross its crowning glory. The centrepiece of Cheapside life for centuries. A dozen workers had been labouring for hours, cutting into it with hammer and chisel, rending it with crowbars. Some began the assault on ladders, chipping away at the engravings on the topmost part. The face of an angel, its eyes gazing upward, pointing the beholder towards the mysteries of Heaven. The face of a saint, eyes looking down upon the crowd, urging the people to pray with him. Each one losing a nose, a chin, a mouth, ears. The hammer depriving the saints of their accoutrements, a blow of the chisel clipping the wings of angels. Bits of stone, plaster and lead falling to the ground beneath the ladders. The crowd responding, some showing their approval with shouts of joy, others abusing the workmen and the soldiers who protected them. A rope was tied to the cross itself and it was pulled down from the top of the memorial, the roar of the crowd surging as it fell to the ground. Shouting, screaming, clapping, swearing. Singing psalms. Uttering curses. Acceptance and protest mixed together. One of the soldiers began to beat a drum, another raised a trumpet, the clear, metallic notes breaking through it all. The workers set to completely destroying it, the column of the Cheapside Cross descending in pieces, stone by stone, panel by panel, angel by angel, saint by saint.

May, 1643. He was eighteen and had been a soldier for a year or so. He had been in Reading with the Earl of Essex's army that year, a fever decimating the ranks, killing more of them than the King's guns. Camp fever. Rows of the dead laid out, turning the encampment into a nightmarish vision, as if they were practising for Doomsday. Rows of them, ready to be rushed into a hasty mass burial. Like with the plague in London four years later.

He tries to push that plague out of his mind, the Little Plague that took such a big chunk out of his life. He tries to remember as much as possible about 1643, makes his mind dwell on that year, trying to relive it. He was eighteen and had been in Reading, witness to the devastation of the fever in the Earl of Essex's army. And in London with the others, summoned by Colonel Powel, making good the will of Parliament. Like that day at the beginning of May, keeping the crowd back and letting the workers bring down the Cheapside Cross. And again, a week or so later, at the site of the old Cross. Nothing left now but a mound of rubble, the most colourful pieces having been taken. A piece of the face of a saint seized by someone who held to the old faith, to be hidden in a church or home. The nose of an angel taken by someone who adhered to the new mode of worship, a memento of the victory over the papist remnants of the old pagan times. The lead was taken on the very day of the destruction of the Cross, seized by soldiers before they left the scene and carted off to one of the armouries in the city to be melted down and turned into bullets. The Army of the Saints at work: turning crosses into weapons of war. And so nothing but a mound of rubble was left when he returned to the site. Debris and stone, devoid of meaning. The devastation of war. Aftermath of a siege. Like the walls of Wexford and the ramparts of Drogheda. Some weeks later, Colonel Powel asked them to come back to that same site once again, this time to keep the crowds back from the fire. They were burning *The Book of Sports*, proclaiming that the Sabbath was the day of the Lord alone, announcing that the old pastimes were no longer to disrupt Sunday prayers. The roar of the crowd swelled with the flames. Acceptance. Protest. Shouts of joy, curses called out. Some singing psalms. Others crying out verses: remember the Sabbath day, keep it holy. The flames rising higher, paper burning, and the smoke carried off into the wind.

Rhisiart Dafydd walks past the site. There's nothing left to show what happened here, not a bit of the cross left. It's like every other spot in this part of the lane, but Rhisiart knows exactly where it is. There's a small cart there right now, full of empty baskets – their contents already sold – its owner standing in front of the horse, having paused to talk with some acquaintance. Rhisiart continues on, leading his own horse, heedless of the racket around him. Shouting, calling out, laughing, barking. Onward through that mass, that noisy, stinking press of humanity.

He has left Cheapside and is walking up a narrow street. It's not half as busy and he is able to move along unhindered. Although he cannot see the brewery, he can smell it; the familiar sourness irritating his nose and giving his stomach a turn. And then he comes to the gate. There, on the right, in the middle of the biggest building on the street, the only building with an open gate rather than a small wooden door. He leads his horse through the gate and the short passageway to the courtyard. The tidy cobbles are different from the uneven, muddy and muck-spattered street outside, and his horse's hooves make a pleasing sound on them. This brings a young stable boy out of a small door in the far wall, the lad running towards him, shielding his eyes from the sun and reaching out to take the reins.

He suddenly realizes that a soldier is standing beside him. He has been there the whole time, no doubt, but Rhisiart only notices him after his horse has been led away. He's a young man, with a smooth face, in the uniform of a dragoon or cavalryman. A large coat of buff leather dyed yellow, tight around the waist with two belts, one of heavy leather with a sword hanging from it, and higher up a wide red cloth sash holding two long pistols. No armour, no helmet, only a simple woollen hat, the same colour as the sash. Exactly like Rhisiart himself, except that he has put his pistols in a bag behind his saddle and is wearing a large black hat with a wide brim. The two soldiers recognize one another as belonging to the same brotherhood, though they have never met before. Each knows that the other is in the service of Colonel Powel. In the service of Parliament and its government, but answering first and last to Colonel Powel.

Rhisiart puts his right hand into his coat, pulls out the letter and shows it to the young guard. His left hand rests on the hilt of his sword, fingering it lightly. He studies the young soldier as the other examines the letter he's holding. How old is he? Eighteen? Twenty? Has he cut flesh with that sword? Hardly. Has he shot at a man with his pistols? Not likely. Unless he has been in the Low Countries. Has he seen bodies on the battlefield, has he looked upon a *memento mori* of his own making, looked upon the eyes of the dead before the crows came and plucked them out? Hardly, unless he has served on the continent. Lucky him. One of the soldiers of peacetime.

The lad gives the letter back to him, then turns on his heel and leads him to one of the small doors along the interior walls of the courtyard. He says something as he opens the door, some courtesy or other, though Rhisiart doesn't catch it. Rhisiart removes his hat as he crosses the threshold and begins to climb the steps, his heavy footfall striking the dark wood, the echo loud in his ears.

It's quiet inside, yet not as quiet as he has been expecting. Some low voices can be heard coming from the other end of the building through partition and wall, occasionally one louder than the others. Someone laughing somewhere, even, surprisingly raucously, and another voice joining in the hilarity, all within earshot of Rhisiart, though the dark wooden panels of the walls dull the sounds somewhat. It's surprising, and the unexpected sounds sharpen his senses, refreshing him and reawakening him from the weariness that has overtaken him after the long journey.

He has not been in this part of the building before – only in the rooms beside the stable at the back, between the courtyard and the back of the big brewery that faces the next street – and he imagined that it would be different somehow. He expected that everything would be quiet inside. He imagined that silence would roll down the corridors like mist on the surface of a river, that quiet would collect in the chambers like water gathers in a fountain's pool, turning sound to vapour and dulling the ear, keeping secrets secret. For that is what is dealt with and discussed in those chambers. Secrets. And the master of the secrets is Colonel Powel.

–ΔΩ–

He swims as fast as possible between the waves, trying to reach some sort of refuge. Wave after wave comes, fiercely regular, tossing him on as helplessly as if he were a rag doll. Every time he feels the power of the water surging behind him he holds his breath, his heart in his throat, half-expecting this to be his last moment on this earth. Ending his time on earth in the sea, a body bruised from the sharp rocks, slipping back into the water – a bit of dead flesh, a toy for the waves to play with, until he sinks and becomes food for fishes and the creatures of the deep.

But he doesn't hit the rocks and he doesn't surrender to the cold water. The dark of the night, the chill of the water, the cruel waves are all against him, but there is still strength in his legs and his arms. He swims on, striving to reach the land he cannot see. He thrusts with his entire body, striking out with his arms, kicking with his feet. Moving. A huge wave comes, one that feels much larger than the others, and it lifts him up and tosses him right out of the water, hurling him on to the dark of destruction.

He hits hard, the force of the impact knocking the wind out of him and delivering a hard blow to his jaw. But he's alive. It's not the sharp rocks that are beneath him but small round stones. Shingle.

A beach.

The shore.

America.

—2—

He's moving slowly. At times he has to crawl on his belly, but at other times he crawls on all fours across the shingle. Moving is important, up the beach away from the sea. Every joint and every muscle in his body aches and there are some other, sharper pains, but he's not stopping. He can hear the waves pounding the shore behind him – the roar, the groan, and then the crash of the water hitting the shingle. Tiny stones hurtling down the beach in the wake of the crashing wave, and then, in a matter of seconds, it all begins again. Roar, groan, crash and a rush of stones. Wave upon wave striking the shore, searching him out with their watery claws. He doesn't know whether the sea is ebbing or hasn't yet reached high tide, and he is fearful. Afraid of pausing, afraid of resting, afraid of passing out, lest the waves move nearer, follow him up the beach and drag him back to the sea. He lifts his head and tries to see some sort of shelter in the darkness around him, but the beach is on an incline. A small steep slope running up from the sea to whatever is on the other side of the shore, and all he can see is the slope itself, that patch of unwelcoming land. And so he creeps along with his head down, like a yoked horse straining hard in his harness, gravel slipping and rushing down, frustrating his attempts to crawl forward and escape the grasp of the waves. His body shakes the whole time, from the effort and the cold. He's wet and cold and every time he lifts a hand to move, the effort feels too much for him, every yard of the slope a mountain to be climbed. The shingle moves beneath him continually, and every now and then becomes a miniature landslide, a torrent of tiny stones pouring down the slope in the direction of the waves and dragging him down with the flow. He climbs back each time, head down, crawling, pulling with his hands, kicking with his legs as if he were still swimming in the sea. Pain in every joint in his body, every muscle aching. Doing all he can to move forward.

–ΔΩ–

The room is large and relatively bright. There are two windows in the far wall, rows of small panes of glass in a web of lines of lead, the sunshine that reaches the narrow street outside streaming into the room. The large candlestick in the middle of the table helps too, eight candles burning in it, throwing their light on the maps and the mountain of papers that take up most of the big table. There are six chairs around the table, but only two are currently occupied. Rhisiart sits at attention in one, his left hand on the hilt of his sword and his right hand holding his hat on his knee. Colonel Powel leans forward, his hands folded under his chin and his elbows on the table. His dress is simple – plain black, suggesting a preacher or a lawyer. He wears no sword and has no other weapon. He dressed differently in the old days when he was leading soldiers on the field, but since taking charge of these offices in London he has changed his manner. Someone who does not draw attention to himself when he walks down the street, who moves quietly in the shadows. But his face is the same – broad, a moustache and a sliver of beard: a short, thin line in the middle of his chin, white like the hair on his head. His eyes shine in the candlelight, studying Rhisiart across the table, the air charged with that feeling which attends occasions like this. Two men who know each other well but haven't met face-to-face for a long while.

'The years have changed you, Rhisiart. Where has that young lad gone, tell me? His face smooth and his hair short around his ears?'

Rhisiart smiles slightly but says nothing. He has let his hair go its own way since he returned from Ireland seven years ago, the tidy Roundhead turning into a wild animal, a long mane of thick brown hair falling to his shoulders. He has not grown a beard as such, but he doesn't shave regularly either, and today there is a week's worth of growth on his long face, the stubble mottled with white, complementing the wrinkles around his eyes and making him look older than he is. Thirty-one, and a soldier for fourteen of those years. Years of the sort that change a man.

'I know you, Rhisiart.'

Rhisiart sits at attention and remains silent.

'Do you remember the first time we spoke, Rhisiart?'

Silence.

'I remember it well. Thirteen years ago, but I remember it as if it happened last week. But you have changed so much. I'm sitting here, you see, feeling that I'm having the same conversation with the same man, and that nothing has changed during those thirteen years, but…' He raises his hands, fingers extended, palms towards Rhisiart as if saying 'Look, my hands are empty'. 'But…' He moves his hands so as to frame Rhisiart's face. 'But yet it's not the same man who sits here with me. Do you remember that conversation, Rhisiart?'

'I do, sir.'

'When you first came to me, from Reading?'

'Of course, sir – that was when I joined your regiment.'

'Yes, yes – but do you remember the subject of our conversation?'

'I do, sir. Many things. A bit of my history. You wanted to confirm what you had heard. But before that… the preaching of Isaac Huws. And we spoke about the Earl of Essex as well.'

'That's right, Rhisiart. Robert Devereux, the Earl of Essex, has been in his tomb for upwards of ten years.' He was moving his fingers now, striking imaginary strings, creating a melody that no one but he could hear, accompanying his own story. 'And that tomb is in Westminster Abbey. I was there at the funeral. Ten years ago. He died following an accident that occurred while he was out hunting deer. Amazing, isn't it, when you remember that banner that some of the King's men followed during the first war. Do you remember it? A large green banner with a stag's head and the words *Cuckolds Here We Come*? To make fun of the Earl of Essex?'

He puts his hands back on the table. Smiles. 'There we are, my boy. I never succeeded in dragging a bad word about Robert Devereux from your lips. You haven't changed in that respect.' He smiles, moves his chair slightly before speaking again. 'Burial in Westminster Abbey, the most important men in Parliament paying homage to him. But what happened a few months later? Hmm? Some of our own soldiers destroyed the carving on his tomb. The grandees of the Army of the Saints extol the dead man, and the common soldiers – the common saints – dishonour him.'

Although Rhisiart has not had chance to see the Earl's tomb either before or after being defaced by the 'common saints', he can easily imagine it, having witnessed the destruction of many images. Chisel and hammer at work. Chunks of stone and plaster falling. Dust rising. Someone holding up the nose of the departed, and the crowd baying shouts of approval.

'I'll say one thing, sir. Those soldiers must not have stood with the Earl at Edgehill. I'll say something else too. Not one of us is a saint.'

'To be sure, Rhisiart, to be sure. But don't misunderstand me. I'm not joking. My point is this: it doesn't matter what we think about that part of our past, it's gone. Essex has been in his grave for years. And the wars are over. But what about Isaac Huws? Do you remember his sermon?'

'I do, sir. Revelations. The four horses.'

'A common enough text, isn't it? Every travelling preacher and chaplain was preaching on it at the time.'

'But Isaac Huws was the preacher with us in Reading, sir.'

'Yes, yes. It was he who gave your name to me, Rhisiart. I remember that too.' He leans on the table, pushing his chair back a little, the wood squeaking. He stands. '"And I saw, and behold a white horse: and he that sat on him had a bow; and a crown was given unto him."' He pauses for a moment, straightening his back. '"And he went forth conquering, and to conquer... And there went out another horse that was red: and power was given to him that sat thereon to take peace from the earth, and that they should kill one another: and there was given unto him a great sword."' He pauses again, his eyes on Rhisiart. '"And lo a black horse; and he that sat on him had a pair of balances in his hand."'

The Colonel pauses again, and it's Rhisiart who speaks this time, his eyes on the table, avoiding the other man's gaze.

'"And I looked, and behold a pale horse: and his name that sat on him was Death, and Hell followed with him."' He raises his eyes to meet those of Colonel Powel. 'That was the main theme of Isaac Huws' sermon in Reading. Because the Earl of Essex's army was in the grip of disease at the time. Camp fever. Death was on a wild rampage through our ranks.'

'There you are, Rhisiart, exactly. The pale horse is the plague. The red horse is warfare. We have heard plenty of sermons from the chaplains on that subject, God knows. And after that, the black horse is famine, which follows war every time. And the fourth one, the white horse?'

'Conquest.' Rhisiart continues to look John Powel in the eye, even though tears are welling in his own eyes. Weariness, he tells himself. His eyes itch, they ache. Weariness. But he doesn't move a muscle to dry them.

'That's right. Conquest. That was difficult to explain before the war came to an end. In my opinion, that is. It didn't make sense. I heard Morgan Llwyd preaching on that text in Bristol in the early days. A wonderful sermon. But he said something about the white horse that no one could understand, you see. Awfully complex. I saw him some years after that and indeed, I asked him to go over that old sermon and explain it to me, but he refused. He said he was sorry, but he refused. He said that he had never preached on the subject of the four horses since that time in Bristol. Wise man. Knows his own limits.' He sat back down, his chair creaking under his weight. 'I can't remember what Morgan Llwyd said about the white horse. I remember words well usually, but for the life of me I can't remember that sermon. It was too complicated, too obscure. But I do remember what you said to me about Isaac Huws' sermon when you came to me from Reading thirteen years ago.'

Rhisiart moves now, shifting his weight on the chair slightly, and with his left hand quickly wipes the tears from his eyes, shakes his head for a moment and puts his hand on the table in front of him.

'Isaac Huws said that conquest precedes war, famine and plague because it… because it was the conquest of the ages. This great and wondrous turn of the world that had transformed everything. The conquest of the times, the fact that this amazing age had come at last. That is what set the other horses free to run roughshod over the land.'

'This wondrous turn of the world. Not the conquest, victory, which comes on the day of the battle, but a higher conquest, one that compels the other horses to run free and restore the old order.'

'Yes, sir. That's it. That's what he said. You remember well.'

'Yes, Rhisiart. Sometimes. Some words are easy to remember.'

The colonel turns towards the windows, staring at something. Rhisiart thinks that he is looking through the glass, as if he were studying something he sees off in the distance. Not the dust that is floating in the pale light, not the bricks and wood of the building opposite that's pressing too close to the windows across the narrow street outside, but distant vistas. Beauty. Mountains. The sea. Green meadows. Rhisiart remains silent. He's waiting, respecting the silence that the older man is claiming for himself. Nothing is moving in the room except the dust in the air and the shadows the candles are throwing on the table. Then Colonel Powel turns to him.

'I'm going to tell you something, Rhisiart. Something I've not told to anyone. Something I don't even admit to myself very often. But it is possible that we will not meet again on this earth, and I want to say this to you.' He's not looking at Rhisiart, but has turned his eyes to the windows again.

'I do not believe in many of the things I believed in at the time of the wars. I can't...' He laughs softly, sadly. 'All those lovely words. I don't believe most of them now. I don't.' He takes a step towards the window, but he turns slightly, quickly, looks at Rhisiart out of the corner of his eye. 'And I think that you are like me in that respect.'

He turns away again. Slowly, he takes a step or two, three, and stands beside one of the windows, his hands folded behind his back. Although he can't see his eyes, Rhisiart is certain that they are fixed on that distant scene again. He can see John Powel moving the thumb of his right hand. His two hands are folded tightly together in an attempt to keep them still, but that one thumb has broken free and wants to escape, a lone indicator of the nervous energy inside his body.

'It's a bold thing I have to say, but I believe I know your heart, Rhisiart. And I believe you've lost more than me. That's why I've let you stay away for so long. It has been a dilemma, you see:

what to do with a man like you these days. But I have an idea now.'

Rhisiart moves his chair to get a better look at the back of the man. He can't help himself. He would prefer to stay just as he was, calm, attentive, and appearing dutiful. But he can't help himself. He has to understand all of it, every aspect of this extraordinary moment, though there's nothing to see apart from the Colonel's twitchy thumb, its tiny movements betraying a body that is otherwise completely calm.

'But before I ask you, Rhisiart, I want to tell you this. Something I've never said to anyone else. I don't believe all those things now. I don't. But I continue to believe one thing.'

He turns quickly, his eyes finding Rhisiart's and fixing upon them, the light coming in through the window behind him igniting his white hair somehow, making it glow.

'The conquest of the times, Rhisiart. I continue to believe in that. It's not what all the preachers say it is. It came not with the war nor with the death of the King. I don't believe it has come here, to England and Wales, even. In that, all the scholars are mistaken. But I believe in it, Rhisiart. I believe in that conquest. I believe that we have to do all we can to help it come.'

He walks back to the table, his hands still hidden behind his back. 'And you have to believe in it too, Rhisiart. You don't, but you have to. I know you, you see. Know your heart. If you don't believe in the great conquest, then you have to admit that everything you have done has been done in vain.' He lifts his hands and holds them, folded, in front of his chest, as if in prayer. 'You have to believe in it or everything you have done will be meaningless.' He moves his hands up to his chin, holding something deliberate inside of them. 'I know you, you see. You have to find a way of doing something significant or you will have lost it all.' He opens his hands suddenly, tossing that unseen thing from him, his palms open, hands empty. 'Otherwise, my boy, you have nothing at all.' He sits down again, leaning on the table, his head angled to look Rhisiart in the eye around the candlestick. 'Otherwise, my boy, you have nothing at all.'

He waits for an answer, but Rhisiart remains silent.

'But the great conquest doesn't come in the form of a white horse. The two of us know that. It doesn't carry a bow or wear a crown. It comes in an entirely different way. Bit by bit. By continued small pushes. And I'm asking you to help it, Rhisiart. Help give it a small push in the right place.'

–ΔΩ–

He moves slowly up the slope, crawling across the shingle. The tiny stones shifting under his hands and legs, but he doesn't slip this time. He crawls on through the darkness of the night, the roar of the waves behind him, though the sound is not as loud in his ears now. His body seized by shaking, every joint, every muscle aching, and some sharper pains in one ankle and his side. But he doesn't yield to his weariness. He moves on, crawling up and up.

And then he feels something soft under his hands. Grass of some sort. And he sees that he has reached the brow of the small hill: the end of the slope up the beach. He falls to his belly and grips the wet growth with his hands, dragging his body up to the level ground. He is lying on a carpet of soft grass. And there he stays. Exhausted.

–3–

He awakens from his stupor, reviving slightly, but cold and wet, shivering. Bruises everywhere, every part of him hurting, some more than others. He trembles. He has turned onto his back somehow, though he doesn't remember doing that, and when he opens his eyes he finds himself staring at the sky. He sees that a hole has been ripped in the layer of clouds that had been darkening the night so completely, and that a number of stars can be seen. Only five or six of them, but those tiny bright points comfort him. It's not raining now either, and there's comfort in that too.

But it is so cold, his wet clothes are sticking to him uncomfortably, and the trembling shakes him. He knows that he has to move, knows that he ought to search for shelter and warmth. He tries to rise, but he's too weak and in too much pain. He's not able to rise enough even to sit up. He falls back onto the wet grass, staring at the sky. That little cluster of stars wink at him. The opening in the clouds has widened and the stars are multiplying. Mustering in the sky and driving off the dark of the night.

–ΔΩ–

Colonel Powel leans forward, his elbows on the table, his fingers folded together into a big fist on which he rests his chin. He lifts a finger to stroke his small, thin strip of white beard. Reflections from the candles dance in his eyes.

'And that's how it is, Rhisiart. They are things I don't say, but I feel that you have a right to hear it all.'

It's difficult to see by now. It's dark outside, so the only light comes from the candles on the table. The colonel got up once to change them – by himself, not summoning a servant who could do the job more skilfully for him. No one disturbed them, the two men secluded in this room, the one talking and the other listening as afternoon gave way to evening.

He has been explaining a great deal, explaining the nature of his activities in recent years. Rhisiart knew that the old officer was working for Cromwell, moving in the shadows and doing things quietly. Identifying traitors, listening out for plots, guarding against dangers of which most of them were not even aware. Working in a way that could not be discussed openly.

Although many secrets have just been revealed to Rhisiart, he is not surprised. He knew in a general way the nature of the Colonel's work, though he did not know the details. Until today. He knew that he himself had been serving two masters for years, John Powel and Oliver Cromwell, but he didn't know the nature of the relationship between those two. A relationship that, according to what he has just heard, has changed recently.

'There we are, Rhisiart. I am walking my own path now. He doesn't know that. Only a handful of people know that, and you are one of them now. But I have to work in my own way without him knowing. I don't see a future here, not anymore.

'In fact, it is really he who is walking a different path. And it's not a path that leads to that great conquest, Rhisiart. Nothing but perdition is at the end of the road he is following now. All hopes have been shattered – that's the plain truth. And so I have to do some things myself, you see. For the sake of those who will come after. They are the ones who will enjoy the fruits of the great conquest, Rhisiart, if we can help to win those fruits for them.'

'I don't fully understand, sir. I'll need to be enlightened with respect to some things.'

'I know, Rhisiart, I know. Be patient, enlightenment is on the way, or as much light as I can shed on things.'

And then he describes the path he's been on since he lost faith in Cromwell, coming back again and again to the same short phrase: give a little push.

'Give a little push every now and then. That's what I do, you see. Give a little push to those that deserve it. Those who can help prepare the way for better days. Those whom I believe I ought to help.'

'How do you know which ones to help, sir?'

'I don't, not every time. And I've made plenty of mistakes in the past. But I always learn from my mistakes. And sometimes I have to undo something I have done. Help thwart those who have had a little push in the past but who are now standing in the way… thwarting those who better deserve the help today.'

'Colonel, with all respect, I don't understand you. You are speaking in riddles.'

John Powel laughs. 'Let me continue, Rhisiart, and make it as clear as I can, as clear as the light of day.' He slaps the table with one hand, not too hard, but hard enough to topple the nearest pile of papers. 'The new age is not dawning, Rhisiart. You know that. Not one of us believes all that passionate preaching of recent years. The hopes of the Ranters and the Levellers. Those who claim that the Fifth Kingdom has come. All the other hotheaded seekers who have said that the new age is about to dawn. It's not. Not today. Not tomorrow. Jesus Christ is not coming to rule over the end of time.'

Rhisiart could open his mouth and say that Colonel Powel is right, confess that he doesn't believe all the prophecies and foretellings, say that he has come to scorn those men who prophesy. All the mystical, symbolic words one hears in the camps, almost as frequently as one hears the commands of the officers, as if guidance about the Last Things is as good an education for a soldier as military instruction.

Stand to arms!

Behold the trumpet of the millennia sounding!

Brace to receive!

The great day of the Lord is coming to seek us and to test us!

The seven seals were being opened on the tongues of men every day in every one of the camps of the Army of the Saints, and some of the common soldiers were following the prophecies just as zealously as their chaplains.

Rhisiart could open his mouth and say all of that to him, but he chooses not to. The discussion has taken hours as it is, so all he does is nod, show his assent, agree with the Colonel silently.

'We're preparing, Rhisiart. Not preparing for the second coming of the King of Heaven, because we know that he is not coming, not like that. Men like us have learned one thing. We have to prepare the way as best we can. Help those who can make this sinful world better. And we have to turn our sights across the sea. The saints have been moving to the New World for years. Plymouth. Salem. Boston. Here and there along the coast of America.' He begins to shuffle through his papers, searching for some specific document in a big, untidy pile.

'They're English, most of them, the ones that have gone across the sea. Plymouth. Salem. Boston.' Having finished searching one pile, he moves over to begin on another stack of papers, looking and talking at the same time.

'But I have continually worried about the place of our people, Rhisiart. The small handful of the remnants of the Welsh nation who still inhabit this earth. Our place in the great plan of Divine Providence. And the way I will be able to use the power that God has seen fit to give me to help secure that place.' His busy hands find that piece of paper he has been searching for – a letter, by all appearances – and he holds it on the table in front of him.

The hairs on the back of Rhisiart's neck stand up when the Colonel speaks those familiar words. The exact quote comes to him: 'There is, for that small handful of the remnants of the Welsh nation who still dwell in their own land, a multitude of very great and severe causes to consider, and to acknowledge God's mercy towards them.' From *Carwr y Cymry*, 'The Friend of the Welsh', one of the two small books that were in Rhisiart's possession throughout the wars, kept safe along with his Bible. *The Soldier's Catechism* was the other. He knows it is a sinful, pagan idea, but Rhisiart can't think of them as anything other than two talismans or charms. One of them reminding him of his early engagement with the Word of God and his original spiritual awakening, and the other a fresh confirmation of the connection between his Christianity and his connection with the army of Parliament. One of the first things that made his heart warm to the Colonel was the man's ability to quote or paraphrase the contents of the two books without realizing he was doing so, a thing that Rhisiart himself did often in the early days.

He returns from that thought with a jolt, sits up, and worries that he's lost the drift of Colonel Powel's words. The older man sees Rhisiart's uneasiness, and lowers his voice, changing the mood.

'You look tired, Rhisiart. Would you like something to eat? Some water? Wine? Are you thirsty?'

'No, sir. I'm sorry.'

The Colonel gets up from his chair again, very slowly this time, and stands behind it again. He rests one hand on the chair, the other still holding the letter. One of the candles is choking quietly in its own wax, its flame fighting for life.

'And that's why I worry about one community in particular over in America.'

The flame goes out, and another of the seven remaining candles begins its own death dance. 'Tell me, Rhisiart, have you ever heard of Richard Morgan Jones and New Jerusalem?'

He tells the Colonel that he has heard of neither the man nor the place.

'Richard Morgan Jones is one of those birds that have flown to roost in many a nest during our time on the earth. One of the birds that fly off before you have a chance to catch it. He's hard to know, you see. He was with William Erbery in Cardiff for a while. And afterwards in Llanfaches with Wroth, Cradoc, Llwyd and the others. And then…' He pauses to look down at the letter in his hand, as if he is searching for a particular bit of information. 'America. Before the first war began. You must have been a child at the time. You wouldn't have known about him, unless you came across one of his old acquaintances who had an urge to talk about him.'

'No, sir. This is the first time I've heard the name.'

'Well, then. This bird flew all the way across to America years ago, and a flock of his followers with him. And every now and then, since that time, an occasional Welshman joins them. You know, someone who sailed to Plymouth or Boston or Salem, and then decides to leave that place and join his fellow countrymen. Alright, fine, you'd say. But as I said, I believe we have to give a little push wherever we can to our fellow Welshmen in the new world. And it is possible that it is there that such conquest as we will get will come. It is possible that Divine Providence – if we can believe that that's what it is – has decided that it is in America and not on this island that our people will flourish. There are signs to this effect, Rhisiart. Who knows that it won't be like that? I can't turn my back on them. I have to give them a little push.'

'Right, sir.'

'Right. But it's not as simple as that, Rhisiart. As I suggested, Richard Morgan Jones is a bird who knows his own mind. He and his followers believe that all of us have lost the way. Believe that we have not understood correctly the true mission of Calvin.'

'Calvin, sir?'

'Yes. I got a careful report once from a friend who heard Richard Morgan Jones preach. Years ago, before he and his people left Wales. A sermon against free will, it was. That is, a sermon against the idea. He attacked the value of good deeds, saying that they are not what saves a soul, and that it all depends on the predestination of the elect.'

'I don't understand, sir. What's unique about that?'

'Wait there, now, Rhisiart. I know. You have heard this sort of thing before. Hundreds of times, in sermons in camps and possibly in the old days before the war.'

Another way of preaching fire and damnation. Harsh words of judgement and condemnation.

'Exactly, sir. Predestination. The elect. Saying that good deeds on earth do not save a man.'

'You've heard it all before, a hundred times and more.

'I have.'

'Yes, yes. I too. We have lived that creed, Rhisiart. Believing that good deeds on this earth save a soul from judgement would be a step back into the old superstitious age, to the popery of the dark ages, when the rich could give land and money to the church and alms to the poor and rest easy in their minds that by doing so they could buy their way into heaven. But Calvin has led us to believe that God, in His immeasurable wisdom, knows who is among the elect, having known before the beginning of time who the elect are, and so the attitude of a man who believes that his alms and all his good works reveal that he has been chosen to join with the vast eternal in heaven is nothing other than impudence. A small, finite creature using his animal cunning to deceive the Almighty. We've heard it all before. Yes, yes. We have said similar things ourselves. Every one of us. Accepting the doctrine of predestination and election… and then searching frantically in a cold sweat for signs that we are among the elect. Which implies that we believe – without saying that we believe – that good deeds count, because we are hoping to deceive ourselves that our good deeds in this life are among the signs that show that we are among the elect.'

'And so the Calvinist deceives himself into thinking that he is better than someone who believes in good deeds, and so he weighs his good deeds differently.'

'Precisely, Rhisiart. The Calvinist thus is not earning his way to heaven with good deeds but tricking himself into thinking that he is among the elect. We've all done it, Rhisiart. Justification for our alms. Driving all the strife we've been responsible for… believing that we are improving the world in accord with God's will. We have lived it, Rhisiart.'

The Colonel pauses. His emphasis on the word *have* is a confession that draws the two men closer together. We *have* believed, *have* lived, *have* done. Saying things that Rhisiart would not, at this time, express publicly to anyone else, though he utters them silently to himself, and those words create a bond of iron and blood between them. But he doesn't yet understand the connection between their joint confession and the job the Colonel has summoned him to do.

'And so what was different about Richard Morgan Jones' preaching?'

'Ah, well, yes, to return to the nub of the thing, Rhisiart. My friend said that brother Jones ended his sermon by saying that we have not gone far enough. He said that we are all going astray. He said that the real work of the Christian in this world is to find a way of living that allows him to live the doctrine… though I think that "truth" was the word he used.'

He pauses again. He closes his eyes for a moment, his mouth working silently, as if he were trying to remember something he heard a long time ago, searching for the exact words and the proper tone. Rhisiart's mind moves back and forth between the power of the present moment, here in Colonel Powel's room, and the past, all the sermons he has heard. Behold, the trumpet of the millennia sounding.

But the Colonel opens his eyes again and speaks slowly, emphasizing every word. 'It was not the words themselves, but the sense, the intent behind them. That's what my friend said. That's what made such an impression on him. Not the words, but the way Richard Morgan Jones spoke those words. He was not a man who was taken in easily, my friend. The fact that the thing unsettled him was enough for me to realize that there was something to his concerns.' Moments of silence, of thinking, of gathering information in the mind. 'Anyway, everything I've heard since then makes me believe that my friend was right. We do have reason to worry. It seems he has taken a path which can only lead to ruin. If only I knew.'

'Knew what, sir?'

'If I'm right to worry, Rhisiart. If they are following that path to the end.'

'You're not certain?'

'No, Rhisiart, I am not certain. That's the thing. No one has heard a word from them for years. But a little information has reached me. Rumours mostly. It's difficult to know the truth.' He holds up the letter and shakes it. 'This is the last I heard. A letter that came from New England a year ago. But it was written months before that. One of my acquaintances from around Boston. Miles Egerton. He heard a story from a traveller who had been in a place called Strawberry Bank, and that traveller had heard a story there from another man who had visited New Jerusalem recently.' He lets go of the chair and starts to walk around the table. 'He says that what he heard is a cause for concern.' He comes up to Rhisiart and hands the letter to him. '"That which I have heard suggests that they know not what they do." His exact words. Look.'

Rhisiart reaches for the letter, but his eyes are on the Colonel.

'I wrote back to him, to Miles Egerton. I asked if he would be willing to visit New Jerusalem.' He waits, looking at Rhisiart. 'And that's why I asked you to come here, Rhisiart. There's something I want to ask you.'

'Sir?'

'I haven't heard a word from Miles Egerton since then. He is English. I'm thinking I made a mistake, Rhisiart, in asking him to go there. They're Welsh, after all. That was Richard Morgan Jones' idea, you see. Create a home for Welsh saints in America. And that's why I wrote to you, Rhisiart.'

'Sir?'

'Will you go to America, Rhisiart? Will you go to New Jerusalem?'

–ΔΩ–

He tries to sit, but the pain is too much for him. He starts to rise, but he doesn't have the strength to do it. He falls on his back, the stars above him glittering, offering their cold comfort.

–4–

He feels some strength returning to his muscles. He can move again now, and does so. Slowly, he turns on his side, then completes the turn until he is lying on his stomach. With his hands under his chest and his palms open, he pushes against the earth. He draws his knees up under him a bit, pushes, until he is on all fours. The pain is great, the shivering is intense, but he can move like this. He goes back a bit onto his toes until his heels touch the ground. Cautiously, shakily, he rises – there is a terrible pain in one ankle, but he doesn't fall. He's standing, all his weight on one leg, but he's wet, cold, weak. The wind on this autumnal evening pierces through him. He starts to shiver again, the shivering so strong it keeps him from moving.

–ΔΩ–

Three days after the long meeting with Colonel Powel, Rhisiart is aboard ship, at anchor in the Thames.

The *Primrose* is a galleon, a kind of vessel that hasn't changed in design for many decades. About 100 feet in length, three masts, capable of carrying 180 tons of cargo. But the long deck in the belly of the ship has not been filled entirely with goods. There are around forty passengers, and so open spaces have been left between the piles of casks, packets and boxes, and those spaces are now filled with temporary chests and beds for the passengers. The *Primrose* is served by fifty officers and crew, a total of ninety souls, as the captain says, adding that on its last trip to New England it carried as many as a hundred and fifty.

The captain, Thomas Marlow, is English, like most of his

crew. He's also a devout man, unlike most of his crew. He learned years ago that he would be waiting on the shore for a lifetime if he accepted none but true Christians to serve on his ship. He says often that sailing is his life, and that he has come to the conclusion that it is better to sail with a bunch of pagans and papists than to stay idle on dry land wishing for the impossible. He holds a service every day on his ship, acting as an unordained minister as well as captain, and the fact that an occasional mariner has experienced conversion in the middle of a voyage or near the shore is something that makes the captain think that Divine Providence has guided him in the true direction.

At present, Captain Marlow is waiting for the tide to turn, and so the *Primrose* lies at anchor beside Deptford docks. Most of the crew – whether Christian, pagan or papist – are busy at their jobs, but some are standing idle, like the passengers, looking at the bustle of the docks and the other ships awaiting the turn of the tide.

There is only one other Welshman on the ship. Colonel Powel mentioned him towards the end of their meeting. 'Owen Lewys will be travelling with you, Rhisiart. As far as Boston. After you land, you'll be heading north to Strawberry Bank and then on further to New Jerusalem. Owen will be heading southwest, on completely different business. But I want you to become friends with him during the voyage. You'll see his character and his worth. I'm putting a great deal of my hope in him. I believe that his venture is the greatest hope we have now, truth be told. If my fears about New Jerusalem are realized.'

Rhisiart stands next to Owen Lewys now, the two men leaning on the ship's rail, surveying the scene. The other ships, the workers on the dock, the houses, the shops and the warehouses on land. People everywhere: coming and going, preparing, concluding business. The smell of the river is strong, filthy and living, suggesting the freshness of the sea and the putrescence of human excrement at the same time. The loud, high-pitched cries of the seagulls blend with the deeper voices of men, shouting and calling, greeting and confirming. Yes, that's what my master says. Yes, this is the ship. And the clamour of the birds rising and falling. The Babel of the shoreline, sounds of a region neither water nor land but an intermingling of the two.

There is a striking similarity between the two men, and it's no wonder that some of the seamen and the passengers think that they are father and son. Rhisiart shaved clean in the morning before boarding the ship, thinking that he would not be shaving again until after the voyage. Owen Lewys' face is also long and clean-shaven, and his nose and jawline are strong. He is at least twenty – and possibly thirty – years older than Rhisiart. Like Rhisiart's, his hair falls to his shoulders, and has not greyed very much more despite the difference in age between them. He is tall, like Rhisiart, his body strong despite his years. But his face shows his age, the skin wrinkled like old leather. The face of one who has spent years travelling the roads, in deep winter and high summer. He wears a dark hat with a broad brim, similar to that of his fellow traveller, but it, like the man wearing it, is a bit older and shows its age.

'You and your father are far from home.' A seaman's passing remark. He has heard them talking, and has spent enough time on Britain's docks and ships to identify the language. He knows very well that it is Welsh and that the two men are a great distance from their homes. He supposes that the older man doesn't know English. But before either of the two Welshmen can respond, the seaman has gone on, continuing with his work.

Owen Lewys smiles, his blue eyes brightening. 'Who knows where our homes are now? Isn't that so, Rhisiart Dafydd?'

Rhisiart smiles too, responding more to his companion's

words than to the Englishman's comment. He knows well that the two of them will come back to that subject during the coming days and weeks, but for now he says nothing.

'Here we are, at the edge of this world and about to venture into another.' He waits politely for a response, but since Rhisiart says nothing, he turns from the busy scenes and looks directly at Rhisiart.

'John Powel said nothing at all about the nature of your business in America, only that you are doing his work.'

'And so we are not on equal ground, I'm afraid. You don't know much about me, but I know what you're about. He told me of your mission – to seek out a home for the Welsh Quakers.'

'You know that John Powel acts with purpose. He doesn't leave anything to chance, does he? He must have some idea or hope that you could help me. After you have finished whatever task he gave you to complete there. And then again he doesn't expect me to help you, and so he decided that I didn't need to know anything about the business that brings you to America. And I won't ask.'

Rhisiart smiles, enjoying the way the other's words close the door that he would not be comfortable opening, and opens another, one that leads to friendship. This is the first time he has spoken to a Quaker. He has sometimes seen one preaching or speechifying, has heard things about them, but he's never had the occasion to have an extended conversation with one.

Owen Lewys tells a good deal of his history to Rhisiart. He has been with George Fox in England and knows James Naylor too. And he has been with John ap John near Cardiff.

'Did you know that our friend is the one who arranged for John ap John to be set free when he was imprisoned?'

'Colonel Powel?'

'Yes, John Powel. Though almost no one knows that. He works through others.'

And through the two of us now, Rhisiart thinks.

'He's been helping us very quietly for years, though that's not well known.'

Helping. Rhisiart thinks about the Colonel's favourite phrase, 'give a little push,' and smiles.

Owen says that he was with James Naylor and his friends in London that summer, before they decided to move to Bristol. Rhisiart remembers a conversation he heard between two of his fellow soldiers a couple of months ago.

'Isn't Cromwell beginning to talk about doing something to suppress Naylor and his friends?'

'That's certainly possible, Rhisiart Dafydd. I believe that Oliver Cromwell would like to silence all of us now.'

'Why? Aren't you free?'

'Oh, we are, Rhisiart Dafydd, ever since the constitution of 1653. The law is on our side, and many of us know how to use the law.'

Rhisiart remembers the amusing story about a Quaker who shouts out in the middle of a service, interrupting the minister, demanding: 'What authority gives you the right to preach here?' The minister tells the authorities, and they drag the Quaker before a judge. And then, when the judge begins to read the charges against him, the old Quaker cries out, interrupting him, saying: 'What authority gives you the power to persecute me like this?' This goes on until his manner and stubbornness offend everyone, and he is finally brought before no less than Oliver Cromwell himself. And the Lord Protector decides to let him go free.

'But I thought that he was not entirely against you.'

'No, Cromwell was not against us. To be completely honest, he didn't know what to do with us. The first time George Fox went to speak to him, Cromwell said that he was not certain that we were not part of the original plan. He confessed that he did not know what God's will was, and he hesitated before agreeing with some of his counsellors, the ones who said we were dangerous heretics. Cromwell wasn't so sure.'

'So why did he change his mind?'

'Ah, well, Oliver Cromwell is a Calvinist, Rhisiart Dafydd – at the end of the day that's what he is, a good Calvinist. That Calvinism showed itself in an unmistakable way the last time George Fox went to see him. He said he did not agree with what the Quakers say about the light within. He had been discussing the matter with some of his theologians, you see, and he was prepared. Had armed himself against us, so to speak.'

Rhisiart says nothing, but the look on his face encourages Owen to go on.

'You'll find the information in John's gospel, Rhisiart.'

Rhisiart waits for him to explain.

'"That was the true Light, which lighteth every man that cometh into the world." You see, Rhisiart Dafydd, John was sent by God to testify about that light, so that everyone would believe through it. And what was that light but the true light that lights everyone from within. That's what we do, Rhisiart Dafydd, testify like John before us. Testifying about the light that shines within everyone and shows the way in the same manner to everyone.'

Although Rhisiart hasn't participated in such discussions for some time, he is used to discussing theology, and those occasions have sharpened his mind. The Army of the Saints was practically a school of theology, a theoretical whirlpool bubbling with an abundance of different ideas, the soldiers discussing them constantly. And so he readily took in what Owen Lewys said and came to his own conclusions.

'Your belief that the light is inside everyone suggests that the Holy Spirit or even Christ himself is inside each of us. But Cromwell is a good Calvinist and therefore believes that only the elect have the Holy Spirit inside them. And once the argument is presented in that way, your beliefs sound like blasphemy and you appear to be dangerous heretics.'

'Exactly, Rhisiart, exactly. That's the real nature of our quandary. We can't do differently, only continue to testify to the light within, and if the devout decide that we are preaching blasphemy and heresy…'

'You're doomed.'

'I said that plainly to James Naylor, but he didn't want to listen. "My work here in England is not done, Owen Lewys." That's what he said to me before leaving for Bristol. But there are some Welshmen who agree with me completely. Possibly because they arc Welshmen.'

Rhisiart understands. Our own people. The remnants of the race of the Ancient Britons, hiding in a corner of their old island.

'And John Powel understands, and has decided to help.'

Give a little push here and there. Reawaken the ancient race of Brutus, in the form of a Quaker polity over in America. A Millennial pragmatist playing with the madness of history.

'But I don't know what to expect, Rhisiart Dafydd. It would be presumptuous to say anything with certainty before I get there. I once heard an English preacher who was on the verge of sailing off to America. He said he was going off into the dark heart of that pagan continent in order to kindle the candle of the light of God there.'

The two men turn to consider the scene again, Rhisiart thinking, his mind working through the theological issues as he contemplates his new friend's last words. The difference between one metaphor and another, between an actual candle and a light within. The difference between preaching and testifying, between seeking to kindle a flame and knowing that there is already a flame there. But before he has finished contemplating these things and is ready to offer his interpretation, Owen Lewys is speaking again.

'Presumption, Rhisiart Dafydd, that's what it is. Presumption and arrogance.' He gestures towards the scene before them, compelling Rhisiart to focus on the houses, the taverns, the warehouses, the activity on the docks and the laden ships. 'This too is one of the dark places of the earth. Remember that, Rhisiart Dafydd. It does no good to say that this place is dark and another place darker still, and that a light kindled by people from this dark place can light that other dark place. It's inside where the light is. Remember that, Rhisiart Dafydd.'

Hours later, they're sailing past the Essex saltmarsh, some woods seen in the distance beyond them. Mist from the river clouds the scene, and it is as if Rhisiart is seeing the land in a dream. As the sun begins to sink, the red of the sunset turns the mist into a ruby-coloured mantle, like the veil on the hat of a noblewoman in the days before the wars. He can still see the river, the salt marshes and the trees, but through that radiant red veil.

A pity that Owen Lewys is not there with him; he'd love to share this otherworldly experience with someone, but has no desire to start up a conversation with another of the passengers. Owen went below a little before sunset to help a woman. It happened that an Englishman, David Farmer, had begun to talk to them – or rather to Owen, as Rhisiart only stood by – saying that his wife was afraid of the voyage, and to such a degree that she could only lie on the blankets that served as their bed and shake. He worried that she would become ill if she couldn't calm down, but he didn't know what to say to her to help her. 'Shall I offer to pray with her?' Owen asked, and reached out to reassure the Englishman. 'And if that fails, I will tell her a nice tale which will divert her from her present worries.' And so Rhisiart has been left to himself, gazing through the ruddy mist and following the flight of some sort of large bird – a heron perhaps – that has lifted up from the marsh beside the river.

As he stands there, he feels something pressing against his leg, against his high boots. He steps away from the rail to get a better look – it's a big cat, black with a splash of white on its tail and paws. It presses against him again, purring loudly. The ship is noisy with the voices of the sailors, the ropes grating, wood creaking, and the sails slapping in the wind, but he can hear the cat purring. He bends down to pet it, scratches its ears, runs his hand along its back, pulls gently on its tail. The cat purrs on, leaning into the stroking hand. He sees it's a tom, unusually large, healthy and strong.

'We call him Nicholas, or Nick.' A sailor is passing by, a young, pink-cheeked fellow, smiling warmly. 'He's the best friend I have on this ship.' Another sailor, the one who spoke to him and Owen earlier, comes up. 'Old Nick, I calls him. He's as black as his father the devil.' He's an older man, thin lipped, eyes too small for his head. 'And Robin here's too fond by half o' that devil of a cat.'

Rhisiart straightens to talk to the man, but they see that the captain is looking at them.

'To it, Robin lad.' The sailor says it loud enough for the captain to hear, giving the young man a little push. And then, more quietly, 'Leave the devil to his own work.' The two of them move away, making a show of getting on with their tasks.

Rhisiart bends down again, picks up the cat and cradles it in his arms. He scratches its ears, enjoying the feel of the warm fur beneath his fingers. The cat begins to purr again, and Rhisiart squeezes its paws lightly. 'You're not all black, Nicholas, are you?' The cat extends its claws a bit, sampling Rhisiart's hand. 'Very well, you've got work to do too.' He lets the cat jump down out of his arms, and the animal presses against his leg one more time before moving on in pursuit of some unseen mouse.

It's a fine morning and the *Primrose* is ploughing the waves, Cornwall visible in the distance. She's sailing west, land to the north. Rhisiart wants to view it, study it, lose himself in the moment, but he can't. The bell has announced a shift change for the crew: one half coming out of the sleeping quarters in the fo'c'sle, and the other half in the process of leaving their work and taking the places of their fellow sailors before their hammocks get cold. But this is also when Captain Marlow holds his morning service. Two seamen stand on the upper deck in the stern, their hands on the whipstaff, governing the rudder, and others doing necessary work with the sails, but most of them join the service.

The captain stands with his back against the main mast of the ship, the sailors and passengers in a half-circle around him. All have removed their hats, as is the ship's custom, and Rhisiart notices that Thomas Marlow is bald. Although he is not a tall man, he seems large. Solid. His face is round and clean shaven, and he has a thick nose suggesting some kind of hound. The ship's carpenter, Edward Epsham, stands in front of the captain, facing him, holding the large Bible open. Rhisiart notices that the carpenter too is balding, though wisps of reddish hair hide the back of his neck and his ears. Marlow has a deep, fiery voice, every word exploding from his mouth and carrying a great distance.

"'According as His divine power hath given unto us all things that pertain unto life and godliness, through the knowledge of Him that hath called us to glory and virtue.'"

He is talking about Simon Peter, servant and apostle of Jesus Christ, and Rhisiart feels that the captain is beginning to suggest that each of the sailors and passengers could be like Peter, one of the servants of Christ, but he has lost interest in the sermon itself. Owen Lewys is standing next to him and has removed his hat like everyone else. A question sits on Rhisiart's tongue: don't you resist giving in to what you see as a meaningless religious custom? Don't you reject acknowledging the authority of any person rising up as a minister for you and over you? But then his attention is caught by the open book. He remembers himself as a young lad sitting on a cask beside the door of the smithy, reading his Bible by the light of the moon. He remembers himself as a young man browsing through the book in camp or barracks. He recalls the pleasure of remembering all the words, the strength that would come when calling them easily to his tongue.

And so he finds himself enjoying translating the reading to himself, remembering the Welsh words that correspond to what the captain is reading.

Megis y rhoddes ei dduwiol allu…

But something else catches his attention: Nicholas, the black tom, is weaving his way through the crowd towards him. Rhisiart notes that the sailor who calls the cat Old Nick sees that he is not following the sermon, and shoots him a sly grin. He makes a motion with his eyes to show that he sees the cat – which by now is rubbing against Rhisiart's leg – and he pulls a face that expresses surprise and mischievous pleasure. Rhisiart imagines him saying, 'Ho ho! Now you're showing your true colours, answering the call of the Black One rather than listening to the Word of the Lord!'

'"Brethren, give diligence to make your calling and election sure: for if ye do these things, ye shall never fail' *Frodyr, byddwch ddiwyd i wneuthur eich galwedigaeth a'ch etholedigaeth yn siccr…*

Half of the sailors exit through the fo'c'sle, longing for sleep, and those newly woken take up their duties. Captain Marlow climbs the narrow ladder to the upper deck to speak to the sailors that are working the whipstaff, hat back in place, his baldness hidden again. Rhisiart and Owen Lewys put their hats back on too. The older man speaks.

'Thomas Marlow is a man sure of his election. And he preaches as if he believes that others can show evidence of their own election as well.'

'What would Calvin say?' Rhisiart smiles at his facetious question. But the question he looked forward to asking the Quaker dies on his tongue; he doesn't want to banter or tease, preferring to enter into a discussion that will put the two of them solidly on the same side.

'Yes, indeed, Rhisiart Dafydd. But I ask you, what would the great Calvinist theologians back in England think?'

'I feel certain that Captain Marlow considers himself one.'

'Possibly, Rhisiart, but I don't plan on asking him that.' With an amused look on his face he turns and walks away. Rhisiart knows that he is going to visit David Farmer and his wife. I must learn her name, he tells himself: Owen is fond of them. He bends down to stroke Nicholas, but the cat has disappeared.

The two men are leaning against the railing of the ship, holding their hats lest the strong wind rip them off. They turn their glance north. The *Primrose* is running with the wind through open sea, and it's difficult to believe that such a thing as dry land exists anywhere in the world, but Robin, the pink-cheeked sailor, says that Ireland can be seen to the north. He has just finished adjusting the ropes near the top of the main mast, and he saw Ireland from his perch. 'I'm the best climber on board. Born to it, like my friend Nick.' But the cat is not climbing today, he's down in the dark hunting his dinner. 'And now it's the mizzen mast for me.' After he's gone, Rhisiart and Owen peer at the horizon, searching for land, but there's nothing to see but the waves.

'You said that you had crossed the sea before, Rhisiart Dafydd?'

'Yes. Some seven years ago. Sailing from Bristol' – he nods and gestures towards the horizon – 'to Ireland.'

'That's what I thought.'

'Early September, fine weather – like today. Landing in Dublin, then moving on. At full speed, no rest. Reached the walls of Drogheda by nightfall.' Drogheda: a siege ending in a sea of blood. Cromwell giving orders to kill them all. The garrison at Drogheda, every one of them. Over two thousand men, most of them struck down in cold blood after surrendering. It was mass execution, not battle. But it was too disorderly to be an execution. No ceremony, no drum beating, no chance for the condemned to say his last words. Just cutting them down. Mass murder, the dirt on the ground and the cobbles in the street stained red.

'Is that so?'

'Yes, yes. And… afterwards… after finishing our work… sailing back at the end of October. After we seized Wexford.'

Wexford. There is no word for a day like that. Killing as many of the enemy as they did at Drogheda, but also many innocent civilians. Women. Old men. Children. Hundreds upon hundreds of them. And then burning the town. The red horse leaving Wexford in dust and ashes under its hooves, and power given to him that sat thereon to take peace from the earth. They, the soldiers of the Army of the Saints, were mounted on the red horse. An army that believed it was a Church gathered in His name. That's what some of their preachers said: We are a gathered Church, doing His work. Doing His work in Drogheda and in Wexford.

Rhisiart has not seen Isaac Huws since he returned from Ireland, but his face appears in his mind's eye often, and his heart and his guts ache every time he thinks about him. Like a schoolboy looking for an enemy on the street, trying to start a fight and hoping to land a fist in the face of his opponent. He has searched for Isaac Huws in camps and barracks, in the middle and on the fringes of every service. But the preacher was granted a living in Wales a while back, and no longer travels with the armies. Rhisiart has not had the opportunity to face him, his words like fists, and ask: look at Drogheda and Wexford – ashes and blood. Is that the white horse you preached about? Is that him, with his rider wearing a crown on his head? Is that the way of your conquest?

Rhisiart turns to tell Owen that he can't see anything but the sea, and realizes that he is alone. His friend has slipped away quietly, unbeknownst to him, leaving him there gazing at the horizon. Rhisiart crosses to the other side of the ship and stares at the opposite horizon.

The four of them are talking in the evening. It's dark on their deck, but the night is clear outside and a bit of light reaches them through the wooden hatches. Owen Lewys made arrangements with some of their neighbours so that David Farmer and his wife Elizabeth could move their things close to them. Rhisiart has come to know the young English couple by now, and the four of them speak together often.

Elizabeth, he thinks. Of course. It would be that name. She has come to terms with the ship by now, but rough weather sends her back into the grip of her old fears. The ship is rocking a bit tonight, but it's not stormy, and so Elizabeth is quite at ease. Her husband speaks of the life he and his wife will be living in New England. He speaks quickly, excitedly, but Rhisiart is not paying close attention. The Englishman's skin is very white, and his short, clipped hair is so fair you can almost see through it. But the bit of hair that shows from under her cap is dark, and her skin is like the sunshine of summer. 'A Boston merchant… acquaintance… uncle… letter of introduction… and a start… for five and six…' Rhisiart likes the young man, but doesn't follow his conversation closely.

It's different when Elizabeth joins in. 'Our child will be a girl, this I know.' Her husband tries to silence her, tenderly, saying they ought not to imagine what Divine Providence has in store for them, but she stands her ground, quietly but with confidence. 'That I know as well, David, but I cannot help myself.' Their two heads are close together, the weak light catching the fair hair of her husband and shining in her own blue eyes. 'It is as a certainty inside me.' The young man says they can't be certain of anything apart from the will of God, adding that that too is hidden from them, mere mortals, most of the time. 'It is certain. I don't know why, but I do know that. She will be a girl, and we shall call her Faith.' After that, the four of them are silent for a moment. Rhisiart considers the words he has heard hundreds of times. Faith alone saves. Faith alone insures. If you have Faith, you will lack for nothing. Then he remembers the words of the Colonel, his recent confession. We *have* believed… we *have* lived… we *have* done. *Wedi credu, wedi byw, wedi gwneud.*

He senses, despite the darkness, that the others are looking at him, and he realizes that he's been talking to himself out loud. Rather than asking him about it, Owen Lewys starts talking in English again, telling an amusing story about Caerphilly craftsmen. But Rhisiart is not listening. He's focusing on those Welsh words, turning them over and over inside himself. Have believed, have lived, have done. Of course. Elizabeth is her name. What else? I have lived, have believed, have done.

It's a fine, sunny afternoon. The wind was against them for close to a week, but it turned during the night and has been filling the sails of the *Primrose* ever since, much to the pleasure of the captain. Giving thanks for the wind was the subject of the service held before the mast that morning. Rhisiart stands in the open air, without hat or coat, enjoying the warmth of the sun on his face and the wind through his hair.

A rope breaks free somewhere and is whipping in the wind,

hitting against the mast. The bosun shouts an order, there's the sound of feet drumming on wood as a number of sailors run to take hold of it. But Rhisiart doesn't watch them. He tilts his face to the sun, his eyes closed, and all the sounds of the ship are like a whisper in a dream. This is the world, he thinks, and this is the life I have lived. The heat he feels on his face has the warmth of skin: like another cheek pressing against his own cheek. Living fingers playing with his hair, a hand caressing his skin playfully.

The four of them are sitting on their chests, having finished their meal of dry oat bread and water. The cheese and butter were used up days ago. The day is drawing to a close, but there's still a bit of light filtering through the hatches. Rhisiart is eager to finish and go up on deck to watch the sunset, although the captain and the bosun have warned the passengers, telling them they should keep out of the way when it's dark and stay below on their own deck. But Rhisiart risks it whenever the evening is fair, staying to watch the sun slowly set, the way its colours paint the sea, and no one bothers him about it.

It's getting increasingly difficult for him to eat like this. The hold of the ship is directly beneath them, and the wooden floor of their deck doesn't stop the stench from rising and threatening to choke them. It's a damp smell; saltiness mixed with the sourness of refuse and rot. He asks his friends to go up with him and eat in the fresh air when possible, but the captain has forbidden that today. Some of the passengers bring too many things with them at mealtimes – bottles, blankets, baskets – and these get under the feet of the sailors. So they eat on their deck in the murkiness of the bowels of the ship, the stench of the hold taking away their appetites and the sound of the rats scuttling in the dark corners reminding them that people are not the only creatures eating in this gloom.

He sees that Elizabeth is able to eat under these circumstances.

She's been showing for some time; one of the other women had to help her alter her clothing somewhat in order for her to move about comfortably. David has been talking to her while they eat, comparing different stories he has heard about voyages and various accounts of pregnancy to figure out whether the baby will be born before the end of the voyage or not. At first, Rhisiart thought that Elizabeth would tease her husband and remind him that he was the one who believed that one should not try to guess what Divine Providence had in store for them, but instead she eagerly joined in, relishing the accounts and the conjecture. Of course, he thinks, the wind is with them now and she's enjoying herself. This is the life she's living. Bless her.

Elizabeth says again that she's certain the child will be a girl. Owen Lewys suggests that they name her Primrose if she's born on board ship. The three of them laugh, Elizabeth along with the others. 'Her name will be Faith if she's born on ship.' She reaches out and takes her husband's hand. 'And her name will be Faith if she's born on shore.' They all laugh.

Rhisiart rises and excuses himself, saying he doesn't want to miss the sunset. He has to duck down to avoid hitting the beams that hang low across the whole space. Carefully, he moves between the chests and casks towards the small ladder. The hatch is open above him, and light flows down the ladder, like water down rocks in a waterfall. Before reaching the ladder and placing a hand on a rung, he hears a scurrying in the shadows off to the side, but he moves on, having no desire to look at the rat.

It's midday and the weather has improved a bit. It's still raining, but not as heavily as it was, and the sailors welcome the hopeful sign. The *Primrose* is ploughing through huge waves, surging forward then diving, up and down, each wave pounding as it hits the prow of the ship. It's hard to distinguish between the raindrops and the spray cast up by the constant rhythmic tension between wave and wood. The other passengers have stayed below, at the captain's request, because of the unpredictable motion of the ship. Every letter of his command was unmistakable: I am not going to imperil the life of another just to bury a body that is nothing but a piece of clay. But Rhisiart wants to be there and no one gets in his way. It's the pink-cheeked young sailor who's being buried. Robin. He fell from the main mast in the early hours of the morning, breaking his back as he hit the deck. He probably lived for a while, but the passengers below didn't hear about the accident until after dawn. A third of the crew have to go about their work, so only about thirty of them have gathered to hold the service. Rhisiart is the only passenger. Most of those present hold on to railings or ropes to keep their footing against the motion of the ship, but Captain Marlow leans his back against the main mast, his legs apart as if he is astride a horse, his body moving in rhythm with the motion of the ship. The waves at work and the light rain falling, the water splashing off the captain's bald head.

The ship's carpenter has been holding the large Bible before him, but then it slips from his hands and the holy book falls onto the wet, slippery deck. After he's picked it up and dried it, the captain orders him to hold on to it, and Marlow finishes the service without its help. It isn't hard for him – he knows the words well, having spoken them often: the Day of Judgement, and the sea giving up its dead.

With the congregation so small, this sea burial is very different from the last two. Two of the passengers: a wizened old lady of an age that made Rhisiart wonder why she had ventured the voyage at all had died near the end of the first month, and then a healthy-looking man in midlife died a week or so after that. Fearful rumours spread through the crew and the passengers alike, everyone concerned that he had died of some infectious disease and that the plague was about to seize them all. But it wasn't the plague that had visited the ship after all, and no one else died until this morning. Pink-cheeked Robin has been wrapped in sackcloth and the rough shroud has been stitched together to form a large, neat bundle. The cat's comrade, having fallen to his death from the same mast the captain is now leaning against, saying the last words over his corpse.

The sea will give up its dead, as the earth and hell will give up the dead that are in them too, and each of them will be judged according to their deeds. And here comes Nicholas taking his part in the service, weaving his way boldly between the legs of the mourners, testifying to the good deeds of the departed. Rhisiart considers. He is unwinding the captain's sermon in his head, his mind putting his fingers on all the holes in the reasoning. Nicholas finds him, and though he can't hear it over the voice of the captain, Rhisiart is certain the cat is purring softly to him, testifying to the virtues of his lost friend. It's not the place for it, but Rhisiart can't help smiling: the marine theology of the cat is superior to the captain's faulty Calvinism.

Amen, amen. Four of the sailors lift the body in its shroud of sackcloth and carry it to the edge, their feet slipping and their knees bending with the motion of the ship. Rhisiart worries that one of them will fall, that Robin will land again on the wood that killed him, but the four keep their footing. With the last words, they release the large bundle into the sea. They can't hear the body hitting the water, the other sounds are too loud – waves striking the ship, sails pulling at their ropes, wood creaking, water sloshing. But Rhisiart knows that the body has hit the water with a splash and immediately disappeared beneath the waves. Rocks from the ballast in the hold had been put next to Robin's feet before they bound the shroud tight, bits of dry earth going with him on a trip through the deep. This short life having been lived. Amen, amen.

He doesn't like to do it in front of his friends for some reason, but now he has no choice. He has done it a number of times in the last few weeks, usually seizing the opportunity when the others go on deck to enjoy a bit of fresh air. But Elizabeth is spending much of her time lying down now, and so he has no choice. Owen Lewys is not there, but David Farmer is sitting on a chest beside his wife's bed. Rhisiart knows that the young Englishman is interested in the long, thin bundle he keeps beside his own chest. He knows that he has been waiting for this opportunity to see the soldier unwrap it, take out the weapons from the old blanket that conceals them, and he has no choice this time but to finally reward his curiosity. Now they're lying on the blanket that serves as Rhisiart's bed, having been unwrapped slowly in front of David. Elizabeth is sleeping, or at least her eyes are closed, but her husband is watching every move the soldier makes, and he makes a little gulping sound, like a child swallowing a mouthful of porridge, when he sees the sword, the musket and the two pistols placed down on the bed. Rhisiart opens his chest and takes out a small, soft ball, an oily cloth wrapped in another cloth. He opens it in his hand as he sits on the floor, his legs crossed. He puts the dry cloth on one knee and the damp cloth on the other. He draws the sword from its scabbard slowly and lifts it, turning it carefully to catch the bit of light that's coming in through the hatches, searching for signs of rust. Then he places the long weapon across his legs, takes the oily cloth in one hand and with the other hand grips the hilt of the sword in order to hold it still. He rubs the blade with the oily cloth, pausing over those areas that concern him most. As he lifts the sword again, the light glints on the oily blade, and he takes the other cloth and wipes it dry. After cleaning that weapon, he picks up the first pistol, holds it up to the light, and inspects the metal parts.

There's scarcely a cloud to be seen in the blue sky, but the Atlantic wind is cold. The sailor is naked to his waist and has been tied to the foremast. It's the man with the small eyes and thin mouth. He was dancing and singing last night. Tom. Lucky Tom, some of the other sailors call him. Despite his rough-looking face, he's a man who enjoys a good time and innocent mischief and is fond of making his fellow sailors laugh. But Lucky Tom has broken Captain Marlow's laws. His punishment is to stay like this, shivering in the wind, for an entire day. So he can learn to keep his feet still, says the captain. Every member of the crew not engaged in essential work had to gather when Lucky Tom was tied to the mast that morning and listen to the captain describe the man's offences and his punishment. Idle pleasures in a wanton manner. Endangering the devotion of others to their work, that is, and endangering the souls of others as well. Some of the passengers came also, as solemn-seeming as if they were attending a funeral, but Rhisiart knows well what motives drive a person to witness the suffering of another. The show had lost its novelty by midday, and now Lucky Tom is shivering silently, without an audience. Rhisiart has not come to look at him, but is walking, deep in thought, and has reached that end of the ship. Tom looks at him out of the corner of his eye, being careful not to move his head. Rhisiart winks at him, in a conspiratorial way. He feels an impulse to offer his coat to the man, but he knows that open warfare with the captain would not be a good thing. He winks again and moves away.

Owen Lewys comes with him to the mast that night when it's time. One of them is carrying a blanket and the other a small brown bottle – rum that was donated to the cause by one of the other passengers. But they are unable to reach Lucky Tom because a number of his fellow sailors are there before them. The offender, his punishment at an end, has been untied and wrapped in several blankets already. He's unable to stand, and so a number of hands have taken hold of him and supported him.

'Well now, Rhisiart Dafydd, the business is over.'

'We were foolish. We should have known that they'd look after one of their own. They're a family.'

'We are all a family, Rhisiart Dafydd.'

The two turn and begin walking back, going to return the undrunk rum to its owner and the blanket to Owen Lewys' bed. They walk slowly, discussing the arrogance of men who believe that the right to define sin and mete out punishment has been conferred upon them.

It's night. They ought to get to sleep, but the two of them are awake and talking. David and Elizabeth are no longer there, the couple having moved at the invitation of another woman, so she can help Elizabeth. The woman, Anne Creale, has helped birth babies before, she says, and she has things in her chest that will prove useful when the time comes. And so, with Richard and Owen helping David carry their things, the English couple left the two Welshmen's corner. Owen still spends much of his time with them during the day, and Rhisiart too makes sure that he calls on them at least once a day, but he's glad of the opportunity to speak nothing but Welsh in the evening. They're sitting on their blankets. In the dark they look remarkably alike, each of them with a mane of unkempt hair falling to their shoulders, framing a long face, looking even longer now with the beard that has grown during the voyage. There's not enough light to reveal the wrinkles on the older man's face. In these shadows they're the same, each a mirror of the other.

Theology is the subject of many of their conversations – or rather the religious contradictions of the age. The arrogance of men who define sin and mete out punishment, the arrogance of men who say they know that what they're doing is God's work. Rhisiart likes to think about these long discussions as the parliament of the heretics, but he doesn't say that to his friend. He imagines sometimes that he hears the voice of John Powel joining in, leading the heretical prayer: we *have* lived, we *have* believed. Tonight they have been talking about the wars, Rhisiart referring indirectly to his service in the army. The older man is listening to the sketchy story, and doesn't ask for details. He has never asked, for he is a man who does not urge a friend to discuss such things. The Quaker has also experienced hardship. He has been in prison a number of times and in hiding on other occasions, and has seen close friends perish in filthy cells and cellars. But he doesn't ask Rhisiart to discuss unsavoury details, so he hasn't heard the whole story of Wexford, Drogheda and Naseby. Rather the ongoing discussion focuses on philosophy, erroneous belief, and the folly of men who try to justify the impossible. But tonight Rhisiart comes close to talking about his own history, closer than ever before.

'For some time now I have thought about it as hammer and anvil. The life of a soldier in the Army of the Saints. Like shaping iron with a hammer and anvil.'

'How so, Rhisiart?'

'The shaping between the two. In wartime. Imagine the life of a soldier, the life of one of the soldiers in the army of Parliament. Moving between conflict and camp. On the one hand, there are all the experiences on the day of battle. Hardship. Terror. Seeing things, feeling things, doing things. On the other hand, there's all that time in camp, and all the discussion. Even without counting the chaplains and the itinerant preachers, thousands of ordinary soldiers become self-appointed preachers and theologians. Discussing ideas and cross-examining the foundations of each other's faith. Reading. Arguing. Discussing. Clarifying teachings. The army was a kind of academy. Thousands of ordinary soldiers playing the role of teacher, one reading out the lesson to another. Sometimes in agreement – a Gathered Church, as some would say – and sometimes disagreement, a maelstrom of contradictions and opposing doctrines. But there was one thing that brought the whole together.'

'What was that, Rhisiart Dafydd?'

'The business we did on the day of battle. Everyone talked about the value and significance of the war. The reasons for our work. The justification. As set out in the *Soldier's Catechism*.'

'I can't say I've read it.'

'It's a small book which shows in various ways that a soldier in the army of Parliament is doing God's work on the battlefield. You would find it abhorrent.'

'There must have been some sort of good in it for you to have cherished it so back then.'

'We all took to it. It gave us the very thing that we needed to hear at the time. I memorized the ready answers to the various questions. Words worth keeping in your heart on the day of battle. "To fight in the defence and maintenance of the true Protestant Religion, which is now most violently opposed. God now calls upon us to avenge the blood of his Saints. The whole Church of God calls upon us to come to the help of the Lord and his people against the mighty."' He laughs again. 'I was young. Seventeen, eighteen, twenty years old.'

'But there were others who weren't so young, Rhisiart Dafydd. Men old enough to reason, who yet still believe those things. Why do you see it in a different light now, while so many of those other men who travelled with you through those bloody days continue to believe the same as before?'

Rhisiart doesn't answer his friend, and after a brief silence the Quaker speaks again. 'Those days are over, Rhisiart. You cannot revisit yesterday or the day before. What you do today is all that matters. That, and the path you'll be following tomorrow.'

Path: one of Colonel Powel's favourite words. Rhisiart is silent for a moment, and when he speaks again his voice is unsteady, the words sticking in his throat.

'The *Catechism* told us how we should perceive the enemy, too… it helped us… to see men who could have been friends or brothers as enemies. It was easy in the case of the Catholics who came against us sometimes.' He pauses, swallows.

'So great the old hatred of the sons of the Whore of Rome.'

'Yes. Because that old hatred was so strong, it was easy in their case.'

'But not in the case of fellow Protestants who fought on the side of the king.'

'Exactly. That's what pricked the conscience. Fighting against a fellow countryman. Friends. Cousins. Brothers.' He coughs, clearing his throat. '"Is it not a lamentable thing that Christians of the same nation should thus imbrue their hands in one another's blood?" That is the question.'

'And the answer?'

'The author was English. Robert Ram. He was writing for the English. That was his nation. But for me it spoke of my fellow Welshmen.' My people. The remnants of the race of the Ancient Britons.

'And how did your *Catechism* answer that question, Rhisiart Dafydd?'

He clears his throat once more, coughs, and then speaks softly. '"We are not to look at our enemies as fellow countrymen, or kinsmen, or fellow Protestants, but as the enemies of God and our Religion, and those who take the side of the Antichrist."'

He pauses again, letting these last words land on the ears of his friend. Those who side with the Antichrist. Then he continues, louder. '"Those who take the side of the Antichrist, and so our eye is not to pity them, nor our sword to spare them."'

'Heaven help us!'

'Indeed. God help us. That was the thing, you see. To try not to see them as fellow countrymen and brothers. There were a hundred Welshmen in the King's army for every one who bore arms in the name of Parliament. A hundred and more. For each one like me. They were there facing me. By the hundreds. By the thousands. At Edgehill. At Newbury. At Naseby.' He doesn't tell him that he heard some on the other side shouting out in Welsh in the midst of a press of pikes at Edgehill. Nor does he say anything about the women at Naseby. He's said too much already.

'I'm sorry, Rhisiart Dafydd. I got you away from your subject. The hammer and the anvil.'

'I don't think that's my subject any longer.' He clears his throat again. 'Only a subject of wonder.'

'Be that as it may, you were saying that a soldier of Parliament was as if formed between two poles.'

'That's right. Yes. But they were not two poles, but two things... two kinds of tools. Like shaping iron between anvil and hammer.'

'To wit, the killing and the dead on the field of blood and all the questioning and discussing in the camps.'

'Yes. At least that's how I thought about it for a long time.'

'Which one was the hammer and which the anvil?'

'I don't know. I don't know.'

The sides of the *Primrose* are creaking more loudly by now, the two men moving with the ship as they sit, the ship rocking and rolling. The weather has deteriorated over the last few hours, and it's threatening to turn into quite a storm. The conversation has wandered on to other aspects of the subject, and now the finer points of Calvinism are under consideration in the parliament of the heretics. The two of them agree, though they express their points of agreement in different ways.

'What right do they have to say that the light shines within the elect only? Knowing that the true light shines within him is the greatest wealth and gift of every living soul. By what authority does a man believe that he can tread on that gift and steal that certainty from another soul? That kind of arrogance is the theft of hope and understanding, and if there is such a thing as transgression in the realm of the spirit, then that has to be the greatest transgression.'

'I see it as hypocrisy more than anything. Listen to the thrust of their sermons. There's nothing worse in the view of a Protestant than papistry, Catholicism. And a fiery Calvinist certainly believes that he is a better Protestant than any other kind of Protestant, and therefore he hates papistry even more. The Whore of Rome. False empress of Babylon. Handmaiden of evil. More often than not, that old needle stitches the fabric of their sermons. And the word 'papist' in itself is enough of a curse, as bad as a swear word in their mouths. But Calvin is everything with them. They elevate him as an image higher than any saint worshipped by the Catholics. A holy image and the stuff of idolatry. They certainly don't believe in the Trinity, because there are four names that are the objects of their faith: the Father, the Son, the Holy Spirit, and Calvin. It's a quaternity, not a trinity.'

'Who would not call that blasphemy, Rhisiart Dafydd?'

'Indeed. That is the nature of their blasphemy.'

Almost as if the word 'blasphemy' had called it forth, Rhisiart glimpses a rat walking along the top of one of the chests beside them. A dark form, just a shade lighter than the darkness surrounding it, meandering across the lid of the chest. Owen Lewys sees that something has caught his friend's attention, and turns to look. But before either of them can move to do anything about it, another form, blacker than the darkness around it, springs onto the chest, white paws flashing.

A screech. Tumbling. Small bodies, each stronger than its size would suggest, pounding the wood. And then the two of them fall, in a tangle, from the chest to the floor between the two men, in a wrestling match. The rat is bigger than most of its race, but Nicholas is a big strong tom, and before long the battle is over. The rat is too big to be carried easily, so the cat drags it into the shadows between the chests, like a soldier dragging the body of an enemy to a burial pit.

Thump, thump. Rhisiart can't see it, but he knows that it's the cat's tail making the sound as it strikes the floor. He knows what the other sounds are too: small bones being crunched, teeth tearing flesh. He can hear it all over the creaking of the ship's timbers and the roar of the wind outside.

'And such is its end.' Owen Lewys is scratching his chin, playing with the beard he didn't have a few weeks ago. 'An end it did not foresee when it chose to climb the rope from the dock to the ship, or to go rummaging about in a cask or chest that was then brought here from a warehouse or shop. It was following its animal instinct, whatever it did, whatever brought it here to its end in the mouth of a cat. But here's the question, Rhisiart Dafydd: is the way that the most insignificant instincts lead an animal to its death essentially different from the way that most men follow their instincts to the end?'

'I don't know about that. But given the little I do know about ships, it's likely that the rat neither climbed a rope from the dock nor arrived in a chest.' He makes a fist and hits the floor. Thump! Louder than the sound made by the cat's tail. 'Their world is under us. All the putrefaction of the hold, down there in the shadows. There is as much filthy water and refuse there by now as there is of stone ballast and cannon balls. I can hear them sometimes, when I happen to be standing by the hatch that leads from the deck down into the hold. Rats. Dozens of them. You can hear them if you listen by the hatch. And I think I can hear them through the wood of this floor sometimes too.

Scores of them. Like a flock of birds singing in a tree. But they're not singing. They're squeaking. Squeaking and scurrying.' He points to the shadows where Black Nicholas has gone with his prey, but he's not sure whether his friend can see the gesture. With his outstretched finger he makes a motion like a teacher chastising a child. 'It did not come aboard like us, we passengers. No. That rat was born down there in the rot below us.' With his fist he pounds the floor again. Once, twice, three times. Thump, thump, thump. 'Down there. Born here. Living here. Dying here. In the hellish, rotting dark. That's their life, their world. It's all they know. Their own living hell.'

A hump of grey skin breaks through the waves, fifty yards from the ship. 'There he is again!' Rhisiart can't restrain himself – he's as excited as a small child. Owen Lewys is his father and he's seeing an otter in the river for the first time. But the whale is as big as a ship, a mountain of an animal, a living hillside. 'And again!' The two Welshmen are holding their hats in their hands, leaning against the rail. The wind is making twisted banners of their long hair, and sea spume douses them every now and then. Rhisiart squeezes salt water from his beard and pushes strands of his wet hair away from his eyes. 'There he is again! Look at him! Look!'

Captain Marlow has removed his hat too, and his bald head shines in the afternoon light. He has come to the rail to drive the men who have been standing idle beside the two Welshmen back to their work. There's no wonder on his big, round face but another look altogether: deeply serious, like a judge passing sentence. 'Leviathan' is the only word that comes from his mouth. He says the word again, under his breath, as he turns and walks away. Leviathan.

'In Isaiah, Leviathan is a serpent.' The voice of Owen Lewys is quiet and contemplative, and Rhisiart moves closer to hear him better. 'A serpent or a dragon, not an animal like this.' He continues, more emphatically: '"In that day the Lord with his sore and great and strong sword shall punish Leviathan the piercing serpent, even Leviathan that crooked serpent, and he shall slay the dragon that is in the sea."' A moment of contemplation, and then he speaks again, quietly as before. 'This animal is not a twisted serpent.'

'More like the Leviathan in the Book of Job, isn't it? The one who leaves a shining path behind him, so that one would think the deep hoary white.'

'Quite right, Rhisiart Dafydd. Look at the path he's cutting through the foam. And doesn't one of the Psalms say that Leviathan is playing in the sea?'

'It's as if he's escorting us.'

'Indeed. If I believed in such signs, I'd say he's showing us the way.'

The whale disappears completely under the waves, leaving only the trace of him in the foam. Rhisiart studies the face of his friend.

'But you don't believe in such signs.'

He doesn't answer. Rhisiart continues to look at him. The bones in his cheeks and his jaw are strong, but the wrinkled skin betrays his true age. There's more grey hair, too. He has aged during these two months at sea. He's an old man. An old man that Colonel Powel has pushed forward, sending him across the sea to seek a better world. A Moses of his people, preparing to lead Welsh Quakers to a new land, to create a peaceful realm for the remnants of the race of the Ancient Britons in America. Is there enough strength in him to carry that dream on his shoulders?

Owen Lewys is smiling shyly, as if he's been reading Rhisiart's mind.

'I would like to believe in such signs, Rhisiart Dafydd. I am trying my best to follow the light within, but it would be nice to get an outward sign to point the way every now and then.' He pushes back from the railing, testing his legs. He takes hold of Rhisiart's arm and gives it a squeeze, puts on his hat and turns to go. As he walks he calls over his shoulder, his voice strong again. 'I'm going below to visit Elizabeth and David and tell them about Leviathan. I'll make a story of it that will bring a smile to Elizabeth's face.'

Rhisiart turns back to the sea. The grey back of the whale surfaces again, closer this time, the water churning foamy white around him. Rhisiart smiles. There he is. Again. So close. Look at him. Look.

Playing in the sea. A shining path behind him.

–ΔΩ–

He's shivering. His fatigue has sapped his strength and he hasn't enough energy left to withstand the cold. He sees trees in the distance, or at least he thinks he sees the outline of trees in the darkness of the night. His eyes are watering and his mind fails to focus. He tries to take a step, forcing his legs to move, but he's too weak and the shivering overcomes him. The cold wind lashes him like the waves of the sea. He moves one foot forward, aiming in the direction of the trees, but that's the best he can do. There's nothing left in his muscles. He falls heavily onto his face, not even extending his arms in time to break the fall.

–5–

He's lying face down on the ground, just as he fell. Has been lying there for some time.

I have lived, I have done.

Shivering is all his body can do. He can't feel his hands or his feet. He knows he'll die here if he doesn't move.

Have believed, have lived, have done.

He tries to remember how to move a leg and what stretching an arm feels like. Amazingly, he is able to find one of his hands, squeezed between his chest and the ground. Also amazing is the realization that he is able to move a little. His hand pushes against the ground, enough to enable him to roll over onto his back. But that's all he can manage. The rain comes down again, hard. The wind is stronger too, sweeping over him, lashing the shore. His wet hair feels like grass, a growth that's part of the ground beneath him. Water is dripping off his beard and cheeks and running in small streams into the ground, watering the growth, as he becomes one with the earth.

–ΔΩ–

Land is sighted. One of the sailors shouts it out, then another one. Although the storm has not yet come upon them, the sea is very blustery and the *Primrose* is being tossed mercilessly upon the waves, so Rhisiart is the only passenger who comes on deck to see. It is closer than he expected. As he climbs up into daylight, he thinks he sees a low line of darkness on the horizon. Yes, that is the coastline. He can see the colours of the rocks and also the greenery in the distance. Seagulls are flying, being driven wildly by the awful weather. Birds of New England.

The intensity of the storm grows steadily throughout the afternoon, the ship faltering more and more as the waves push it this way and that. Rain comes too, and later, with the night, thunder and lightning. The captain orders him below with the rest of the passengers. It is too dangerous to look for anchorage: the waves would push the ship onto the rocks, break it to pieces. The only choice is to try to turn towards deeper waters and wait out the storm. The rain grows heavier and heavier, and waves cascade over the side of the ship. Even with the hatch doors closed, water pours in. Some of the passengers scream, others praying as they feel the salt water reaching them, the prayers of those who know the end is near. Heavy waves have smashed one of the doors, and a torrent of water rushes down through the open hatch now in concert with the cruel rhythm of the storm. 'I know not but that we are below the sea already,' one woman screams over the roar of the waves and the creaking protestations of the ship's timbers. 'God have mercy, for we are surely drowned!'

Rhisiart is thrown onto his face by the blow. Sharp and violent like the blast of cannon on the battlefield, and all the timbers of the ship vibrating. He is lying on his side in inches of water, wet blankets wrapped around his legs like seaweed. The darkness is filled with shrieks of terror and the pained wails of those injured by falling casks and chests. Rhisiart recovers somehow and reaches the narrow ladder. The ship is still leaning on its side, and he has to grip the rungs tightly because of the weight of the water pouring onto him through the open hatch. A shower of cold death, trying to push him back down. He climbs.

When he reaches the top, he sees that the ship is on the rocks. Although the waves continue to pound it hard and cruelly, it is caught fast on the jagged teeth. Sailors crawl on their bellies, clinging to whatever might support them and keep them from slipping over the side. Rhisiart hears the deep voice of the captain shouting off in the distance, but he can't make out what he is saying. He climbs out of the hatch and takes hold of a section of the wall of the upper deck beside him. Creeping and climbing. He looks around for the captain and finally sees him: he has lashed himself to the main mast sometime during the storm, his wet, bald head shining as lightning flashes, his voice calling out, shouting, sounds of human madness and animal rage. Rhisiart looks for someone else who might know what to do, his eyes questioning and his hands shaking. Then he sees something moving along the railing on the high side of the ship. Not a sailor, not a person, but a cat. A tomcat. Black Nicholas, working his way through the rain, his claws letting him travel along the wet wood, moving towards whatever end awaits him.

Rhisiart fights his way slowly back to the mouth of the hatch and calls down. Owen comes wading through the water, and the two of them speak hurriedly, shouting over the crashing of the waves and the thunder. Rhisiart says he will come down to help them, but Owen doesn't want him to. 'They're waiting, like everyone else. Hoping that the captain will get us to land.'

'He won't, Owen.' And he tries to explain the reality of the situation, but the older man merely says, 'They can't move, Rhisiart.'

'Wait a minute. Stay there. I'll go and see.' Rhisiart crawls away from the hole again to go and get help. There is a knot of sailors pressed against the railing on the low side of the ship, trying to hold on to the wood as the waves wash over them again and again. Another one hangs in the ropes from the aft mast, howling like a man on fire. And the captain is there still, held fast to the main mast, his deep voice reduced to that of a child by the severity of the thunder that drowns out his words. And so Rhisiart makes his way back to the hole, as quickly as he can, and shous down to his friend again.

'Come, Owen! Come on alone if they can't come. Come on!'

Rhisiart can't hear his reply, but he knows well what he's saying. He's saying he won't come. He's saying he's going to comfort David and Elizabeth. Another lighting flash, and Rhisiart sees that Owen is waving at him, smiling through the stream of water pouring down the ladder onto him. A second later he's gone. Vanished in the dark and the water.

Rhisiart has already decided what he is going to do. He crawls along until he can get hold of the wall panel and then he pulls himself up, gripping the wood, half walking, half climbing. Up and up, until he reaches the railing on the high side of the ship where he saw Nicholas moving earlier. He looks over the side, like a man on the steep roof of a house gazing down at the ground below. The rocks appear and disappear with the motion of the waves. He looks towards the land and sees it in silhouette when there's a flash of lightning. Half dragging himself and half walking, he moves along the railing towards the stern of the ship. When he comes to the ladder that leads to the upper deck, he climbs it. After reaching the aft upper deck, he inches his way along the railing to the stern of the Primrose. He looks over the side again, holding tightly to the railing, waiting for another flash of light. A minute, then another. Death awaits him. Finally, a flash, and it reveals no rocks below him. He climbs onto the railing, sitting on it like a man on a fence, still holding on tightly. He hopes for another flash of light so he can make sure there's nothing but water down there. The waves are treacherous as the sea rises and falls. How high up was he the last time he could see? He waits, but no light yet. A series of big waves come, the biggest yet, and the last of them nudges the ship off the rocks a bit. It's moving, the timbers creaking and snapping as it breaks up. There won't be another opportunity. He pushes himself up until he's standing on the edge of the ship, and jumps.

The Atlantic in autumn: the cold water instantly sucks the warmth from his body and the air from his lungs. But he doesn't hit rocks. Down he goes, somersaulting in the cold water, vanishing into a pit of oblivion. This is the mouth of Hell. Not a fiery, searing pit, but an endless pool of icy water dragging him down away from the light.

But he surfaces, a living cork, and starts to swim.

–ΔΩ–

I am wet grass.

Nothing but wet, cold grass, adhering to the earth. The wind tries to blow me away, but my hair has put down roots in the ground. Here I remain. I have lived, have done, have believed. And now I believe that here is where I shall remain forever.

Rhisiart has closed his eyes. He doesn't feel the rain that strikes his face or the blood that seeps from the wounds he received when he fell. He sinks deeper into the earth, the black hole closing around him.

II

Light unto Dark

1630–1656

Mae gan bob dyn ddigon o gyfrwystra i'w dwyllo ei hunan.

Every man has enough cunning to deceive himself.

Morgan Llwyd

1630

Rhisiart is five years old, and he is caught up in the excitement of the moment. He stands before his father, who is holding a new book, embracing it and handling it lovingly. There is no one taller than his father anywhere in the world. He imagines that not even King Arthur is taller, but he's not sure about Rhita Gawr and the other giants whom Arthur fought against. He looks at his father's face, so big and strong, looking down at him from high above. He almost touches the ceiling rafters. No, it's not possible to believe that Rhita Gawr is bigger than his father. But he's more like King Arthur than any giant. The hero of his imagination. Defender of his family's realm. And his father is all excited, his hands moving constantly, turning the book, embracing it, fondling it. He has never seen his father like this, and so Rhisiart himself is excited.

'See here, my boy.' His voice trembles but he's sure of his words. 'The Book has come into our house. It will dwell here in our home and in our hearts from this day until the end of our time on this earth. It has come at a momentous time in your life, my boy, for you have seen five years. One for each of the Trinity – Father, Son and Holy Spirit – and one each for your mother and me, your own flesh and blood. Five years, and lo, the Bible has come into our house. Learn to read it every day, and you will love it for the rest of your days.'

Later, the four of them are sitting at table. He looks at his sister Alys. She's seven years older than him. Two brothers and three sisters were buried before Rhisiart came into the world; he knows that somehow, though no one talks about it. He doesn't even know their names, but he thinks about them. So now there are but two children, the first and the last, like two bookends on a shelf that is otherwise empty, and nothing between them. Alys has had a big part in raising him, so she's more of a third parent than a sister. But he doesn't think of her as sister or as parent, only as Alys. Her face is beautiful and her hair long and dark, making her a mirror image of her mother. Remarkably similar but prettier: the years of hard work, birthing seven children and burying five of them has dimmed Rhisiart's mother's beauty. But she appears younger tonight, her eyes shining in the candlelight, she too greatly excited by this momentous occasion.

His father opens the book, slowly and humbly. He pauses, studying the page before him in silence, savouring the moment. He lifts his eyes and looks thoughtfully from his son to his daughter, and then turns to his wife. There are tears in her eyes by now, tiny drops glistening in the candlelight. Her husband sees this, and tears begin to gather in his eyes too.

'The first book of Moses, which is called Genesis. Chapter 1.' He swallows, clears his throat, and begins, slowly. '"In the beginning God created the heaven and the earth."'

1631

It's a warm day, and he has been helping to plough their fields. His father is following the plough; his mother is leading the horse. Rhisiart's job is to stand to one side watching, making sure the rows are straight. Alys is there too, but he's the one doing the real work. Every now and then he takes his mother and father a drink of water. Alys has to help with the carrying, but it is he who gives them the water, doing the important work.

The field has been ploughed and the sun has not yet left the sky. It's still warm. When they reach the end of the last row, his parents agree that his mother will see to the horse and Alys will clean the plough, leaving Rhisiart and his father to go to the river.

They reach the little pool, a bend in the river where the water accumulates before flowing out between the rocky banks. Rhisiart is naked and the water is cold, but the sun is warm on his arms and shoulders every time he comes up to the surface. He can stand on the bottom with his head out of the water, but he prefers to dive in and swim. His father taught him some months back, and he's glad to have this opportunity after a busy day.

'There you go, Rhisiart!' His father's voice is lively and clear, complementing the sunshine and the clear water of the river. His father is still talking, but Rhisiart has ducked his head under the surface and can't hear what he's saying. He realizes this and comes up again, finding his feet again. He is standing there in the middle of the small pool, water running off his hair, the sun warm on his shoulders. He faces his father, obediently, listening.

'Nobody in the county will be able to match you, Rhisiart, I guarantee it. Fear of water is one of the chief weaknesses of the Welsh. We live on an island, you know, with the sea around us everywhere. Our mountains and our valleys are full of lakes and pools and rivers, but very few Welsh are able to swim. Don't drown in sight of the shore – there's nothing more wasteful of life. Go to it, now! Show me!'

He's a water hound, let loose on the hunt by his master; laughing, jumping, splashing with his hands, then diving. He comes up swimming, across the pool to the shore and then turning to swim back to the other side. He goes as fast as he can, begins to tire but doesn't slow down. He wants to move fast and skilfully, to show his father.

Again, he jumps and dives, but not careful enough this time, and the rocks at the bottom scrape his hand and elbow. The pain overwhelms him; he tries to stand, but he can't put his feet on the bottom. He sinks down again, swallowing water, thinks he's going to drown, but it's only a few moments of terror. In no time at all he's standing, coughing, spitting out water. Blood is welling up in the grazes as he walks towards his father, not sure if he's crying or not.

'There, there, Rhisiart, come now.' A moment later he's standing in the grass, his father drying him with the tail of his own shirt. Rhisiart puts his clothes back on, his father helping him.

'Come along now, and I'll show you some otter tracks.'

'Will we see the otter?'

'I don't think so, Rhisiart. The otter prefers to come out in the evening or early in the morning. And he'll have been scared out of his wits by all your noise. He's sure to be hiding in his lair.'

Rhisiart has finished putting his clothes on, thinking about the otter in his hole. That's one of the things he thinks about often these days: animals that disappear into the earth. Rabbits, foxes, badgers. And especially the mole, more at home in the dark ground than in sunlight. Warm animals, their fur soft, burrowing into the old, hard earth, living in hidden chambers and making tunnels that go down and down. He heard an old man say once that moles travel down as far as Annwn. He asked his mother what Annwn was and she said that not 'what' but 'where' was the question, because Annwn was a place. Then he asked what sort of place it was and she said she wasn't sure, that some said that it was the land of the *Tylwyth Teg*, the Fairy Folk, and others said that Annwn is the land of devils, like Hell. He knew very well what kind of place that was: a place full of demons and goblins, dancing around in front of the flames. Rhisiart had a number of other questions, but his mother said that it would be better not to talk about such things. He is thinking about the world under the ground as he walks back to the house with his father, his body exhausted after all the swimming, his hair slowly drying, the sun slowly setting. He imagines a mole burrowing deep and reaching Annwn, then being frightened by the goblins. What would he do then? Scramble back up, certainly, clawing through the dirt till he reaches the surface, and the goblins after him, their teeth long and yellow and their horns pointed.

Before going to sleep, Rhisiart tells Alys about his plan. 'I'm going to search for mole hills tomorrow. I want to find every one and put a huge rock upon it.'

'Why, Rhisiart?' She's embracing him, holding him close to her, and there is a hint of laughter in her voice. 'Are you going to catch moles? Skin them so I can make you a coat out of them?'

'No, Alys. I want to cover up their holes. Cover them up forever!'

'Why is that, Rhisiart?'

'To keep the goblins and devils from coming out. I want to keep them under the ground in Annwn.'

1632

It's late, but he's not ready to go to sleep yet. He is still in his clothes, like Alys and his mother. The house is empty except for the three of them – all the visitors and sympathizers have been gone for a while. Alys has been tidying up and restoring a degree of order. Rhisiart is sitting in front of the fire with his mother, and now Alys joins them. When she speaks, she forces energy and strength into her voice, saying with every syllable that she is capable enough to look after them.

'I'm going to let the fire die, Mother. We'd better go to bed. There's no point in us staying like this for the rest of the night.' She forces a smile onto her face, and Rhisiart notices how different she is from their mother, their mother who has come to look so old and weak lately. But when she speaks, she doesn't have the voice of an old woman, only one who is weary to her bones.

'Alys, what will we do? You could go into service, or even marry if an offer comes. But what will we do, Rhisiart and me?'

'I'll do the work, Mother.' He tries to affect the same confidence in his voice as Alys and talk like an adult, but he doesn't succeed. It's the voice of a seven-year-old, the voice of a little boy who has just buried his father.

'You couldn't, Rhisiart. It's too much.'

'It won't be too much if I'm here also,' says Alys. 'And I will be here. And that's that.'

And that's how they are for six months or so. Alys and Rhisiart and their mother, trying to do all the work on the land all by themselves. Alys and her mother speak sometimes about getting someone to help out, but they have no means of paying anyone. Sometimes they talk about marriage, if an acceptable man chose to marry Alys and move in with them, one who could work hard and restore balance to their home. Or if the widowed mother remarried. But they don't have much time to get out and about and socialize. Even time to talk about such matters is scarce, with all the work filling their days. Rhisiart thinks that it is all that hard work that brought them to the graveside of their mother in the end. What will you do, the neighbours ask Alys, now that you have buried both your mother and your father this year? What will you do?

The answer comes all the way from Denbigh, in the form of their uncle. Rhisiart and Alys have their travelling clothes ready and their chest packed. He's a big man, bigger than their father, and all the mud on his travelling clothes makes him look wild, like some monster from the wilderness. His voice is deep and gruff. He doesn't speak in sentences at first, but rather greets them in solitary words. Sometimes a phrase. 'That's it' are the words he says most often. He says something about the trip, about the fact that this is the first time he's seen Caernarfonshire for some years. Rhisiart withers under the eye of the man, hardly believing he can be related to this wild-looking monster. A part of him wants to look to see if he has long, yellow teeth and horns under his hat, but another part of him feels guilty for harbouring such unchristian thoughts.

Then the big, grimy giant bends down next to him, squatting, and hands something to him. A small, slender volume. 'This is for you two. You and your sister.'

Rhisiart takes the book cautiously from the big hand. 'Thank you, Uncle.' Alys' voice is cheerful and confident, her hand on Rhisiart's back, encouraging him tenderly. He mumbles his thanks, echoing his sister's words.

'That's it. Something small. But large. In terms of its significance, that is.'

Rhisiart opens the cover and reads the words aloud, possibly so Alys can hear but also to show his uncle that he can read. '*Carwr y Cymry*, "The Friend of the Welsh", urging his beloved people and his fellow countrymen, for the sake of Christ and their souls, to study the Scriptures as Christ commanded.'

Hearing the boy read has loosened the man's tongue, as if he now knows that he is on familiar ground. 'That's it, Rhisiart, that's it.' He gets up and takes a step back so he can look the two in the face as he speaks. 'Your mother and father have endowed you with the Word. That and much more than I can give you. But I want you to take this book. As a pledge. As a pledge of my aim to do my very best for you. Anyway. It will be better guidance than the little bit of learning I have to give to you.' He laughs, a huge sound, similar, Rhisiart thinks, to the bellowing of a bull.

They thank him again, Rhisiart more readily this time.

'Come along now. Enough of these hellos. I've come a long way, and I'd like some food and a good night's rest. We'll leave before dawn.'

1638

It's a warm evening in summer and he's sitting on a water cask beside the door of the smithy. He had to put the lid firmly on the barrel first and then climb up on the seat and lean his back against the wall, a thing he learned to do a few months back when the lid suddenly slipped and dropped him into the water. He was reading in the moonlight, but a cloud has drifted in and taken away the light, so he closes the Bible. He caresses the book with his hands, as if he was stroking a cat.

'It has come at a momentous time in your life, my boy. Learn to read it every day, and you will love it for the rest of your days.'

Alys often reminded him of those words. She, being so much older than him, remembered many things their parents had said and made certain that her little brother remembered too by repeating them often, trying to make those small parts of their dead mother and father a part of Rhisiart. She succeeded. He doesn't see his sister often these days, but he no longer depends on her to keep these pieces of their family history alive in his memory. By now, he himself can quote things that his mother or his father said, though he doesn't know for sure whether he heard his parents uttering those words with his own ears or whether he remembers Alys repeating them, thus hearing his mother and his father through the ears of his sister. He considers this perplexing question sometimes, but the answer doesn't trouble him too much. He takes comfort in the fact that these words are a part of him.

'See here, my boy. The Book has come into our house. It will dwell here in our home and in our hearts from this day until the end of our time on this earth.'

He marvels every time he sees Alys. Twenty is so old! Old

enough to get married. She has been old enough to get married for a long time. But she's a maid in Plas Araul, and so she doesn't marry. That's why their uncle secured a place for him as an apprentice in Wrexham rather than in Denbigh: he knew that Rhisiart would get to see his sister every now and then when she comes to town for her mistress. This happens barely once a month, but it does happen, and Alys always gets permission to stay longer in the town so she can see her brother. More often than not, Rhisiart is in the middle of some task he can't set aside when his sister comes, and so Alys stands in the door of the smithy and talks to her brother as he carries on with his work.

He's touching the cover of the book tenderly with the tip of his finger, as if he were touching a child's cheek. Alys gave the Bible to him when she went to work for the family at Plas Araul. 'Keep it, Rhisiart. Ieuan Watcyn is a religious man. I won't be deprived of the Word in his house.'

He tried to say it should be otherwise, that he would be able to buy his own Bible when enough wages had come his way. But his sister only smiled and put the book in his hands. 'No, Rhisiart. Go with it, to wherever you go in your life. And go with my blessing too.'

He wanted her to take *Carwr y Cymry*, and when she tried to refuse he said that he had memorized all of it by then anyway and it would be more difficult to see her leaving unless at least one of the two books accompanied her. Reading the two books together had been a nightly custom throughout their two years in Denbigh. *Carwr y Cymry* first, and then the Bible. But beginning with the *Carwr* every night for two years.

> For Holy Scripture is like the garden of Eden, or earthly Paradise, and by reading or meditating on the Word man is in the midst of the garden as it were, conversing with God as did Adam before, and eating of the tree of knowledge of good and evil unforbidden,

> yes, and getting to eat of the tree of life which is in the midst of God's Paradise. And that tree is Christ, and its fruit is sweet in the mouths of the faithful, and they rejoice in sitting in its shade.

Their uncle would sit with them too, on those rare occasions when he didn't have to travel for his business, but he never participated in the reading. He would only sit and listen, every now and then making some sound in his throat, punctuating and commenting wordlessly. And because Rhisiart thought that his uncle was like a bear, he imagined sometimes that that would be how you would say 'amen' in bear talk, but he didn't share that with his sister. Sometimes, when it's too dark to read at night, he recites from memory bits of wisdom from the *Carwr*. Man will be in the midst of the garden of Eden or earthly Paradise, eating of the tree of life, and its fruit sweet in the mouths of the faithful.

He's reflecting on that right now, but cultivating thoughts of another kind. He's an apprentice to Edward Wiliam, and Edward Wiliam is a good man. But Rhisiart is not completely certain that he is a religious man. He believes he is, he wants to think he is, but he doesn't know for sure. Alys always says that her master and mistress are religious people, but he doesn't understand how she can say that with such conviction. He would like to ask her, but more often than not Edward Wiliam or his wife or one of their daughters are around when Alys is visiting. He feels uneasy, thinking that he's doing his master an injustice by letting this question take precedence in his thinking. Judging. Who has the right to judge others? And Edward Wiliam is a good man.

His master's smithy is Rhisiart's world now. He's learning to work the bellows and wield a hammer, learning how to handle iron – the secrets of beating and shaping, everything that happens between the heating in fire and the cooling in water. Learning how to create. He loses himself in the pounding, in the singing of hammer on anvil. There is no sense or measure of time beyond this singing and hammering, as he beats day into week, week into month, month into year. Yes, and year into another year. Only on Sundays does he remember that time has structure, and the respite from work gives him the opportunity to note that another week has gone by. He is excelling in his work, and his master says he is going to let him take up some tasks by himself, tasks that most smiths would not entrust to such a young apprentice. Edward Wiliam is a quiet man who doesn't speak if he doesn't have to, so the fact that he praises Rhisiart warms the lad's heart.

The family goes to church, like everyone else, and Rhisiart with them, to listen to a sermon and to say the familiar words. Afterwards, he gets to enjoy a bit of fun and Sunday leisure. These occasions afford an opportunity to familiarize himself with the town, walking to the church and then joining in sport with some of the other youths of the town, playing ball or wrestling. He almost never loses; long hours at the smithy have made him stronger than most boys his age, and he possesses a degree of determination that, he supposes, borders on sinful pride. But he enjoys winning, and he almost always does.

Just as he loses himself in the music of the hammering during the day, so he surrenders to the words of the Scriptures at night. He tries to read the Bible every night before sleeping. When he has a stump of candle, he'll read in the little loft above the smithy where he sleeps. And sometimes, when the weather is mild and the moon is bright, he'll sit on the water cask beside the door in his nightshirt, reading.

Something else also weighs on his mind tonight, something apart from the piety of Edward Wiliam and his right to judge him. He thinks about his own gift.

Slowly but surely he has come to realize that words are ringing in his ears with the echo of the hammer when he's at work, and he is turning words over in his head, remembering bits of Scripture and reflecting on certain verses. He notices that he has begun to play with all these words. Now he's in the habit of rearranging them, working with them and mixing them with colloquial words and expressions that aren't in the Bible.

And so he has begun to work words just as he works iron. As Rhisiart's arms grow strong with the physical activity, so too some internal faculty strengthens within him. He recites verses silently to himself, verses that he himself has composed, and he recites them to the accompaniment of the hammer. He delivers sermons to the fire in the forge, fashions an address to the iron in elaborate language about this thing or that, the polished words coming one after another, accompanying the ringing of the hammer on the anvil. He has never written down a word – he has neither paper nor the time to use it – but he's composing works in his head as if he were intending to record them some day. Religious verses. Elegies to his mother and his father. Poetic greetings to his sister. An ode to the smith. A host of sermons, numerous flowery orations. And although he has not put one of them down on paper nor shared them with anyone, he sometimes feels that he is sharing them with the world. They become a part of his work, an element in what he produces, his words penetrating the iron that he hammers, becoming part of the gate or the horseshoe or the knife he's creating. All his words recorded in secret writing in the metal.

He leads a horse from the forge, its new shoes leaving bits of Rhisiart's poetry in the muck and mud along the streets of the town. *The loveliest trefoils that ever were.*

When the new fire irons in the Swan tavern are used for the first time, some of the smith's apprentice's flowery language rises with the flames. *And we, the remnants of the race of Ancient Britons, remember.*

The new gate at the church opens for the first time, revealing part of a sermon as it squeaks on its hinges. *In the name of Jesus Christ, who shed his heart's blood for us, the wretched children of Adam.*

Brightness. Light. Not much, but enough for his young, strong eyes to see the letters on a page. The cloud has moved and let the moon show its face again. He opens the book and finds his place in it.

> By night on my bed I sought him whom my soul loveth: I sought him, but I found him not. I will rise now, and go about the city in the streets, and in the broad ways I will seek him whom my soul loveth: I sought him, but I found him not.

A familiar voice is calling across the smithy courtyard from the direction of the house. 'What would my father say? You sitting there in your nightshirt!'

It's Elisabeth, his master's eldest daughter. He looks up. She's but a pale shadow in the doorway, but he knows exactly the shape of her head and the curve of her mouth. He knows that her eyes are laughing at him, teasing and provoking him. What would my father, your master, say? He closes the book and slides off the barrel onto his feet so he can stand to answer her. 'That doesn't concern me as much as what you think of me.'

1640

John Davis will come tomorrow to fetch the sword. The first that this forge has produced. It's a sample sword that will show the old soldier that Edward Wiliam and his apprentice can make weapons for the militia. One piece of work that will secure more work for them. John Davis said that it was Ieuan Watcyn who suggested that the smith ought to have a chance, even though he was not overly familiar with that kind of work. Rhisiart knew well where that impulse came from: the servant girl whispering in the ear of her mistress, her mistress whispering in the ear of her husband, and, to the great surprise of John Davis, here's Ieuan Watcyn telling him one day that he ought to give the smith, Edward Wiliam, the opportunity to serve the militia. John Davis is not a man who likes to listen to other men, but he has to defer to the nobleman. Although he doesn't hide his feelings easily, he's not entirely displeased; he has admired the sturdy fire dogs at the Swan and the new gate at the church, and he knows very well which smith made them. All right, he says to himself, give them a chance to beat ploughshares into swords. Edward Wiliam gives thanks to Divine Providence for this opportunity. Rhisiart gives thanks to his sister, Alys.

The day's work was finished some time ago. It's been a while since Edward Wiliam went out of the door of the smithy, washed in the cask's clean water, and walked across the yard to his house. And as he does at the end of every work day, Rhisiart has been straightening up their workplace. Sweeping up the ashes that have fallen to the floor. Arranging the tools. Making certain there is enough firewood in the pile for the next day.

The new sword shines on the long table next to the wall. They don't have a scabbard for it, and so the naked blade reflects the light from the fire's glowing embers. He walks over to it and carefully grasps the hilt. He raises the weapon and tries to hold it as he imagines John Davis will hold it tomorrow. With each passing week Rhisiart takes more and more pleasure in his work. The hammering and the composing. The magic that he puts into his creations. The secret words he encloses in them. He composes a sermon for himself and puts it into the metal. He makes a poem in praise of his master and hammers it into a part of the object. He sings a love song to Elisabeth and folds it into the hot iron.

He imagines what will happen in the morning. John Davis will come to inspect the sword. Rhisiart lifts the sword and tests its balance. Looks closely at the blade. He holds it up and stands as if he were facing another swordsman. He strikes the air with it, killing his imagined foe. Striking, stabbing, turning, and striking again, Rhisiart's words flowing from the blade. *Who can ask the iron tool about its lot and its lifetime, who but the smith who made it?*

Rhisiart pauses, the sword hanging uncertainly in the air, his attempts to imitate the soldier yielding to different thoughts.

He heard Walter Cradoc preach for the first time earlier that year. Cradoc and others around Llanfair, some who had been preaching in the district before going to join the new church that was being organized in Llanfaches. A heart opening a heart. Words compelling him to consider the truth of the Word. Voices calling on him by his name, sinner, to see his own life in a new light. He has turned his back on the Sunday games, although some of his old friends call to him to join in the fun when he walks home from the church with Elisabeth and her family. He believes he ought to turn his back in like fashion on much of his composing, reject the desire to compose praise poems and love songs, and devote himself only to pounding religious verses into the iron. But he can't obey his own conscience. He can't control his poetic inspiration nor renounce his gift. Words come unbidden into his mind to the accompaniment of hammer blows, and he can't stop them any more than he can silence the echo of the blows on the anvil.

And so, after testing the balance of the sword in his hand, he asks himself, what words have been sunk into this metal?

Edward Wiliam has taken him to hear the itinerant preachers. His wife and his daughter Elisabeth come sometimes too, when it's possible and appropriate. Together they have heard Walter Cradoc preach. And they've heard Vavasor Powell with their own ears, saying that it's the grace of God rather than human will that counts, preaching as if he were speaking directly to them – friend to friend, or a brother counselling a brother or sister. They've witnessed the power of a young preacher by the name of Morgan Llwyd. And they've heard a number of others as well, some who have touched their hearts even though they have not won as much fame among the faithful as some of the other preachers, some who have done their work and played their part even though future ages will not remember them.

Everyone who is acquainted with Edward Wiliam knows that he is a quiet man. Some have mistaken his silence for apathy or lack of courtesy, or even the animal dumbness of one who cannot engage in proper speech. But he is gradually becoming known as a quiet, contemplative man these days. The silence that people had taken as a defect is now considered a sign of presence, of depth. The people of Wrexham – or at least those inhabitants who are concerned about such things – say that Edward Wiliam is a religious man. His house is sought out by people who are called faithful believers by their friends and zealous extremists by those who don't agree with them. Occasionally one will ask the smith about the change, and he says, in his own quiet way, and in as few words as possible, that it is his apprentice, Rhisiart Dafydd, who is responsible.

Rhisiart comes to the house every night these days to pray

and read together with the family. Edward Wiliam has bought a Bible for the family and it sits in the middle of the table with a candle on either side of it. But it's removed from that place of honour each night after the family has finished the meal so they can read it and discuss it. Sometimes Rhisiart recites from the *Carwr* from memory before they open the Bible.

> For Holy Scripture is like the garden of Eden, or earthly Paradise, and by reading or meditating on the Word man is in the midst of the garden as it were, conversing with God as did Adam before.

Rhisiart looked at Elisabeth once as he recited those words, thinking about Eve, and blushed. Edward Wiliam saw his apprentice's discomfort, and thought that the cause of his embarrassment was forgetting the words of the book. So he bought a copy of *Carwr y Cymry* and gave it to Rhisiart, to help him. The lad thinks he ought to tell his master the truth, but he's fifteen years old and he finds it hard to discuss the subject. He can pound the words into the iron easily when he's working, but he can't find them when he wants to use them in conversation.

Just as he can feel the power in his muscles, as he knows that a smith's strength is in his arms, he knows that there is power of another kind inside him. The Word has penetrated him and become a part of him, just as something of himself has become a part of the iron he hammers in the smithy.

But something preys on his mind as he stands there in the shadow of the forge, the sword in his hand. What good is the power in his body and the strength in his will if he's not using them to defend that which is right and true? It's not uncommon when the faithful gather in the open air to listen to one of the travelling preachers for a crowd to rise up against them. Jubilation turning perilous, the religious experience becoming a very different kind of experience. Once, when William Webster was delivering a sermon, Rhisiart found himself on the opposing side in a confrontation with a couple of the youths he had once played with on Sundays.

'Look – Rhisiart Dafydd has gone to listen to an open-air sermon with the English fools!'

Rhisiart tried to enlighten them, tried to say that that special light is as much for the Welsh as for the English. He quoted from the *Carwr*, saying that the minority could become the majority if they would only open their hearts. He stood against them, attempting to silence their curses and their threats with words from the book.

'There is, for that small handful of the remnants of the Welsh nation who still dwell in their own land…'

– beastly screaming from his antagonists –

'a multitude of very great and severe causes to consider…'

– threatening shouts –

'to acknowledge God's mercy towards them…'

– mocking laughter –

'because of his constant succour and goodness to them…'

In the end he had but two choices: defend himself with his fists against his former friends, or turn and run. He chose the latter and fled from his tormentors, telling himself that the scornful tirade and mocking laughter were a price worth paying for turning the other cheek. He opened the *Carwr* that night so he could see the sentences he already knew by heart, and thought he found new meaning in the familiar words:

> You, hearkeners eager to study the Scriptures, will be ready to fight in the ranks of your ministers against your opponents, like soldiers fighting in the ranks of their Captains. Bold and confident you can be on behalf of the truth, when you hold the sword of the spirit, that is the Word of God, a ready weapon against ignorant and wicked men.

Shortly afterwards he heard Vavasor Powell telling in a sermon how Satan had tried to deflect him from the path by sending persecutions to frighten and torment him. Once, when that godly man was travelling in his native district, two noblemen who were relatives of his, men he had rebuked for their sins, attacked him with a cudgel. He was wounded but he escaped with his life, and grace and the ability to forgive came into his heart. Another time, as he was going to worship on the Sabbath, there were four men waiting beside the road, armed and intending to kill him, but their plan was thwarted when a company of travellers passed by and he managed to escape with his life once again.

Rhisiart told himself that that was the way of a soldier, fighting enemies of the ministers of God. Turning the other cheek and letting deliverance come in accord with His mystical providence was the way of the sword of the spirit. He told himself that it was the Word of God which was the true weapon when ignorant men attacked and denied and mocked the truth. And yet he could not dismiss the feeling that the Spirit was moving him to read the words of the *Carwr* literally and become an actual soldier for that Word now.

And then Edward Wiliam got the opportunity to serve the militia, provided he and his apprentice could first fashion a sword that would satisfy John Davis, the captain who directed them at the request of Ieuan Watcyn. His master was not certain they could manage the unfamiliar work, but Rhisiart said that he was confident that they could give it a good try if they could get a well-made sword on loan to check and examine. He spent a good deal of time with that weapon, noting how it felt in his hand and how it sliced through the air. He cut stalks and wood, noting the action of the blade. When he felt he understood the nature of the weapon well enough, he and his master set to work, finally producing the sword that he brandishes tonight.

He lifts it up, holding it at an angle, and then turning it until the little light that remains in the smithy touches the blade.

He thinks about the persecutions that would come to torment a true Christian. He remembers Vavasor Powell's stories. Wouldn't it be better for a righteous Christian to arm himself and trust in God? Wouldn't He guide his hand if it were necessary? The grace of God, not man's will. In what way does the one prevail over the other? How does one know the true path of grace? He remembers how Vavasor Powell took up the Word against the club of his persecutors and escaped alive without resorting to violence. Yes, escape safely and receive grace, that grace bestowing the ability to forgive those who want to be your enemy. He thinks to himself that this is the way of the Lamb.

But Rhisiart cannot completely cast out the desire. He feels the force of the sword in his hand and imagines what he could do with it. He raises it, turns, strikes, pierces, his words pouring from the blade.

1641

Evening is coming on and the shadows are long. Autumn has come upon them swiftly, as it does every year, and night comes earlier than expected. Most of the enclosure, including the smithy, the stable and the house, is in shadows, but although the sun has retreated quickly in the last hour, it hasn't yet disappeared entirely. A patch of light remains close to the smithy, because the roof of that building is not as high as the others. Here they meet. Here, on this tiny island of light, among the heavy shadows of autumn.

Rhisiart had come from the door of the smithy to fetch more firewood for the morning, but paused in the light, closed his eyes, and turned his face to the sun. There he stands, when Elisabeth comes to him. She had been on some other errand but saw Rhisiart and walked over to him, quietly, out of the shadows into the middle of that little pool of light. He opens his eyes and sees her standing there in front of him, the late sunlight enhancing the glow of her cheeks and the lustre of her blue eyes.

They stand there for a moment, looking at each other, the sun bathing them with a shower of light. Rhisiart smiles at her, and she smiles back. He walks on then, silently, but as he steps past her his hand brushes her hand. Lightly, for less than a second, almost accidentally. But connecting nonetheless, before moving out of the light into the shadows.

July 1642

Sweat drips from his brow and his cheeks. He feels it running down his neck too. His shirt hangs wet on his body, as drenched in sweat as if he'd been swimming in his clothes. But he doesn't move. He knows that the men on either side of him are reeling; he can hear the pikes shaking in their hands and their laboured breathing suggests that they are on the verge of collapse. The midday sun is roasting and the day is still, the air motionless. But he doesn't move an inch. He holds his body in the proper position: left foot forward, knee bent, right foot stretched back and slightly to the side, his weight forward. His hands hold the long pike at an angle, the sharp iron tip waiting in the air to stop an imaginary horse, the other end of the shaft secure against his right foot.

It's an open field with no shade at all, and within earshot of some of London's busiest markets. A patch of grass amidst the urban tumult, but today that patch has been turned into a drill field, and the grass has been trampled beneath hundreds and hundreds of feet. The recruits can hear the cries of merchants in the background, mixed with other sounds from the crowded streets, but every one of them hopes to hear just one particular voice. Every one of them is awaiting the next command from their officer, longing to hear it and be released from their misery. It's been forever since he ordered them into this position; like the other soldiers, Rhisiart expected the officer to follow it immediately with another command. The men are growing angry: he's playing with us, he's enjoying abusing his authority. But he's testing – testing their stamina and their obedience at the same time. A minute passes, then two, three and more. Rhisiart hears men struggling throughout the ranks. He hears the pikes shaking in their hands, but he doesn't move.

I am iron, iron purified in fire.

A wasp circles through the air, its unwelcome buzz coming nearer and nearer. He can see the insect now, moving in the air in front of his face. Buzzing nearer still, and then some silky part of its little body brushes the skin of his cheek – a wing or a leg or a stinger, feeling him, testing. But it doesn't sting. And Rhisiart doesn't move. He clenches his teeth, but he doesn't move his head. He doesn't move an inch. A second that is painfully long, and then another second. And then the wasp flies off, buzzing and winding his way through the heat of the treeless field.

Rhisiart has been in London since the beginning of the month. King Charles had published his Commission of Array in order to swell the ranks of his army and prepare for the conflict that was coming. The faithful from around Wrexham heard that the authorities had come to Chester to force the men of that district to obey the King's call. They feared that their town would be next, and so rather than wait to be dragged into the ranks of the Royalist army like sheep being driven into pens, a number of them decided to travel to London, the stronghold of the cause of Parliament and the Saints. Rhisiart received permission from his master to break the bonds of apprenticeship and go with them.

He got permission from Elisabeth, too.

The two of them stood by the door of the smithy for a long time, the moon lighting their faces. She spoke of the future: war wouldn't come; the King would surely waken from his foolishness. And even if war did come, it wouldn't last long. Rhisiart would be back in Wrexham after a few months, back to her. They would be together again soon, probably before winter. Rhisiart spoke of the present, beautiful words flowing from him. They were living in an earthly paradise already. He would take that paradise to London with him, in his heart. Knowing that she would be waiting for him was enough; loving from afar is still love, and true love is paradise on earth. That certainty outweighs the uncertainty of the times. All those words came effortlessly from him; he uttered them with the sureness of one who speaks from the heart.

A dreamlike week on the road, walking the entire way from Wrexham to London. A knot of the faithful walking together, talking excitedly about the good days to come. Frequently receiving the kindness of strangers in village and farmhouse, but sometimes forced to draw back and hide when they feared that the King's men were nearby, and then going along footpaths between fields and along hedgerows until they thought it safe to return to the main roads. And then, finally, London: a city they would normally have thought of as Gomorrah or Sodom or Babylon, a cesspool of filth and sin, the destination of those who worship money and pleasure. But weary after dusty days on the road, with sore feet, stomachs half empty and their hearts swelling with the knowledge that they had arrived safely, that's not how they looked upon the streets of London. London for them then was the destination of hope, of justice, the seat of the Parliament which gave succour to the Saints.

Their little drop of Welshness is lost in a sea of Englishness. Rhisiart is now living in a warehouse that has been turned into a barracks, bunking and training with hundreds of Londoners. Apprentices of every kind. Craftsmen. Small merchants. Boatmen from the Thames docks. Young men who were doing who knows what before enlisting along with a host of others and following the regimen of the London trained bands. Volunteers, soldiers of the Saints. They come to this field every day, drenched in the rain, sweating in the sun. Preparing.

The news came three days ago: the King had raised his banner in Nottingham. *God save King Charles and hang up the Roundheads* is the blasphemous war cry of the forces who follow that flag, but Rhisiart and his fellow volunteers know that they are the soldiers called by God. It is they who are training to do

His work. The travelling preachers who visit the barracks in the evening and on the Sabbath tell them that they are like a church gathered in the Holy Spirit. They know that this is true. They pray together like a church. They move together like a church on the practice field too, preparing to face a false enemy on the day of battle and stand, shoulder to shoulder, like a church gathered together in the Holy Spirit. And here they are, in the punishing sun of July. Training. Preparing.

Rhisiart hears something close by: a heavy sound – a body falling, hitting the ground heavily – and right after, the lighter sound of a pike bouncing as it lands on the grass, the long shaft rattling. He hears similar sounds further down the row, but he doesn't turn his head to look. He remains still, unmoving, the sweat running down his face, rolling down his neck and dripping down his legs and arms. The wooden shaft of his pike feels slippery in his hands, but he doesn't lose his grip.

And then, finally, the voice of the officer shouting, cutting through the air like a trumpet: 'Order your pikes! Stand! Order! Pikes to your inside!'

October 1642

They are moving again after standing for so long; marching in formation, disciplined. They are lost in the several rhythms of their march: hundreds upon hundreds of feet pounding the ground, blending with the beating of the drummers, swords clanking on thighs, the shaft of an occasional pike improperly held clattering on the shaft of another. They move on, marching in a column down the road, in the direction of the hill.

Rhisiart is in the front row of his group of pikemen, so it's the musketeers who are marching directly in front of him, their weapons on their shoulders. Each of them marching, part of the rhythm of the whole, contributing to the myriad sounds filling their ears. It was raining earlier and therefore no dust raises to blind and choke them. A blessing. But it didn't rain hard, so they aren't marching in mud either. Another blessing.

Rhisiart is marching in step, disciplined, holding his long pike on his shoulder, his sword slapping his thigh with each stride. His head is a bit warm in the helmet, but it doesn't bother him. He's got used to the heavy breastplate; it no longer feels like extra weight, only a part of his body. A shell, hard skin. The sun is warm but the wind is cool, so the marching is not difficult.

There's a letter in his knapsack, but he doesn't need to take it out to read it, for the words are all in his head. He can read them slowly and tenderly, caress the handwriting letter by letter, word by word. The first three words melt his heart: 'My dear Rhisiart'. Three words, strengthening their bond, expressing love. And the last words: 'Be true, be safe, be well'. Words conveying the solace of a prayer or a charm. And finally, the name: Elisabeth. She says in the letter that she'll be on her way to London before long. Ieuan Watcyn has secured work for her father in one of Parliament's armouries there, so the whole family is moving.

Rhisiart's sister has moved there already, because the Watcyns have relocated most of their servants from Plas Araul to their house in the city. Elisabeth says she can't wait to see her again: 'Alys, whom I will get to address as *my* sister before the end of the year.'

Before the end of the year. If Rhisiart comes back to London alive. He will be true, will be safe, will be well.

He marches on, his body yielding to the rhythm and helping to create it at the same time. Hundreds upon hundreds of feet pounding the ground. Drums beating. Weapons clanking, creating a counterpoint to the main rhythm of the march. He can see more of the hill now, its summit growing as they draw near.

A heavy, booming sound drowns out the rhythmic beat of their feet, louder and deeper and new. It's coming from the direction of the hill.

More loud booms. Cannon firing. He can't hear the shots landing; the enemy must be firing at their lead troops. But the sound is blunting his fellow soldiers' courage. He can hear the rhythm of the march changing as some of them flinch and others stumble, the ranks falling out of step. He hears the voice of an officer shouting in the distance: he can't make out the words but he knows the officer is calling on them to move on, calling on them not to lose heart.

As the cannon continue to pound, one of the men begins to sing, and before he finishes the first line others are joining in, soldiers throughout the column adding their voices and swelling the song.

My shepherd is the Living Lord
Nothing therefore I need,
In pastures fair with waters calm
He sets me forth to feed.

He did convert and glad my soul,
And brought my mind in frame
To walk in paths of righteousness
For His most holy name.

The thunder of the cannon mingles with the song, an intermittent series of bass counterpoints to the hundreds of voices. The marching becomes more rhythmic again, the soldiers' feet pounding the ground confidently, accompanying the psalm they are singing. Rhisiart sings too, but the Welsh words come naturally into his head as the English lines flow from his mouth: *Yr Arglwydd yw fy mugail i, ni bydd eisiau arnaf.*

Now they are leaving the road and being led into an open field. The singing has ceased and Rhisiart is praying silently. He remembers hearing Vavasor Powell say in a sermon that the true saint can pray anywhere, whether standing, walking, or even talking. His marching is his prayer – each foot striking the ground, the strength of his arm holding the pike, the way he stands tall as he marches: that is his prayer. I do not fear harm, for Thou art with me.

They move from their column into rows, an officer telling them where each rank should stop and stand, forming them into battle lines. Rhisiart can see some of their standards along the line, fluttering in the wind, small splashes of moving colour floating in the air. One of them is close enough for him to read the words on it, large black letters on a field of bright yellow: *God With Us.* He sees the lines of the Royalist soldiers at the foot of the hill in the distance, their own colourful standards catching the eye. He hears horses behind him; he can't turn to look but he knows that some of Parliament's cavalry are moving from behind their ranks, being repositioned in another part of the field.

Another booming salvo, and he can see the smoke rising from the Royalist cannon in the distance. Sounds come from another place this time too, from behind and to the left, their own big guns answering. Finally. And now yet another kind of sound, an evil whistling in the air, coming nearer and nearer as the enemy's cannonballs pass over their heads. One of them strikes the ground heavily some twenty yards in front of him, sending a spray of dirt into the air.

The wind has turned and smoke from their own cannon blows through their ranks, bringing the taste of sulphur to their mouths and tears to their eyes. More blasts and more smoke, and Rhisiart can see nothing in front of him but the odd patch of colour in the distance. A rare star twinkling through the occasional tear in the clouds, but those clouds are on the ground, surrounding them, choking them.

A thunderous sound, coming closer and closer. Hundreds of hooves pounding the ground, men shouting, their cries swelling with the sound of the horses, nearer and nearer. Rhisiart cannot hear the officer's command, but he senses the line moving and he knows instinctively what to do. He puts his left foot forward, bending his knee and moving his pike at an angle at the same time. A slight movement then to make sure that the end of the shaft is sitting firmly against his right foot.

But the direction of that surging clamour has changed. The King's cavalry has moved to the side, past the middle of the line. He can see the last of the squadron through the smoke now, crossing in front of them to the left. And then a series of shots – the musketeers next to his own line of pikemen are firing. He thinks he sees a man falling from his horse, but a new cloud of smoke blocks his view before he has a chance to get a better look. Other sounds now from the far end of the line to the left. Horrible noises as the attacking Royalist cavalry reach their army. Metal on metal, screaming, shots, horses whinnying wildly.

God help them.

Once again, a roar coming from the foot of the hill and growing rapidly. The sound of another Royalist squadron racing across the field. Here they come, they're charging right at us, Rhisiart thinks. These are coming at me. He shakes his pike a little, making sure that it's firmly secured at his right foot. But they're not coming at him, they're following the same path as the other Royalists, galloping past the middle of the Parliamentarian army and striking at the flank.

The sounds of the fighting coming from that direction are different, rather like the roar of waves striking a beach, lapping different sections bit by bit, the sound moving further away from Rhisiart, further to his left and maybe a bit behind them too. Words nervously exchanged along the line, coming now to Rhisiart: some of our cavalry are there on the left, but they have broken under the weight of the onslaught by the Royalists. They're retreating, fleeing, with the enemy in pursuit. They have broken.

God help them.

Something moving rapidly in front of him. Horses, five or six of them, galloping madly, not at him but past him, a few yards in front of the tips of their pikes. Although he didn't get a chance to see his face, Rhisiart knows who one of the riders was – the Earl of Essex. He is about to turn to try to follow his path, but something in front of him catches his eye: the earth around the foot of the hill appears to be moving, and the land is coming towards them. Rhisiart strains to see, but another puff of smoke is obscuring his view. A moment, another, and the air clears enough for him to see better. It wasn't the land that was moving, it was men, long lines of infantry who had been standing, waiting, along the foot of the hill. Thousands of men, on the move. The main army of the Royalists moving, thousands of foot soldiers coming nearer and nearer.

God help us.

Whispers and words, percolating all down the line: they're coming, they're coming. Nervous talk. Hold your ground, lads. Hold. God is on our side. Hold. Another message being delivered from man to man along the line, one that's spoken enthusiastically: the Earl of Essex is standing with us – he has dismounted and is standing in the front rank with us.

Hold fast! Here they come! Hold fast!

They're coming, they're coming. Hold your ground, Rhisiart, he says to himself. God is on our side, so stand firm and hold your ground. You shall not want.

He notices that parts of the enemy front line are stopping, standing, the Royalist musketeers preparing to shoot. He thinks he hears one of their own officers calling on their musketeers to hold and wait until the enemy has come closer, but he has not succeeded in controlling them. Shots explode down the line as the men shoot before the Royalists have chance to fire their own weapons. He sees a few in the enemy line falling, but only a few. The ranks close immediately; it has had almost no effect. Then a series of answering shots, the Royalist musketeers shooting, and smoke rising in a patchwork of small grey clouds. Rhisiart hears one of his comrades screaming somewhere down the line, but he can't see the man falling.

The enemy pikemen come nearer and nearer. The colourful spots on their banners have grown now, and he can see an occasional design clearly. A tree. The head of a stag. A crown. He can't read the words yet, but since so many rumours have reached them in the last week, he knows well what words are on them. *For King and Church. For King and Queen. Cuckolds Here We Come. Death to all Traitors.* Their officers shout commands, and their pikemen lower their weapons, ready for the encounter. Stand, hold your ground. The Lord is my shepherd. My dear Rhisiart, you shall not want. Hold your ground. Stand.

Row after row of muskets on both sides fire away, just before the lines come together. Out of the corner of his eye he sees men falling, some Royalist, some Parliamentarian. Everyone is shouting as the pikes collide, animal screams of men mixed with the clashing of weapons. Wood striking wood, metal hitting metal. Long shafts colliding, pressing, pushing.

Rhisiart is in the midst of the press of pikes, enclosed in a shifting forest of wooden shafts weaving through each other, striking each other, moving up and down. Some of the soldiers on both sides have dropped their pikes entirely and drawn their swords, and they are trying to move laterally through the press of shafts. But the smoke comes endlessly, puff after puff, cloud after cloud, drying the throat and bringing tears to the eyes. Rhisiart feels something, a jolt, the tip of his pike has gone solidly into something, but he can't see exactly what. Has it sunk into flesh? Has one of the enemy grabbed the shaft? He gives a slight push, moves forward a half step, but he can't see. Then the smoke clears, enough for him glimpse the faces of the enemy, right in front of him, not more than the length of a pike's shaft. Faces distorted in fear and fury. Frenzy. One is coming nearer, pushing himself along the shaft. He has dropped his pike and drawn his sword. Rhisiart steps up, drops his pike, his right hand feeling for the hilt of his sword.

So easy. He strikes once, twice, then his blade finds the man's neck, just below his chin. Striking, thrusting, metal on metal, metal sinking into flesh.

The man beside him has not had time to drop his pike and draw his sword, and so it's even easier, the blade finding a neck, a hand coming up too late.

He turns to the next man. He is ready, but can't withstand Rhisiart. Striking, driving, finding flesh. Bold and confident, fighting in the name of truth, bearing the sword of the Holy Spirit. Rhisiart Dafydd playing his part in the Battle of Edgehill.

He is seventeen years old. He is killing men who are very much older than him. He kills an occasional lad who is younger than him too. But age, name and every other human consideration are of no concern to him in the press of pikes and the choking smoke. He is a timeless creature, a guardian angel, one of the messengers of the Lord. He is a soldier in the Army of the Saints.

May 1643

Cheapside again, about a week after they demolished the Cross. Smashing and crushing every bit of it, pulling it down, utterly destroying it. Of course, Rhisiart didn't do any of the work himself, only guarded and protected, stopping the crowd from interfering with the workmen. Influential members of Parliament had been afraid it might turn violent, and since Colonel Powel's men were in the city at the time, they had asked him to ensure that the work was done without incident. Rhisiart heard angry shouts that day, an occasional curse, some threats. But most of the crowd there were cheering. Even so, the soldiers still had to keep them from interfering with the workers for fear that bits of stone, plaster or lead would fall on someone and injure them. And so Rhisiart is here again, with some of his comrades, stopping the crowd from getting involved in the show. He has just left the Earl of Essex's army and become a dragoon serving under Colonel Powel, only to find that his first service is not to be on a battlefield, but here, on the streets of London. Protecting the workmen, watching the crowd.

This time there are only four workmen. Three of the men who were arranging the wood for the fire are now standing by, holding buckets of water in case the fire spreads, and one man is holding the pitchfork. It's a long tool, the wooden shaft wetted down well to keep it from burning, and he holds it straight up like a soldier holding a pike during an inspection. But the top is weighed down with something, and the man has to work hard and use every muscle in his arms to hold it high in the air. It looks like a small, thick pennant, but on closer inspection one can see that it is a book. The tines of the pitchfork have been stabbed through the book, and it is held like that, in the air, over the heads of the crowd and the soldiers who are keeping them back from the flames.

Rhisiart knows who this man is, though he doesn't know his name. He's the hangman. The official executioner of the district.

He also knows which book is about to be executed. It's *The Book of Sports*.

The preacher who came with the soldiers steps forth and begins to address the crowd. The hangman begins to walk slowly around the fire, waving the heavy 'pennant' slightly: they're making a drama of this act of destruction, the words and movements chosen carefully to create an effect on those gathered here.

Rhisiart is not focusing on the show. He stands quietly, confident that his armed presence is enough in itself to keep the crowd in its place. But his mind is not on the crowd, the minister, the hangman, the book, nor the fire.

Tonight he will marry Elisabeth. Colonel Powel has given permission to leave his service for three days from the end of the book-burning. After the crowd has dispersed, he will bid farewell to his fellow soldiers for a while and make his way through the web of busy streets that lead to the new home of Edward Wiliam and his family. Edward Wiliam, his former master and his soon-to-be father-in-law. The entire family will be awaiting him there, and also Alys, who has received permission from Ieuan Watcyn to be present at her brother's wedding. John Griffith, the chaplain of Colonel Powel's company, will be there waiting to perform the ceremony. And Elisabeth will be there for him. And his mind is there now, far from the show in Cheapside.

But he can't ignore the cry that comes from the mouth of the hangman as he approaches the flames: 'Thus I make an end of *The Book of Sports* and thus will I make an end of any who doth still cherish it.'

Someone in the crowd makes a threat, cursing the hangman and Parliament. And then another voice from elsewhere in the crowd, cursing and threatening in a similar way. But Rhisiart doesn't turn to try to find the blasphemer. He doesn't want to drag anyone into court today. He's a soldier doing his work, and nothing more. Let others prosecute the blasphemers if they want.

The hangman is widening his stance a bit, almost like a pikeman readying his weapon to receive the enemy. But he doesn't set the bottom end of the shaft against his foot and hold the tool at an angle. Rather he lifts it higher and higher, then lowers the book that's impaled on the tines of the pitchfork bit by bit, lower and lower, into the fire.

The flames take hold of the paper, and the sound of the crowd grows with the flames. There's some protesting and cursing, but most are approving. Some begin to sing psalms, but not as one chorus – rather it's a babel of different voices singing different hymns at the same time. Many raise their heads and shout for joy.

Today is the Sabbath, keep holy the day.
Remember the Sabbath, to sanctify Him.
No longer will the day of the Lord be blasphemed.

The flames grow higher and higher, and a gust of wind takes burnt fragments of the book, the paper turning into ash before the eyes of the crowd, and the ash filling the air and vanishing into tiny showers of black snow.

A little later, most of the crowd has left and melted into the usual bustle of Cheapside. Small groups of people remain, standing around, talking or holding an impromptu prayer meeting. But the excitement of the book-burning has gone. The show is over. Rhisiart turns his back on the embers and the ashes. He walks off quickly, people moving aside to let the young soldier go by.

June 1643

Rhisiart is sitting, and although he can't see her, he feels her hand on his shoulder. Elisabeth is standing behind him, cutting his hair. It's a fine day, warm, and so she has brought a chair out to the courtyard between their house and the house next door. The little court is very narrow so the shadows keep it dark most of the time, but it is midday and, because they have put the chair right in the middle, the sun is warming them.

She has been talking about colours. Elisabeth believes she could make a good paint colour, but she knows that her father would not be open to such a thing. She worries that he would say that it is vanity. Rhisiart has promised to talk to him. After all, he remembers Alys saying that there were beautiful colourful rooms in Plas Araul, and no one would deny Ieuan Watcyn's piety. He said too that he can remind her father of the ornamental iron gates they made in Wrexham. Don't antagonise him, Rhisiart said. Your father is a quiet man, but he's stubborn. She's yearning for colours: blue, green, orange. She spoke playfully, enjoying the vanity. Talking about colours, decoration, white flowers weaving through each other in beautiful patterns, glorifying the borders of yellowish-red walls.

But they're quiet now. Rhisiart has closed his eyes and turned his face to the sun, forcing Elisabeth to give up cutting his hair for now. She stands there, her right hand holding the scissors, her left hand resting on her husband's shoulder, enjoying the quiet. When she speaks again, it's with a different voice, thoughtful and serious.

'I know what's on your mind, Rhisiart Dafydd.'

He hums a question, a sleepy sound, as if he has surrendered too much to the solace of the moment to be able to speak actual words. The chair comfortable, the sun caressing his face, and

Elisabeth lightly massaging his shoulder through his thin shirt – all of it wrapping him in comfort, as if he had sunk into a feather bed, all set to enjoy hours of undisturbed sleep. The house is between them and the busy street beyond, so that all the sounds of a London day are filtered, like the voices one hears between sleep and waking, just beyond a dream.

'I know, Rhisiart, that you're thinking about the courtyard between the smithy and my father's house in Wrexham.'

'Hmm?' He turns to look at her over his shoulder. 'I am?'

'Yes.' She gives his shoulder a squeeze. 'Because that's what I was thinking about, and I know when we are thinking about the same thing.'

'You do?' He reaches up and takes her hand. 'How?'

'A feeling. Some sense inside me tells me. I don't have to think about it. It's certain. I know when you are thinking exactly the same thing as I am, just as I know that when I open my eyes, I'll see light.' They fall silent, his hand closing around hers, his thumb lightly stroking her wrist. The sun wraps them, the street sounds far away.

'Right then, Rhisiart Dafydd, on with the shearing.' She pulls her hand free and with it pushes his head down to the right position. She clicks the scissors threateningly, next to his ear.

'Shearing, indeed! Those were made for sheep.'

She lifts a lock of hair with her left hand and cuts it.

Snip.

Rhisiart made shears like this, a number of them, in the smithy in Wrexham.

Snip.

He struck his words into the hot iron, enclosed lines in the blades.

Snip.

And when a pair of his shears was used for the first time,

bits of his poetry fell along with the sheep's wool. *Majestic the gentility of the summer sun, even as it comes to an end.*

But no words are shed by these shears, only bits of his own hair. He tries to imagine the smith who made them, but he can envisage no smithy apart from the old one in his mind's eye, his father-in-law's.

Snip, snip.

'There we are. You're a tidy Roundhead now.'

'Hush! He turns in his chair to take her in his arms. 'Don't say that!'

'There's no one here to hear us, Rhisiart.' There's a hint of laughter in her voice. She yields to his arms and lets him pull her onto his lap.

'But it's best not to, Elisabeth.' His voice is tender and soft, but anxious. 'Just in case.'

And he tells the story that he has told her before. Something he saw when he was a pikeman with the London volunteers, before joining Colonel Powel's company. It happened in a camp: a conversation between two of his fellow soldiers, one calling the other *the boldest of Roundheads*. Affectionately – as the two were best friends. But another soldier heard the remark, one who considered every rule of the Army of the Saints akin to the Ten Commandments. He brought the matter to the attention of an officer or the chaplain, and the soldier who had used the word was arrested that evening.

'It's an offence for one of Parliament's soldiers to call another a Roundhead.'

'All right, Rhisiart, but I'm not a soldier.'

'Hush, Elisabeth – it's just better not to.'

He tells the rest of the story, even though she's heard it before. They had to assemble in their ranks the next morning to witness the punishment. The man was bound to the wagon of one of the cannon and the chaplain stepped forth to announce the offence.

Then, with two soldiers holding his mouth open, another one came with a hot iron and burnt the tip of the man's tongue. Not enough to disfigure him permanently, just enough to make sure that everyone would remember the lesson.

'All right, Rhisiart.' She turns slightly and puts her lips against his ear. She whispers, her lips touching his skin lightly like the edge of a live coal, her breath warm in his ear. She says that she will not say it here, outside, but she'll call him that same thing again tonight, in bed, with no one there to hear it. She kisses his cheek and Rhisiart embraces her warmly.

September 1643

There's not much of a sunset. Though the rain stopped hours ago, a layer of grey clouds still hides the sun. In one place the clouds have opened a little, a tiny tear in the encroaching veil of grey, letting a shaft of orange light reach the earth.

And there are bodies spread across that earth. Over three thousand of them, some lying as solitary corpses and others tangled in piles of dead flesh. Horse carcasses can be seen here and there, some with a man's body crushed beneath them. The residue of war scattered everywhere: casks, carts, knapsacks. Guns, swords, pikes, some of the weapons planted in the wet earth, standing straight or at an angle, like saplings stripped of their branches.

The shaft of light that does reach the earth catches on scattered pieces of armour. Fragments of metal reflecting orange, creating an otherworldly illumination. Corpse-candles, Rhisiart thinks, remembering stories from his childhood. These are corpse-candles, glowing and twinkling in a swamp of death. In contrast to these occasional bright flashes are small, dark shapes moving among the corpses. Crows and ravens, jumping from body to body and half hopping, half flying to the top of the piles of flesh to peck, tear, and eat. Over three thousand dead in the middle of the carnage of war. The aftermath of reaping on the field at Newbury, the result of twelve hours of fighting.

Rhisiart walks slowly, his body heavy and his clothing uncomfortably wet. Wetted thoroughly by the rain last night, and sweat from the day's efforts soaking it again before he had the chance to dry completely. A night without sleep on wet ground, the rain lashing him, and an entire day of struggle and battle. But Newbury is in their possession now, and the Royalists have retreated and left the road to London open again. Rhisiart walks carefully, stepping over bodies without bothering to look at them. Without bothering to see if they're alive, even. He's looking for his horse, any horse, so he can rejoin the rest of Colonel Powel's men. He walks on, stumbling sometimes, falling to his knees in the mud. He stands up slowly, shoulders back, blinking the fatigue from his eyes. Across the field he spots two horses, apparently unharmed. Slowly, he walks towards them.

A fortnight and a half of hard days and comfortless nights, ending here on the field at Newbury. It began on the first of the month with the review. Fifteen thousand of them, infantry and cavalry, gathered together in ranks for the Earl of Essex to inspect. And then the tough riding. Powel's company was set to protect the vanguard of the London volunteers. Riding out to inspect the land and the villages and then returning quickly to tell the infantry officers what sort of terrain awaited them down the road. Rhisiart helping to protect his former fellow infantrymen – they marching slowly, carrying muskets or pikes, he now in his dragoon's uniform, mounted on a horse. He hoped to have the opportunity to pause with the main army and look for some of his old friends, but it didn't come. Back and forth, moving quickly: reconnoitring, assessing, and reporting back. On the second day of September there was a small skirmish near Hook Norton, but Rhisiart did not get a chance to fire his pistol or draw his sword. It was over minutes after it began. The thousands of foot soldiers coming up the road behind them were suffering from the lack of food and water, so the Colonel had ordered them to ride further than usual in front of the main army to search the villages and farms outside Gloucester.

'Be damned, you traitors – you thieving Roundhead traitors,' the old man shouted after them as Rhisiart and his companions led the farmer's pigs away. Rhisiart, Dafi, Owen, and Siôn. Names the Colonel spoke like a child's rhyme. Rhisiart, Dafi,

Owen, and Siôn. Owen and Dafi had dismounted; Owen was driving the pigs in front of him and Dafi was leading their two horses. Still mounted, Rhisiart and Siôn were keeping their eyes on the undergrowth and trees around them, just in case. As they drove the pigs back in the direction of the main army, the old Englishman continued to call after them – 'Damned thieving traitors, you damned crop-eared devils.'

'Don't listen to him,' Owen said to the others. 'The old fellow is a papist. He got what he deserves.'

'And the pigs?' Siôn called to him. 'Did you ask whether they were papists, Owen?'

On the fifteenth, there was a minor battle outside Cirencester, but Colonel Powel's men were stationed a mile away to guard the camp, and so Rhisiart did not come face to face with the enemy that day either. By evening the infantry had taken some two hundred enemy soldiers prisoner. And more important than that, they had found significant stores of food in the town.

And so it was: searching, taking cover, fighting an occasional skirmish, and stealing food from the inhabitants of Wiltshire. Until they reached the vicinity of Newbury on the nineteenth of the month and found thousands of the King's soldiers there waiting for them, guarding the road and compelling Parliament's army to take to the field. The Colonel said they would be leaving the London volunteers: the infantry was moving to the crest of a hill on the other side of the field, and his company of dragoons was going to link up with the rest of the cavalry in the woodland bordering the fields and the little lanes. And then came the rain, cold and heavy, coming down all night. Siôn suggested they leave their position beside the dyke so they could sleep with the horses, thinking that the warm bodies of the animals would keep them warm too. 'No, we won't do that,' Rhisiart said, 'and for two reasons. First, that would mean ignoring our orders. And second, a horse isn't quiet in the night. He can step on you if you're sleeping beside him. Break a bone, or worse.' So sleeping beside the dyke on the other side of the woodland it was. Or trying to sleep. Wet and cold. Shivering through the long hours of the night. Trying to keep their powder dry.

The rain stopped with the dawn. And then cold comfort: the rain ceased and the battle began. Twelve hours of struggle for Rhisiart and his companions, with Colonel Powel's company called upon again and again to fill the gap or push the head of the line. Shooting and wheeling back around. Attacking and retreating. Leaping from their horses and fighting on foot. Sweating and bleeding, wounding and killing. Soldiers fighting on the side of righteousness. Boldly and confidently, fighting in the cause of truth, striking hard with the sword of the Spirit. And at the end, victory of a sort. The Royalists retreating from the field, leaving the road to London open. Leaving the corpses of Newbury to the pale light of this feeble sun.

Rhisiart reaches the horses. The first one shies away when he tries to take hold of its reins, tossing its head, its eyes wild. Rhisiart makes another attempt to take hold of it, but the horse responds fiercely this time, rearing and kicking out with its front legs. Rhisiart jumps to the side, avoiding its hooves by a hair's breadth. He falls smack on his face on the wet ground, and by the time he rolls over and scrambles back up, the terrified horse has galloped off. The other animal is tamer, and although it backs away from Rhisiart, it doesn't run off. Rhisiart walks slowly up to it and takes hold of the bridle. He strokes the animal and whispers in its ear, bringing his head close and letting the horse see his eyes.

Soon after climbing into the saddle, he hears a stomach-turning sound nearby. Grunting and tearing; a greedy, wretched mouth, chewing flesh and crunching bones. He turns in the saddle, trying to find out what is making such a hellish commotion. It is maybe ten yards away. He turns the horse in the direction of the sound and urges it forward. The grey of evening has given way to the gloom of twilight by now, but he can make out the scene well after getting a bit closer. A corpse, the body of one of the Royalist musketeers, with a large boar feasting on it. The animal has pushed up the buff coat so he can stick his snout into the middle of the man. A raven sits upon the corpse's head, its beak hollowing out the eyes, but Rhisiart can't hear the bird because the boar is eating so noisily. It is rooting and sucking, chewing and gulping.

He sits there for a while, the horse submissive and quiet, considering killing the boar. If he has any dry powder left, he'll load his pistol and shoot the beast through the head. Or dismounting, draw his sword and slit its throat. It would make food for a number of them that night. But weariness overcomes him. He sees other soldiers coming his way, searching the field, sifting through what's left from the battle. He decides to leave the boar to them. He turns the horse gently and spurs it forward, leaving the wretched beast behind them.

Christmas 1644

The six of them are sitting at the table. At one end is Edward Wiliam, and at the other end his wife Ann. Marged and Ani, their two younger daughters, are sitting on one side, and Elisabeth and her husband Rhisiart on the other. They are not celebrating Christmas as such, since they are a religious family who have rejected the old secular customs, but they are enjoying this simple meal with each other, especially because this is the first time Rhisiart has been with them for months.

Their food sits in front of them – bacon, bread, cheese, butter, pickled onions, wine mixed with water in wooden cups – and Edward Wiliam has just finished his prayer. 'We remember today, Lord, the day your Son came into the world. Let us remember in a way that is fitting in your sight, and give our bodies and our spirits this day, as on all other days, into your service. Amen.' Silence for a moment, each one meditating quietly. And then Edward Wiliam speaks again: 'Amen. So be it.'

The parents and the younger daughters begin, contented sounds of a family eating filling the small room. But Rhisiart and Elisabeth are not reaching for their food. They sit there quietly, holding hands under the table.

This is the first time they've seen each other since she lost the baby. The letter came to him, finally, about a month after she sent it, and he received it in camp in the middle of July, shortly after the battle of Marston Moor. *My father says that it is the Lord's will. He says that there is unseen good in all of His works, but all I can feel is sadness and loss.* Rhisiart squeezes her hand. He knows that she is thinking the same thing he is, that the child would be here by now if it had reached full term and been born alive. It would be here with us tonight.

She pulls her hand free and puts it on his shoulder, leaning towards him and whispering in his ear. 'You came home. You are here tonight. You're alive. That has to be enough for us.'

'Isn't this a celebration?' Marged is thirteen years old and always inquisitive.

'No, it's certainly not.' Her father's voice, coming through a mouthful of bread and cheese. 'We are eating. Remembering the day properly, not celebrating the Nativity with a feast.'

'But what if I'm enjoying the meal? What if I'm feeling so happy that I almost want to laugh?'

'Yes!' The voice of Ani, fifteen years old. 'And what if these weird things my little sister says make me want to laugh?'

And then, unable to hold back, the two of them break into laughter. Their father stares in wonder at them, his face reddening a bit. He swallows, then opens his mouth as if to speak, but the words don't come. He closes his mouth, his face growing redder.

'I see no harm in it, Edward Wiliam.' Rhisiart is defending his sisters-in-law, his tone reflective. 'We ought to celebrate life. Rejoice in our lives together every time we are with each other. That's what the girls are showing us tonight.'

Edward Wiliam heaves a sigh, and whatever words he had begun to produce die on his tongue.

'What better way to show our gratitude to the Creator?' Rhisiart adds.

'Amen,' comes from the mouth of Edward Wiliam.

Elisabeth leans closer to her husband, pressing up against his shoulder.

June 1645

The hammer is heavy in his hand. So heavy that his arm aches. He can feel the pain flowing through his body, rolling up from his hand and arm and gripping his shoulder. He tries to lift the hammer. He has to. He has to lift the hammer and finish this piece of work. He has to finish pounding the words into the hot iron. Has to finish the poem. *Rhisiart, Dafi, Owen, and Siôn, walking along the river. And the day gentle, fair and happy and the market in Rhiwabon.* No, that was not it. That wasn't the rhyme. The words won't go into the iron; he can't finish the work. It's too heavy and something is tickling his cheek, making it difficult for him to find the words. *Rhiwabon.* Yes, Siôn was from Rhiwabon. Yes, but he didn't go to the market. He was killed in a skirmish on the lane. Is that what the rhyme was? *He was killed on the lane.* Dafi lost his leg on Marston Moor. Almost a year ago. He's in London, or back in Wales, living on alms. *Rhisiart, Dafi, Owen and Siôn. Where are the four happy Welshmen?* Is that what it was? He can't lift the hammer, can't finish the poem. Where are they? Where is the hammer? He tries to lift it again, but it's too heavy and his arm is too weak.

The sounds are familiar: groaning, screaming, crying for help, calling for a lost comrade, whinnying. The aftermath of battle. Where is he? He's lying on his back. He has a headache and his right arm hurts. He opens his eyes: late afternoon sun and a few white clouds in the blue sky. He turns his head to the side: the dead horse is lying on his arm. The arm is under the animal's neck, and its mane is tickling his cheek. He rolls towards the horse, as if he is embracing its neck, bringing his left hand up to take hold of it. He pushes, tries to get up; pushes again, and there's enough movement for him to pull his right hand free.

Where is Owen?

Where are the boys?

Even though Rhisiart is only twenty, he thinks of them like that. The boys. The young Englishmen who came to fill the ranks at the beginning of spring. Thomas, Philip, Henry and John. Is there material for a poem here? Enough to fill a line? No. Maybe. *Thomas, Philip, Henry and John.* He can turn any name, any word into the stuff of poetry. If he has the strength. Anyway. Where are the boys?

Two or three years younger than Rhisiart. Except Henry, who is the same age as him. But he thinks of them as boys. He became both father and teacher for them when the four of them joined at the beginning of spring. Boys from religious families, capable of handling horses, confirmed in the cause, but inexperienced. Owen didn't show much interest in the new recruits, but Rhisiart set about educating them and helping them to become men. Preparing them.

They're travelling with Oliver Cromwell's army, the new army. *New Modelled.* But Rhisiart tells the boys every day that it hasn't been necessary for Colonel Powel's company to bend to the new rod of Cromwell's instructions. The Colonel had formed his dragoons along similar lines from the beginning. He chooses his men carefully. He makes certain that they have the ability and the instruction and the motivation. Iron purified in fire. But the men who came with Cromwell that summer showed the same stamina. Thousands upon thousands of them: the Army of the Saints in its new form, on its way to demolish the King's men. Here is the end of the journey. Here, on the field at Naseby.

He holds his right arm on his chest, searching it carefully with his other hand. Feeling. Testing. Probing. Examining. It's sore, badly bruised, but he doesn't think it's broken. It's not a wound, only a bruise. No. Wait. He examines his right hand carefully, feeling the fingers one by one. No. He's not completely free of injury. His little finger hurts terribly. He can't move it at all. It's crooked. One little finger. Not much of an injury, considering. Not much at all. Where is Owen? Where are the boys?

He is their teacher. He is their guardian. He got a new booklet at the beginning of the month, at the beginning of the journey that would lead to this field. A little book by Robert Ram: *The Soldier's Catechism*, composed for the Parliamentarian Army. A booklet. Catechism. He used it to teach the boys. To lift their hearts and help them to become men. It gave him comfort too, conveying some of the feeling he remembered from his youth, when he would read *Carwr y Cymry* with his sister Alys. The same helpful questions and answers, the same strengthening and comforting, the answers telling him that he was doing the right thing. Sitting beside the fire at night, after taking care of the horses and eating what food they had. Teaching the boys, Owen sitting at the edges, listening, but pretending he wasn't interested. Rhisiart holding the booklet before him, even though he had learned most of the words already:

'What Profession are you of?'

The four voices answer together, schoolchildren reciting:

'I am a Christian and a Soldier.'

Owen listening, smiling slightly, but refusing to join in.

'I fight in the defence and maintenance of the true Protestant religion, which is now violently opposed.'

The flames lighting the faces of the earnest youths. The sound of the fire, wood crackling and sizzling as it burns, punctuating the recitations.

'We take up arms against the enemies of Jesus Christ, who in the King's name make war against the Church and People of God.'

Sometimes other soldiers would come by. Some would sit with them and join in the lessons, others stood at the edges, trying to look as if they knew it all and hiding their interest, like

Owen. But sometimes it would grow into a significant crowd, and Rhisiart would have to stand and project his voice. A preacher addressing his flock. A schoolmaster examining his pupils:

'But is it not a lamentable thing that Christians of the same nation should thus imbrue their hands in one another's blood?'

A chorus of voices chanting the words in unison:

'I confess that it is, but it is impossible to avoid the need which has been placed before the godly people of the land.'

'God now calls upon us to avenge the blood of his Saints that has been shed by the godless ones.'

'The whole Church of God calls upon us to protect and maintain that Freedom and that Teaching that Divine Providence has given to us.'

'We are not to look at our enemies as fellow countrymen, or kinsmen, or fellow Protestants, but as the enemies of God and our Religion, and those who take the side of the Antichrist. Our eye is not to pity them, nor our sword to spare them. They are the natural enemies of the soldiers of the Lord.'

The soldiers are speaking with one mind, chanting heartily. They are a gathered church. A church that Rhisiart is leading and shepherding.

Where are the boys now? And Owen? Where is he?

They were together that morning. Weary, having ridden through the night. Colonel Powel said that they would join up with the rest of the dragoons under Colonel Okey in the dykes alongside the field. Hiding in the woodland like birds once again. Like at Newbury. Their horses being held behind them, as they lay low there, pressing close to the line of small trees which served as a border between the thicket and the open field. But it was dry that morning, very different from Newbury.

They were tired, not having slept all night, but at least they were dry. There was Rhisiart, leaning against the branches, his musket ready. Philip was on one side of him and Owen on the other. He could see the field through the branches. Not good land for the horses. Uneven. Gorse growing here and there, breaking up the smooth run of the land. Rabbit holes everywhere. Up the slope on the right was Parliament's main army, in long lines, row after row of pikes standing to attention, braving the morning sun. The familiar battle flags waving in the wind.

And in the other direction, on the left, the Royalists. The little restless flutterings of their flags catching the eye. A few officers wearing colourful uniforms on horseback in front of the massed ranks, moving back and forth.

'There are Welshmen over there.' Owen was beside him, resting his musket on a low branch, nodding his helmeted head in the direction of the enemy. 'There are hundreds upon hundreds of Welshmen there. The regiments of Rhys Thomas and Sir John Owen.'

Rhisiart looked, scrutinizing the long rows broken into smaller units. Sir John Owen's Regiment of Foot. Welshmen from Gwynedd. Fellow countrymen. Kinsfolk. Childhood friends. The youths he used to play with on Sundays. 'Look – Rhisiart Dafydd has gone to listen to an open-air sermon with the English fools.' There is, for that small handful of the remnants of the Welsh nation who still dwell in their own land, a multitude of very great and severe causes to consider, and to acknowledge the mercy of God towards them. Our eye is not to pity them, nor our sword to spare them. They are the enemies of God and the true faith. Be ready to strike, boldly and confidently, in the cause of the truth.

The Royalists began shouting 'God and Queen Mary!' An answering shout came from the brow of the hill: the Parliamentary forces shouting 'Religion! Religion! Religion!' Rhisiart moved his head a little from side to side, loosening up the muscles of his shoulders. Then he leaned forward, checking that his musket was resting firmly on one of the branches. 'Religion!' the Welshmen shouted, in their own language. He looked closely at them. Fellow countrymen. Kinsmen. Enemies of God and His Church.

Mercifully, the King's cavalry came past their hiding place first, not the Welsh infantrymen. Prince Rupert's cavaliers, the officers splendid in their velvet, their silk, their lace. The work was easy. Shoot through the undergrowth, load and shoot again. Thinning the ranks of the cavalry as they galloped past. The Royalists didn't even turn to face them, just galloped on up the hill, charging Parliament's cavalry and leaving an assortment of dead and wounded horses and men strewn along the uneven ground in front of the woodland.

Then an order to fall back to their horses. He couldn't see the field at first, but he could hear the tumult that indicated that the front ranks of cavalry of the two sides had clashed. Sounds of metal and flesh coming together. Shooting and whinnying and hellish screaming.

They waited, then, hidden in their thicket, listening to the thunder of battle, imagining the scene. The two colonels, Powel and Okey, came galloping along their line, shouting orders. Load pistols. Prepare. Ready yourselves to charge to the top of the wooded area and across the field. The front ranks of their infantry are there, spread out. It's an opportunity, boys, to show what you're made of.

Thomas was thrown before they reached the enemy, his horse stumbling or breaking a leg in a rabbit hole. Philip vanished from his side when the enemy musketeers turned and fired, a few moments before they reached the end of their charge. Owen was still there, his horse panting, the two of them drawing their swords. The first time charging the enemy like this, the first time fighting like true cavalry. Swords ready to strike, ready to find the heads of enemy infantry. Turning to evade the pikemen, and aiming for the musketeers, who had turned their weapons upside down and were holding them like clubs, stepping backwards, already beginning to break.

And then they clashed. The noise, the contact, the striking. Their horses hitting live bodies, and they wielding their swords. Rhisiart like a boy working with his father, billhook in hand, cutting through undergrowth. Up and down, up and down, the branches falling. His father alongside him, encouraging him, the two of them cutting and cutting. His sword found an arm, found a neck. Found head after head after head. Turning his horse in circles in the midst of men. They were no longer infantrymen but unprotected creatures trying to escape, running here and there like chickens, trying to jump out of the way of the horses' hooves. Most of them had thrown down their weapons by now, putting their hands up to try to protect their heads. But in vain. Up and down, cutting back undergrowth. His sword ringing as it found an arm, a neck, a head.

And then his horse lurched to the side, falling, as Rhisiart fell from the saddle. He landed on all fours, but had lost his sword. He rose, turned to his horse. The animal had also begun to rise, but as Rhisiart moved to take hold of its bridle the horse fell again, heavily this time and for good; Rhisiart going down under it. His head struck the ground hard, his arm caught under the weight of the dead horse. Sounds began to fade as he descended into a pool of darkness.

'Thank God!' A familiar voice beside him. Owen, bending over him, proffering a hand to help him. Familiar sounds: moaning, screaming, calling. Wounded horses whinnying.

'Where are they, Owen?'

'They've fled.' His friend misunderstands. 'The King and what's left of his army have fled.'

'No, Owen. The boys. Where are they?'

April 1646

He walks as quickly as possible. The streets are busy, busier than usual. He has dismounted so he can lead his horse through the crowds. One step at a time he goes, pushing past the congestion of square, corner and street. He walks on, not noticing faces or listening to voices. He's very close, almost there, but these last minutes have been a time out of time. He's walking in a dream, the world seen through a magical filter and every step an unreasonable effort, his feet frustratingly heavy. He pushes on, squeezing past tight knots of people. In a hurry yet moving slowly, people in his way, but he's close. He's coming home, coming home to her.

Everyone knows that the war is over. Oxford has not fallen yet, but the Scots have seized the King. It is expected that they will hand him over to the Parliamentarian army before long. And the siege is tightening its grip on Oxford, the Royalists' last stronghold. But the war is over. The King has been imprisoned and the sun is beginning to rise on a new realm. Colonel Powel said that they had wasted enough of their time waiting for Oxford to open its gates. He said that Parliament had other work for them in London, and gave permission to everyone who lived in the city to ride ahead of the company so they could spend some time with their families before the rest of them arrived.

It's a mild and fair day. The April breeze brings a variety of freshness and life that all the rot and stench of London cannot hide. It's a lovely spring day, the sun is shining brightly on a new order, and he's on his way home to her.

There are the familiar small windows.

There's the gateway.

He leads the weary horse under the arch that half closes the gap between the walls, its hooves clattering on the cobbles, the echo filling the enclosed space.

Although shadows have darkened most of the small, narrow courtyard, some afternoon sun has slipped over the roof of the building opposite and catches the door. He had imagined stepping up to this door, opening it, walking through it, closing it behind him. But in a dreamlike state it's quite different. It has an otherworldly sheen in the shafts of sunlight: the gate of the Court of King Arthur or the Temple of Jerusalem, the Gates of Heaven. He steps nearer, the horse's hooves clicking on the cobbles. The image turns into something else. He sees that the wooden door has been painted: a bright orange, and myriad white flowers woven into a beautiful pattern around the edges. The colours are bright and clean. They sparkle. The image changes again. The gate of the Court of King Arthur. The Gates of Heaven.

The sun sinks from view behind the roof and the colours fade slightly as the sun leaves the courtyard The image changes yet again.

And then the door opens and Elisabeth is there, rushing out and running towards him.

July 1646

Owen rests on a low wall, his face red and glistening with sweat.

'Is there a Welsh word for them?'

'There's a Welsh word for everything on this earth.' Rhisiart is sweating too, the summer sun roasting him inside his clothes and armour, but he stands firm.

'Really? What's the Welsh word for them, then?'

'I'm not sure what they are, to be honest. It's hard to put a name to something when you don't know what it is.'

'Levellers.' Owen pulls out a handkerchief and wipes his brow and his face. 'That's what they are. Levellers.'

'Yes? That's what they are?' Rhisiart is trying to sound serious, but there's a laugh in his throat that's threatening to break out.

'Yes. Levellers. That's the word.'

Rhisiart can't hold back. He laughs. 'And what language is that, Owen Huw? Welsh or English?'

'I don't know. Both.' But he's uncertain, like a schoolboy thinking that the master is about to catch him out.

'Both?' Rhisiart laughs louder, reaches over and pats his friend on the back. 'That settles it for good! You are quite the scholar, Owen.'

As he stands there, he looks up, studying the fortress on the other side of the street. It has high walls, towers in several places, and the shining White Tower rising in the centre, higher than the rest. Owen stands too.

'Is that where he is? John Lilburne?'

'Yes. Somewhere in the Tower, as far as I know.'

'Do you remember Samuel Lamb?'

'The one who was killed in Torrington?'

'That's the one.'

'I do, I do remember him. Why?'

'He was serving with Lilburne in the Earl of Manchester's army before joining up with Colonel Powel.'

'He was?' Rhisiart sounds thoughtful, and speaks quietly. His friend can barely hear him above the hubbub of people and animals thronging the street. 'Every one of them was serving with someone else before the Colonel called.'

'Almost every one. Jenkins and Smyth and Joiner were with him from the beginning.'

'Almost every one. What about Samuel Lamb? Did you know him?'

'A little.'

'And what did he say about John Lilburne?'

'I don't remember exactly. Words don't stay in my head like they ought to. But I do know that he was fond of him. He said that he was a good man. Brave. Faithful. Zealous. He said that Manchester himself praised him on numerous occasions. I do remember that.'

'And now he's been imprisoned for speaking against Manchester.'

'More than speaking against him, Rhisiart. He said that the Earl is a traitor who's giving succour to the King. Said too much about a man who led Parliament's army on the field.'

'Said too much. And he's paying for it now.' Rhisiart nods in the direction of the Tower.

'Will Parliament hang him for that?'

'Hang John Lilburne? Somehow I don't think so. Silence him. Give him reason to think twice before speaking like that again. But I don't believe they could kill him.'

'They could, Rhisiart.'

'No, they couldn't.'

'Why not?'

'It's a legal matter, for one thing. What would be the charge? Slandering an earl? Maybe, but such slander is no cause for death. And here is something else: Lilburne has many followers. His faction is growing.'

'The Levellers.'

'If that's what you call them.'

'That's what David Smyth calls them.'

Rhisiart doesn't respond. He's looking around, inspecting the press of humanity filling the street. Studying the crowd, looking for signs. Travellers. Merchants. Townspeople. But no sign of a crowd gathering. No sign of men acting out of the ordinary. Owen is being more attentive, remembering his responsibility, and he too begins to eye the crowd closely.

'Where are they, anyway?'

'I don't know.'

'But the Colonel was thinking they might be gathering here.'

'He wasn't sure, Owen.'

'But he wanted us to watch them. Listen. Just in case.'

'Yes. Just in case.'

'Does he suspect Lilburne's people?'

'I don't think he does – not yet. To be completely honest, I believe the Colonel respects Lilburne. But Parliament is afraid.'

Owen leans close to him, looking around quickly, his eyes watchful. He whispers to Rhisiart, 'Afraid of what?'

'Afraid of losing too much of the army.' Rhisiart is not whispering. He knows no one is listening to them. 'Afraid of Lilburne's party gaining popularity in the ranks. If the army is listening to a man like him, Parliament will lose its power base.'

'What do you think about it?'

'I don't know enough to judge. But I believe that I have heard something like it.'

In camp, barracks and field. The heated discussions. The arguments. The planning for the coming of the Kingdom of Heaven. Soldiers preaching to fellow soldiers. Stump-top orators. Self-appointed teachers. Prophets, reading the signs of the times.

An army that was a church and a school and a public forum and a pulpit. The faithful agreeing on one point and disagreeing on another. Philosophy, religion and politics bubbling in the cauldron of their discussions, and various men putting various kinds of fuel on the fire and throwing different kinds of ingredients into the pot. Soldiers trained to move obediently and uniformly in battle at odds in their discussions. They would split into factions, their beliefs ecstatically unorthodox. There were a small number of silver threads drawing one and all together – their belief that the army was a means of creating a better realm and their certainty that it was they who were the true Protestants fighting to preserve the purity of their religion – but the different multicoloured threads of religion and faith that were woven together in the fabric outnumbered those unifying strands.

Really?' Owen's response is uncertain, his mind is wandering.

'Yes, yes. Many times over. But, again, there must be something exceptional about John Lilburne. Some unusual zeal. I don't know.'

'Rhisiart?'

'Yes?'

'Do you think Colonel Powel will be leading us on the field again?'

'The war is over. Why should he take us to the field again?'

'I know. But… I was just thinking.'

'About what, Owen Huw?'

'Do you like the sort of work the Colonel gives us these days? Watching. Gathering information. Eavesdropping on other soldiers. Searching the nooks and crannies of the city for nameless shadowy threats. That's not what it is to be a soldier, is it? I long, sometimes, for how things were.'

'I don't agree with you, Owen Huw. And I can't believe that

you believe that in your heart. Go to war again?' Put yourself in front of enemy fire? Kill your fellow Christians? Your fellow countrymen?'

'Is that how you think of them, Rhisiart?'

The old catechism. What Profession are you of? I am a Christian and a Soldier. Is it not a lamentable thing that Christians of the same nation should thus imbrue their hands in one another's blood? I confess that that it is, but we are not to look at our enemies as fellow countrymen, or kinsmen, or fellow Protestants, but as the enemies of God and our Religion, and those who take the side of the Antichrist.

'Rhisiart?'

'What?'

'There's no point.' Owen heaves a deep sigh. 'They're not coming. Not today.' He removes his helmet. His hair is wet, as though he has been standing in the rain.

'You're right, Owen. Come, let's head back.'

November 1646

They're watching the fire die down. There's but a single, small flame left, a weak one at that, anchored in the few embers that continue to burn. They sit in front of it, their feet stretched out, nearly touching the embers. There's no other light; the candles have long since burned down. Elisabeth's parents and sisters have left them alone. It's late and the house is unusually quiet. They can hear a dog barking in the distance, in a courtyard or back street, its call a challenge which is answered by another bark from a different direction. And then silence again. Rhisiart looks at her: her long, brown hair looks black in the dark, framing her face with soft shadows, but her eyes sparkle in the weak light of the tiny flame. He takes her hand, gently pressing her fingers.

Rhisiart is leaving in the morning. He will be travelling to Southampton and staying there for some months, doing work for Colonel Powel. He has not discussed the precise nature of the mission with Elisabeth; there is no place for that in this quiet room tonight. Rather the two have been talking about their eventual reunion, imagining the season and the circumstances. In the spring, and she still pregnant. Or perhaps in the summer, the baby having arrived before his return. They had spoken of all the help she would get, from parents and sisters. Alys would certainly get permission to come and look after her sister-in-law. They had thanked the Lord for family, for His care, for seeing fit to surround her with a protective family.

But they're not talking now. They sit quietly, their feet stretched towards what's left of the fire. The glow of the embers is fading, the fire surrendering to the ashes.

Christmas 1646

He thinks he sees a light in the distance.

Only a pinpoint of light. The smallest dot winking at him from afar. Not clear, nothing more than a new promise of something other than darkness. A kind of hope. Night fell a while ago, and the cold has its claws in his flesh. He knows he shouldn't continue to ride, that he should dismount and walk, lead the horse and make sure it doesn't stumble and break a leg. But he's too cold and too tired. The snow arrived on the uplands a few hours after he left Exeter. It was unexpectedly heavy, covering the moors on both sides of the narrow path. He ought to walk and spare the animal, but he's afraid he'll succumb to the cold. At least the warmth from the horse reaches up to him, a way of keeping the frigid claws from reaching his heart.

He tries to count the days of the journey, sketching a map in his head. Southampton. Bournemouth. Dorchester. Exeter. And now on his way to Okehampton – today, on Christmas Day. In the dark and in the middle of a region he has never seen before, the cold sapping his strength, the horse plodding along fitfully under him. He's hunting a fox, a fox running far in front of him and keeping out of sight. Leading him on a frustrating hunt from place to place, through unfamiliar territory. Southampton. Bournemouth. Dorchester. Exeter. He knows in his heart that the hunt won't be over until he reaches the furthest point of the Cornish peninsula. On the trail of the treachery of Edward Samington. Who was the man? Papist. Ghost. Fox. Bogeyman of children's stories, turning up everywhere. And nowhere. He was in Southampton. Then he turned up in the vicinity of Bournemouth. No, he sought cover with friends in a village near Dorchester. No, not there, the secret Royalists of Exeter are sheltering him. Not there either, the old man was certain:

they are meeting in Okehampton. Samington and his fellow English papists are meeting with the Royalist conspirators of Cornwall. Foxes, hiding in their holes. Out of view in their deep dens, moving in tunnels beneath this frigid moorland. A web of tunnels leading down and down to the edges of Annwn, to the mouth of the Otherworld. Conspiring foxes dancing with goblins before the fiery flames.

Will the journey take him all the way into Cornwall? Will he hear that language, which they say is similar to Welsh? He heard an English comrade describing the language of Cornish prisoners who had been taken in the Battle of Sourton Down. He said that they sounded Welsh, but that there was more of an *awl* in their speech. More of an *awl*? Yes, that's what he said. 'Spake like Welsh, but with more of an awl to it.' What kind of a sound was that? Perhaps he would meet a Cornish man before long and hear him speak. It's possible that that's what the foxes and the goblins would speak in their fiery holes. A language similar to Welsh but with more of an *awl* in it.

The horse stumbles but does not fall. Rhisiart leans forward and strokes the animal's mane.

'There, there, You're fine.'

It walks on. Relief: it's not hurt, but it's tired; not much left in it.

'We're fine. Just a little bit further.'

Rhisiart smiles; talking to the horse heartens him. He tries to remember details of the stories he heard from the old people when he was a young lad in Arfon. The devils of Annwn. The Cave of the King. He tries to recall the voice of his father as he stood before him.

See here, my boy. The Book has come into our house. It will dwell here in our home and in our hearts from this day until the end of our time on this earth.

It's not his father's voice that he recalls, but the voice of his sister, Alys, relating the incident to him during their years with their uncle in Denbigh. Encouraging her little brother to keep hold of some of their former life. Wanting him to remember their mother and their father. Did he remember them? A little. How much? Difficult to say. The memories came and went, and the line between an actual memory and one sown in his mind by Alys was very fine.

He talked about these memories with Elisabeth sometimes. Times when she would ask about his childhood. When she would probe the depths of her husband's heart and mind. And when he questioned her curiosity, she gave the same answer every time.

'Why do you want to know so much about that?'

'Because that is my right. To know you. I want to dig deep into your mind, I want to know the depths of your heart.'

You have already plunged to the bottom of my heart. That's where you are. Ever since that night at the smithy in Wrexham. What would my father say? You sitting there in your nightshirt! That doesn't concern me as much as what you think of me.

He sits up in the saddle.

Yes, there is a light. There in front of him. A bit lower; the land must drop down into a hollow or valley. It must be a house or tavern there. Some structure with a window, and a fire inside burning brightly, the light of the fire beckoning to him through the dark and the snow. A light of promise, of hope.

'There, there, you're fine. We'll both walk.'

He pulls on the reins and the horse halts. Rhisiart dismounts. He can feel the snow wetting his legs halfway up to his knees. He strokes the horse's mane, then begins to trudge through the snow.

'It won't be far now. Let's go.'

1647

He is standing there, looking at the door.

He hasn't moved for a very long time. The rain has wet him to the skin and he is standing in a pool of water. There's a slight hollow in the middle of the narrow courtyard and the rain has filled it, creating a pool. He stands in the middle of it, his feet underwater. Soaked to the skin. But he doesn't move. He stands and stares.

Ugliness. The beauty has been transformed, turned to ugliness.

A big red cross, painted hurriedly, carelessly. A big ugly scar in the middle of the orange door. Red paint dripping down from the arms and bottom of the cross, over some of the white flowers. Ruining them forever.

He had been near Plymouth at the beginning of the week, but he received permission to leave and travel to London. To come home.

The Little Plague. He has heard some call it that. Its visit to the city mercifully short, its assault mercifully light. That's what everybody says: it was minor compared with significant plagues of the past. Only some three or four thousand dead; not many, compared with the tens of thousands taken by past plagues.

> And when the angel stretched out his hand upon Jerusalem to destroy it, the Lord repented him of the evil, and said to the angel that destroyed the people, 'It is enough: stay now thine hand.'

Entire streets had not lost a single soul. Whole families without cause to grieve. The Little Plague. Only some three or four thousand dead.

Three or four thousand, and Elisabeth one of them.

Elisabeth and her father and her mother, and her sisters Ani and Marged. Yes, and Alys her sister-in-law, who had come to assist with the birth. He doesn't know whether Elisabeth died before giving birth or after. He doesn't know whether the baby came into the world alive or not. Probably not. No one has said a word about it to him. He enquired about their graves, but no one knew exactly which field had been used. A good many of them had been dug, many common graves had been opened for the dead of the Little Plague. But no one was able to tell him which one it was.

And so he came to this street. He walked slowly, without a horse to lead. He came past the small, familiar windows. To the opening. Walked under the arch that half closed the gap between the walls, his feet sloshing through the puddles.

And here he stands, in a pool of water. Soaked to the skin. Staring at the ugliness of the door.

1648

'I'm happy to get to speak.'

Rhisiart can see a bit of the man's face through the small hole. There are four of these tiny windows in the wall. Small, oblong holes, no glass. No iron bars either. They weren't necessary: the holes were too small for a man to put his head through, even, let alone squeeze his body through and escape. A guard by the door said that the prisoners were Welsh, and Rhisiart came to the hole and called to see if that was true. One of them answered, ready to talk, eager to recount his story.

'Back in March. It started at Pembroke Castle, you see. And suddenly, people throughout South Wales were coming out on the side of the King. I don't mind saying that now, even though these stone walls are between us, and God knows what will happen to me. But there you are. You can hang me, you can shoot me, doesn't matter which. I am proud to say that I came out in support of the King again.' The man shakes his head as he speaks, and different parts of his face appear in the shadows through the hole as he moves. An eye and then another eye. Blue or grey. A small, snub nose. Thick dark hair on his upper lip. Cheeks long unwashed. The soil of battle, of the road.

Rhisiart has just arrived in Bristol. He's been travelling with a cavalry company, on their way to join Cromwell's army. Colonel Powel had let him remain with the garrison at Southampton over the last year, but when the Royalists took up arms again, he ordered him and a number of others to go and reinforce Cromwell's army. An army heading for south Wales.

Rhisiart, too, on his way to Wales for the first time in years.

He has heard much about the condition of the country from other people over the years. He heard about the fire that destroyed a quarter of the houses in Wrexham in 1643. One house in four left in ashes. Some of those he must have done ironwork for. Gates, hinges, hooks. Fine pieces he had forged on his master's anvil, releasing his words into the wind when they were first used by their new owners. Now swept away with the ashes and the rubble to rubbish heaps, and new houses raised up where the old buildings stood, new hardware by other smiths holding their doors.

He heard about the devastation in Shrewsbury, Oswestry, Bangor and Caernarfon. Houses outside the town walls torn down to deprive would-be besiegers of hiding places. Other houses burned by besiegers or by a passing army. He heard about ships off the coast of Anglesey and others attacking Bardsey Island. He heard news of the deaths of people known to him, and of the deaths of other men he didn't know but whose names meant something to him. The cousin of an old acquaintance. The son of a certain squire. One after another. Welshmen, like him, his own people, cut down by the wars.

He heard about the women of Naseby.

Rumours.

Whispers.

Terrible stories, tales to frighten children.

Only a rumour at first. Fellow soldiers whispering quietly after the battle. But it didn't make sense; he knew he couldn't have heard the story right – and he didn't ask for more details. Better not to. And then another rumour. And another. And then travellers who had been visiting Wales bringing the story, having heard it from some of the families, those that backed the King. A story, and then another story, similar to the first. Some of the details varied, but the sum and substance were the same. The accounts agreed, the rumours completing the picture, and the picture revealing the fate of the women of Naseby.

He had been on the field at Naseby. In the middle of the attack, their horses colliding with living bodies. The sound, the sensation: striking and striking and striking. But his horse went down, he fell from the saddle. He lay on the ground for a long time, his arm pinned under his dead horse. He did not go forward with the cavalry. Did not see the action. Only heard of it, afterwards, when the rumours and accounts came to his ears. Over and over again, hearing their rumours and whispering between clenched teeth: the story of the women of Naseby. Again and again until the stories turned into fact.

'Where are you from, eh?'

The face is moving up and down on the other side of the small hole. An eye staring at him. A blue or grey eye. Lips half-covered with thick dark hair, opening to greet him.

'Wrexham. I was living there before the first war began. But…'

The face is still now, bright eyes gazing at him from the shadows.

'But… since then, I've been here and there.'

'Where's your home now?'

'Here and there. I live the life of a soldier. I don't have a home as such. Not now.'

'No? I hate to say so, but it's not much of a life, is it?'

'No, not much of a life at all.'

1649

The cry of seagulls.

A playful gust of wind spraying his face with sea spume.

The smell of salt filling his head.

Rhisiart leans against the rail of the ship, holding tight and enjoying feeling his body move with the rhythmic pounding of the waves. The ship lurching with each blow, his own body bouncing against the rail, wetted by spray from the wave.

He feels the blows bruising him, in his shoulders and right to his bones, but he's enjoying this kind of pain.

The sea is punishing him, knocking his history and his old self out of him, saying that there is neither past nor future, only this great present. Nothing at all but the cry of seagulls, the smell of the sea, the water wetting him and the blows of the waves, each one saying, Surrender to this and forget. Surrender. Surrender. Surrender.

It's other men who interfere. This is what man is: an imperfect creature interfering with the perfection of creation. The world is like the garden of Eden or an earthly paradise, and man is crushing the sweet fruits under his feet, smashing the promise of eternal peace.

He hears men talking behind him. Sailors, working, calling to each other. Other soldiers, laughing, enjoying camaraderie, gloating over their victory.

He sees other ships every time he opens his eyes. Some are fairly close, some distant, ploughing through the waves, the sailors only specks, busy handling ropes and sails, soldiers in their red uniforms appearing as small splashes of colour. Other men are experiencing the blows from the waves rattling their bodies, the cry of the sea birds in their ears, and the salt tang of the sea in their noses. But Rhisiart knows that these other men are not like him. They are not surrendering to this great present and forgetting. They're thinking about the past and the future, offering prayers of thanks for the victories they won in Ireland and considering whatever activities await them in England. Not Rhisiart. Surrender, he says to himself, and the word echoes the cry of the seagulls. Surrender. Surrender to the present.

He had asked permission from Colonel Powel not to rejoin the Colonel's company in London. He instead chose to go with Cromwell's forces. The King was in his grave and Oliver Cromwell was turning his attention to Ireland. In June, Parliament had appointed him Lord-Lieutenant of Ireland, responsible for leading all the armed forces that were going to sail to the island that year. The word spread throughout the army that summer: Oliver Cromwell is getting ready; he's taking the best of his Newly Modelled Army, the cream of the Army of the Saints; he intends to pay the soldiers well and ensure that they lack for nothing and he has persuaded Parliament to sell lands that belonged to the King and his church in order to raise the money. An army drawn up precisely in line with the wishes of the Lord-Lieutenant himself; they would lack for nothing. Rhisiart volunteered. He asked and received permission from Colonel Powel. Choosing to go. Crushing the fruits beneath his feet. Mainly to avoid returning to London. Losing himself in work. Not thinking. It was he who chose that path, not Divine Providence. No one but him. An imperfect man, choosing to trample the garden.

He turns and looks back; he can't see land behind them, only more ships and the endless waves. Ireland has slipped over the horizon. Wexford is behind him. Drogheda is behind him. He looks ahead: no sight of Wales or England, only the fleet bounding fitfully through the waves.

He sailed with the fleet in the middle of August. More than thirty ships, one of them carrying Cromwell himself. Ireton, his son-in-law, brought another fleet and met up with them in Dublin, where Colonel Michael Jones was waiting with his forces. All the forces were united under the leadership of the Lord-Lieutenant – twelve thousand experienced soldiers, the cream of the Army of the Saints. And thus they came to the walls of Drogheda.

The walls of Drogheda: twenty feet high, strengthened by a number of towers. The main part of the town lay along the northern bank of the River Boyne, and a drawbridge prevented anyone who succeeded in seizing the southern part of the town from crossing. Sir Arthur Aston and his soldiers waited behind those walls, confident in the strength of their fortress. Waiting. Expecting. Little news reached the common soldiers, some saying that Aston was considering surrendering, others saying that he was refusing to. Some sharing humorous stories about Aston and his wooden leg, click-walking along the town walls. Talking, swapping rumours, waiting. But no sign of movement. Waiting, expecting and watching. By the middle of the second week Cromwell had had enough: the cannon began to fire, taking aim at the town defences. The Lord's judgement, striking down blasphemous men. By the end of the afternoon on that first day, breaches had been opened up in the walls. Rhisiart, with his fellow cavalrymen, waited and watched the first attack. Some of them went upriver to find a ford and cross it; their task was to surround the northern part of the town and make sure no one escaped. But Rhisiart and the rest waited, ready to support the infantry when the time came.

And the time came. A wave of soldiers of the Saints rushed the breaches in the walls, but the defenders of Drogheda held their ground. Bravely and decisively. Firing from their hiding places in the towers and in the rubble where parts of the walls had fallen. Some of the Parliamentarian soldiers reached one of the breaches, but they didn't get through. Many of them fell there, their bodies blocking the gap. In the end, eager to finish the job, unwilling to wait any longer to fulfil the judgement of the Lord, Cromwell himself led the attack. He went at the head of another wave of soldiers of the Army of the Saints, pushing through the walls of bodies and squeezing through the breaches, pouring into the streets of Drogheda and releasing their fury and their anger on its inhabitants.

By the time some of the gates were opened for the cavalry, the work in the southern part of the town was done. Rhisiart saw their bodies, lying like an uneven carpet along the streets and gathered into small piles at the gates. Aston and those of his men who were still alive had retreated to the other side of the river and sought refuge on Millmount Hill. The last stronghold of the Royalists – a large mound with a low wooden wall surrounding it. Rhisiart and some of his fellow cavalrymen paused there briefly while the vanguard was lowering the bridge across the river. After the hill had been taken, a soldier who had been at the front of the battle with Cromwell described Aston's last minutes to Rhisiart.

'The wooden wall came down like wheat before a herd of pigs, and we rushed at Aston and the remains of his company. Spare no one, that was Cromwell's order. Even after they surrendered. Guns were turned into clubs and used to strike them dead. Like killing rats in a sewer. Those were the orders: spare no one. Come,' he said, 'come and see. There Aston lies in his own blood. I'll show you. There he is, without his wooden leg. I saw his death with my own eyes. He fell head over heels, the fool. One of the lads grabbed hold of his wooden leg and pulled it off. There he lay, kicking his only leg in the air, the stupid fool. He, Sir Arthur Aston. Turned into an object of derision, holding on to his pride, his blasphemy and his treason. Rolling on his back and kicking his only leg in the air. They beat him to death with his own wooden leg. That's true, used his own leg as a club and beat him to death with it. The fool. Come, I'll show you.'

Rhisiart declined and moved on with the rest of the cavalry to the river bank. The vanguard had crossed the bridge already; Rhisiart and the cavalry had to remain there, lest some of the enemy tried to cross again and escape. He didn't even have the opportunity to unsheathe his sword, just waited on the riverbank, watching and listening. A hideous chorus of voices, most of it unintelligible howls, most too far away to hear any words clearly. But some words he could hear: a word in English, an occasional sound he knew was a word but in a language he couldn't understand. Fires breaking out across the northern section of the town. The church tower in flames. Only afterwards did Rhisiart hear that some of the enemy soldiers had sought refuge in the tower and that Cromwell had ordered them burnt alive. The Judgement of the Lord. He heard the boasting afterwards. Late that night, as they left the rubble and ashes of Drogheda and its thousands of corpses to await the dawn. Boasting. Killed the townspeople too. Irishmen. Papists. The Judgement of the Lord. And yes, there were priests too. Asking to be punished, even more than Aston's soldiers. Papists, servants of the Antichrist. Occasionally taking the time to hang one of them, but otherwise just cutting them down on the spot. Boasting of the exploits of the Army of the Saints, doing the work it was created to do. The Lord-Lieutenant himself said that the fate of Drogheda was payment for the evils of a host of papists, and who can naysay his word?

And afterwards, Wexford. Before the end of the month, their lines closed in a siege on both sides of the River Slaney, the town held firmly between their ranks and the sea. They didn't have to wait too long: it fell before the middle of October. Rhisiart watched from a distance this time, part of the thin line of cavalry that was positioned to stop anyone who tried to escape overland. Most of them failed to reach the land; they drowned in the river and the harbour, leaping wildly into the water, driven by the Army of the Saints. The red horse galloping through the streets of Wexford and grinding everyone and everything into dust beneath its hooves. Rhisiart saw some of the bodies the next day. Those the waves washed ashore. Men of every age. Women. Children. Bodies spread like human driftwood all along the shore. Wexford was a shipwreck; the corpses that moved sluggishly in the shallow water along the riverbanks were all that was left of it. The Judgement of the Lord.

Rhisiart leans against the rail of the ship, closing his eyes and holding tightly to it. He is wet and cold but doesn't move to seek protection from the wind and waves. The fire of the cold flames purifying him. There is nothing beyond this present. The seagulls cry: surrender, surrender, surrender. The smell of the sea. The waves pounding the ship, and the blows beating his history and his former self out of him.

1653

The argument fills the room. His comrades, all of them English, are discussing the obligations of Parliament towards the ministers, those it had set to work and later decided to discharge. Some of them are now without shelter or lodging, living on alms. Godly men, servants of the Gospel, betrayed by the Commonwealth they had served so diligently. Some of the soldiers want to start a petition calling on Parliament to reinstate these servants in their livelihoods. Others disagree, and the discussion turns into an argument, their clamour reverberating between the stone walls, their supper left forgotten on the tables.

Rhisiart gets up from the bench. He hasn't been speaking at all, just focusing on his food, eating quietly with his head down. He has no interest in the discussion and he doesn't want to get dragged into the argument, so he rises and walks out of the warm room, shaking his head to clear the thunder of voices. The door closes on his comrades, who have begun to roar angrily. He enjoys the freshness of the breeze on his face as he meanders up the lane in the direction of the fields, leaving the church towers of Portsmouth behind him.

He holds a small book in his hand. It came by messenger yesterday, a little parcel wrapped twice: once in a sheet of yellow paper and, under that, in a layer of linen. Inside the cover was a piece of paper with handwriting he recognized on it. *Here's another of the works of Morgan Llwyd. Read it. Consider.* Nothing else. Only the familiar shape of the letters showing that it was Colonel Powel's hand.

He walks on slowly, one hand holding the small volume to his chest. He spots a large flat rock beside the road, a grey platform rising from the middle of the gorse. He sits on it and opens the book, his eyes warming to words that are already becoming familiar. Words that deny words: *Nid mewn papur ag inc y mae bywyd yr enaid*. The life of the soul is not contained within paper and ink.

His debate is here. Not with the Englishmen in the refectory, but here with this Welshman who is addressing him through printed words. He wants to argue with him, disagree, say that words of the true kind turned into substance are powerful things, a living connection between imperfect man and higher knowledge. He wants to say that he has felt the power of words – when he was beating them and folding them into the hot iron. He senses that he has not fully grasped the depth of this other Welshman's argument, but he's enjoying the intellectual struggle. Here is a man who is speaking in new parables. A man whose words are remarkably concrete and enticingly elusive at the same time. He presents meaning in one sentence and then contradicts it in another sentence. He says laughingly: No, read it again. And think. I'm saying something that I'm not saying. It's agonizingly simple and delightfully complex.

> *O Bobl Cymru! Attoch chi y mae fy llais, O Drigolion Gwynedd a Deheubarth, Arnoch chi yr wyf i yn gweiddi. Mae'r wawr wedi torri, a'r haul yn codi arnoch.*
>
> O People of Wales! To you my voice is calling, O inhabitants of Gwynedd and Deheubarth, I am calling on you. Dawn has broken, and the sun is rising on you.

He looks up and closes the book, keeping his place with his thumb. A small bird is flitting above the gorse. He follows it with his eyes until it swoops down and vanishes. No, in that too is my argument. Dawn has not broken. There is no sun other than the sun of this world shining down on him. He opens the volume again.

O People of Wales!

O inhabitants of Gwynedd and Deheubarth.

Birds are singing: Awaken, Welshman, Awaken.

He is distracted by another sound; not the singing of birds, but human voices. Two men, walking up the road in his direction, talking leisurely, in English. The two are continuing the suppertime discussion, evidently agreeing with Parliament's decision and with each other.

'Diligence is needed. Lest purity of purpose be forfeit.' Rhisiart looks at the book again, ignoring the two Englishmen and closing his ears to their words.

1655

The Wild Welshman, that's their name for him. On account of his long, tangled hair, and his thick beard. Maybe because of the look in his eyes, too, and that fact that he doesn't like to talk to his fellow soldiers any more than necessary. He utters ugly guttural noises when he answers their questions, grunting his yes and groaning his no instead of making normal human sounds.

'The Wild Welshman, he will have Penruddock's head.'

He will, he will, the others agree enthusiastically. He'll come back to Southampton with Penruddock's head on a stake. He'll come back screaming a savage battle cry, John Penruddock's head in one hand and Joseph Wagstaffe's in the other. And then, after soaking them in oil and vinegar and putting them under his pillow for safekeeping, he'll go to the north, galloping to find the Earl of Rochester, and will bring his head back as well.

One of the young Englishmen refers to him as 'The Old Welshman.' He's thirty years old, but the young soldiers think of him as the mad old man or the wild old Welshman. A timeless character. Fabled. A wild-eyed prophet out for the head of a wicked king.

It's a week since they left Southampton on the trail of the rebels. Bournemouth. Dorchester. Exeter. Travelling fast, galloping past company after company of infantry on the march for the same purpose. Everyone on the trail of John Penruddock and his supporters. The rebels who have risen up in the name of the exile they call Charles II. They succeeded in seizing Salisbury and are on the move in Devon now. At least some of them. On their way to Cornwall possibly, to gather more Royalists under their banner.

But a messenger came in haste from the other direction to

meet them, a few miles outside of Exeter, to say that Crook's cavalry had beaten the rebels in some place called South Mount or South Mouth, or something like that. The rebels have all been killed or captured and imprisoned. John Penruddock himself is in Crook's hands. Wait here until word comes from the north. They say that the Earl of Rochester and the others have fled. Escaped to the continent, they say. It appears that the short-lived rebellion is over.

That night, as they sit around the fire eating bread and cheese and onions, there he is, the old Wild Welshman. Having to content himself with onions rather than the head of a rebel. Leave him be, lad, or he'll take your head off your shoulders before you can say ho dandy.

He doesn't look at the young Englishmen.

He chews his food quietly, staring into the fire.

Late Summer 1656

He hesitates in front of the gatehouse.

He's in a hurry. He needs to get through the gate and into the hubbub of the bridge, squeeze through the crowds, work his way along the swarming streets and reach Colonel Powel. See him and hear his message from his own mouth. Learn why he has been dragged back to London. But right now he can't move. Some spell has beguiled him and he remains there. Sits like that for a time, the horse standing obediently still, people pushing past him to plunge into the crowd on the bridge. He needs to wait, pause, and think. Has to study the heads that are rotting on pikes, reflect on the ornaments on the bridge's gate. Skulls half visible through shreds of grey and red and purple flesh. Ravens and seagulls hopping from head to head to peck holes and search. *Memento mori*. Remember that you too will die.

He shifts the reins, bends and slips from the saddle to his feet. He walks on, slowing enough to stroke the neck of his horse. Then he pulls lightly on the reins, leading the horse into the bustle of activity on the bridge, pushing through a sea of faces, each one a mask of flesh hiding a skull.

Remember, remember that death is near.

III
Another World

Nenachihat sakimanep peklinkwekin.
Wonwihil lowasha wapayachik.

The chief was a watcher; he looked towards the sea.
And this time the white men came,
from the north and from the south.

Walam Olum

—I—

He wakes and discovers that he is dry and warm, and lying on something soft. He knows that some kind of blanket has been spread beneath him because he can feel the material on his skin, along his naked body. He's conscious of aching in his muscles, especially in his arms and legs, and of more intense pain in his ribs on the left side, and in one ankle. Dull throbbing on the skin of his knees, his hands and his face. Extreme weariness. But he feels lucky to be here, on this side of death.

He knows he's under a roof, though he can't see well yet: it's dark except for a little light emanating from a smouldering fire next to him. There are different smells, some familiar, some not. Smoke from a wood fire. Leather. And then some kind of oil or other unfamiliar fragrance.

He turns his head slightly and sees someone standing between the fire and the wall. A man. He's tall and well built, wearing leather clothes. He squats down next to Rhisiart. His skin is fairly dark, his face beardless. The front part of his head has been shaved bare, but long black hair hangs down his back. He checks the fire, using a stick to poke it back to life. A few small flames brighten the man's long forehead, and Rhisiart sees that that part of his head has been decorated with red paint. The man turns his attention back to Rhisiart, his eyes bright and his face kind. He talks softly to him, but Rhisiart can't understand the language.

Akwi sagezo.

He holds a small wooden bowl in front of him, places his other hand under Rhisiart's head, raises him up a little and brings the bowl to his lips.

Mitzi. Akwi sagezo.

The broth is warm, tastes of meat of some kind and other flavours Rhisiart can't identify.

Mitzi, mitzi.

He can see more of the small room now. Walls of birch bark supported by simple wooden poles. A low roof, rising in a kind of dome in the centre. A few leather bags and other things that he can't see well sit in the shadows. The whole of it reassuringly domestic and yet extraordinarily strange at the same time.

The door opens and a little pale light comes in – moonlight. It's the middle of the night, but it can't be possible that it's the same night. Rhisiart doesn't have much time to think about it, as something else attracts his attention. Another man enters, closing the door behind him, a man similar in his dress and his hair, but somewhat older. The first man looks at the newcomer, rises and greets him carefully.

Kwai Nijia.

Kwai, kwai.

They stand there, speaking face to face. It's a long conversation. At times the words flow rapidly, at other times they slow down to repeat some things. Rhisiart notices the repetition of certain words or sounds over and over, punctuating the conversation, as if they were questions and answers and exclamations.

Nebi.

Sobakw.

Senojiwi.

Tegoak.

Kichi Niwaskw.

Rhisiart tries to thank them in English, but he's not strong enough to sit up and speak properly, only to turn and look at them. The two fall silent and listen to him, but there's no sign that they understand him. They begin to address one another again.

Tegoak. Nebi. Senojiwi. Sobakw. Kichi Niwaskw.

And so on, the two speaking softly, their words wrapping around Rhisiart like the warmth of the room. He feels sleep coming on, closes his eyes, and surrenders to it.

Akwi sagezo. Gawi, gawi.

He wakes every now and then. Sometimes it's quiet in the room, apart from the low crackling of the wood that's smouldering in the fire, and at other times there are voices there, speaking softly. All of it comfortably familiar and remarkably strange: someone's home, and that someone has saved him.

Once when he wakes he hears female voices. Girls or women, speaking softly with the men. *Kichi Niwaskw. Senojiwi. Tegoak. Nebi. Senojiwi. Sobakw.* Women speaking a language he doesn't understand. He can hear them between sleep and waking, their words intermingled with the crackling of the wood. He's in Ireland.

He turns his head to try to get a look at them. He's in Naseby, but not lying on his back, his arm pinned under the dead horse. His body aches and he's tired, but he's not lying on his back. He stands there, looking at them. He's been riding with the rest of them. He did not dismount from his horse and the animal didn't fall on him. He went forward, riding with the others, chasing the Royalists from the field. On and on. Leaving the field of battle. Nothing can stop them. The charge of the red horse; on and on and on. And then there they are, standing before him. He leaps from the saddle – not falls; leaps, effortlessly. And he stands there, looking at them. The women of Naseby. Several hundred of them. Speaking a language he doesn't understand. He looks again, and some of the faces are rather familiar looking. Not dissimilar from Elisabeth and Alys. Over there's an older one, her face like what he remembers of his mother's face. He continues to look, listening intently to them. The language is no longer foreign. He can understand it. He can understand the women of Naseby.

Gawi. Kowawtamenô. Gawi, gawi, gawi.

He opens his eyes and sees daylight, flooding in through the partially-opened door. Someone enters the room, and then someone else. He raises his head and looks: there are five people sitting around the fire. The two men who kept him company last night are there, along with three others. One of them is a young man – a youth really, fifteen or maybe a little older. The front of his head has been shaved, like the other two men, and the red that adorns it is brighter, as if it has only just been painted. Two women are there also, their dark hair long, very different from the style of the men. Little stars blink through the dark locks: metal jewellery in their ears catching what light there is in the room. The man who was tending him in the night is reaching for something from beside the fire. It's a vessel of some kind; he holds it with a piece of cloth and pours liquid from it into the wooden bowl.

Rhisiart sits up slowly, and tries to hide his nakedness with the blanket as he turns to rest his back against the wall. He reaches out to take the bowl, gratefully.

Mitzi. The man smiles before sitting again. The eyes of the five are watching Rhisiart closely, observing how he drinks from the bowl as if they were searching for some sort of sign. When he has finished, he puts the bowl down by his feet, gratefully again.

The man who proffered the food turns and signals to the young man, who stands and moves nearer to Rhisiart. The others move back to make a place for him to sit beside the stranger. The youth bends towards Rhisiart, the redness of his forehead darkening in the shadows.

Kwai, kwai.

He smiles widely and extends a hand. Rhisiart sees his intention and offers his own hand. The young man takes it in both his hands and shakes it, smiling.

'I can *iglismôniwi.* Speak like the English. Can you?'

'Yes, I can. I can speak English.' He says that he is grateful to them for saving his life, that it is a debt he cannot repay. The youth sits between Rhisiart and the man who fed him. The man speaks to him, quickly, shooting questions and making observations under his breath. Rhisiart hears some words being repeated.

Pilewak. Iglismôn. Plachmôn.

'My father says you are not English. You are not *Iglismôn. Nda, nda.* My father says you are not *Plachmôn*, not French either. *Nda, nda.*'

'He's right. I'm a Welshman.'

The youth turns to explain, and the other four, the two men and the two women, are talking excitedly. The word is not a familiar one, but Rhisiart explains to the boy and now he explains it to them. A Welshman, Wales. The remnants of the race of the Ancient Britons.

Wli, wli, wligo. Good, they understand. Welshman, not *Iglismôn*. Good. *Wligo.*

'We are *Alnôbak. Wôbanakiak.* The English call us Abenaki.'

And so on, the talk brisk. The youth speaking to Rhisiart and then turning to explain to the others, pausing to join in their discussions, asking their questions for them and trying to answer Rhisiart's questions. The five of them laugh sometimes, enjoying seeing that the boy can't translate it right for Rhisiart, but he is smiling with them anyway, enjoying the company and the conviviality. Rhisiart thanks them again and again, and the boy translates, conveying his gratitude to the others. *Wlioni, wlioni.* More talk, questions, laughter and thanks, and it's time to share names. He says his, Rhisiart

Dafydd, and they repeat it, forming it in their own way in their mouths as Isiad Dawi.

Malian.

Asômi.

Msadokwes.

'My father's name is Pene Wons. The English call him Penewans. I am Simôn. I have another name, but that is what you can call me. Simôn.

Pene Wons is trying to intone his own name in the English style, turning the corners of his mouth down coyly and stretching out his vowels. 'Pe-ne wans.' He pretends he's speaking the language, making meaningless sounds that imitate the sounds of *iglismôniwi*, the look on his face complementing the comic performance. 'Pe-ne wans. *Se se with with me se se fith.*' He tries to keep his face like that, contorted into a mock-serious look, but he can't keep it up. He laughs, and the others join in the laughter. Rhisiart laughs too, imagining the Englishman that Pene Wons is mocking.

There is joy here. They have saved this man from the grasp of death. Him, the man who came to their shores from the grip of the waves. He's a *Pilewak*, yet not one of the *Pilewakak*. He's a newcomer but he's not one of those other strangers. No. The chance to save him was given to them. His life was given into their hands. Theirs, and no one else's. And they know that that's how it is. Here, sharing the joy with him. Talking. Asking. Laughing.

Malian.

Asômi.

Msadokwes.

Pene Wons.

Simôn.

Isiad Dawi.

—2—

The care was tender and the attention thorough. He slept much of the time, but as far as he knows he was never left alone for even a minute. At least one member of the family was with him all the time. Simôn, Malian or Pene Wons. The son, the mother or the father. They brought him food four times a day – different kinds of broth, smoked fish, or something similar to porridge but tasting of plants and fruits rather than oats.

Rhisiart knew by the second week that he could stand and limp slowly on his own, but every time he rose, Pene Wons insisted on helping him. At first the only occasions were when he went out to pass water or otherwise relieve himself. Since he was still naked, he would wear his blanket like a cloak and lean on Pene Wons' arm. The two would walk past the fire that burned day and night, and out through the door.

The family's home stood in a broad clearing, with birch trees of different sizes around the edges and tall pine trees beyond. There was but a single other structure in the clearing – the home of Asômi and Msadokwes, a small house made of bark and birchwood, just like Pene Wons' house. There were also a number of long mounds with some dead, brown growth on them: gardens denuded by the harvest, with nothing but the residue left, bits of roots and vines slowly decaying into the earth.

The two of them would walk carefully, slowly – arm in arm, like lords in a procession. Onwards to the woods at the edge of the clearing, and then Rhisiart would do whatever it was he had to do. Sometimes they would talk while walking, Pene Wons encouraging him in a friendly and sociable way with a string of words that the Welshman understood none of apart from his own name: Isiad Dawi.

He would answer in Welsh, thanking him and making observations about the weather, the sun, the colour of the leaves. The leaves of the birch trees had just begun to turn the first time Rhisiart came out into the clearing, but after a few weeks of this quiet, tranquil life, the green of the edges of the clearing had been displaced by brilliant red and yellow leaves, with the dark green of the pine trees in the background providing a counterpoint to these splendid, glorious walls. By the time the leaves finished turning, the talk of the two men had become more meaningful.

And so here they are walking today. They walk in the direction of the *abaziak*, the woods, looking at the beautiful colours of the *maskwamozi*, the birch trees, and raising their eyes, *koaikok*, to the pines beyond. *Pamgisgak* is what they are walking through; Rhisiart originally thought that it was the word for the clearing, but he's beginning to think it might refer to the present, or possibly to today. *Kizos*, the sun, is directly over their heads, meaning it's midday. After reaching the woods, urinating, and returning to lean on Pene Wons again, he straightens his blanket, the *maksa*. When they get back to the *wigwôm*, Rhisiart pauses and thanks his new friend in his language: *wlioni*.

Pene Wons nods his head, the red paint on his forehead glistening in the sun. He opens the door and leads Rhisiart carefully through the opening, calling him *nidoba*. It's a word Pene Wons uses often in their conversations, one that Rhisiart understands fully: my friend.

–3–

He's been asking them for days – imploring, begging, explaining his wishes explicitly in English to Simôn, and trying to persuade Pene Wons with those words of their language that he has learned, and he has finally succeeded. Pene Wons knows that Rhisiart is well enough to travel beyond the clearing. He also knows that he cannot deny this trip to his friend.

The three of them set out in the morning. Pene Wons, Simôn and Isiad Dawi, leaving the clearing *sôkhipozit kisos*, at dawn. Rhisiart learned another new word that morning. Malian, Asômi and Msadokwes stood there wishing them farewell: *Wlibomkanni.* A word wishing them a safe journey, a successful trip, a swift return. And the journey has gone smoothly so far. It's a fine, dry day, although the wind is bracing. Rhisiart believes that it's been some three weeks since the ship sank; he doesn't know the exact day, but he knows that it is October of 1656. Pene Wons says that it's *Penibagos*, the month when the leaves fall. Most of the leaves are still on the trees. They move along in the shadows of the tall pine trees most of the time, their dark green crowns filtering the sun over their heads and the dead pine needles forming a scented brown carpet under their feet. Broadleaved trees appear in small multicoloured groves every now and then, their yellow and red leaves bright in the sunshine.

Rhisiart is wearing his own clothes again, but they're not the same. After washing the salt out of them and drying them in the sun, Malian set about repairing the big holes in the knees of the breeches and the elbows of the shirt, and so patches of light hide have replaced the lost material. It doesn't feel any different on his skin, for the deer hide has been worked in such a way that it is as smooth as the best material Rhisiart ever put on. He has been given shoes too, ones that he has learned to refer to as *makezenal*. Leather shoes, the soles harder than the rest and yet flexible. He's wearing the same long leggings as his friends, fitted out with some kind of colourful buckles that connect his shoes with the bottom of his breeches. He doesn't have a cloak like theirs, and so he wears his blanket, *maksa*, around his shoulders. The father carries a bow and has arrows in a long pouch attached to his belt. The son carries a musket. They were discussing weapons last night in preparation for the journey, and Simôn explained that they had got the musket from the English the preceding year. It's not as dependable as the bow and arrow, but Simôn's father insisted that he use it since they were embarking on important business. This told the English and other natives alike that Pene Wons' family was able to use the *Iglismôn*'s weapons. Like the English that Simôn can speak, this is an important matter. Father and son are also wearing metal knives they got from trading with the English. Rhisiart is travelling without a weapon of any kind, for the first time in nearly fifteen years.

Rhisiart walks a little behind the two of them. Sometimes they stop and listen, focusing on the source of some sound, holding their weapons at the ready. But there is nothing to see except birds and squirrels. And what do these creatures see? What would another man see if he came across them? Two natives, one a middle-aged man and the other a youth, the fronts of their heads shaved and decorated with red paint, the black hair of each falling in a tail down the back, their faces hairless. And the third man – his face pale, his greying brown hair in disarray, and half of his face hidden by an unruly beard, his clothing a mix of the world he came from and the world his friends have welcomed him into.

They don't take a break to eat, instead passing around dried fish, which they eat as they walk. It leaves a salty taste on Rhisiart's tongue, so he doesn't notice at first that he's breathing sea air. The trees have thinned out and their feet are now walking on grass and brush as thick as the pine needles. He notices that a low, rhythmic pounding is reaching his ears, the sound of waves hitting the shore.

Akwi sagezo, Isiad Dawi.

Pene Wons is by his side, his hand on his arm, leading him. *Akwi sagezo*, Isiad Dawi, *akwi sagezo*. Simôn explains that his father is telling him not to worry. He thinks he'll be afraid to return to this place, the place where he was in the grasp of death. Rhisiart thanks him and walks out of the shadow of the last trees across the grass. Here and there are hillocks of brush and also outcrops of dark rock breaking through the ground, like skeletons of monsters from an ancient age.

He comes to the edge of the beach and stands there looking down the hill to the sea. The slope is not as long or as steep as he remembered it. He steps down from the grass to the rocky beach and feels the shingle shifting under his feet, his legs slipping and his body beginning to move down the slope against his will. He doesn't fall but he doesn't try to walk any further. He stands there, remembering that night. Feeling the stones slipping under his hands and feet. The pain in his muscles, his ribs and his ankle. The shivering wracking his body. Effort bordering on despair, weakness approaching death.

He sees shapes of different kinds and sizes littering the beach. Not the solid bones of the dark rocks, but things that appear more fragile. Most of them are wood, some small pieces, splinters, and some large pieces, even the size of a horse. Bits of the ship that one can half recognize. Bits of fabric here and there too. Parts of a sail or hammock, half full of stones anchoring it on the beach, the free edges moving dreamily in the foamy waves.

He stands there a long time, his eyes sweeping across the wreckage, searching for remains of another kind. He's afraid he'll see them, and yet he needs to know, and so he's straining to see, searching for the bodies.

Simôn comes to stand next to him. The wind is up, tossing his hair, its dark tail whipping in the wind behind him. Rhisiart feels the wind tugging at his own hair and hears its rush in his ears, mixed with the roar of the waves on the rocky beach. But he can still hear the voice of the youth beside him, even though he's speaking normally.

'My father asks me to tell you the story.'

Story? A tale? He turns and studies Simôn's face. The young man is not looking at him but staring out to sea. Rhisiart sees the straight line of the red paint that decorates the front of his head, a line that's parallel with his hairline where it's been shaved. His hair blows in the wind, and his eyes are watering a little. He speaks slowly, thoughtfully, keeping his eyes on the waves the whole time.

Msadokwes and Asômi saw the ship one afternoon. The two of them had gone to the shore to take advantage of the tide to hunt shellfish and catch fish in the surf. And there it was, like a monster rising from the waves. The ship, larger than the small ones they had sometimes seen sailing up and down the coast. A monster. A fictional creature. It was coming closer and closer, like it was intending to land, though there were no English ports in the area. Rather than going about their business, the two of them went straight back home and told the the others the news. It was decided that Pene Wons should go back with Msadokwes to see what the ship was about. But the storm was raging by the time the men reached the coast, and the ship had disappeared from view. By morning the storm had run its course, and all five of them went back to search the shores. They had to walk for half a day before they found the area where most of the wreckage was. Bits of the ship in the shallows bobbing in the waves, together with the bodies of the dead. A single body lying halfway between the beach and the woods, still alive. Pene Wons and Msadokwes brought the live body home. Malian, Simôn and Asômi remained to take care of the rest.

The three stand there for a while, quietly contemplating. Rhisiart thinks about all the bodies he has seen on the battlefields. Bloating in the heat of the sun. Growing cold under the moon. Ravens, crows, gulls picking at them. Pigs coming to root around in them. Dogs creeping around furtively to tear into an arm or leg. He asks Simôn what happened to the bodies.

'Come, Isiad Dawi, we will show you.'

There is a line of earth nearly rock-free, far from the clutches of the waves. On the western side the branches of giant pine trees shade the graves, but the eastern side is open to the wind from the sea. There are nine of them, each one a rectangular mound, the top of the grave a mixture of soil and tiny stones and shells. A small cross stands at the head of each one, two pine branches stripped of their bark and tied together with leather string. Nine of them. The sea must have taken the rest to other shores or else pulled them down to the bottom with the ship as it sank. Rhisiart feels he ought to ask for more details. Were they men? Women? What age? What colour hair? But he can't force the questions out. He walks around the line a number of times, his steps encircling the nine graves, taking in the extent of the small new cemetery. He walks slowly, eyes down, studying Malian, Simôn and Asômi's work. Rhisiart stands at the foot of the first grave, bowing his head, praying.

> Death brings the soul of a godly man into communion with God in joy and eternal glory. It frees him from the wretchedness and

misery of this world and is the means of releasing himself from the grasp of sin. It opens the door to the kingdom of the living God, the gate of the heavenly Jerusalem. Death puts the soul in possession of the full, present inheritance and all the blessedness that was promised. It fulfils that which Christ promised you in his own words, establishing for you that which he purchased with his own blood.

It's an old, old prayer, one that he had memorized before he heard Walter Cradoc preaching for the first time. Alys, his sister, taught it to him; she said that those were the words that were spoken when their parents were buried. Rhisiart knows that he has reworked the prayer, putting it into his own words. He vaguely remembers pounding the words into hot iron in the smithy in Wrexham. But he can't remember which parts came from Alys and which words are the fruits of his own imagination. All he remembers is the fact that it's an old prayer, formed in his memory before he began listening to the itinerant preachers.

He raises his head and walks slowly to the foot of the next grave. He gazes at the little cross. Studies the mixture of earth, rocks and shells. Closes his eyes and bows his head. Prays again. Death brings the soul of a godly man into communion with God. Raises his head and walks to the foot of the third grave. Pauses. Prays. Death puts the soul in possession of the full, present inheritance. And so on, again and again. Nine times. He is aware that Pene Wons and Simôn are standing there silently, and he wants to turn and ask them. An old man? Young woman? Hair colour? Owen Lewys? Captain Marlow? David? Elizabeth? But he doesn't have the power to ask the questions. He can't turn and ask them, only walk slowly, staring at the graves, and praying. But his internal voice is asking quietly:

Owen?

David?

Elizabeth?
Elisabeth?
Alys?

Finally, he turns from the cemetery and walks over to Pene Wons and Simôn. He stands with them for a while, looking at the sea. The tide is rising, and has already swept some of the remains of the shipwreck from the shore. He can still see some pieces, the biggest ones standing like rocks and the smaller ones moving in the grip of the waves, small stuff bouncing in the foam: driftwood of the dead.

He asks Simôn about the crosses. 'Are you, then, a Christian?' The youth says that he has not renounced the faith of his people, but he knows that the English like to be buried in this way. Then he apologizes, saying 'I am sorry, Isiad Dawi, I know you are not an *Iglismôn*.' Rhisiart says he's right, explaining that the passengers were English. All except one. Owen Lewys. He pauses for a moment, thinking again that he ought to ask if it's possible for Simôn to describe the corpses that were buried, but the question still won't come out. He asks instead about the crosses, and although he's not a Christian, Simôn is eager to show that he understands much about the faith of the *pilewakak*, the foreigners' religion. He was studying English with Moses Walker, the Englishman who said that he had come to bring light to the darkness of their forests. The youth learned the man's language, but did not embrace his religion. He learned many other things about the English too, things that were strange and things that were shocking. He had just returned to his family a few days before the shipwreck, his head newly shaved in the style of his father. He pauses to explain to his father in their own language what he has been discussing with Isiad Dawi. Then he turns back to the Welshman and continues in English. 'I tell my father that it is a very strange thing. Here I am, come back home from the world of the *Iglismôn* and then we find all of you washed up here on the beach, washed all the way from England.' He apologizes again. 'But I know you are not English, Isiad Dawi.' The remains of the race of the Ancient Britons, wild prophet of the old ages, whose hair and beard are unkempt, wearing clothing of two worlds, standing here between forest and beach, taking in the ocean wind.

Alosada.

Pene Wons speaks softly. Let us go now.
Alosada.
The three men turn and walk past the little cemetery.
Wlibomkanni.
Safe journey to the gates of the kingdom of God.
Farewell.

The three walk on, leaving the graves and their crosses behind. The grass beneath their feet yields to the fragrant brown carpet of pine needles. The sun is setting, and the shadows of the forest are heavy across the path. Rhisiart follows the other two, his mind on the ship, the shore and the graves.

He notices that the other two are not walking only a moment before he bumps into the back of Simôn. The father and son stand there, their heads turned to one side, listening, and their eyes boring into the shadows. Pene Wons unslings his bow and draws an arrow. They remain very quiet. Looking and listening and getting ready. Rhisiart sees that something is moving in the gloom, something that's darker than the forest shadows. It moves swiftly towards them, challenging his eye to follow it. He senses that the father and son have relaxed somewhat. The creature is not large and Pene Wons is not going to shoot it. It comes nearer, moving swiftly, white paws holding whatever light is left. Another second and the black tomcat is there, weaving through Rhisiart's legs.

'Nicholas!'

He bends down and picks him up – another who came out of the *Primrose* alive. He holds the cat tightly to his chest and lifts a finger to tickle him under the chin.

Nidoba.

Pene Wons and Simôn are laughing, enjoying the surprise. *Widôba*, his friend. *Widôba*, Isiad Dawi's friend. Rhisiart joins in, laughing and talking. *Nidôbasizek*. This is my little friend Nicholas. *Nidôbasizek*. The three of them walk home in the shadows of the trees. Pene Wons carrying his bow, Simôn carrying his musket, and Rhisiart carrying the black cat.

–4–

Rhisiart is sitting in the grass, his legs crossed, his back straight. There's not much wind and the air is warm, though October is drawing to a close. *Penibagos*: the month when the trees will lose their leaves. A storm the night before last brought down many of them. A bit of yellow can still be seen surrounding the clearing, but holes have appeared in the bright walls, gaps that reveal the skeletons of birch trees with the dark pines behind them.

Pene Wons promised they would be going before *Penibagos* gave way to the days of *Mzatanos*, before the leaves stopped falling and the frost began to form. The storms have passed and all signs say that the weather will be fine for quite a period, and so it has been decided that they will leave tomorrow. He has no desire to leave. London is a world away from this clearing, and there is a world of another kind between the man who sits here in the grass and the one who sat in Colonel Powel's room two months ago. But he promised John Powel and Pene Wons has promised him. They're going before the leaves stop falling. They're starting on their journey tomorrow morning.

He can't see Malian, but he feels her hand tugging at his hair. Pulling and pulling on one lock and *snick!* as the knife cuts it, his head snapping forward a bit each time. Then she takes hold of another lock and begins pulling again. She shaved his face first. She asked if he wanted her to shave the front of his head too, get it ready for the red paint. He hesitated before answering through Simôn, her son, their translator, worrying that he would offend her, but the five began to laugh and he knew that she was joking. She said that she had never shaved a face before, but she accomplished it quickly without nicking the skin once.

The beard had grown, the beard of the wild man, the sign of the prophet living in the wilderness: all of it fell there in the grass in front of Malian, Pene Wons and Simôn's *wigwôm*. There was laughter and talk, Simôn translating the comments.

Asômi says that you are like her husband now.

Msadokwes disagrees; he's handsomer than that.

Malian asks if she should shave the cat next.

Pene Wons suggests that a cat's bare backside would be more like Msadokwes' face than Isiad Dawi's is.

Malian had to stop a number of times because her hands were shaking with laughter, but she didn't cut Rhisiart once. She moved behind him, got down on her knees again, and began to cut his hair just above his shoulders, as he had asked her to do. *Wdupkuanal*, hair. He understands when she says that word. Other than that, he has trouble understanding Malian because she speaks more rapidly and more softly than the others. But he likes the sound of her voice, just as he liked the feel of her hand on his face when she was shaving him. Rhisiart understands something else she says. Nita, her name for Nicholas. Simôn said that she calls the animal that because he springs so quickly. He's over there and then, *nita!*, he's here. Nita. Nicholas is sleeping beside Msadokwes' legs, his fur unshaven and shining black in the sun.

Msadokwes calls him something else, a long name that Rhisiart can't remember clearly. He's understood it as Makawiganô, though he's certain that's not the whole name. He knows that the name refers to the animal's colour: The Black One.

You have as many names as the Devil himself, Rhisiart thinks. Nic. Old Nick. Nicholas. Makawiganô. Nita, able to swim to shore, arriving alive. The Devil looks after his servant well. Nonsense, Rhisiart. He swam. Just like you yourself. There's no one looking after us but ourselves.

He feels Malian's hands on his shoulders, massaging them

gently. She says something about his *wdupkuanal* and Rhisiart knows that she has finished cutting his hair. He turns around to thank her.

Wlioni. Thanks. *Wlioni*, Malian, *nidoba*.

Everyone is laughing and Simôn explains. He says that his mother can't be *nidoba* to Rhisiart. Simôn is *nidoba* to Rhisiart. His father too is *nidoba* to him. And Rhisiart is *nidoba* to them. But his mother cannot be *nidoba*. She is *nidobaskwa*. Rhisiart tries to pronounce the word.

Nidoba sgwa.

Everyone laughs again, and the sound awakens the cat. He stretches his legs slowly and looks around haughtily, a king surveying his kingdom. After stretching his legs again, he walks leisurely towards Rhisiart.

Nidôbasizek.

–5–

They pause for a while to savour the dawn. There's a huge rock rising up from the middle of the woods, and Pene Wons says they should climb it and stand there to watch the sunrise.

They started out in the sunless grey light. Malian, Msadokwes and Asômi came to the edge of the clearing to bid them farewell. *Wlibomkanni. Wli nanawalmezi.* Go safely. Malian gave her son a long embrace, and then released him with some comment that Rhisiart didn't understand but that made everyone else laugh. She embraced her husband then, and they stayed entwined like that for a long while. And then the three men walked to the forest. Black Nicholas followed in Rhisiart's footsteps; the cat had been with him on short walks over the last few days. Simôn called back to the three remaining at the edge of the clearing, and was answered with laughter. It was no wonder that Nita chose to go with Isiad Dawi; he was afraid that Malian would shave him bald if he stayed in the *wigwôm* with her. And so the trio became a foursome. *Wli nanawalmezi.* Go safely. *Wlibomkanni.* Farewell.

Pene Wons and Simôn are wearing long leather coats with a kind of cowl that can be pulled up as a pointed hat to protect the head if it rains. Rhisiart has his blanket over his shoulders, a cloak to match his patched clothes. He holds Simôn's musket, and the youth carries a bow similar to his father's. The father and son walk softly, avoiding making any unnecessary sound, and Rhisiart tries to do the same.

His body is moving instinctively, doing familiar work, his muscles remembering. He's walking with a weapon in his hands, trying to see before being seen. He moves in a line, following Dafi and Siôn, searching the woods on the outskirts of some village in England. Sliding into concealment in the undergrowth on the brink of battle. Then his mind swings back to the present. He's following Simôn and Pene Wons, two men in their own land. *Ndakinna*, my land. That's what Pene Wons said at the beginning of the journey. I know every inch of this land, because it is my land. He knows every trail, every clearing, every rock and cliff. When Simôn says that his father wants them to climb to the top of this rock to see the dawn, Rhisiart half thinks that Pene Wons has planned the journey this way so that they will reach this rock at this exact time. He smiles.

Black Nicholas has been making his own way, close on Rhisiart's heels sometimes, following at a distance at other times. Every now and then he disappears, following some sound in the undergrowth, but he always comes back, bounding onto the trail to rejoin the small company moving almost noiselessly through the shadows of the trees. For some reason, Rhisiart worries that the cat will not understand that they want to climb the rock, so he shifts the musket to one hand and bends down to pick up the cat with the other. The animal slips free of his grasp and Rhisiart thinks he wants to jump down and escape, but Nicholas only climbs up his arm and sits on his shoulder, his claws gripping the blanket cloak.

Although it is not very high, it is high enough to rise above the trees around it. They stand there at the top of the rock, looking in the direction of the sea. The sun begins to rise, and as it climbs higher and higher the light changes from grey to red. Between them and the coast is about half a mile of trees: some without leaves and reaching their bony fingers into the sky, but a good many of them still wearing their mantels. It is a riot of colour, a mixture of brown, yellow, red and green leading to the sea. The sea itself is a green veil, dark, stretching towards the horizon, the approaching dawn splashing it with streaks of red. Simôn and Pene Wons are talking animatedly; Rhisiart doesn't understand the conversation and he doesn't ask the youth to translate. He stands there, Nicholas perched on his shoulder, watching the sun climb to claim the sky. Father and son have fallen silent, and Simôn now stands next to him. After a moment he raises his hand and points: *Wôban.* The light of the dawn. That's what we are. The people who live in the land of the dawn. *Wôbanakiak.*

> Listen my brother. The dawn is breaking. Look you at the light. Ask for a fountain of understanding and drink frequently from it. Awaken, awaken, awaken, and walk like a child of the day. I say again: here is the dawn, and the sun is rising to claim this place just as it has done every day since the beginning of creation. Here I am, receiving the light, here, with the People of the Land of the Dawn. The dawn has broken, and the sun is rising on me. The birds are singing: Awaken, Welshman, Awaken. And if you do not believe words, believe deeds. Look about you and see. I look. I see.

–6–

Today is the second day of the journey and it's a magnificent day. Pene Wons says it ought to be colder, but he's grateful for the unseasonable weather. He talks of the warm breeze, light as the breath of summer. But the breath of winter will come before long, he says. It could come tomorrow or the next day, or three days from now, he says, but he's grateful for today. Red and yellow leaves crackle beneath Rhisiart's feet, a dry and pleasing sound. He believes that more of the colours of autumn linger in the branches above them now too. Pene Wons says that is probably true: they are travelling south and those who observe such things know that the leaves cling longer in the south. A day and a half of walking can make a difference. On the other hand, he adds significantly, trees everywhere are in the grip of *Penibagos*, and they will, one and all, have to shed their leaves before long. But not today; he gives thanks again for this memory of the breath of summer. Simôn translates his father's words – although Rhisiart learns and remembers a number of new words every day, he's not able to understand the stream of Pene Wons' words when they're flowing freely.

He was surprised yesterday when he learned that they were journeying south. Rhisiart is a man who thinks about maps; he forms them in his head when he's travelling and likes to say to himself that this place is west of that other place and note that the journey has taken him in that direction. For some reason he had thought that the ship had sunk somewhere between Boston and Strawberry Bank, so he had expected Pene Wons and Simôn to be taking him north. But no, they're going south; the *Primrose* sank on the coast north of Strawberry Bank.

A good two and a half days to the north, according to Pene Wons.

The smells of the forest have filled his head throughout the journey – a mixture of the unmistakable freshness of the pine trees and the dry, earthy smell of the broadleaved trees – and their beautiful colours adorn the world above his head and under his feet. It's a rocky land, with outcrops of different sizes breaking a patch of land or hill. He remembers his childhood in Caernarfonshire: swimming in a brook with his father and looking up to contemplate the mountains. This land is almost as rugged, but it's also completely different, hard in different ways in places and soft in different ways in other places. He decides that the earth exhibits different remains in different parts of this great world. The sea comes into view occasionally, that green veil, its extent immense, continually rolling towards the horizon, with an occasional island or rocky eruption breaking the waves here and there.

They've been walking in silence for a while, the three men following a narrow path through a thicket of pine trees, and the black cat trotting along beside Rhisiart. He went off the path once, and returned with a mouse in his mouth. What will Nita eat in the winter, Pene Wons asked, when the mice are sleeping in the earth? Birds, answered Simôn. And when the snow is too heavy and the birds are resting too high up? his father asked back. Isiad Dawi will provide food for his friend, the lad answered. Laughter then, the two of them chewing over familiar words. *Widôba*. Nita. He, the Black One. But they've fallen silent by now, and the four are travelling quietly, the scent of pine filling Rhisiart's head.

Up a hill then. The land is rockier here and the trees are thinning out. On they walk, following a trail down into a small valley, the sound of a brook charming them, the whisper of water rushing over rocks mixing with the crackle of the dry leaves under Rhisiart's feet. Pene Wons speaks, saying something to his son, too quick for the Welshman to understand.

'My father says I should tell you about the dying times.'

By the time they reach the brook Simôn has explained. He is going to tell the recent history of their people, all that has happened to the People of the Land of the Dawn since the Frenchman and the Englishman came to these shores. The history of the days of death that came with the *Plachmôn* and the *Iglismôn*. Rhisiart stops and picks up Nicholas before stepping onto the first stone and crossing the stream. When they reach the other side, Rhisiart puts the cat down again, and he bounds along in front of them. Safely on the other side, Simôn begins his story.

Yes, there was warring. Attacks, fighting, killing. But that was not the source of the dying times. It was death of another kind. A death that came along a different path. Coughing. Bloating. Sweating. Fever. Disease. Plague. *Akuamalsowôgan*. The Great Death came back time after time, sometimes killing four of every five in a village and sometimes killing nine of every ten. Whole villages disappeared sometimes, the woods swallowing up homes, fields and gardens. Wave after wave, a sea of death smashing the living land of their people. In the time of his great-grandfather. In the days of his grandfather. In his father's time. And although he's not very old, Simôn himself has witnessed it. Wave after wave sweeping whole families from the tribal record, snatching villages in their entirety, making people scarce in the Land of the Dawn. Wave after wave pounding the shore, coming back again and again and again. Their name for it is a long word, and Rhisiart generally has a hard time remembering long words, but he knows in his bones that he'll remember this one.

Akuamalsowôgan.

Rhisiart asks Simôn why his father has chosen to share this

history with him at this time. Are there graves nearby? Vestiges of an old, vanished village?

The boy speaks rapidly with his father and then translates the answer. No, no. Not at all. The water of the brook, rippling cheerily between the rocks: it's the happy sound that stirs sad memories.

Rhisiart begins to ask if they have lost family and friends but he clamps his mouth shut after uttering the first word. *Have…* Not *have you…* Not *have you lost*, only that single word. Of course they have lost. They've lost much. Whole families. Whole villages. They are a people who were living in large villages – of what does their community consist now? Five people living in two houses in a clearing. Two families, one childless, and Simôn the only child. They're the remnants. He knows that there are other communities of People of the Land of the Dawn living in this district, but they too are remnants. He has an urge to say something else, to share his own history rather than ask the question. Say that he too has experienced the destruction of that Death. The pale horse galloping through the ranks of the army in Reading. The Little Plague taking his whole world from him in London.

But he can't form the words. It's a kind of cowardice – failing to share his loss with those who have lost more than him. Rhisiart knows that that's what it is, but he cannot share this history and he doesn't speak. He looks up and notices how the afternoon sun has lit up the yellowish-red leaves over the trail. Breathtaking beauty. Happiness that comes with sad memories.

–7–

Pesgatak was.

Pene Wons says these words smiling broadly, and then immediately says something and his son laughs. Simôn tries to explain: there are names and there are names, some we use continually and some come and go. Since they came to these shores, the Frenchman and the Englishman have adopted some of these names and rejected others. Sometimes they take words that are not names and turn them into names. Pene Wons likes this one especially: *Pesgatak was*, the water is looking dark.

They are standing on a bare slope, studying the broad river. There are small islands close to the near shore and a longer one can be seen on the far side. These slopes have been despoiled of trees, so Rhisiart can see the view clearly – the river opening into an estuary and then the sea beyond, lead-grey water turning dark green as it reaches the sea. He sees a large, wooden structure near the shore beneath them, not a house of wattle and birch bark but a strong, rectangular building with a stone chimney. Reminiscent of English houses, but slightly different in its structure. He spots a few more houses on the far shore and on some of the islands, but they are mere specks.

He senses the strong presence of his friends. He turns to see their solemn faces, which then break into smiles and laughter. Pene Wons speaks quickly, and then presses something into Rhisiart's hand, a thin booklet wrapped in soft material.

'We made this for you. My father drew the land and I wrote the names. All for you.'

Simôn says it's an *awikhigan*. Says it will help you on your journey from here to your destination. It brings together much information; his mother and his father consulted at length with Msadokwes and Asômi, mining the memory and analyzing stories heard from travellers. It's a good and detailed *awikhigan*. It will be a faithful companion. And with that Pene Wons clasps his arm.

Wlibomkanni, Isiad Dawi.

Go safely, Rhisiart.

Go safely, *nidoba*, my friend.

Pene Wons bends down to stroke Nicholas, and when he straightens there's a smile on his face. Simôn says that bidding farewell happily is always better. A smile on his face too.

This farewell has come suddenly, unexpectedly, and Rhisiart isn't ready for it. He hoped to say more. Deliver a paean of thanks. Sculpt words that would express his feelings. But suddenly they are leaving, and he has no chance to search for those words. He is speechless and the silence is painful. But he finds two words before they turn and walk swiftly up the slope.

Wlibomkanni.

Wlioni.

Farewell.

Thank you.

He picks his way carefully down the slope, noting the occasional stump gathering moss amid the grass. Remnants of lost woods. Trees that have been cut down, the wood used for ships or houses. Firewood to warm a home or feed a furnace.

He reaches the door of the house. Shouts hello. The cat disappears, following the path of prey underneath the house. Rhisiart shouts again.

He's about to knock on the door but a voice stops him.

'I saw you from the bank. I am Thomas Fernald.'

The accent is English but he can't quite place the region. Somerset? Devon? A taste of Oxford, yet different?

'My name is Rhisiart Dafydd. I sailed on the *Primrose*, a ship which foundered off these shores some weeks hence.'

Before he can finish that sentence, the cat is at his feet, a mouse hanging limply in its mouth. The Englishman takes notice and the two stand there for a moment, looking at Black Nicholas, one in amazement and the other glad of the opportunity to stop talking. The only sound is that of the crunching of small bones in the cat's mouth and the final whimper of his prey.

'Well! I see you have not come to my door alone!'

Rhisiart says nothing; he doesn't want to share any more of his history with this man. And so he remains silent, his eyes on the contented cat at his feet.

I have not come alone, no. This one came ashore a friend to me. I, the one man who made it to land with the breath of life in him. I plunged deep into the dark waters, I went down to the dark mouth of Hell. It's not fiery and hot but icily cold. Down I went into the grip of that mortal cold, down far from the realm of light and life, but I came ashore alive.

–8–

It's not a town. Not even a village; that is, not like the villages of Wales and England. There are about forty houses and the occasional barn, workshop and mill squeezed in along the shores of the river, with a few more on the biggest island. Although the community does not have a centre as such, most of the buildings are on the south shore, so Thomas Fernald arranged for a boat to bring Rhisiart across the water. Piscataqua is what he called the river, the word rolling smoothly off the Englishman's tongue.

He was very friendly and ready to be of assistance, but also eager for the Welshman to know that he was a man of importance in the district. A son of the late Renald Fernald, the famous old doctor, a man who had received a lease on the land along the north shore of the Piscataqua from no less than Sir Ferdinand Gorges himself. Although Rhisiart did not know of Thomas Fernald's father, he did have some dim memory of having heard the other name before – a fellow soldier from London or Bristol, perhaps, mentioning the name of Sir Ferdinand in passing. But he showed neither his ignorance nor his knowledge, only listened courteously to Thomas Fernald's account of his claim on the land, his history and his standing. Rhisiart sat there apparently attentive, a look on his face the Englishman could construe as respect, but his mind wandering to recall the words of Morgan Llwyd.

Ond mae pob un yn ymbalfalu fel dall.

But everyone is fumbling around like a blind man. 'If people were to bow to me as to God, I would be a grand man,' says one man.

> 'If I could fill my chest and my coffer with the riches of the earth, I would sleep peacefully and I would be blessed,' says another. But O, Welshman, not one of these men knows grace. The people are trying to live among the dead and they are searching for the sun in the deep pits of the earth.

Since arriving on the other side of the river, he has been handed from house to house and from family to family. He is tired of repeating his name and has tried to hide his irritation when the English settlers call him Richard Davies. Although English comrades in the army often called him this, something inside him resists the name now. He prefers the Wôbanakiak's name for him, and suggests that they call him Rhisiart Dawi. It's Richard Dewy in their mouths, and he leaves it at that. And so the day goes, Rhisiart going from house to house and from family to family, until someone, towards the end of the afternoon, hits upon the right place for him. 'But of course, take him to the Welshman.' The Welshman. The only Welshman in the community. The Welshman of Strawberry Bank. And that's where he is tonight, sitting in front of the fire in the home of Gwilym Rowlant, learning that he's no longer the Welshman of Strawberry Bank but the Welshman of Portsmouth.

'There you are, Rhisiart, my boy – the name of our town was changed some three years ago. I know the petition by heart. I had a part in putting it together, you see.' Gwilym Rowlant's name has changed too –he is called William Rowlands by the Englishmen of the new Portsmouth – but he's pleased to be able to speak to another Welshman. Another person who can say his real name.

He's a big man with a belly that shows he enjoys life and food, and the chair groans audibly when he shifts his weight. A narrow white beard adorns his moon-shaped face, and his hair falls in curly locks onto his broad shoulders.

'The others signed their names to it. Pendleton, Fernald, Haines, and Sherbourn. But I had a part in writing the petition. As big a part as any of them. And I remember it word for word.' He raises a hand and points a finger at his temple. 'It's here. Here, deep in my mind.' He moves his substantial body a little, the chair creaking its displeasure, and begins to recite in a loud voice, his accent extraordinarily English. '"To the honoured General Court at Boston, this present month of May 1653, the humble petition of the inhabitants of the town at present called Strawberry Bank, showeth…"' Lofty words to soften the heart, earthly gems to satisfy the eyes. Men deceiving themselves, letting their blindness lead them to think that position, wealth and power are the sources of light. The rush of the dead stumbling in the world of the living, walking with their eyes closed to the sun. Gwilym Rowlant talks on, some of his words grating on Rhisiart's ears. *Honour. Commonwealth. Captain. Court.* Each word an ensign, a banner that's trying to claim a piece of land. A vain boasting of wealth. '"The desire of your humble petitioners is that this honoured Court would grant us the neck of land… Strawberry Bank, accidentally so called by reason of a bank of strawberries found in this place upon the first landing, that we now humbly desire to have called Portsmouth."' He leans forward a little, the chair threatening to collapse beneath him. 'You see, my boy, the name is well chosen, because we are living here next to an estuary. There will be a port here, you see, one to marvel at. It is only spring here now, but when autumn comes, and we have seen the fruits of our labours, the world will see that we have the biggest port in New England. Bigger than Salem, bigger than Plymouth, bigger than Boston. This will be the place, my boy, and here I will be, ready to claim my share of the wealth that will flow through it.'

Rhisiart listens attentively, showing the proper courtesy towards this man who has welcomed him into his home, but also for another reason: he has been stirred again by his mission. The day has brought with it a slow awakening. Leaving one world and coming into another, the Land of the Dawn receding from the front of his mind like last night's dream fading in the light of day. As he is passed from house to house and from family to family, as he meets Englishmen with names like Fernald and Cutt and Haines and Smyth, he slowly wakes to this present: New England. And now here he is, sitting in the house of the only Welshman of Portsmouth, speaking his mother tongue and pondering the mission Colonel Powel has given him. Will you go, Rhisiart? The Englishman Miles Egerton failed, and that's why I'm asking you, Rhisiart. Will you go?

After dining, the two men return to their chairs in front of the fire. Gwilym Rowlant is a widower. He has one living child, a son, but he has gone to sea, captain on a ship. Gwilym has a manservant and a maid, but they have disappeared into the kitchen and left their master with his guest. The cat sleeps in front of the fire; he too has gone from home to home with the newcomer, a subject of wonder, some finding it amusing, some tut-tutting. Only now, after hours in each other's company, does the old merchant take notice of Nicholas.

'Watch out, my boy, if you come across those hot-headed believers. They'll think you're a witch, with that little creature following you around everywhere.' He winks playfully at Rhisiart, lifting his long, clay pipe and sucking deep on it. He offers one to his guest, but Rhisiart declines. Tobacco smoke curls into the air, its bitter smell mingling with the warm aroma of the wood burning in the fireplace. Gwilym Rowlant takes the pipe from his mouth and points accusingly at Rhisiart, using the clay stem like a long finger.

'And your clothes.'

'My clothes?'

'Yes, my boy. We have to get something else for you to wear.'

'Why?'

He motions with his pipe again, pointing at the knees of Rhisiart's breeches. 'There's the mark of an Indian's hand on that stitching. Don't try to tell me otherwise. People will talk, Rhisiart. You shouldn't draw attention to yourself like that. Doesn't pay, my boy.'

He puts the pipe back between his teeth and takes a contented draw on it as he leans back, the chair responding. Rhisiart doesn't mention the People of the Land of the Dawn, doesn't name Pene Wons, Simôn nor Malian. But he doesn't try to deny the truth of Gwilym Rowlant's accusation either. The old man enjoys hearing the sound of his own voice – more so, probably, because he's getting to speak Welsh for the first time in years – and so Rhisiart lets him talk. He speaks at great length and in detail about the history of the dealings of the English with the natives. He describes the war with the Pequot twenty years ago, the destruction and the losses. He explains what happened some ten years later when John Eliot came from England with a commission from Parliament itself and plenty of money to establish a strong Christian mission among the Wampanoag.

'And many are Christians now. Praying Indians, we call them. But they're doing more than praying.' He winks again and takes a long pull on his pipe.

'I don't understand. What else are they doing?'

'Aha! Well, my boy, that's the nub of it. It's a remarkably good plan. It was decided to establish them in new villages around Boston.'

'I see. A series of fortifications around your most important centre. Defence. Protecting the settlers.'

'Precisely, Rhisiart. A line of villages guarding Boston and vicinity in case the others attack again. There are a number of them lying hidden in the unpopulated areas, you know. The

Narragansett. The Massachusett. The Abenaki. The Mohegan. The Nipmuck and the Pocumtuck. There are many of them to be found. And so it's good to have Christian Indians as a defence, as you say. A strong line between us and them.' He sucks vigorously again, his cheeks working hard, but no smoke rises. He takes the pipe from his mouth and looks at it disappointedly as he sees that the tobacco is gone.

'But there's one thing about the plan that's wrong.'

'What's that?'

'The Christian Wampanoag are guarding Boston and vicinity, but they're not guarding us. The line is too far to the south and to the west. We here in the north have to look after ourselves. And thus the clothes.'

'The clothes?'

'Yes, my boy. The clothes. We have to get new clothes for you. It won't pay for people in these parts to think that you're too friendly with the savages.'

Gwilym Rowlant talks on and on, imparting wisdom and giving advice. Every now and then he pauses to ask a question, but he doesn't show much interest in the answers. Again and again he comes back to his favourite subject, commerce. He takes it for granted that Rhisiart has come to America to make his fortune.

'It pleases me to see that another Welshman has come to these shores. There's not enough enterprise in we Welsh as a rule. That's my experience. The Welsh are too tied to the past. Ploughing up the same old lands as their fathers, following the same plough, walking the same path. But there are adventurous men among the English. The prize comes to those who take chances, that's one sure thing about this world, Rhisiart. And these shores are the place to take a chance, I'm telling you. If you want to stay in Portsmouth, I can help. Give a little push here and there. Set you to a venture which will pay off.'

'I am indeed grateful for your kindness. But I have family further to the west. I'm hoping to find them and begin anew there.'

The old man rests his cold pipe on his knee, one hand stroking his beard, his eyes looking intently at Rhisiart.

'Other Welsh? In these parts?'

'Yes, a number of them.'

The merchant turns and stares into the fire.

He remains silent for a spell, and when he speaks again his voice is dreamily distant.

'I know the ones you are talking about, Rhisiart.'

'Can you help me, then?'

'It's not a matter of help.'

'I don't understand.'

The other man doesn't respond to him. He looks down, studying his plump fingers, which are busy filling the bowl of his pipe with tobacco. When he's finished, he leans forward, about to rise, but Rhisiart stands first. He picks up a dry twig from the basket beside the hearth and holds it in the fire, then offers the flame to Gwilym Rowlant, who nods his thanks. With the clay pipe clenched firmly between his teeth, he takes the twig from Rhisiart, pushes the flame into the bowl, and puffs hard. As the smoke begins to rise, he tosses what's left of the twig towards the fire and takes the pipe from his mouth, the smoke wreathing around his big round face.

'You won't find them, my boy.' He pulls on his pipe again and blows the smoke from his mouth. 'You should surrender that hope.'

He is studying Rhisiart's face, trying to assess the effect of his words on him. When he speaks again his voice is kinder and warmer.

'They say that New Jerusalem has failed. I'm sorry, my boy, but that's what I've heard. There's no one there. They're gone.

They all died, more than likely. A plague or the savages. Everyone has disappeared. Everyone and everything.'

He sucks again, raising his chin and blowing a smoke ring towards the ceiling. 'There's nothing there but wilderness. The dark of the forest has swallowed everything.'

Rhisiart stares at the fire, avoiding Gwilym Rowlant's eyes.

–9–

It's a dark night, but Gwilym Rowlant's servant has left a candle burning in the room. Rhisiart sits on the edge of the bed, leaning over a small table, the gift from his friends in his hands. He begins to unwrap the soft material. Animal skin, but it's not rawhide. Must be deer. The flesh has been eaten, the bones made into implements of various kinds, and the skin turned into something else. A rectangular patch was cut by skilful hands, and those hands then worked it and worked it and turned it silky soft. There's a packet of paper inside. A slender booklet. Rhisiart inspects it more closely, holding it nearer the candle, and sees that it's not paper but bark. A section of birch bark pulled carefully from the tree by skilled hands and worked and worked and turned into something else. He sees that in fact it hasn't been bound like a book, rather the thickness comes from the way it's been folded upon itself. He opens it, fold after fold, and places it on the bed.

Awikhigan.

He holds the candle over the beautiful forms. It's a country, a tiny world revealing itself to him in the shadows of the night. He grasps the meaning of the forms intuitively. Here are rivers, lakes, mountains and communities; their lines finely formed, sometimes playfully complex and sometimes stoically simple. The words are written in another hand. Rhisiart's eyes wander to the edge of the page and see that there is a large river opening out to the sea, with the words *Pesgatak was Piscataqua* written along it. And over there is a tightly woven black spot. He looks closer and sees houses squeezed together and little men everywhere around them, the angle of their bodies suggesting density, and the words *Straebery Banke Portsmouth* under it all. Rhisiart smiles. This *awikhigan* was made to direct him in the world of the *Iglismôn* as well as lead him through that of the People of the Land of the Dawn. Fine lines and evocative shapes described in a mixture of the English language and the words of the Wôbanakiak, channelling memory, information and advice. And all of it created in order to guide him.

Carwr y Cymro Hwn. Friend of this Welshman.

Awikhigan Isiad Dawi.

—10—

A taste of winter.

The wind is blowing through the trees, shaking the smaller branches of the pines. There's an edge to the cold and it gets into the skin. Rhisiart knows before finishing his breakfast that the last of autumn is behind him. He'll be walking into winter today.

The weather was grand when he started out a week ago, a memory of the breath of summer still in the air, but every night growing cold. He woke today to a cold wind announcing that winter is on the way. He's wearing clothing that he received as a gift from Gwilym Rowlant: high leather boots with good, hard soles, breeches of a heavy material, two shirts under a long coat of buff leather, a hat with a wide brim. A sword hangs from his belt and he wears a pack on his back, his blanket folded and tied to the top of the pack. He carries a musket, the best the merchant could buy. Rhisiart thanked him repeatedly for his generosity. The older man smiled. 'Since I can't keep you from going, at least I can ensure that you're ready to face the wilderness.'

Gwilym Rowlant had spent the first two days Rhisiart stayed in his home trying to persuade him not to go on the journey. He said it was foolishness. A waste of time at best, a waste of Rhisiart's life at worst. But by the third day he realized that there was no way to dissuade his new friend, so he set himself to helping him prepare. Rhisiart said farewell to Gwilym and Black Nicholas at the same time. The old merchant had taken to the cat and his maid was full of praise for the work he had done in getting rid of mice, and since he had claimed a place in the home, Rhisiart decided he should stay. Be well, Nicholas. Farewell, Old Nic. *Wlibomkanni*, Nita. You won't go back to sea; your wandering days are over. Stay here, pursue leisure and sleep soundly next to Gwilym Rowlant's fire. He received one last favour from the inhabitants of Portsmouth – a boat trip across the perilous breadth of the Piscataqua – and then he departed, a man alone, walking along the northern shore of the river.

He has been journeying to the north-west, following the fine markings of the *awikhigan*. He has come to recognize the nature of the great trees: the subtle variations in the greenness of the pines; the broadleaved trees, their branches bare as bones, inhabiting the edges of a clearing or marsh. Different kinds of birch – sometimes strikingly thin and tall, sometimes less impressive; sometimes a lone birch in a grove of pine and sometimes tightly clustered together. Time after time he has noticed that birches tend to grow in clumps of three, their bare branches woven together. He has often stepped over a dead birch that has fallen across the trail, its white bark giving way to brown as the tree returned slowly to the earth.

He has learned to recognize the different kinds of wetlands. Marshes full of rushes, sometimes with water visible amongst them, and sometimes completely filled with vegetation, instinct alone telling him that there was water under the rushes and dead leaves. The various shapes and forms that occur when a stream meets a marsh or pool, bright, clear water mixing with dark mustiness. Lakes of different sizes, and the differences between lake and lake – bright rocks seen through the translucent waters of one, and dark, peaty depths hiding the mysteries of another. Wide lily leaves adorning the surface of some pools, and the shore of some lakes reshaped by the work of a beaver, a dam of branches built at an angle, drawing the eye from land into the water. It can be difficult to tell the difference between river, estuary, marsh and lake, but the *awikhigan* has led him faithfully through it all so far.

He has learned to recognize different kinds of rocky land also. Huge hunks of granite appear here and there, sometimes as crags rising high out of the land, and sometimes as hard ground half-covered by moss, grass, and dead leaves, as if someone had spread a thin carpet over the hard rock that constitutes the ground. This land is rock; the cover of moss that tries to hide the granite under his feet is a green lie.

And there are mountains. They are tree-covered for the most part, the green of the pines clothing them, but now and again there is a cliff or promontory that is naked or half-naked, looming over the trees like the head of a giant, his nose turned to the sky and his eyes closed.

It started raining one night, and one night only, but since he had taken shelter under a shelf of rock that formed a comparatively dry cave, he wasn't much worse off when he woke the next morning. He sees quite a few deer during the daytime, and he could have shot one for his meat, but he has enough bread and cheese and smoked, salted fish in his pack, and he doesn't want to make any noise. He stops to drink water from fast-flowing streams, but his practice is to eat as he walks. Occasionally, he stops to think and to study the *awikhigan*, comparing this picture or that symbol with the characteristics of the land around him. He goes from the shore of a lake to the bottom of a hill, along rivers and through mountain passes, the fine lines from the hand of Pene Wons leading him further and further from the settlement of the *Iglismôn*, all of it directing him to one corner of the *awikhigan*. In that corner there is a detailed sketch, a complex of lines suggesting houses and people similar to the one labelled *Straebery Banke Portsmouth* by Simôn. But the depiction of the little people there is not as playful. Nor is there a name on the place, but

Rhisiart knows what the picture means. *U tali.* Here, it is here.

And so he prepares for another day of walking. After replacing some things in his pack, he studies the *awikhigan* which will lead him to that place. *U tali.* He should arrive after about three more days of walking. Should get there before the snow gets too heavy to stop him, but his breath turns to steam before his eyes and he knows he'll be walking into the grip of winter.

He folds the bark paper and puts it safely into a leather pouch he carries. He rises quickly, fastens his coat against the cold, puts on his pack, lifts his musket and begins to walk, the wind whistling through the pines above his head.

—11—

He stands still.

He feels he ought to disappear into the shadows. That he should try to shrink himself. That he ought to hide. But he also knows that he'd better not move and draw attention to himself. Keeping still is his only choice. As still as the trees around him.

He's been walking along the base of a slope. This is the rockiest land he has seen so far on his journey; the stony bones of the land make it difficult for tree roots to get a grip, so there's an occasional bare stretch interrupting the trees. In the middle of one of these bare stretches he saw something moving a moment ago. There, some hundred yards up the hill. People. Three people walking quickly across the open land. People of the Land of the Dawn, probably. He's sure they're not English. Perhaps some other native tribe. And there they are, before his very eyes: the first people he has seen since he left Portsmouth. He stands there, stock still, seized by the thrill of knowing that he is not alone.

At times during the last few days he has had the feeling that he was being watched. But he can't be sure. Every time he has paused to look closely at the shadows under the trees, there was nothing to be seen there. But now there they are, moving quickly across the open, rocky land, on a mission.

Before they vanish into the woods again, one of the three turns to look. He doesn't pause, only turns to look at Rhisiart. There is no sign of wonder or concern of any kind at all in his demeanour.

Only a glance as he walks, nothing more, as if he were casting an eye over a familiar scene.

Rhisiart stays still for a moment, and another. He doesn't hear anything. He sees no sign that there are other people around.

He starts walking again.

—12—

Rhisiart strayed from the paths of the *awikhigan* the day after he saw those other people. The day before yesterday. Only after reaching the far end of a narrow valley that he'd been tramping through for hours did he realize that he hadn't seen anything he could connect with the lines on the map. His only choice was to turn back. He had to retrace his steps for an entire day before he found a familiar place again. A stream winding its way between four large rocks, clearly indicated on the *awikhigan* by Pene Wons. Confirmation.

He's sure he's following the directions of the *awikhigan* today, but he's travelling towards a place marked on the map with a symbol he doesn't understand. It's a circle, the shape created by small dots similar to raindrops. Inside the circle are many thin lines intersecting each other, darkening the space and suggesting a shadow or a cloud. He can see clearly that he's headed for this place – he has spotted that hill and that river – but he doesn't know what kind of place it is.

Towards the end of the afternoon, the sun beginning its descent to the horizon, he reaches the spot. He comes to a large opening in the woods, too large to be called a clearing. As soon as he steps from the shadow of the trees he sees that there are gaps or passages within the space. There are traces that suggest former boundaries of some kind – a great circle that was almost exactly in the centre, and a number of rectangular fields between the edge of the circle and the forest. When he gets to the circle itself, he sees that there are traces of other shapes inside it. Although trees have begun to reclaim the place, the birch and maple saplings cannot hide these remains completely; mounds can clearly be seen in the grass, sometimes one with a small tree growing in the middle, and a few withies still standing on others – what's left of what were once walls.

Remains of homes, scores of them.

Land that people were living on.

Fields where food was grown.

Remains of a village – a large one.

An entire community that fell victim to plague. *Akuamalsowôgan*. Disease. The Big Dying.

He now understands Pene Wons' map. The symbol. They're not raindrops, they're tears. This is a place defined by tears.

Rhisiart doesn't pause here. Although night is nearly upon him, he walks on, determined that his camp will be as far as possible from this place. But he knows that his dreams will not be free of the grip this village of death exerts on him. When he turns in his sleep on the hard earth, he will hear the hooves of a horse striking cobbles. He will open his eyes and see the large red cross disfiguring the orange door, paint like blood dripping over the white flowers.

–13–

Each day is colder than the last. That's the first thing he notices upon waking every morning. A wind that is sharper and more biting than the previous morning is whistling restlessly through the trees, digging into his skin, its icy breath whispering in his ear: winter is tightening its grip. But although frost is decorating the vegetation and ice is clogging every stream and pool, it hasn't snowed yet.

He tells himself before going to sleep each night that he's been here before. Says that he will wake in the morning to a heavy layer of snow on his chest. He expects to open his eyes and see a white blanket covering the land, every trail obliterated. He fears that the rest of the journey will be like that journey to Okehampton, his horse struggling through the icy landscape, and he searching desperately for a light in the darkness. But he doesn't have a horse and that land is not this land, and although Pene Wons and Simôn have assured him that *Mzatanos* will come with a world of snow in its wake, it hasn't come yet.

And so he sets out this morning, the leaves and frost crackling and crunching under his feet. He remembers his childhood musings, how he used to think about the warm animals living beneath the earth, every paw at work digging, extending the network of tunnels that lead down and down into the darkness.

On he travels, along valley bottoms and around marshes, getting his bearings from the top of a mountain or the location of a lake, following the information in his *awikhigan*. He makes his way through a sea of pines, with an occasional clearing or pool or rock appearing like small islands in the vast forest, some broadleaved trees claiming the borders of a place where there are no pines, their bare branches extended to the sky. Sometimes he sees a trio of birch along a stream or on the slope of a hill, three white trees pressing together, like a symbol rising from the hardness of the earth, but he sees not a living soul.

He trudges mile after mile, feeling that he is travelling through the seasons as he crosses the land: leaving autumn further and further behind him with every step. He heads – decisively and resolutely – into the embrace of winter.

–14–

He is awakened by a sound. A presence.

A visitor.

There he is, a strange creature rummaging in his pack.

Rhisiart sits up, the noise dragging him from his sleep, and reaches for his sword, but he doesn't unsheathe it. He sees he doesn't have to; there's no threat to his life, only to his food. There, in a shaft of moonlight filtering through the pines, is the animal. His shape is similar to a bear's, but he's no bigger than a corgi. A long striped tail, and a black mask around his eyes. He was searching in the pack with paws that moved like a man's hands, but Rhisiart's movements have frightened him. There he stands now, quiet, bent over the pack, his small black eyes shining in the moonlight.

It's one of the goblins of Annwn come up from the warm depths of the earth, but he presents no threat other than the theft of a smoked fish from the pack. A moment later the creature decides it had better search for food elsewhere, and turns and walks from the scene on all fours.

Rhisiart stays there for a while, sitting up, the sword in its scabbard lying across his knees, staring into the shadows of the trees. He hears nothing other than the howl of the wind.

He sets the weapon on the hard ground beside him, stretches his arms and his back. Another minute and he's lying down again, the blanket pulled up to his chin. The ground is hard and cold, but the moon offers the comfort of its light. It comes to him through the patchy ceiling overhead, the branches of the trees weaving between him and the distant moon, creating a web of dark shapes.

–15–

He walks with the determination of one who is about to reach the end of his journey. He knows he is very close; the *awikhigan* tells him so. Intuition tells him so too; there is a difference in the woods and a look to the trail which both suggest that people have been passing by here frequently. People who can't move without leaving a trace.

He hurries. The path is clear, following a stream that twists through the woods, the tall pines shading its banks. The babbling of the bright water across the rocks in the stream has accompanied his progress all the morning, but now the rush of the wind and the rustling of the branches are filling his ears, just as the combination of the scent of pine and the smell of the promise of snow is filling his nose.

The trail has forked. Straight on it goes along the bank of the little stream, but another route splits off from it here, bearing left into the trees. He inspects it and sees evidence of use of this new path. Looking up, he sees some difference in the trees in that direction. The quality of the light indicates that the tall pines are thinning out; there's a suggestion of space, that there's a large opening behind the curtain of pines. He sets off again, turning to the left, leaving the stream.

The wind brings an aroma to his nose. Smoke. The smell of smoke from a wood fire. He picks up the pace, hurrying along the path. He hears a noise, and then another. Different sounds mingling, getting louder as he draws nearer. Some more clearly – a hammer ringing on an anvil, a distant but clear striking calling him to a smithy he can't see. Dogs barking. An axe splitting wood. Voices calling, talking. The everyday sounds of a village.

Another moment and he's able to see something through the thin curtain of the trees: a large open space and more trees beyond it. As he comes closer he sees that they're not trees. This is a landscape formed by human hands. The open land is fields, with the broken stalks left in the wake of the harvest clearly to be seen. And it's not a forest he sees beyond these fields, but a wall. A wall of tall timber that has been felled, worked and raised as a defence. And another rising up beyond the first wall. Walls. The path leads through an opening in the first wall, but there is a gate or some kind of door, closed, in the interior wall. He can see nothing but shadows in the space between the two walls.

It has begun to snow. By the time he has moved from the woods to the open land, large flakes are falling quickly and heavily on the path before him. The wooden walls are close, looming high and dark, but dimmed and softened by the whiteness of the snow. He feels the frosty touch of the flakes on his face.

A shout: a man's voice calling loudly. Although his eyes are watering, he can see a figure moving on top of the wall above the opening. A man. A guard.

Rhisiart walks on through the snow. He's coming closer and closer, the walls rising higher and higher before him.

The walls of New Jerusalem.

IV
New Jerusalem

Ye are the light of the world. A city that is set on a hill cannot be hid. Neither do men light a candle, and put it under a bushel, but on a candlestick; and it giveth light unto all that are in the house.

Matthew 5:14–15

Diamau yw, fy nghymydog, mai'r hwn y bo dyn yn was iddo, gan hwnnw y caiff ei gyflog, pa un bynnag fo, ai llygredigaeth ai anllygredigaeth.

It is undoubtedly the case, my neighbour, that a man receives his wages from the thing to which he is a servant, whatever that master be, whether corruption or purity.

Morgan Llwyd

—I—

Mid November 1656

There is order to everything, and reason lies behind that order.

Two wooden towers rise above the walls, one facing the other across the village. They rise from the interior wall, one at the southernmost tip of the settlement above the gate, the other defining the northernmost point, forming an unseen axis across the very middle of the village and compelling everyone to live within this compass.

The walls are round and enclose all the buildings in their perfect circle. First, the low outer wall – a row of slender pines stripped and shaped into posts, their tops cut into sharp points, ten or twelve feet in height. Next, three wide paces from this external wall, the higher inner wall, some twenty feet high and constructed of large pine trunks that have been worked more smoothly and carefully than the smaller ones that form the outer wall. The tops of these trees have also been cut into sharp points, but because there is a substantial thickness to each individual tree, there are gaps between these points for the guards to look through. The guards stand on a narrow wooden walkway attached to the inner side, so those guarding the walls can walk along the ramparts of the wooden fort. There's a small door on each side of the two towers that opens onto the parapet. Four men guard these walls at all times, day and night. One stands atop the south tower above the gates and another atop the north tower, and the other two walk back and forth along their half circle of wall from the north to the south and back from the south to the north, one watching the western side and the other the eastern side. They usually walk slowly, and the rhythm is significant: the heavy tramping of the guards is a constant reminder of the hammers that shaped the wall they are guarding.

The gates of the external wall are not different from the wall itself from the outside, but have been made to exact measurements to make certain that they meet the internal wall when they are open, thus creating a small, three-sided pen to hold those who are waiting for the interior gates to open. Upon opening these gates, one can walk through the south tower at ground level to see the top of the north tower rising in the distance above the houses.

In the dead centre of the village, halfway along the unseen axis that runs between the two towers, there is a structure that has more meaning than the others. Its roof is twice as high as the other buildings around it, about half the height of the two towers. It's a strong, rectangular building, its door facing south and opening onto a path leading directly to it from the gates. There's nothing on this path, so one can see clearly the whole way from the gates to the door. This is the house of worship, the focus of the community. There are small, glassless openings – like all the windows in the village – perforating its thick walls, each one big enough for a defender to shoot from, but too narrow for anyone to get through. It has been designed like a castle keep, the last stronghold if the enemy breach the walls. Though its walls too are of wood, it stands like a rock in the middle of the perfect circle of New Jerusalem. The church is a rock, and that rock is a fortress, and the fortress is a protection from every evil.

Twelve of the village's houses – most of them – have been set in a circle around this central point, about half the circumference of the circle of walls that guard them from the outside world.

Halfway from the gates to the door of the house of worship, the main path reaches a crossroads, where one can turn to the right or to the left and walk along another path – the circle road, as it is called – which leads from door to door around this inner circle of houses. Four other houses are inside the circle, built entirely of wood like the other houses, but somewhat larger. They stand beside the four corners of the house of worship, halfway between the big structure and the circle road. They are the ministers' houses. In the open space between these buildings and the house of worship, what remains of the summer gardens can be seen, large brown traces of vegetation showing through the thin coating of snow that has been falling intermittently in recent days.

There are seven houses outside the inner circle, breaking the regular pattern of the plan. One of them is the smith's home and forge, standing on the eastern side of the path leading from the gates to the inner circle. And then there are six other houses dotted here and there between the twelve houses that surround the middle and the big wall that encloses the whole. The risk of fire explains why the smithy has been located as far as possible from the other wooden houses. Dangers of other kinds compelled their builders to situate these seven other houses at the edges of the community. They were built for those who had not been accepted as full members, those who had yet to prove that they were among the saints.

There is order to everything, and reason behind that order, even behind these things that appear to the uninformed as a lack of order.

Rhisiart noticed two other prominent places as he was being led through the gates that first day. On the way to the inner circle, some ten yards after he passed the forge on the right but before he came to the crossroads, he saw two sites, one on each side of the path. On the east side, fairly close to the smithy, stands the community well, enclosed by a low stone wall. There is a pavement of smooth stones around it, creating a round space in which the well is the centre point: a circle within a circle. On the other side, facing the well across the narrow path, there is a wooden platform some six feet high.

He has not yet had an opportunity to enquire about the platform, but Rhisiart has learned a good deal about the plan of the community in the three days since he arrived. Plan. Division. Order. Reason. There are twenty-four buildings, not counting the two towers, and twenty-four is a good, ordered number. There are sixty-two inhabitants. Another good, ordered number – twice the number of the founders. Thirty-one sailed from Bristol over fifteen years ago, but now there are sixty-two. Despite every adversity and peril, they have doubled their number. Exactly twice. Proof. A definite sign, which cannot be denied.

Rhisiart has been given lodging in one of the houses standing between the inner circle and the wall, a vacant building being used as a community storehouse. The barrels, baskets and chests have been moved aside to make room for Rhisiart to spread his blanket beside the small fireplace. The wooden floor is hard, but no harder than the ground that was his bed on his journey. He has been told that Rowland Williams the carpenter can make a bed for him if he chooses to remain among them. He has been given food. His clothes have been washed. Enough wood has been brought to his lodging to keep him warm.

Rhosier Wyn led him around during those first days. The others refer to him as the Elder. Rhisiart cannot guess his age, but he must be at least fifty and possibly closer to sixty. His face suggests that he is older, but he moves with the vigour of a young man. He's bald, apart from a few wisps of fine hair hanging above his ears. He smiles frequently, his thin lips opening to reveal a row of gapped, crooked teeth. He's very short and pot-bellied, and his arms are unusually long, but despite this apparently malformed body, he moves briskly, strides ahead of Rhisiart to show the way and talks rapidly.

'All the way from Strawberry Bank, is it?' His voice is high and grates on Rhisiart's ears, but the genuineness of his broad smile makes up for the shrillness.

'Yes.'

'Really? The whole way from Strawberry Bank?' Another smile, showing his crooked little teeth.

'Yes, but now they call it Portsmouth.'

'All the way, all by yourself?' Another smile.

'Yes.'

'Well, well! And you reached us as healthy as the day you were born.' And then he smiles and takes Rhisiart's arm, taking him from the door of his lodging and leading him between two houses to the circle road. Although it's cold and snow covers those patches of ground where there's not much traffic, it is a sunny day and people can be seen here and there, carrying water from the well or a bundle of firewood, some pausing to talk and be neighbourly. They all wear good quality clothing. Simple and unadorned as a rule, in sober black, grey or brown, but clothing of good quality, expertly made. They all pause to greet him, each one wishing his guide a 'good morning' by name, calling him 'Rhosier Wyn' or 'Elder.' Smiling at Rhisiart too, some greeting him by the name he has given them: Rhisiart Dewi. Some contrary instinct within him keeps him loyal to the Wôbanaki version of his name. He has gone through many worlds and those worlds have changed him. Rhisiart Dafydd. Isiad Dawi. Richard Dewy. Rhisiart Dewi. All names suit him, and yet none of them do.

As the two of them walk around the circle road, the sound of voices reaches them. Rhisiart turns in their direction, but before he can open his mouth, the Elder nods with his bald head and gestures with his ungainly arms in the direction of the house of worship.

'The children.' A broad smile, his hands moving excitedly, urging Rhisiart to imagine the classroom hidden by the thick walls of the building. 'There at school, happy in their activities.'

The voices rise higher, reciting their lessons in unison. 'There are fourteen of them in the school. The youngest is three years old and the oldest fifteen. They leave their lessons at sixteen, that's the plan. Each one healthy, all of them blessings to their parents. Fourteen of them. Half of them are Mansels.' The smile is even wider this time, as if he has cracked a joke, but before Rhisiart has a chance to ask for clarification, Rhosier Wyn gesticulates vigorously towards another building, one of the four houses sharing the inner circle with the house of worship. 'This is the only empty house in New Jerusalem. That is, apart from the one serving as your home at present.' He smiles, his voice rising in a squeak. 'But that's not empty now, since you're living in it.'

He opens his mouth as if he is about to say something else, but reconsiders and stops. He sets off again, his hand lightly on Rhisiart's shoulder, keeping him close.

'The houses of the ministers. That's what someone told me yesterday. Four of them?'

'Yes.' The thin lips close tightly. Rhosier Wyn folds his hands behind his back and walks more slowly, letting his belly lead his short legs. He looks down at the path, his eyes pensive.

'Four?' Rhisiart prods again, but it's as if the talkative and cheery little man has changed into someone very different – someone silent and serious.

'Yes, four. But one of the houses is vacant at this time.'

'Why are there four? For such a small community?'

Rhosier Wyn stops, and turns to look into Rhisiart's eyes.

'That's the way New Jerusalem was designed, you see.' His

sentences are short this time and lack the usual smile. 'Exactly as planned. Four ministers, one for each of the four offices.'

'I don't understand.'

'How well acquainted are you with Calvin, Rhisiart Dewi?'

'I don't know. I'd say that I'm familiar with the principal ideas of Calvinism, you know. That is… I have read some and have heard more… in sermons and discussions...'

'But you are not familiar with his thinking regarding the arrangement of the ministry?'

He walks on slowly, his hands springing to life again, punctuating his discourse. 'Calvin explained it all, you see. Just as he revealed the means for us to understand the higher order, so also he revealed the order to be followed here on earth. He gave it all to us, you see: the entire foundation of the kingdom, the way to instal it here on earth in order to construct a system that would turn our eyes towards heaven. The foundations of the Kingdom of Heaven, that's what they are, Rhisiart Dewi. Nothing less than the foundations of the Kingdom of Heaven.'

Rhisiart sees that the little man is smiling again, but in a different way. The sincerity and warmth on the face of Rhosier Wyn is of a kind that Rhisiart has never seen before.

'And as part of that entire splendid system, Calvin explained that there are four offices to that ministry.'

They are walking side by side now, spanning the narrow road. The little man lifts his hand and raises one finger.

'The Doctor. He guards the purity of the creed and the constancy of doctrine.'

He lifts another finger. 'Second, the Minister. That is, the Preacher, the one who's responsible for preaching and holding the regular services. Pyrs Huws. You can hear him preaching tonight.'

The shadow of a smile vanishes right after reaching his thin mouth. Rhosier Wyn pauses and turns to face the empty house they have just passed by. Rhisiart does the same.

'The Deacon, the emblem of Christian charity. That's it, the Deacon's house, but it's empty since old Edward Jones died.'

The two men pause there for a moment, silently studying the building. Shutters of the sort that can be seen on all the houses of the village have been fastened tight over the windows and no smoke curls from the chimney. The children's voices ring out again from the house of worship as they recite in unison, and Rhosier Wyn beams his contentment.

'Come.' They recommence their walk.

'Pyrs Huws is the Preacher?'

'Yes, the Minister. Although all four are ministers, the one filling the office of Preacher is the one called Minister, you see.'

'What about Richard Morgan Jones? I would have thought that he would be the Minister.'

Rhosier Wyn takes his time before answering, and when he does he speaks softly and slowly.

'He's the Doctor, you see. It's true that he filled all the offices at the beginning, before we had a chance to build and arrange things properly. But since we established order that first year, he has been serving as Doctor only. But he's the one who showed that we had established a True Church.' He gestures in the direction of the house of worship to indicate the Doctor's residence, hidden on the other side of the large building.

'I see. I was half expecting to meet him. After I arrived. After I said that I had come to find you, all the way from Wales.'

'Ah… well… Doctor Jones is not well these days. Some ailment has taken hold of him in recent months, and he is not a young man.'

'Can I see him soon?'

'He doesn't leave his house these days, you see.'

'Can I go there to see him?'

'He's not well enough. It's better to leave him to his prayers. He doesn't have enough strength for anything else these days, more's the pity.'

They walk on, silently, along the circle road.

'Three ministers.'

'Hmm?'

'You've named three ministers. Three offices.'

'Yes, yes.'

'What is the fourth one?'

'Well, the Elder, of course.'

'Of course… You.'

'Yes, that's right.'

'And what is the function of the Elder?'

'Discipline, Rhisiart Dewi. That's the function of the Elder… Discipline.'

There's order for everything, and a reason behind that order.

There are nearly sixty of them sitting on simple benches in eight neat rows. It had been growing steadily colder during the day, and by the time they got to the door of the house of worship for the evening service, the wind was promising more snow. The cold is taking hold now, bringing chattering teeth and shivering bones with it, but body heat is beginning to warm the large room. In the same way, the voice of Pyrs Huws is warm and distracts the congregation's minds from the cold.

'God decided through His divine decree whatever fate he desired in the case of every man.'

He's a tall man, thin as a skeleton, his beard and his reddish hair also thin and patchy, as if there isn't enough flesh for the hair to take root in. He's about five years older than Rhisiart, and had been a very young man when they came across to America – a man who matured here, as Rhosier Wyn stressed. Rhisiart went to meet him after he had asked for a second time if he could see Richard Morgan Jones, and received the same reply: Doctor Jones' health is very poor and no one may disturb him. And so instead Rhosier Wyn took him to see Pyrs Huws and his family, as a kind of consolation prize.

They sat around the table in the minister's house, wood crackling cheerfully in the fireplace. Catherin Huws did most of the talking, in contrast to the silence of her husband, asking Rhisiart for news of England and Wales, about the fortunes of the saints in the Old Country, the standing of the Faith on the continent. Their young sons, Jeremiah and Joseph, joined in at times, asking the kind of personal questions their mother avoided. They were about thirteen and ten years of age respectively, speaking courteously like their mother but unable to rein in their enthusiasm. Had Rhisiart been a soldier? Really?! And what was the Army of the Saints doing now that the wars were over? What sort of ship had brought him across the sea? A shipwreck?! How far had he swum? For how long? This was the only time their father joined in the conversation, offering an impromptu prayer and saying that Divine Providence had brought Rhisiart ashore for some reason. Otherwise, he looked thoughtfully at Rhisiart, studying his face, listening attentively to his answers, but leaving it to his wife and his children to carry the conversation. Rhosier Wyn sat there quietly also, content for others to do the talking for once.

And then Jeremiah, the older boy, asked the question that neither Rhosier Wyn nor anyone else had asked Rhisiart since he arrived. Why had he travelled so far to visit New Jerusalem? Rhisiart had considered how he would answer the question, searching for a way of presenting himself that would be honest and would satisfy them without revealing too much. He had told Gwilym Rowlant, the Welshman of Portsmouth, that he had family in New Jerusalem, but that lie wouldn't wash here. And so he had no answer to the lad's question except the truth.

'I came at the request of my former commander, Colonel John Powel.' He spoke directly to the children, avoiding the eyes of the adults. 'Colonel Powel was helping Richard Morgan Jones in the days before your parents and their friends left Wales.'

'This is the first time I've heard that.' Catherin Huws spoke candidly, and then turned to her husband with enquiring eyes. Pyrs Huws raised his eyebrows and frowned, as if the story was news to him too. He shrugged his shoulders as if at a loss, his clothes hanging loose on his bony frame.

Rhisiart looked at Rhosier Wyn and saw something in his eyes that suggested that all this was no surprise to him. Rhosier Wyn noticed that Rhisiart was staring at him.

'There we are. Some of us are older than others, and remember better than others. That's how the aged instruct the young, you see.'

'And the Elder is older than most.' It was Joseph, the younger son, who spoke this time. Despite his mother reaching a hand across the table towards him and moving her lips as if she were about to shush him, the boy went on, speaking rapidly. 'But he's not as old as Doctor Jones. Or Rhys and Gwen Edwart. Or Rachel Morgan. Or Sarah Williams. And not half as old as Hannah Siôn. That's six who are older than the Elder.' His mother was smiling by now, having pulled her hand back and folded it with the other on the table. She looked down a bit, trying to hide her amusement, enjoying the cleverness of her child despite the fact that he had spoken when he shouldn't have.

Making lists, thought Rhisiart. Just like Rhosier Wyn. The people here like lists. Naming. Counting and seeing meaning in numbers. Listing, and finding significance in the arrangement.

'There you are, my boy, there you are.' Rhosier Wyn himself seemed to be enjoying this light moment in the conversation.

But Pyrs Huws was not smiling. He continued to study Rhisiart's face, waiting for the others to talk.

'He's a studious man, you see,' Rhosier Wyn explained after they left the family. 'Pyrs Huws came here a young man, and he has matured in his faith here in America. Here, the years of building New Jerusalem have turned him into a light to lighten the darkness.

Rhisiart has had to wait until tonight to understand the thrust of the Elder's words. The man who stands before the congregation in the pulpit is totally different from the quiet Pyrs Huws Rhisiart visited at his home.

'Yes!'

He repeats that one word, like shots from a gun, shooting across the room and filling it with their echoes. Yes, yes, yes.

And then he lowers his voice a little, though he still speaks loudly enough for those in the back benches to hear him without difficulty. There, at the back of the house of worship, is where Rhisiart is sitting, and every syllable of every word the Preacher utters reaches his ears clearly, even though by now his voice is as if he were whispering secrets of the heart to a bosom friend.

'God decided what fate will befall every single person. We know all this. We know that not everybody is created equal. Some have been preordained to eternal life and others to eternal damnation. This we all know, dear friends.'

Rhisiart has heard some of this before. From travelling preachers who nurtured the conceptual maelstrom of the Army of the Saints. From enthusiastic soldiers who turned camps into religious academies and philosophical battlegrounds.

'And accordingly, as each has been created for one or other of these ends, it is not proper for us to seek to deceive ourselves. No, it isn't, brothers and sisters. Let us confront this fact every day of our lives and walk in that knowledge, the knowledge that each has been born to one of these two fates. Some are preordained to eternal life and others to eternal damnation.'

Pyrs Huws pauses, and lifts a hand to wipe the sweat from his brow. The breath of the congregation rises as steam above their heads in the cold, but the Preacher perspires under the burden of his passion and his efforts. He speaks again, a little louder this time. His voice is shaking by now, like the hand that mops his brow and pushes locks of thin, reddish hair away from his eyes.

'We know all of this, brothers and sisters. Some have been born to life. And others have been born to death.'

Silence. The Preacher stands there for a good while, letting the echo of his voice die within the wooden walls. The only sound is breathing and the coughing of those with colds. Not even the smallest child is moving a finger on the benches. It's a clear night, and the shutters on the narrow windows have been opened to let moonlight flood into the large, rectangular room. There are four windows in each of the two long walls, all of them high up, and all of them narrow. There is a large chest under each of these windows, furniture that fulfils two functions. In them are stored muskets, bullets and powder – weapons for defending this place. And the chests are high enough for men to stand upon them comfortably and aim out of the windows.

There is order for everything, and reason behind that order.

Evan Evans, the leader of the New Jerusalem militia, explained its structure to Rhisiart not long after he arrived. Every man has been trained in the use of weapons, but only six men carry arms at all times. Those six are all unmarried and live in a small barracks at the bottom of the north tower, where the only other store of weapons is kept. Although Rhisiart has left his sword and musket in his lodging since he arrived, everyone knows that he was armed when he arrived in New Jerusalem, and the rumour has been going around that he served in the Army of the Saints. That's how Evan Evans greeted him that first time, as one soldier greeting another soldier. He is thirty years old, a bit younger than Rhisiart, and crossed the sea with the original company when he was fifteen. Like Pyrs Huws, he's a man who came of age here in America. He's one of the few who has never married. He's strongly built, with a square, cleanly shaved face and hair cut short to his ears. He speaks in short sentences, detailing the extent of his militia, like a proud officer parading his soldiers on the field, though there are only five to respond to his commands.

'There are six of us. The standing militia. Six.'

Rhisiart has had a chance to meet each of them in recent days. Owen Williams, about the same age as Evan. An ox of a man, larger than his leader. One who could claim some authority for himself, but he's quiet, almost like someone whose spirit has been broken.

Huw Jones, grandson of old Edward Jones, the recently deceased Deacon. He came over as a child with his parents and grandfather, but now he's the only member of the family still living. He's young, about twenty, and unmarried.

Tomos Bach, whose parents died shortly after they arrived fifteen years ago, when he was too young to remember them. He was raised by Gwen and Rhys Edwart. At seventeen, he's the youngest of the militia.

And then the two Englishmen, Ben Cotton and David Newton, both in their mid-twenties. They came three years ago, exiles from Boston. There were three other religious young men who had set off with them, but the others died during the long journey to New Jerusalem. The two survivors found refuge here with the Welsh Saints; they concur in every aspect of the Faith, and they understand Welsh very well by now, though they speak English to each other.

‘Six, you see. Two of us walking the walls continually, day and night.’

Rhisiart learned that they have need of volunteers too – other men to help with this important work, walking the walls and standing guard atop the two towers. There is a list of young men who volunteer, two serving each watch, every eight hours, to ensure that the militia men have time to complete their other duties and to sleep. John Williams, the eldest son of the carpenter, does more than his share.

‘He’s very fond of the work of the militia, you see, very fond. He’d rather carry a musket and walk the walls than farm.’ This is as close as Evan Evans comes to humour. He’s a man who takes his job and his status seriously, and the questions he asks Rhisiart are serious ones. He asks him about training, about the order of march, about setting the lines on the field of battle. Rhisiart has no desire to discuss such matters, and so he tries his best to avoid the leader of the militia without giving offence.

Evan Evans sits on the same bench with him now, his head rising confidently above the old woman sitting between the two men. Which two were on duty tonight? Rhisiart saw Owen Williams on the way in, his broad shoulders filling the doorway, and Tomos Bach with him. He thought he recognized David the Englishman from the back of his head, but he wasn’t sure. Ben Cotton and Huw Jones, maybe? One walking each of the two half circles, back and forth from the south tower to the north tower, their feet rhythmically striking the wooden ramparts behind the parapet of pine wood. Military deployment, regular, all of it familiar to him. An officer selecting his guards, each with his appointed hours of duty. Like the plan of the defences, Evan Evans hardly need explain. Layer upon layer of defence, like peeling an onion, before reaching this hard centre.

Rhisiart looks left out of the corner of his eye. The old

woman who sits between him and Evan Evans is Hannah Siôn, the oldest member of the community according to Joseph Huws, her face a network of deep wrinkles and the little hair showing beneath her cap pearly white. She has closed her eyes, her head bowed in prayer. The old widow, the oldest, living in a house all alone – one of those on the corners, outside the main circle of the village, close to the storehouse that is temporary home to Rhisiart. On the other side of her, Evan Evans sits straight-backed, his eyes riveted on the Preacher.

Along with the shafts of light from the moon coming in through the narrow windows, there's light from the candles – some in simple iron holders along the walls between the windows, and another row of them on a low bench in front of the pulpit. Though they give decent light, these candles also smoke, and every now and then a gust of wind blowing through the glassless windows sends small clouds of thick, black smoke across the room. A strong, acrid smell assails Rhisiart's nostrils, a smell that says the candles were made from some kind of animal fat.

'God decided through his holy omniscience whatever fate he chose for every single man.' Pyrs Huws is preaching loudly now, his voice echoing from the wooden walls, the light from the candles dancing in his eyes, the patches of red beard on his chin and cheeks appearing as tiny flames kindled here and there across the pale canvas of his face.

'I say again!' He strikes the pulpit with his fist, his voice full of earnest fervour. 'All are not created on equal terms, but some were preordained to eternal life and others to eternal damnation. And therefore, since each one has been created for one or other of these ends, it is not proper for us to deceive ourselves. No, it isn't, brothers and sisters.

'Yea, listen! I say again!' Two more blows, his fist hitting the wood of the pulpit. 'Let us confront this fact every day of our lives and walk in this knowledge, the knowledge that each has been born to one of these two fates. Some have been preordained to eternal life and others have been preordained to eternal damnation.'

Rhisiart admires the man's gift. He has been dealing with words that were important to Rhisiart once, yes, and he can recognize the ability and appreciate the effort. He did the same thing in his youth, though he had no congregation of the kind listening to Pyrs Huws now. He worked the words in the smithy of his master, his soon-to-be father-in-law. He composed sermons and folded them into the hot iron. No congregation ever heard the words he composed, but when the new church gate was opened for the first time, they creaked out through the hinges. *In the name of Jesus Christ, he who shed his heart's blood for us, children of fallen Adam.* When a horse was led from the forge along the streets of Wrexham, the fair words of his songs would remain in the wake of its hooves. *The sweetest clover there ever was, come to me to keep a tryst.* And when the new fire-dogs of the Swan tavern were used for the first time, parts of his orations rose with the flames. *And we, the remnants of the race of the Ancient Britons, remember.* And the test sword that he made, striking and cutting the air for the first time, Rhisiart's words pouring from the gleaming blade. *Who can ask the iron about its life and times, who but the smith who made it?*

Where did they go? The sword possibly broken on the field of some battle during the wars. Many of the fine pieces he had shaped on the anvil of his master destroyed when much of the town burned in 1643. One of every four houses in ashes, and the gates, hooks and hinges Rhisiart had created dead and mute, carried with the rubble to the rubbish heaps. Was the church gate still there, rusting on its hinges? And where did the words go? With the wind. With the smoke that was carried on the wind.

He dealt with words in the first war too. Yes. Educating the young soldiers, centring on *The Soldiers Catechism* and making it as much a part of them as *Carwr y Cymry*, taking ownership of words and moulding them to his own voice. Speaking the words confidently, leading the camp catechism.

> What Profession are you of?
>
> I am a Christian and a Soldier. I confess that that's how it is, and it is impossible to avoid the need that has been placed before the godly people of the land. We are not to look at our enemies as fellow countrymen or kinsmen or fellow Protestants, but as the enemies of God and our Religion, and those who take the side of the Antichrist. Our eye is not to pity them, nor our sword to spare them. They are the enemies of God and Religion, not fellow countrymen and kinsmen. Those who take the side of the Antichrist, natural enemies of the soldiers of the Lord.

He was the one who explained everything to Owen, his closest comrade during those tempestuous years, translating and explaining. There's a Welsh word for everything on this earth. But bit by bit he has lost his grip on words. Life has knocked them out of him. All the fighting. Wexford and Drogheda. The Little Plague in London. The young Welshman fervent in the cause and confident in his judgement has died and left an older and different man in his place. The Wild Welshman, his hair long and beard tangled, making tired, gutteral noises to answer his fellow soldiers, refusing to be caught up in discussions. All the words that were so much a part of him have been carried away with the rubble of his years to the rubbish heap of his being.

But Rhisiart can recognize the gift of this preacher.

'Although we have seen this, we can never see the reason or the cause. The urge and the reason and the cause are the hidden counsel of God, and that is beyond our imagination and our understanding. That is what accounts for election and rejection alike – the hidden counsel of God. We know all this, though we cannot know that hidden counsel itself. We know that that is what decides the birth of a person into election, yea, and we know that that is what determines which are born into damnation. There is no nature within man himself, be it good or be it bad. No, there is nothing at all but the hidden counsel of God, who has decided everything.'

Pyrs Huws lifts his hands and stretches his arms wide, as if he were about to embrace everyone sitting before him in this house of worship.

'We can recognize that hidden counsel sometimes as God's mercy, but we know that there is no way for us to understand or comprehend the true nature of its source, that hidden counsel which ensures that some are born to election. We know that that election is not a reward for any human virtues, we know that it is not payment for whatever goodness man has tried to spread during his life. It can't be, because it is a fate that was decided before the birth of each man, a fate decided beforehand through the hidden counsel of God. By the same token, those who are born to damnation have been sentenced to damnation that is right and flawless, even though it is also a sentence that is incomprehensible to the powerful who cannot understand His mind and His intention and His hidden counsel.'

The Preacher's hands are back on the pulpit and he is leaning forward, the candles on the bench below him throwing flickering shadows on his chin and cheeks.

'But… but… we consider God's calling a sign of election, justification another sign. It is true that one cannot examine either one sign or the other until one comes to the Divine Presence, but we know that God lets these signs show themselves to us. We know that God seals the elect through His calling and His justification. In the same way we know that through depriving the rejected of knowledge of His name and the sanctity of His spirit, God is showing signs of the damnation that awaits those rejected.'

He recognizes the passion too. The zeal of one who knows. Like the travelling preachers and the soldiers who elevated themselves into ministers for a while in camps and barracks and on the field. The planning for the coming of the Kingdom of Heaven. Prophets reading the signs of the times. Self-appointed theologians of an army that was a church and academy and lecture hall and pulpit. But the theology of New Jerusalem is different. Since his spiritual awakening in Wrexham, Rhisiart has been witness to counterpoints and arguments. The Army of the Saints especially was a melting pot of beliefs, with believers agreeing on one point and disagreeing on another, a stew of point and counterpoint bubbling away in the pot of their discussions, soldiers who had been trained to move obediently and uniformly in battle out of step in their debate. They would divide into a host of factions, ecstatic in the variance of their beliefs. There were a number of fine threads pulling them together – their belief that the army existed to create a better kingdom and their certainty that they were the true Protestants fighting to protect the purity of their faith – but there different threads of belief and faith of many hues woven together in the endless fabric. Many of the multicoloured threads of their motley beliefs had been spun from the tenets of John Calvin, but there was no consistency in their weaving. But here in New Jerusalem is a single, unified Calvinism of a sort he has never encountered before.

He remembers another voice, Owen Lewys', reaching his ear above the height of the storm, the sides of the *Primrose* protesting loudly as the ship groaned and rolled in the grip of the wind and the waves. What right do they have, Rhisiart Dafydd? What right do they have to say that the light shines only within the elect? What authority lets a man believe that he can trample that gift and take that certainty from another soul? And his conclusion: it's a quaternity that Calvinists of that sort worship, Owen, not a trinity, and who would not say that that is blasphemy too?

Shuffling and moving, people standing, the session over. No hymn was sung and Rhisiart did not notice any words bringing the service to a close. He turns and offers support to Hannah Siôn. The old woman takes his arm and mumbles her thanks. They move towards the door, the rest of the congregation waiting for those from the back benches to leave first. Rhisiart notices for the first time someone who was sitting on another back bench. A woman. Girl. By herself. She turns to look at them for a moment before stepping through the door and into the night. A young face, open.

And then Evan Evans is walking slowly in front of them, Owen Williams following him, his large frame filling the door as he passes through it. It's Rhisiart's turn next and he leads Hannah Siôn carefully, walking sideways down the steps so she can lean on his arm the whole time. As they reach the hard ground outside, Rhisiart sees that another layer of new snow has hidden the path.

'Thank you, Rhisiart Dewi.' The old woman knows his name, as does everyone else.

Before he has chance to answer, the young woman is beside them, smiling shyly at him, and then looking away quickly.

'Come, Hannah Siôn, I'll walk you home.'

'Thank you, Rebecca, it will be nice to have your company.'

Rhisiart stands there, unsure of what he should do, but before he is able to decide, Rhosier Wyn appears, gesticulating with his long, ungainly arms as he talks.

'There you are, there you are.' He see that Rhisiart is watching the two women walking away, the old woman leaning on the arm of her young neighbour. 'The widows helping each other. That's how it should be.' And then he takes Rhisiart's elbow, leading him away from the door of the house of worship as he brings the conversation back to his favourite subject.

'I said that the light shines through Pyrs Huws, didn't I?' There's enough moonlight to see that the man is smiling, his thin lips revealing the crooked, gapped teeth. 'The light illuminates the darkness.'

'He has a gift, without doubt.'

'More than a gift, Rhisiart Dewi, more than a gift. Come now, I'm sure you would like to stretch your legs before sleeping, as I would.'

He leads Rhisiart along the circle road, though the blanket of white is hiding the greyness of the path itself. The snow crunches under their feet, and their breath rises as steam as they trudge slowly in front of the houses that surround the house of worship and the houses of the ministers. They walk past Pyrs and Catherin Huws' house, and on past Rhosier Wyn's own house. And then on past the empty house of the Deacon and then to Richard Morgan Jones' home. Rhisiart sees that there's some smoke coming from the chimney, but he can't see any light behind the closed curtains at the windows. Although he wants to ask again if he can meet Doctor Jones, he has no desire to broach that difficult subject at this moment. His mind wanders far from the repetitive words of Rhosier Wyn. When he tries again to concentrate on the tedious monologue, Rhisiart notices that the little man is still on the same subject.

'That is certain, you see. The light was ordained by Divine Providence to illuminate this darkness. You have just witnessed it, Rhisiart Dewi. You cannot refuse to acknowledge that. I would be satisfied to claim that you too have just witnessed the strength of New Jerusalem. Yes, strength and mystery. There are so many signs, aren't there? You can't deny them. We have established ourselves here in a city on the hill, the light illuminating the darkness.'

He's beginning to list and name and count again. Sixty-two of them, exactly twice the number that sailed across the sea fifteen years ago. Although a number of them have died, others have come to fill the houses and swell the ranks of God. Sixty-two. Exactly twice. Sure proof. He carries on, striding ahead of Rhisiart at times, his big belly shaking above his little legs, gesticulating here and there, urging Rhisiart to consider this fact and that sign. But Rhisiart is lost in his own thoughts: I have believed, have lived, have done.

'That's what happened, you see: the plague.' The words bring Rhisiart back to the present. He listens attentively to the big-bellied little man who is speaking energetically beside him.

'The plague?'

'Yes, the plague. There were many Indians living here, you see. Thousands of them. This place was crawling with them. But the plague came and destroyed them. Wiped them out. It came with the Frenchmen who arrived first, you see, down from the north-east. The Frenchmen first, trading with the natives. Brought the plague with them. The Indians had never known that sort of disease before, you see, and so it went right through them like a scythe through wheat. Destroyed them all, and not long before we arrived. Cleansed all these lands of the savages. Cleared the wilderness of them, ready for us. Divine Providence cleared all the Indians like that, and all we had to do at first was clear the trees. Divine Providence, you see. Divine Providence at work, clearing and preparing the way for us. It was all part of His plan, you see. It's all so clear, Rhisiart Dewi. It was part of the plan, you see.'

There is order to everything, and reason is behind that order.

–2–

End of November 1656

Sssss. Sssss.

The familiar sizzling hiss. A smell not experienced anywhere else, one that says that pure, red-hot iron has just gone into water. A smell sensed nowhere but in a forge.

Having no specific work to do – he, the visitor, the only idle man in the village – Rhisiart is free to wander during the day. And without thinking, without deciding that this will be his route, he comes back here every time. The smithy, the only building standing near the well, halfway between the gates and the centre of the village. He always gets a warm welcome from the smith, Griffith John Griffith. A man born to his work; Owen Williams of the militia is the only one in the village bigger than him. His face shows his years: somewhere between middle and old age, his head completely bald.

'My hair got burnt, you see, when I was a young apprentice, and it never grew back.' A deep, sonorous voice, completely serious, but an eye that winks mischievously.

'Actually he shaves his head every day.' His son Ifan is his apprentice, a youth in his late teens, his dark hair cut short to his ears. 'It's a habit with him.'

'Yes, quite true. I do it every day. Since I burned it when I was an apprentice.' He winks playfully at Rhisiart again.

Griffith John Griffith's wife died soon after they arrived, fifteen years ago. Ifan was a small child at the time. Although he can't say he remembers Wales, the boy has a dim memory of the voyage. A dim memory of his mother also. The counting, recording, listing. Everyone in the village who has chosen to share a bit of their personal history with Rhisiart has told it in terms of the voyage – he was a young man at that time and grew into manhood here in America; she was a very small child and remembers neither Wales nor the voyage; he is a child who was born here in New Jerusalem.

That journey fifteen years ago is the reference point that defines the two ages: the old age in the old land and everything that has happened here, everything that has led to this great present.

The smith and his son are like all the other villagers when it comes to this, but even so Rhisiart feels that the conversation and company he gets in the smithy is different from what he gets with the other inhabitants of New Jerusalem. There's a lighter atmosphere here. He feels that the order is not so strict here in the smithy. Although Griffith John Griffith and his son are godly people like everyone else, they don't watch their words in the same way. The smith even swears sometimes.

'Hellfire, Ifan, this is going to break before it bends any more.' Another blow with the hammer, and then – chink! – a strip of iron breaks on the anvil.

'Hellfire! I told you it would break!'

Although his face is red from the heat of the forge, Ifan reddens even more when his father speaks like that, but he doesn't reply.

'These eyes are the problem, Rhisiart Dewi, you see.' He lifts a big, knotty paw of a hand and shakes it accusingly in front of his eyes. 'I'm going blind, you see. Slowly but surely. I can't see the grain of the iron as clearly these days.'

He's running a hand back and forth across his bald head. 'Alright then, Ifan, that won't make a scythe blade. We'd better start again.' And then he swears once more, under his breath, as he wipes the sweat from his hands on his apron. 'Hellfire!'

Strong language, the importance of words. Such talk would have offended Rhisiart years ago, when the propriety and content of everything that was said was important to him. He saw fellow soldiers punished for cursing in the first war and believed in his heart that the punishment was fair. Loss of pay for the first time, imprisonment the next time. All of it just, a means of cleansing the Army of the Saints of unchaste language. Ensuring that the throng would bend to church discipline, for that's what the army was – a church gathered in the Faith. He chided Elisabeth for speaking carelessly. You're a tidy Roundhead now, Rhisiart. Hush! It's an offence for one soldier of Parliament to call another one a Roundhead. Alright, Rhisiart, but I'm not a soldier.

By the time of the second war he was no longer able to accept that discipline. The taciturn Wild Welshman no longer worried about the gravity of words in the same way as the earnest young Puritan. He had cursed at times then, under his breath or in his heart. When he thought about that Welshman talking to him through the hole in the wall of the prison. I am proud to say that I came out in support of the King once again. I hate to say so, but it's not much of a life, is it? No, not much of a life at all. When his cheeks burned thinking about his own foolishness, having asked Colonel Powel if he could go with Cromwell to Ireland. He would curse his own selfish callousness, having chosen to go in order to have something to do rather than be forced to think. He, content to smite the earth, having chosen the path that brought him to the walls of Drogheda and the shores of Wexford. Part of a line that denied hope to the town. The waves bringing bodies to the shore: women, children, men of every age. Human flotsam and jetsam, remnants of the siege. When the English were arguing about Parliament's obligations towards the ministers, those it had set to work and then decided to remove, and Rhisiart sick and tired of it all, walking away, swearing under his breath. The time of Penruddock's rebellion, and the young soldiers talking about him. There's the Wild Welshman, ready to go. He'll come back with the traitor's head on a stake. And he, living practically like a mute, avoiding saying anything beyond an occasional muttered *yes* or sighed *no*, but cursing in his heart, yes. Ah hell, I swear, damn devils. I'll go the whole way and kill the entire lot by myself, damn it – but not to please you, damn devils. I'll kill the whole lot of them because I can, and that's what I'm good at. Unlike you, you shitty flies. Worthless, every one – go to hell.

These things that he thought to himself set him apart from his fellow soldiers, since no one heard the frequent oaths that took the place of prayer in his heart. Not so the language of Griffith John Griffith. The smith's exclamations are confined to the smithy, and he sits next to his son in the house of worship at every service and prays as fervently as anyone else in the congregation. But the smith's swearing makes Rhisiart feel comfortable, a significant part of the welcome and the warmth in the forge.

During his second visit Rhisiart tells them that he himself was once an apprentice to a smith.

'Hellfire! Did you hear that, Ifan?! Rhisiart Dewi here is a smith too! Hellfire, I knew there was something particularly likeable about him!'

The smith and his son work every day, even when there is no call for their work. Forging a new scythe blade or repairing a ploughshare, though no one will be asking for such things until spring.

'You understand, Rhisiart Dewi. You have to keep the fire hot and the anvil ringing. It wouldn't be a village without the sound of hammer on anvil, would it?'

Working and reworking the iron they had, melting pieces of tools that have broken and reworking them into new things. Keeping the anvil ringing, as much a part of the rhythm of the community as the footfalls of the watchers on the walls.

The rhythm of everyday life. Although he has not lived in a community other than the ranks of the army for many years, the rhythm is familiar. The sounds, the coming and going, the smells. The patterns of life – work, worship, and work. People enjoying conversations with neighbours, children running around, laughing riotously, during rare moments when they are unoccupied, despite the scowl of the occasional adult. And all of it in Welsh. Yes, all of it, except David Newton and Ben Cotton, who speak English to each other. The talk between neighbours, children's school lessons, the praying and preaching, the discussion about winter storage and next year's crops. All in Welsh. Rhisiart finds himself swinging between two states. He's relaxing into pleasure, accepting without question and enjoying the everyday rhythms of the Welsh ways and language in the village, but then at other times he marvels at it all, and the wonder bewilders him. It's entrancingly improbable, and yet it's real. And why not? What about the other communities of New England? What about Salem, Plymouth and Boston? Didn't the English Saints establish them in order to secure the right to live in godliness according to their own will, far from the sins of the Old Country? Why shouldn't the Welsh Calvinists claim the same opportunity? Who can say that they don't have as much right to a new life, having dared the seas to create a godly kingdom for Welsh believers here in America? It was easier to relax and accept it all, wallowing in the familiar and turning his back on the doubts. Accepting, yes, and enjoying. Living in this great present.

That's what plays on his mind when he's trying to sleep, lying on his blanket on the wooden floor of the storehouse, casks and chests for company. That's what keeps him awake for hours. The comfort of the familiar. Yes, that and the success of the place. What will he say to Colonel Powel? That the inhabitants of New Jerusalem are alive and well. The community is thriving. There are sixty-two souls living there, twice the thirty-one who sailed across the sea. And there is meaning, significance and proof in that number. Sixty-two, a sure sign of success. Yes, it's true that they are strict in their doctrine, but they are consistent. And they are blessed. Perhaps that's what he ought to say to the Colonel. Say that he ought to put his hopes in the future of this community. Give a little push when the chance comes, in order to give a strong foothold on this continent for the remnants of the race of the Ancient Britons. The dreams of the Quakers were shattered on the rocks with the *Primrose*. They were drowned with Owen Lewys, alas. Here, in the middle of the forest, within the safe walls of New Jerusalem, that important work has begun. Yes, here that work is afoot. And it is succeeding. But he cannot forget that letter the Colonel had received. 'That which I have heard suggests that they know not what they do.' What rumours lay behind that warning? And what basis did those rumours have? Was it malice? An Englishman envying this opportunity for a handful of Welsh people? Religious suspicion, the author of the letter disagreeing with the theology of the leaders of New Jerusalem? Try as he may, Rhisiart himself doesn't agree with it, and yet he feels that he doesn't have the right to deny this life to them. What right does he have? What basis?

It has warmed up in recent days, and the snow has given way to wet ground. A memory of the breath of summer, though they are on the threshold of winter. Should he venture forth and leave now? Travel back to Portsmouth, or go the whole way to Boston and wait for a ship that can carry him back to Colonel Powel? He has no money, but surely somebody in the governor's employ will vouchsafe his passage when he reveals that he is working for a man as important as the Colonel. But he hasn't seen Richard Morgan Jones yet. Doctor Jones, the Moses who led the flock across the sea after leaving the church in Llanfaches, their doctrine unacceptable. After deciding that he could not maintain perfect communion between community and the True Church except in the middle of this wilderness, far from the sins of the Old Country.

In the end, Rhisiart decides to take his frustrations to the only ones he feels he can share his secrets with.

Sssss. Pure, red-hot iron sizzling in the water, Ifan holding it in the tongs and his father standing beside the anvil, wiping the sweat from his face and his bald head.

'Do you know why I have come here?'

'Yes, I do, Rhisiart Dewi.' The deep voice booming, like waves striking the sides of a ship. 'You've come here to talk. And to enjoy the comfort of the familiar. Because you are a smith in your veins, aren't you?' He winks at him and turns to throw more wood on the fire and stir the flames. He turns to his son, takes the tongs from him and puts the strip of iron in the fire.

'No, that's not what I'm asking.'

After turning the iron over and giving another poke to the fire, Griffith John Griffith turns to him, his bald head glistening with sweat, his eyebrows raised, questioning.

'I'm asking whether you know why I have come here to New Jerusalem.'

'I do. Everyone knows. It's difficult to keep secrets within the walls of New Jerusalem.' He winks at him, turns back to the fire.

'I came here, you see, all the way from London.' He's talking to the back and broad shoulders of the smith, who is still bending over the fire. 'At the request of Colonel Powel. He's a man I trust, you see. I couldn't refuse his request.'

He waits, expecting Griffith to respond or turn and face him. Ifan is still standing beside the vat of water, his arms folded, his face red, obviously listening but feeling uncomfortable. 'The Colonel knew Richard Morgan Jones, you see. In Wales. Before the wars. In the old days. And he's a man who… *acts*, Colonel Powel, you see. Important ears listen to him. And he wants to make certain that all is well. He wants to help you, if need be.'

The big smith turns to him finally, tongs in his left hand holding a piece of iron that's glowing red. His right hand lifts the hammer and he steps towards the anvil, Rhisiart moving out of his way, and he begins hammering the iron again. He studies the work, then gives the iron a final blow before passing the tongs to his son at the vat of water. Sssss.

Griffith walks over to Rhisiart then, wiping the sweat from his face and head with his hand. He faces him, drying his hand on his apron. 'And you think that we need help?' His deep voice is completely serious for once, his face inscrutable.

'No, I don't. I don't believe that you need anything at all, as far as I can see.'

'Well, then. You've finished your work. What will you do next? Stay here with us? New Jerusalem is growing, you know. There are a good many children here. Tomos and Esther Mansel have seven of them. Seven! Joshua, Ruth, Dafydd, Sarah, Rachel, Tabitha, and Dorcas. Seven, you see!' List, name, and count. Sure signs. Significance. Seven. 'There'll be more children here before long too. Believe you me, my boy. We'll have to build other houses. Work. And it's possible we'll need another smith here before long. I'm slowly going blind, and there'll be too much work for Ifan during the spring and summer. At harvest, too. You'd make an excellent smith, Rhisiart Dewi.' That conspiratorial wink again.

'I don't know. But first I have to keep my word to Colonel Powel. Finish the work.'

'But you've done that. You said so. You came here to see New Jerusalem for yourself, and see that everything is fine here. And so your work is over. Go back to Strawberry Bank and write a letter to send back to London with the ships. Say to your Colonel Powel that everything is good here. And then come back to us to stay. Unless, of course, you have someone waiting for you in London or Wales?' That mischievous smile again.

'No, I don't have anyone. But my work is not finished yet.'

'No?'

'No. I have to see Richard Morgan Jones first. He's the one the Colonel knows. He'll want to hear what he has to say.'

Griffith John Griffith leans over his anvil, as if he were leaning over a piece of furniture, his arms folded and resting on top of it. 'No one has seen Doctor Jones for a long time. He's very ill, you see. He hasn't left the house in weeks. Catherine Huws looks after him usually. Otherwise, it's only Rhosier Wyn who visits him. Sometimes Evan Evans goes with him, but mostly the Elder goes to see him by himself.'

He stands up then, rotating his big bald head back and forth. 'Ow! This old body will be going before my eyes do, if I'm not careful!' He smiles at Rhisiart, then turns to his son.

'Ifan.'

'Yes, father?'

'How does that piece look now?'

'It looks good, father. Likely to hold, I'd say.'

'Alright, leave it here with me. Take some of this firewood to the widows. We have too much. Rhisiart Dewi?'

'Yes?'

'You go with him. There's too much of it for Ifan to carry by himself. Take some to Rhys and Gwen Edwart also.'

For the rest of the afternoon, Rhisiart and Ifan go back and forth, carrying armful after armful of firewood. Simple, pleasurable work, Rhisiart enjoying the kind of weariness that comes with it. Serving others in a simple way. Pleasant exhaustion.

First, to the old childless couple, Rhys and Gwen Edwart, who live in one of the houses along the circle road in the middle of the village. Then to the widows, all living in the houses scattered here and there between the inner circle and the walls. Rachel Morgan and Sarah Williams, the two old women living together, helping each other. And then Hannah Siôn, who lives by herself, despite the fact that she is the oldest one in New Jerusalem. And lastly, when the sun has sunk below the wooded horizon and the great wall is casting a shadow over her little house, Rebecca Roberts.

'I'll go home now, Ifan. Remember me to your father, and thank him for the talk.'

'Alright, Rhisiart. Good night.'

'Good night.'

Rhisiart ought to turn and walk in the shadow of the wall, wending his way past the house that Rachel Morgan and Sarah Williams share, and on past the house of Hannah Siôn. Thence past the north tower, the strong building that's the arsenal and home to the six guards, and then to the storehouse that's serving as his home. But he doesn't turn and walk away. Rebecca is still standing at the door of her house, despite the cold that's beginning to take hold as the sun disappears. She has already thanked the two of them, but she thanks Rhisiart again.

'Come in, Rhisiart, and have some food. There's too much for me, and there's a fresh loaf there, thanks to Hannah Siôn.'

The two have eaten and are now sitting in front of the fire. There's no other light in the house. The conversation has died after the one thanking the other over and again, she for the firewood and he for the food. Awkwardness, shyness, and then silence. Rhisiart tries to stare into the flames, but his eyes are trying to pull back to her. After another minute, she takes a deep breath, as if she's about to jump into cold water, and begins to talk. A rush of words, tripping over each other, trying to get it all out before her visitor rises and says good night.

She talks about her husband, Robert, who died of an illness some two months before Rhisiart arrived. He was a farmer, at his happiest in his fields outside the walls. Every crop a victory for him, every harvest making him king in his own world.

She talks about the little lakes. She says she can take him to see them in the spring, if he stays. Each one of them different, each a little world in itself. Some filled with lily pads, the flowers incredibly beautiful, looking like part of the garden of Eden. Some with large, dark fish swimming slowly through crystal clear waters, others muddy-brown, the depths hiding dark secrets. Occasionally there's a beaver dam, the branches forming unnatural shores, running at an angle from the land and vanishing beneath the water. Turtles everywhere, some swimming slowly, others basking in the sun on dead trees that run like bridges to nowhere, from the shore to the middle of the lake. Some delightful with red and yellow stripes, and others sharp-beaked and dangerous looking, like monsters that have swum up from the underground pools of Annwn. Rhisiart wants to tell her that he has seen such places, but he remains silent.

And of course she refers to the voyage, that central chapter in the chronicle of the community. She was eight years old at the time. Yes, she remembers it well. She remembers something of Caerphilly, and remembers the two years in Cardiff. And yes, of course, she remembers the time in Llanfaches too. She mentions her mother and father, and her brother, all of them sleeping in the cemetery between the walls and the north fields, the three of them buried in this good earth.

Another sense of awkwardness comes over her. She apologizes

for talking too much, sure that she's a bore and that he's tired and ready to head off to his lodging.

No, he says, he's enjoying the warmth of the house, enjoying listening to her. She blushes and falls silent again.

And then Rhisiart is talking. He's decided to ask the big question, knowing that he can't share her friendship if he's not honest and open.

'Do you know why I came here to New Jerusalem?'

'I do, Rhisiart Dewi. Everyone knows.' Of course everyone knows. But he wants to hear it from her. And so he asks again, despite feeling at the same time that he's being discourteous, prodding in this way.

'Exactly what does everyone know?'

She's blushing again. She had been studying his face, but she turns and talks to the fire to avoid his eyes. 'Everyone has heard your story. An acquaintance of Doctor Jones sent you across from Wales to see how it is with us here.' She looks at him out of the corner of her eye, with something like concern on her face.

'Yes, except that it was from London that I came.'

'That's it. From London. One of the old Welsh Saints who knew Doctor Jones in the Old Country in the old days. An influential man.'

Rhisiart sees something in her face, hears something in her voice. He can feel it, there, hovering in the air between them. He can't put a name to it, but it's not unlike a feeling that's been nagging him for days, some half-knowledge disturbing him. An as yet unformed question preying on his mind. But he senses that the same thing is disturbing her.

And then he understands. He knows exactly what it is; he can form that question now and ask it. And he decides to ask it of her.

'Rebecca?'

'Yes?'

'There's one thing that's strange.'

She looks at the fire again. It's obvious that she's listening intently, though she doesn't want to look at him.

'This story is not a complete surprise to anyone here, is it? I thought it would be a matter of wonder to people, you know, my saying that I was sent all the way across the sea to search for you. But it's not.'

She turns and meets his eyes.

'It's not a surprise, is it?'

'No, Rhisiart Dewi, not really. Some have been saying that another one would come to look for us. It's not the sort of thing that people discuss openly, but some have been saying that that's how it would be. Whispering quietly when they are among friends. Hannah Siôn, for example, has been saying that to me for some time now. She has been saying that another one would be coming.'

'Another one?'

'Yes, Rhisiart Dewi, another one. A man on a similar errand came some time ago. Miles Egerton. He is buried here, in New Jerusalem's cemetery.'

This good earth.

Rhisiart sees tears gathering in her eyes. She moves her chair so she can lean closer to him, and she whispers pleadingly, 'But no one is supposed to mention him, so please don't say I did.'

'I won't, I won't.' He's whispering too, although he's not sure why – the night is quiet and dark. 'But I could ask Rhosier Wyn. He's answered all my questions so far.'

'No, don't ask him. Don't!' This last word hissed between her teeth, like a mother shushing her child.

'Then I'll go visit Richard Morgan Jones. I'll have to.'

'No, Rhisiart Dewi, no one gets to see Doctor Jones now. No one has seen him for weeks.'

'But I have an obligation, Rebecca. I have to.' He pushes his chair back and stands. 'And thank you for the food and the visit.'

Before he can take a step towards the door she is on her feet too, beside him, taking hold of his arm.

'No, don't!'

He takes her hand gently and moves it from his arm. He pauses for a moment, squeezes her hand softly and looks into her eyes, like a father trying to quiet a child who has woken from a nightmare. But although she is trying to whisper, she's talking like one gripped by fear, dread deepening in her eyes.

'It's not safe, Rhisiart Dewi. Go now. Tomorrow morning. I don't want to see the same thing happen to you.'

'The same thing?'

'Yes… the same thing as… what happened to him, Miles Egerton.'

Rhisiart tries to get her to clarify, but she's not answering his questions any more.

He stands there, shifting his weight from one foot to the other, there in the middle of the only room of her little house, asking for more information, pleading with her. But she refuses. Says she has said too much already. And so he gives up asking. He thanks her once again before saying good night and leaving.

The night is dark and quiet. The only sound is that of the guards' feet moving slowly and rhythmically, striking the wood of the ramparts as they walk back and forth behind the big wall.

Rhisiart walks as quickly as possible, but softly too. To his right are the houses that face the circle road, nearer to each other than the handful of scattered houses that dot the open space between the inner circle and the big wall. To his left is the wall itself, rising as a barricade of blackness darker than the night. The moon has gone behind a cloud and there's no light at all to be seen in the village. He passes Hannah Siôn's house. He can't see anyone, but he senses something – a sound, half heard in the shadows. He stops, listening, looking intently. Nothing; it must be his imagination. He pushes on, walking cautiously, past the house of the two widows, Rachel Morgan and Sarah Williams. Nothing to be seen, the only sound the footfalls on the parapet. He goes on, gliding silently past the north tower on his left, the storehouse where he lodges a dark silhouette some fifty yards in front of him. He's almost home, but he hears another sound, other feet. Not striking the wood of the parapet but walking a gravel path. Has the sound been there all the while, following the light tread of his own feet? Maybe. He walks on, increasing his pace a bit, but before he reaches the door of the storehouse he hears the sound again. An unearthly sensation takes hold: a feeling that someone's eyes are on him.

–3–

Christmas 1656

Rhisiart walks through the village, enjoying the sound of the snow crunching under his feet. Although the circle road and the other paths have been cleared, he avoids them, choosing to walk through the heavy snow. It comes up to his knees, making his stockings and the bottoms of his breeches above his boots wet, but he welcomes the damp cold just as he enjoys the crunch of the snow. He'll be warming himself in front of the fire before long – shedding the boots and stockings and stretching his cold feet towards the flames, enjoying himself – but he wants to feel the winter for now, feel it right to his bones.

Mzatanos, that's the word. Pene Wons said that *Penibagos*, when the leaves fall, would give way to the long, dark days of *Mzatanos*, the coming of snow and ice.

All his thoughts and senses yield to the familiar: the sound of snow underfoot, the feeling when a boot breaks the frosty white surface with a crunch and then sinks slowly into the middle of the damp cold. Many years ago, as a small child in Caernarfonshire, running through the snow in front of his father to see the brook in the grip of the ice. Ten years ago, with ice and snow hanging heavy in his horse's mane, following a small patch of light through the snow near Exeter. There, there, you're fine. We'll both walk. All of it so familiar, yet different. The feel of winter that comes on the wind is colder, and the silence is deeper with the thickness of the snow and the tall pines beyond the walls and the fields stifling sound. Rhisiart wants to feel all of it, to surrender to it; he wants to experience this winter. And so he avoids the paths, getting wet and feeling the cold, and loving it.

He'll be sharing a meal soon. No one here celebrates Christmas as such, but there will be a prayer service and afterwards all will return to their homes to eat. It will not be festive, no, but families and friends will gather to enjoy this simple meal with each other. Let us remember today, Lord, the day your son came into the world. Let us remember in a way that is appropriate in your eyes and give our bodies and our souls this day, as on every other day, into your service. Amen. Rhisiart has been invited to eat at Hannah Siôn's house. Griffith John Griffith and his son Ifan will be there. Rebecca too. It's not the food which will make the meal special, but the company: the fact that friends will gather to share.

* * *

Rhisiart has been dividing his time between the forge and the widows' homes. He helps Griffith John Griffith, though he doesn't have to; there's barely enough work for the smith and his son, but they keep busy, perfecting pieces and experimenting with new ways of making tools. Melting broken pieces, working and reworking their scarce store of iron. Making nails, scores of them. And so Rhisiart joins them, their duo becoming a threesome. Sometimes the three of them compete to make the thinnest nails, with Griffith John Griffith exclaiming proudly:

'Look at this one then, boys!'

He takes pride in his accomplishments, saying that he can feel the iron under the hammer even though his sight is going.

'Men usually make nails with cast iron, using a mould. But we have plenty of time on our hands, and I always think that a nail is a good test for an apprentice.'

Rhisiart agreed, and said that his own master made him make nails.

'Hellfire, Ifan, what did I say? This fellow was taught by the right kind of smith! You see, Ifan? It's easy enough to strike a blow with a hammer. It's controlling the hammer that's difficult.'

Rhisiart agreed again, saying 'amen' to the words; strength comes with the work, but the ability to control and restrain a blow is a skill that's not easy to teach.

'But I would like to teach Ifan to shoe a horse. That's the one thing I would like to teach him,' Griffith John Griffith went on, complaining grumpily because there are no horses in New Jerusalem. It's a painful subject for him, he said. A matter for sorrow, even.

'Isn't there something special about shoeing, Rhisiart Dewi?'

Yes, Griffith, there is, he readily agreed. Shoeing is a completely different art, a job that's totally different from everything else that's done in a smithy. The iron taking hold of the horse's hoof, the item fashioned by the smith becoming one with the living animal. Not unlike creating a small test piece: care is the virtue, not strength.

Sometimes the three of them go off into the woods. The smith fastens a piece of cloth around his bald head before putting on his hat, and they venture into the wider world outside. They walk through the gates and around the wall to the north, past the cemetery. They always pause beside the grave of Griffith John Griffith's wife. Wooden memorials dot the snow, indicators of graves that can't be seen under the white blanket. Their colours range from yellow to brown to grey, depending on the age of the grave marker – a gravestone that's not stone but wood, like almost everything else in this community. The memorial at the head of Ifan's mother's grave is old: its grey colouring shows blotches of green, and the letters are difficult to read. Griffith John Griffith says something about it every time: they'll make a new marker in the spring. Sometimes he says that it's high time they got a stone memorial instead of a wooden one. On they go then, past the open white space of the fields to the woods, each of them shouldering an axe.

After finding a suitable tree, one that has fallen and whose wood is not yet decaying, they go at it with their axes. Before picking up the armful of wood they can carry along with their axes, the smith takes off his hat, cursing as he reties the bit of cloth around his head.

'Hellfire, it's not fair – no, it's not, boys! We ought to have horses to carry this wood!'

Rhisiart and Ifan take the firewood to the old people: Rhys and Gwen Edwart, the widows Rachel Morgan, Sarah Williams and Hannah Siôn. And to the young widow, Rebecca Roberts. She needs a bit of help these days; she's pregnant, and by Christmas she's having trouble doing much of the work around the house.

She chose to tell Rhisiart during one of their conversations, revealing that which she couldn't hide forever during one of the floods of words that would come after she overcame her shyness. She was pregnant, yes; had found out before her husband Robert died. She asked Rhisiart to not tell anyone the first time she shared the information with him. Her voice was soft, a nervous whisper showing her fear, asking him to keep it to himself. Why? Rhisiart asked again and again. Why? There's no shame in the matter. It's a natural state. Something to be expected, after all. Sad giving birth as a widow rather than a wife with her husband living, true, but there's no shame and it's not a sin. Why the secrecy? No, she explained, her breath catching in her throat. That's not it. That's not the reason for trying to hide the fact from her neighbours. It's not shame that's weighing on her, but fear.

'Fear of what? There are dangers at the time of childbirth, true, but you are young and healthy. There are no signs of illness, no sign that something is wrong?'

'No, there isn't, Rhisiart Dewi. Indeed not – that's not it. Not fear of the birth, but fear of what comes afterwards.'

He said he didn't understand, but despite pleading with her, pressing and pressing for an explanation, she wouldn't elaborate.

It's been five months by now, and she's showing considerably. Everyone in New Jerusalem knows that another baby is on the way, and it's an occasion for happiness. Another child! A sure sign of growth! But it's not a matter of joy to Rebecca. Every time Rhisiart is alone with her, he raises the subject, and the young widow's answer is the same every time. Fear. The joy of the community is a matter of fear to her.

Rhisiart spends much of his time helping the widows. Cutting firewood, shovelling snow to clear a path in front of the door, carrying water from the well. And he always takes the opportunity to spend time in Rebecca's house and talk. The talk is often domestic and pleasant. They discuss the weather. She describes the wonders of the region in the springtime – the trees budding, the flowers of the field, the little lakes. They share memories. She talks about her husband Robert. A farmer by instinct. King of the harvest.

Gradually, Rhisiart has talked about Elisabeth. Their youthful days, the two of them meeting in the evening in summer, in the courtyard between the smithy and the house of her father, his master. The blessed hours in London. How it was, coming home to her, the horse's hooves clicking on the cobbles. Seeing the small, familiar windows, the gate. The door he had imagined reaching, dreamily different, gleaming otherworldly in the shafts of sunlight. It had been painted bright orange, with hundreds of white flowers woven in a fine pattern around the edges. Yes, truly, it glowed magically in the April sun. The gate of the Court of King Arthur. The Gates of Heaven.

Rebecca talks about her father, her mother and her brother.

Says what she remembers about Wales and the voyage. Rhisiart tells tales of his youth. Every reminiscence a wonderful story. Going with his father to the banks of the brook to look for the otter. Tossing and turning in his bed at night, dreaming about the goblins of Annwn who were certain to come up through the mole tunnels and seize him in his sleep. His father standing before him, the Bible in his hand, his voice trembling: 'See here, my boy. The Book has come into our house. It will dwell here in our home and in our hearts from this day until the end of our time on this earth.' His bear of an uncle, a large, likeable monster, coming to take him back to Denbigh. Alys, his sister, the mirror of his mother, a third parent to him.

She is aware of the degrees of emotion on his face, and she doesn't ask about anything that he hasn't brought up. So he hasn't talked about the Little Plague and the grotesque red cross on the door. But he has been willing to share some of the experiences of the wars. He tries to explain the intensity of that dreamlike week on the road, walking all the way from Wrexham to London. A handful of the faithful having evaded the grasp of the King's forces, walking together on the road to London, talking excitedly about the good days that lay ahead. Receiving instruction with the London trained bands, he himself learning to live the words of Vavasor Powell, learning to pray in any place, standing or walking, or even marching under the weight of his armour and weapons. He has tried to describe the press of pikes at the Battle of Edgehill and the aftermath of the battle on the field at Newbury after twelve hours of fighting, crows and ravens going from body to body and half-hopping, half-flying to the top of a mound of flesh to pick, tear and eat. But he has said nothing about Ireland or about the women of Naseby. She's alert to the passions that play out on his face, and doesn't press and ask further when his account wanders too close to these things.

But the conversation can become awkward. At times, Rhisiart asks her about things, returning to subjects she doesn't want to talk about. The reasons for her fears; what happened to Miles Egerton, the Englishman who came at the request of Colonel Powel. She mumbles her apology, saying there are some things she can't discuss, and then the conversation dies in a slough of silent regret. Sometimes she intimates that he ought to go once winter loosens its grip. And sometimes she pleads with him, saying she wants to go with him, leave the place, escape, before the baby comes into the world. But at other times she says she can't ever leave her home and asks him to promise that he will remain. She says she wants him to stay, to continue to call every day, to talk in front of the fire like this every night. To go with her to see the lakes in the springtime.

And he asks why, why should I go? Of course, he says, you and the baby can come with me if I go, but why? What are you afraid of?

And every time she refuses to answer.

But despite the frustration of the questions he can't get answers to, Rhisiart leaves her house every evening feeling contented. He has found his tongue, and enjoys talking to her.

He also takes pleasure in his friendship with Griffith John Griffith and Ifan. The competition in the smithy, the teasing. Walking together through the snow to cut wood, and Griffith John Griffith longing for horses, regretting that Ifan has not learned the craft of shoeing.

Rhisiart sometimes gets himself to the point of asking them the same questions. He senses the words welling up on his tongue, feeling he's on the verge of asking. Do you know about Miles Egerton? What happened to him here? Why is Rebecca Roberts afraid? But he succeeds in stopping himself every time. He enjoys this friendship, the helpful refuge he finds in the company of the father and son from the thoughts that keep him awake at night, and so he chooses not to ask them these difficult questions.

He's spending hardly any time at all in the company of Rhosier Wyn these days. It's as if the Elder is leaving him to follow his own path every day, although Rhisiart has the feeling sometimes that the big-bellied little man is watching him from a distance. Evan Evans chats with him sometimes, and so Rhisiart agrees to visit the militia's home in the north tower when their leader extends an invitation to him. He doesn't much like the man. Evan Evans is one who enjoys his authority, and though he has but five soldiers under him, it's as if he looks for orders to give so he can show that he can get other men to obey his commands. The two young Welshmen, Huw Jones and Tomos Bach, are slavishly obedient to their bully of a captain. The two Englishmen, Ben Cotton and David Newton, make fun of him sometimes and whisper among themselves, but they jump to obey all the same. And the giant Owen Williams, who has to duck to avoid hitting his head on the roof rafters, and whose shoulders fill the open space in a doorway, moves slowly and quietly. Griffith John Griffith has explained that Owen is a widower too, and that his young son, his only child, died from the fever some five years ago, at the same time as his wife. It was then that Owen decided to quit farming and join the militia, so gave up his house to a young married couple and moved to the tower. The life of a single man, one who doesn't support a family or maintain a home.

Evan Evans takes Rhisiart up the steps to walk the ramparts with him sometimes. 'There we are, plenty of work for the six of us to do. Two guards every hour, day and night.' He explained the arrangement, saying that it was necessary for other men to support them, the volunteers, so that Evans' men could get some sleep.

'Otherwise, six is enough, you see.' Watching, walking the

walls, their feet rhythmically striking the hours of the day and night in New Jerusalem.

Rhisiart doesn't like the leader of the militia, but turning down these invitations would be discourteous. He knows that turning the man into an enemy would not be wise. And Evan Evans respects him because he's a soldier. He asks him about the wars, and Rhisiart makes his answers as brief as possible. What is required, not the pleasure of revelation that comes when he's sharing some of his story with Rebecca in front of the fire.

'How was it, Rhisiart Dewi? Bearing arms in the Army of the Saints, striking out against the enemies of the Faith?'

Our eye is not to pity them, nor our sword to spare them. They are enemies of God and our Religion, not fellow countrymen or kinsmen. They are those who take the side of the Antichrist, natural enemies of the soldiers of the Lord.

But he avoids Evan Evans as much as possible, preferring to spend the day in the smithy or helping the widows. Enjoying talking with Rebecca in front of the fire, sharing memories and discussing the weather.

* * *

Rhisiart walks on, lost in the crunch of his feet in the snow, welcoming the cold that's taken hold of his legs. It's still fairly early in the morning; there'll be time to warm himself and dry his clothes before the service and dinner time. He has just brought a bucket of water to Hannah Siôn, and after a brief conversation with her about the time of the meal they will be enjoying with each other in her house after the prayer meeting, Rhisiart turns to walk slowly back to his own house, turning from the path, enjoying striking out through the deep snow.

'There you are, Rhisiart Dewi!'

A familiar voice, calling from a little way off. He turns and sees Rhosier Wyn waving enthusiastically at him. The little man is standing on the circle road, between two houses.

'Come here, Rhisiart Dewi. I have something to say to you.'

When Rhisiart reaches him, Rhosier Wyn is standing there, his arms folded and resting on his belly.

'Come quickly.' He glances at Rhisiart's wet boots before turning and walking quickly. 'Come. Doctor Jones wants to see you.'

* * *

'Happy Christmas to you, Rhisiart Dewi.'

Richard Morgan Jones' voice is strong, and doesn't seem to fit the feeble-looking old man lying in the bed.

'I'm pleased to meet you at last, but I'm sorry it has to be like this.'

He lifts a shaky hand and gestures towards the bed that he's confined to. Rhisiart can see him clearly. Although the shutters on the small windows have been pulled tight, there is a fireplace in the room, and there is a six-branched candlestick on the table. Although shadows lurk in the other corners of the room, the flames from the fire and the candles shed enough light on the man in the bed. His skin is waxy and yellowed. Rhisiart can see the outlines of the old man's bones and the colour of the veins pulsing under the thin skin of his hand when he lifts it. The face reminds Rhisiart of a carving he saw on a tomb in a church in England before his fellow soldiers went at it, hammering away at the white marble and disfiguring it: the face of the old dead knight vanishing piece by piece, his nose first, and then his eyebrows and ears, his chin taking many blows before cracking and falling to pieces. Richard Morgan Jones' cheekbones are high and strong, but the deep hollows beneath them suggest he is a man who has not eaten well for a long time. His hair is as white as his skin, and so too is his beard. Rhisiart cannot tell whether his eyes are blue or grey, they are so bloodshot now. And they shine unhealthily, as if they are continually watering. It's obvious that lifting and turning his head is a significant effort for the old man, as is lifting his hand, everything shaking.

'This is how it is with me, Rhisiart Dewi, so we have to speak here like this. I've heard about you, and I've been waiting to see you. It's clear to me now that I won't be getting better so there's no point in waiting any longer. Thank you for coming to see me like this.' The voice is strong, although a bit raspy in his throat, suggesting the strength of the man he was, as opposed to the weak, immobile body in which he is now contained.

And then he lifts his head slightly from the pillow, the effort bringing pain to his face, and calls out: 'Go, Rhosier Wyn.'

Rhisiart had forgotten that the little man was there behind him, standing in the doorway.

'Go to the service. Rhisiart will be staying here with me for a while yet.'

Rhisiart doesn't turn to watch the man depart, but he hears the door of the room close as he leaves. He can't take his eyes off this pale image of a man lying there before him. Richard Morgan Jones raises his trembling hand again and points it towards the corner next to the fireplace.

'Bring a chair here beside my bed, so we can talk at ease.'

Rhisiart fetches the chair from the corner, sets it next to the bed and sits, removing his hat as he does so. He sits there, holding his hat on his knee.

'I'm sorry for making you miss the prayer service. Pyrs Huws' sermons are worth attending.'

Rhisiart tries to respond, but he's not sure what he should say. But Richard Morgan Jones is not expecting a response.

'However, it's obvious that that's how it is going to be.' The voice is one that's easy to listen to, rich and clear, despite the rasping that creeps in now and again. 'Here, with me on my death bed, on Christmas Day. There's no vain celebrating here in New Jerusalem, as you know – that's certain. But it is fitting for us to remember the birth of the Lord Jesus all the same.'

'That's how it was in my home; when I wasn't with the army, anyway.'

'I *enjoyed* the festive season when I was young, you know. Before my heart was fully awakened.' A faint smile plays upon his lips and his rheumy eyes are bright. 'The feasting... the presents... the singing. I remember the singing, you know, in the old times past.' The old man has the look of one who enjoyed delicious food, and he's savouring the memories.

Rhisiart has been trying to mind what he says, to think carefully before speaking, but the old man's words have disarmed him, and he says in surprise, 'It's strange to hear you confess that now, since you have come all the way across the sea to leave behind the old sinful ways.'

The old man smiles kindly, then points a finger at him, like a parent reprimanding a child. 'That's a trap which often snares a godly man.' His voice is lively and his eyes are smiling, as if he is sharing wisdom that delights his heart. 'You can't deny the man that was. It's all part of the order of Divine Providence, you know, that which was and that which is now. If it is ordained for you to be that which you are today, this day, then it holds that that which you were is also a part of the great order of Providence.' He pauses, turns his head to lock eyes with Rhisiart. 'It doesn't pay to deny that, Rhisiart Dewi. And so for what would a man try to deny that which was? I *enjoy* remembering things that I enjoyed in the old days, even though I would consider such things unseemly today. It's possible that another person would say that it's just as unseemly for me to think about them and enjoy them today, but I don't agree. It doesn't pay to deny that which was. It would be just as foolish as denying the truth of that which exists now.'

He's been watching Rhisiart's face the whole time, but he's not urging him to speak. 'I knew you would turn out to be a godly man, Rhisiart Dewi.'

Rhisiart says nothing, but he moves a bit in his chair, and tries to avoid the watery red eyes scrutinizing his face. What shall I say in response? Should I answer with Colonel Powel's litany? I *have* believed, I *have* lived, I *have* done. Should I be honest and say that I no longer know what true godliness is, confess that I do not know where I could find the true foundations of grace?

'It's apparent to me, you know. I know that you are a godly man, even though you try to hide from your own godliness.'

Should he say that the last time his soul felt truly awake was when he was talking to Owen Lewys on board ship, say that the next time he has chance to open the covers of the Bible, he will turn straight to those words in the gospel of John? That was the true Light, which lighteth every man that cometh into the world. Should he say that testifying to this light is the only form of worship that makes sense to him now, though he can't work out how to live like that? He could confess that he feels the compulsion to search for that light in his own heart, but that he fails to dive deep enough, and that his own stubbornness keeps him from giving himself up to that means of finding grace.

Rhisiart feels tears welling up in his eyes. He feels warm, as if the heat of his body is responding to the swelling inside his heart, blood rushing to his cheeks and sweat on his forehead. He cannot deny the voice that's calling to him, the voice that's penetrating his being, forcing him to think about those things he has banished from his thoughts for years.

'I know in my heart that that's how it is, Rhisiart Dewi. It has all been made clear to me. But I had to see you before dealing with the road ahead. And here you are, in accordance with the order of Divine Providence.'

Rhisiart lifts a hand to wipe the sweat from his brow and the tears from the corners of his eyes. He shakes his head slightly, like a man trying to awaken from heavy sleep, attempting to shake the embarrassment from himself and straighten up. Embarrassment, and this strange man witnessing his weakness.

'All this I know, please be assured of that.'

The weirdness of the situation throws Rhisiart, sends him reeling. This man saying these things to him, like an ancient white effigy on a tomb in a church turning to him and addressing him, and the voice piercing his heart from the furthest reaches of past ages.

But the voice is not strange or exotic. A patchwork of memories come together with every word it utters. The dim memory he has of his father's voice. There you go, Rhisiart. Come now. Don't drown near the shore. Learn to read it every day, and you will love it for the rest of your days. The voice of Colonel Powel. I know you, Rhisiart. Bits of sermons by Vavasor Powell, Walter Cradoc and Morgan Llwyd. All the voices that succeeded in reaching the depths of his heart. The children of the day who love the Light. There's something in Richard Morgan Jones' voice that calls to him, something that says, sit here with me and listen. Forget about your own stubbornness and everything you blame this life for. Sit, listen, and open your heart. Give yourself up, surrender to this great present.

They stay like that for hours, Richard Morgan Jones relating the history of New Jerusalem and Rhisiart detailing some of his own story. The old man urges Rhisiart to remove his boots and put them to dry in front of the fire. 'Make yourself comfortable. It's easier to turn the mind to higher things if the body is at ease. We are all creatures of flesh, and we should live accordingly on this earth.'

And so Rhisiart removes his wet boots and stockings and puts them on the hearthstone in front of the fire before sitting back down and returning to the conversation. He is surprised to learn that the inhabitants of New Jerusalem know so much about recent events in Wales and England, living as far as they do from the nearest British settlements.

'They come here twice a year, the Wampanoag. Those the English call the Praying Indians. There's a community of them about a week's walk to the south. They come in the spring and at the end of summer. Sometimes the minister Samuel Appleton comes with them. Have you heard of him? They say they have great respect for him in Boston and Plymouth.'

'And they bring news to you?'

'They do. That is, they come here to trade with us. They bring things that we can't make for ourselves. Gunpowder, more iron, and so on. And we give meat and animal pelts in exchange. They could get these things easily, certainly, from the forest Indians, but they come all the way here just to trade with us. They see it as a Christian mission. In order to help support us, you know. And so a bit of news comes to us occasionally.'

Rhisiart's mind wanders, trying to imagine what it's like hearing all that recent news from Wales and England – the wars, the King's execution, the efforts of the new government – from afar in that way. News reaching the port of Boston with the ships. Rumours going from mouth to mouth and from community to community until they're eventually heard by some of the Christian Wampanoag, who then bring the stories to New Jerusalem. The English minister, Samuel Appleton, perhaps receiving a letter from England and able to share news more directly. But truly, what is the value of the story of something that happened months or even years ago in a country none of them has seen for years, and some have never seen at all? Those tales are as distant from their world and their lives as tales of magic and illusion or the feats of Old Testament heroes. Egypt and Canaan, Wales and England.

'But our English brethren misunderstand about the Praying Indians. And some of our brothers and sisters here in New Jerusalem make the same mistake, though I have tried to enlighten them more than once.'

'Really? How so?'

'It's like this, Rhisiart Dewi. The great majority of those who consider themselves saints believe that Satan lurks in this wilderness.' With an effort, he gestures to indicate everything outside of this one room. 'They say that Satan walks about boldly in the dark forests of America, and that the Indians are his children. They believe that seizing these lands in the name of God is our mission. Turning a part of Satan's realm into a little bit of the kingdom of God.'

Rhisiart hears the words of Rhosier Wyn again: 'Destroyed them all, and not long before we arrived. Cleansed all these lands of the savages. Cleared the wilderness of them, ready for us.'

He sees that Richard Morgan Jones is waiting quietly, giving Rhisiart time to follow his line of thinking. The rheumy red eyes are fixed on his face, penetrating and studying.

'Yes. I believe I have heard that sort of argument already. They see signs of the workings of Divine Providence here on American soil.'

'Exactly.' The eyes are smiling on him now, and the voice rises a bit, like a teacher enjoying seeing that a pupil understands his lesson. 'And they take pride in the fact that the Praying Indians have turned to God. They welcome them as Christian brothers and sisters.'

'But aren't they Christians?' The voice of the uncertain pupil now, the lesson having slipped through his fingers just when he thought he had grasped it all.

'There you are, Rhisiart, falling into the same trap that trips up so many these days.'

'Am I?'

'Yes, you are. That's not the right question to ask – whether someone is a Christian or not.'

'It's not?'

'No, no, it's not. The question is this: is a person among the elect or not? If we follow the doctrine to its logical end, then it follows that the Indians who pray to God and call themselves Christians are no more or less likely to be among the elect than the most barbarous pagans who lurk in the shadows of these forests.'

Rhisiart stares at the man. He tilts his head slightly at an angle, unconsciously striking the pose of one who's listening intently and considering what he has just heard, but he says nothing. Although he feels comfortable with the man, he's not about to take issue and argue openly with him. He's there for a reason and he wants to hear more. Is Richard Morgan Jones mistaking his silence, thinking that he agrees with him? Rhisiart moves his head again, and stares at the man's hands, avoiding his eyes.

'Some have been preordained to eternal life and others have been preordained to eternal damnation. All this we know. Some search for signs. They are hoping that a calling from God is a sign of election, and that the godly lives they are living prove that they are answering His call and so testify to their election. But there is no certainty, Rhisiart Dewi. Calvin showed us that. Some are born to life and others are born to death. The true goal of Divine Providence is to gather the elect together in whatever way He is pleased to make that election manifest. We can only recognize it when it is made clear to us.'

* * *

It's late and it has begun to snow again. Rhisiart walks back with Rebecca from Hannah Siôn's house. There, in the old widow's one-room house, squeezed around her table, the five of them enjoyed a meal of simple food. Griffith John Griffith and his son Ifan, Rhisiart, the young widow Rebecca Roberts, and the old widow Hannah Siôn. No Christmas carols were sung and there was no mention of revelry or matins, just an occasion to pray together and then to eat and talk. Christmas evening in New Jerusalem. And afterwards he escorts Rebecca to her house.

Rhisiart stays for a while so he can bring in more wood from the pile beside the door. 'I'll make a fire, so you don't have to bend down.' He comes every day, first thing in the morning and again at night, to carry water and firewood, sparing the pregnant young woman from any work that might be a strain. She sits in her usual chair, thanking him.

Somewhat later, Christmas evening closing in on midnight, the two of them are sitting comfortably, warming themselves in front of Rebecca's fire, making small talk. Referring to what was discussed at Hannah Siôn's during the meal. Exchanging childhood memories. Talking about the snow, Rebecca describing what it is like living through the long winters in this land. And then, after sitting quietly for a time, Rhisiart sits up and begins to talk.

'I got to see Richard Morgan Jones today.'

'Doctor Jones?'

'Yes. Finally. You know I've been trying to see him since I arrived.'

'How was he? I haven't seen him for ages.'

'I can't say. That is, I didn't know him… when he was younger… when he was healthy. So I don't have anything at all to compare him with. He's bedridden. Failing, apparently. But well enough to talk. I was with him for a long time today, all morning.'

'And that's why you weren't at the prayer meeting.'

Rhisiart doesn't answer right away. He's trying to get his thoughts and ideas in order, to ask the right questions.

'Rebecca?'

'Yes?'

'I have to say…' He stares into the fire, as if the words he's searching for are to be found there in the flames, and she waits patiently for him to finish. Finally, he straightens and looks at her. 'I have to confess that I had not expected him to be like that.'

'Like what, Rhisiart Dewi?'

'I don't know… I wasn't expecting him to be like that. So likeable.'

'Are you saying you like him?'

'Yes, I suppose so.'

'Contrary to expectations?'

'Perhaps… Yes, I suppose so.'

'And so you were pleasantly disappointed, as they say.'

Rhisiart laughs to himself, agreeing with her, before turning serious again.

'I don't say I agree with him. I don't believe much of what he believes in. But there we are. That doesn't matter. I have disagreed on certain points with many men I otherwise like.' The religious academy of the Army of the Saints, men agreeing on one point and then disagreeing on another. 'There's much about him that I respect. Though I can't agree with his Calvinism.'

'I'm sorry, Rhisiart, but I'd rather not discuss religion or doctrine,' she sighs. 'Not now, not tonight.'

Rhisiart wants to ask her the questions that he didn't ask Doctor Jones earlier, questions that have been smouldering inside him for weeks. What happened to Miles Egerton, the man who came here at Colonel Powel's request? Why has the doctrine of the ministers of New Jerusalem become a cause of fear for others? What was the foundation of those rumours? A cause of concern: 'They know not what they do.' And he wants to ask her why she's worried about giving birth, why she sometimes says she would like to flee with Rhisiart the first chance they get.

She has come to know Rhisiart quite well by now. They have spent long hours talking here in front of the fire, discussing this and that, familiarizing themselves with bits of each other's history. She has learned that there are things about his past that he would prefer not to talk about, and she knows how to steer the conversation around those personal pitfalls. In the same way, their friendship has survived those painful moments of awkwardness when Rhisiart asks her questions she refuses to answer.

And so she senses that he is getting ready to ask that sort of question, and she has decided to stop him before he opens his mouth.

'I'm so tired, Rhisiart Dewi. Don't ask tonight, please. Don't ask. I will say one thing to you: the women and mothers of New Jerusalem have to shoulder an especially difficult burden. That's all I will say to you tonight.'

Sometime later, as he walks home through the snow, Rhisiart is trying to remember a line from a poem. *Great indeed is the burden of every mother, but Mary is carrying it for us.* He knows he hammered the words into the hot iron one afternoon when flurries of December snow were swirling about outside the door of the old smithy in Wrexham, but he can't quite remember the exact words, or the rhyme or the metre. There was a tune on his tongue at the time too, definitely, but he can't find the beat now. *Great is the burden of the Virgin Mary, and she is carrying it for us.* By the time he opens the door of his lodging and takes off his boots, he's certain he'll never remember the song.

–4–

End of January 1657

There's but a single, small flame left, an ineffectual little thing, fighting for what fuel remains, weakly holding onto the few embers that continue to burn.

Rhisiart rises and throws a few wood shavings into the embers. Then he grabs a slightly bigger piece of wood and puts that into the fire. He waits for a moment, making sure that the flames have begun to take hold of the offering, and then turns and puts more firewood on top of it all, making a stack of logs that will continue to burn for some time. Then he sits, Rebecca murmuring her thanks to him.

The two of them sit together quietly. Rhisiart has told her some of what he's been doing today, but she's not talking much tonight. Even though she's quiet, every time he's about to say goodnight and go, she asks him to stay. And so the two have been sitting for some time in front of the fire, sharing the silence.

* * *

The pattern of Rhisiart's days has changed since Richard Morgan Jones began to ask for him. He continues to spend much of his time in the smithy, enjoying the friendly competition with the smith and his son, each in turn trying to create the thinnest nail or the most beautifully turned hinge or hook. And sometimes he accompanies the two to cut wood, past the cemetery and the fields' white desolation, trudging through the snowdrifts to the forest, axes on their shoulders.

One time, Ifan called his attention away from the fallen tree he was working at with his axe.

'Psst! Come and see!'

Rhisiart had told the smith and his son to rest for a while, saying that he would finish this tree by himself. His axe rising and falling, striking the dead wood dully, sweat breaking out on his brow in spite of the cold.

'Psst, Rhisiart Dewi, come now!'

There was excitement in the boy's voice – he was trying to be quiet but still calling loudly enough to Rhisiart to get his attention. There, some twenty yards away, standing between two birch saplings, was a man. Not one of the inhabitants of New Jerusalem, but a man. He was wearing a leather cloak with some kind of blanket covering his head and shoulders. The front of his head had been shaved to make his forehead long, and it was daubed with red paint. He held a musket, but showed no intention of shooting. He stood there quietly, gazing at the three of them. And then, a moment later, he turned and walked away, vanishing among the pines, birch and mounds of snow.

Griffith John Griffith's weakening eyes had not made him out clearly, so his son described him to his father after the man had left.

'One of them, father, and the front of his head as bald as your own. You should have brought your musket, Rhisiart Dewi. It's not always safe here.'

Rhisiart had been trying to remember the words, wanting to greet the man in his own language, but he wasn't certain if he was remembering correctly, and he didn't find his tongue until after the man had disappeared from view. *Akwi sagezo. Kwai, nijia, kwai. Wligo, wlioni. Wlioni, nidoba, wlioni.* He didn't respond to Ifan. He left the lad to share his excitement and his concerns with his father and turned back to the dead tree, lifting his axe and striking again. Remembering. He remembered the names, if not all of the words. Malian. Asômi. Msadokwes. Pene Wons. Simôn. Yes, and he himself, Isiad Dawi.

He continues to help the village widows every day too, carrying firewood and fetching water from the well. Ifan shows him how to get water from the well in the middle of winter. You have to find a rock and drop it into the well first, to break the ice. Then you can lower the bucket on a rope and draw cold water from the dark depths. Rhisiart asks whether that is wise – won't the rocks clog up the well one day? Ifan answers by pointing to the long ladder hanging on wooden pegs on the wall of the smithy. It's long enough to reach the bottom of the well, and on a warm day in summer Ifan or one of the other village youths goes down into the darkness and disappears into the black water, like someone who doesn't know what fear is climbing down into the watery throat of Annwn. He dives down and brings the rocks up from the bottom, putting them in the bucket for the others to pull up. When he begins to feel the cold, the lad comes up from the black hole and lets someone else take his place. It takes three or four of them to clear the bottom of the well, but there's a good deal of fun, between teasing and daring, each one seeing who can retrieve the most rocks from the black, blinding waters before becoming too cold to continue the work. 'Well-Clearing Day', they call it, some hot day towards the middle of July usually. The young lads look forward to it, each one waiting for the day when he will be old enough to volunteer and go down the ladder to the dark, cold bottom.

Rhisiart lingers when he gets a chance to talk to Rebecca, the two of them enjoying sharing memories and talking about the simple little things that occur in their daily lives, but the conversation grinding to a halt every time Rhisiart tries to get answers to the difficult questions. And Rhisiart, in his turn, avoids revealing certain bits of his history to her. So the two spend time together, the conversation swinging between the comfortably familiar and the restraint of those things that one wants to keep private from the other.

But now the pattern of their days has changed; Rhisiart spends almost as much time with Richard Morgan Jones as he does in Rebecca's home. A messenger comes to fetch him – Rhosier Wyn, Evan Evans, Pyrs Huws, or Catherin Huws – saying that Doctor Jones is asking for him. He has come to expect this request each day, and he's disappointed if the sun begins to set without him receiving a call to keep company with the old man that day, a bit of business unfinished, and unanswered questions preying on his mind and keeping him from enjoying the company of Rebecca or Griffith John Griffith and his son. But the call comes most days, and Rhisiart always complies, hurrying to sit beside Doctor Jones' bed. Sometimes Catherin Huws is also there, though she always closes the door of the bedroom behind Rhisiart so the two can talk privately. But Rhisiart can hear her in the adjacent large room, cleaning or cooking. Sometimes she brings food for the old man – usually broth or some kind of stew – and if Rhisiart has not yet eaten, he accepts the invitation to sup with the Doctor. He helps Catherin to move this white shadow of a man to a sitting position, a pillow set firmly behind his back. And then Catherin brings another chair so she can sit beside the bed and feed the old man, a spoonful at a time. Rhisiart sits in his own chair by the foot of the bed on these occasions, holding his bowl and spoon. And then, after Catherin takes the empty bowls away and they have helped the Doctor lie down comfortably in his bed again, she leaves them, closing the door quietly behind her, and the men resume their discussions.

There's no small talk between them: the two understand each other and they understand that there's not much time. They know that there are many gaps to be bridged in the short time they have, and so they speak openly; complete honesty governs their discussions. It's no secret that Rhisiart has come to New

Jerusalem at the request of John Powel, and he details the nature of his service with the Colonel during the wars and afterwards. Richard Morgan Jones talks about the Colonel lovingly, like one remembering a lost friend, but he says a number of times that Powel 'has strayed'. The first time the old man said this, Rhisiart asked for clarification, and his answer was that John Powel worried too much about the things of this world.

During his second visit, Rhisiart asked him outright what happened to the Englishman Miles Egerton, who had come here some time back at the request of Colonel Powel.

'I'm surprised that no one has explained it to you, Rhisiart Dewi.'

'No, no one has. It's as if they're afraid to talk about him.'

'Well, it's a sad story, that's certain, the man having travelled such a distance only to die in the forest here.'

He told the story in its entirety, beginning with what Miles Egerton himself had told him. Yes, he was a man serving Parliament and working with John Powel. He had come across to New England on some other mission, something to do with trade, but Colonel Powel had asked him to do something else during his time in America. He had agreed: no one who knows John Powel would ever refuse him anything. And so after he completed his work in Boston, Miles Egerton journeyed to the west and to the north, asking the Wampanoag about New Jerusalem. He went from village to village and finally found the ones who visited New Jerusalem twice a year. He came one summer with a letter from Brother Appleton addressed to *my most esteemed brethren, the Ministers of New Jerusalem.* But it was soon seen that the man had begun his journey in London rather than Boston, and that it was Colonel Powel and not Mr Appleton who had sent him. The minister of the Praying Indians was only doing a favour for another godly Englishman.

Miles Egerton was a man who spoke plainly, and it soon

became clear that he did not agree with much of the doctrine of New Jerusalem's ministers. But there we are; he decided to stay through the winter before travelling back to Boston and looking for a ship to take him back across the sea to England and Colonel Powel. He was given lodging and was welcomed among them. Though he was prone to argue, he also seemed to enjoy everyday life in the village. But one day he went hunting in the forest with Evan Evans and Owen Williams, and disaster befell them: a number of Indians, not the Wampanoag but those that had not adopted the ways of the white men, though they did have muskets. Armed by the Frenchmen, no doubt, or by some unthinking Englishman who valued his trading above his conscience. A skirmish took place and Miles Egerton was shot dead. A very unfortunate event. A sad story. And that's it.

The two discuss theology at times, the arguments and counter-arguments coming easily to Rhisiart, recalling the philosophical tumult of the Army of the Saints. He leans forward in his chair, speaking enthusiastically with the old man, the other sometimes with considerable effort lifting his hand to make a point. Sometimes he shakes his head a little on his pillow, his mouth scowling in disagreement. At other times he nods, smiling his agreement.

'Yes, Rhisiart Dewi, we are in complete agreement about that. I have been telling the brothers and sisters that it's not so, but it's difficult for that lesson to sink deeply into their hearts. Like a number of those who cherish the teachings of Calvin back in the old countries, they're still searching for signs. Searching hard, searching diligently, to see signs showing that they have formed the True Church. Signs that would prove that the earthly church they have been supporting is the same as the Invisible Church of the elect.'

Although his voice is somewhat raspy in his throat, Richard Morgan Jones is fully animated, the discussion bringing evident pleasure to him, his eyes shining and a bittersweet smile playing on his lips.

'I myself was searching for signs, Rhisiart Dewi. Yes, yes. I was searching for signs in Llanfaches, and I can say that I was earnest in my desire, searching passionately for signs that would show me that that was the True Church. Yes, yes. And I'm not afraid to confess something to you now: so great was my desire, yes, so great was my need that I almost succeeded in completing the self-deception there. Yes, almost deceived myself and concluded that the True Invisible Church could be seen in that earthly church. Believe this, Rhisiart Dewi: I wasn't looking for faults, but I was looking for signs that this true grace could be found in this world. I searched. I tried. Yes, yes, I searched everywhere and I tried hard, so intense was my desire.'

He turns his head towards the wall, tears running down his cheeks and wetting his white beard.

'So earnest… so earnest… so ready to believe. But there was something there that would not allow me to close the eyes of my heart to the truth. Something that is called Divine Providence by some. I could not close my eyes and my ears and my heart to His will. And so I could not be content there in Llanfaches. I couldn't. I searched there in that church, I did, and I found that church wanting. There were probably Saints there in that congregation. It's possible that some of them were among the elect. But it was a visible church, an earthly church, like a good many other churches, not an Invisible Church of His elect. And after searching and searching and trying and trying, and after failing completely to see anywhere a union between a visible church here on the earth and the Invisible Church, I decided that the only choice was to create that church myself.'

And so on. At times Rhisiart listens silently, enjoying the eloquence of the man even though he doesn't agree with a lot of what he's saying, and at other times he argues with him, offering good reasons for doubting the hard Calvinist stone that Richard Morgan Jones has set as a foundation for the church in New Jerusalem. The old man shakes his head, showing his displeasure when Rhisiart voices an opposing opinion, but he doesn't try to silence him. He welcomes the debate, even when it is heated.

But Rhisiart has not yet asked him to explain why Rebecca is afraid. The question burns inside him and he feels it there sometimes, like a bit of food stuck in his throat which he's uncertain whether to wash down or try to cough up. But he keeps his promise: he won't break his word to Rebecca, so he doesn't ask the question. But he feels free to ask the Doctor about his doctrines, and often voices complaint and judgement – but no matter how much he disagrees, no matter how much argument and counterargument, the call comes again and again.

And so another call today, just as expected. As he is carrying a bucket of water from the well to Hannah Siôn's house, walking along the circle road past the large building that is home to Richard Morgan Jones, the door opens. Catherin Huws is standing there, as if she has been expecting him. There is an urgency in her voice which hasn't been there before. 'There you are, Rhisiart Dewi, come as quickly as you can. Doctor Jones is worsening again today, but he wants to see you. Come quickly, as quickly as possible.'

Rhisiart hurries through the snow to the old widow's house and knocks on the door. He apologizes, saying he is sorry for not being able to stay and talk, then turns and hastens to the Doctor's bedside. The old man can only speak very softly, as if his voice is battling the increasing rasping in his throat, and the words are finding it difficult to reach his lips. But he smiles after Catherin Huws closes the door and leaves them to talk.

'Thank you for coming, Rhisiart Dewi. I am pleased to see you today.' His hands are folded and lying on his chest, completely motionless, as if life has already departed from his body and that body is ready to be enclosed in a shroud, put into a coffin and buried.

'I shall not be long among you on this earth, and I want to finish saying what I have to say to you before departing this life.'

Rhisiart leans over the bed, his hands on his knees, his eyes seeking to discover meaning in the watery pools of the old man's eyes.

'What is it that you want to say to me?'

'I want to say that I…' The words die on his lips, as if he doesn't have enough breath to push them out over his tongue. He closes his eyes, tears spreading over his cheeks, and coughs lightly. Then, without opening his eyes, he begins to speak again, his voice a whisper, like a light wind rustling rushes.

'I… want… to ask… you… something.' He pauses and opens his eyes again, though Rhisiart doesn't believe the man is able to see him. Those unseeing eyes wander up to the ceiling as he begins to whisper again. 'I want to ask… you… to be a deacon.'

Rhisiart bends closer, not having understood the last word, but ready to seize on whatever word comes.

'Deacon,' the old man repeats. 'Deacon.'

'I don't understand…'

But Richard Morgan Jones is asleep, and when Rhisiart goes through the door to the main room of the house, he sees that Rhosier Wyn and Pyrs Huws have come to wait with Catherin Huws. The Preacher's wife goes in to check on the sick man, and then comes back, closing the bedroom door softly behind her.

'He's sleeping now. But he's weak.' She looks at her husband, tears wetting her cheeks and her voice shaking. 'He's weak, Pyrs Huws, he's so weak.'

The minister steps close to his wife before asking quietly, 'But did he get to say what he wanted to say?'

His wife's only answer is to look at Rhisiart.

'Well, then?' Rhosier Wyn's voice is loud, his long, ungainly arms gesticulating agitatedly. 'Tell us! What did he say? Did he have the chance to ask you?'

'Yes, I believe so.' Rhisiart speaks as if in a dream. 'I believe he wants me to be Deacon.'

Pyrs Huws smiles and takes his wife's arm. 'Thank goodness for that. It's good that he's had the opportunity to get his message across today, lest he be leaving us.' He speaks quietly but quickly; Rhisiart has never seen him so fervent outside of the pulpit. 'That's good, that's good. He told me yesterday. He said he had decided that we ought to ask you to stay with us, Rhisiart Dewi, and fill the office of the fourth minister. He said he was going to ask you to be Deacon.'

'But I don't understand. I didn't come here to stay. Only to visit you. I'll be leaving in the spring. I didn't come to join you.'

'There you are, Pyrs Huws, that's it.' Rhosier Wyn is at Rhisiart's side, taking hold of his arm and leading him to the front door, speaking over his shoulder to the others. 'That's what I told you, isn't it? I told you that Doctor Jones had misunderstood things. I told you he wasn't making sense.'

The tall minister stepped in front of them, standing between them and the door. 'No, Rhosier Wyn, no – it must be you who has misunderstood. Doctor Jones must be right, once he sees his way clear and decides how things are going to be. What right do you or anyone else have to disagree with him, eh?'

'The right of a man who knows when another man is sick, Pyrs Huws. The right of a man who is trying to save his friends and his church from making a mistake. Doctor Jones is not in his right mind. He's sick. His mind is wandering. I said that it was a mistake letting this man come here today at all. Why do you two want to disturb the Doctor when he's so ill? He's not well and he's not in his right mind.'

The short, big-bellied man pushes past the Minister and leads Rhisiart out of the house into the cold of a sunless afternoon.

Rhisiart halts on the doorstep, pulling free of the Elder's grip. 'Thank you, Rhosier Wyn. I can get home on my own.'

* * *

The fire continues to burn brightly, the flames dancing merrily, shadows playing across their faces. Rhisiart has been staring long into the flames, watching the gradual victory of the fire over the wood, the hot embrace, the crackling, the surrendering to smoke and ash. Although he doesn't need to yet, he gets up, takes more wood and places it carefully in the bosom of the flames, which lick perilously close to his fingers. He sits again, shaking his hands to cool them, and then turns to Rebecca.

'We have had all kinds of discussions during these last days, you know. He and I. All kinds of things. He even told me the history of Merrymount.'

The story of Merrymount, the history of Thomas Morton: the licentious community, Morton himself bragging about his hedonism in his work, *New English Canaan*, tempting fate and challenging God and man alike. The story was commonly known in the English colonies when Richard Morgan Jones and the rest of that first company came out to establish New Jerusalem, and the contemptuous gaiety and revelry of Merrymount provided a kind of counterpoint to the godliness of the community they were on the verge of creating in the distant forests.

'And he is happy enough for me to argue with him. That is, he lets me say my piece and explain my position. We have argued hotly, you know. Yes. We have disagreed vehemently over the last days. But he continually asks me to come back. To talk to him. Again and again.'

'And so today…'

'Yes, today. Asking me to stay here forever – and more than that, asking me to be Deacon, which means becoming a minister of sorts, doesn't it?'

'It does, Rhisiart Dewi, it does. It means becoming one of the ministers. But you're wrong about one thing. Nothing lasts forever.'

She's looking him in the eye. Rhisiart can't handle her challenging look, and he turns his gaze towards the fire.

'I don't understand why.'

'Doctor Jones sees things differently from other people. And everyone always listens to him.'

'Rhosier Wyn didn't seem happy to listen to him. Not this time. Not in this matter.'

'Perhaps that's true. But others will listen to him.'

'But why? Why me?'

'To take the place of old Edward Jones, the last Deacon?'

'Yes? Why me, rather than one of you?'

'I can't say, Rhisiart Dewi. Only Doctor Jones can answer that question. But it's possible that you are the only one who has demonstrated the virtues he's looking for.'

'How so, when I disagree with him so much?'

'Well, Rhisiart, it's possible that that's the very reason. You are the only one who disagrees with him. And yet he sees goodness in you despite that. Such a quality is necessary in a Deacon. Compassion, good will. The ability to see the other side, even when it's difficult.'

'It's not important anyway. I am not staying here and I am not joining your church.'

'Is it so repugnant to you?'

He looks long into the fire before answering.

'Yes.' He looks her in the eye, searching for the effect of his answer on her, concerned that he has hurt her by acknowledging that that's the way he sees things.

'Alright, Rhisiart – explain, then.' Her voice is quiet and her face open, her eyes demanding honesty, saying that there are no secrets between them.

'Alright, then. This is how I see things… it's as… it…' He pauses, swallows, trying to order his words properly. Then he remembers the book. He remembers the voice that spoke to him through the ink and paper.

'You're not familiar with the books of Morgan Llwyd, are you, Rebecca?'

'No, I'm not.'

'I've mentioned him before, I believe. He was one of the preachers I heard in Wrexham before the first war began.'

'And he wrote books too?'

'Yes. He writes books. Many of them. I have read all I could get my hands on. Even when I was down around Southampton Colonel Powel would sometimes send one to me, knowing that we shared the same pleasure in his writing.'

'Oh?'

'Yes, and there's something he says in one of his books.' He pauses again, to make sure that he's remembering the words, and then he closes his eyes and recites.

'You were born in Hell, and it's there that you want to live. But you do not want to be called by the name of your country, nor to be judged by your works.'

'Those are fierce words, Rhisiart Dewi. Harsh words.'

'They are. He says that man's deeds and actions can originate in Hell even though he may not recognize that. He says that there are men who believe that they are godly, when in truth they are diabolical.'

'He does? And that's what you think about us? About our church here, in New Jerusalem?'

'Not exactly, Rebecca. Not entirely. That is, you and your church are no different from all the saints I have been struggling against through the years. You are no different from what I was doing… how I was living for some time. The doctrines of your church are more consistent, possibly, and more… harsh, to use your word… but you are not fundamentally different as a community.'

Her eyes are questioning and she nods at him as if she's saying: go on, go on and finish what you have begun. Go on.

'I have believed, Rebecca. I have lived. I have *done*. I have been a soldier fighting in support of my captains, and those captains were my ministers. I threw myself into all the work of the Army of the Saints. I believed it all. But the work that was done by me was work born in Hell, and there in Hell was where I wanted to live the whole time I was striving to do that work. An army of Hell is what it was, and I committed myself passionately to the work of that army. It took years for me to assign the right name to that realm and to judge my own labours correctly. And having understood that, I could never consider joining any church that believes that it is the True Church on earth.'

He pauses and looks at her before beginning to speak again, his words falling from his tongue slowly and heavily.

'Soldiers like me believed that the Army of the Saints was a church, gathered together in the work of the Lord, you see. A true church… gathered together… doing the work of the Lord… in Wales… in England… and in Ireland.'

And then he tells her.

He speaks slowly, relating the whole history, finally putting into words things he has never told anyone. He talks about the campaign in Ireland, describing the streets of Drogheda and the shores of Wexford. He relates every single detail he can remember.

And then he tells another story. He looks her straight in the eye and tells her about the women of Naseby.

The Women of Naseby

First of all, he says, there are many things about war that are strange. One of those things is the way the history takes shape. It's not like the writing of history, like reading about the kings of the Old Testament chapter by chapter. Living through it is different. It's confusion, it's untidy. The ordinary soldier witnesses some things – some chapters, those he's living through, those he's playing a small part in – but he knows nothing about other incidents until later, and then he's dependent on gossip and rumour. Sometimes he gets bits of the recent history in pamphlets from the English presses, but he can't rely on things like that, since they are nothing more than the product of gossip and rumours. And so Rhisiart saw much, witnessed much, took part in a movement or a battle or a siege. But he heard very much more, and what he heard was often a hotchpotch of gossip and rumours and the sanitized homilies of itinerant preachers.

He had heard about the course of the wars in his homeland, though he had not visited Wales himself for some time. He had heard about the fire in Wrexham in 1643, one out of every four houses in ashes. He had heard about the death of kinsmen, people he had known in his youth. Familiar names, Welsh names. His fellow countrymen, one after another cut down in the wars – most of them Royalists, enemies of the true faith. His fellow countrymen. He had heard about these things.

He had also heard about the women of Naseby.

Quiet whispers. Dreadful stories. Tales that were told by one soldier to another in the camp at night. It was only a rumour at first. Comrades whispering quietly after the battle. He didn't understand the story, it didn't make sense. He was sure he had not heard correctly. And he was cowardly, too cowardly to ask, to search out those who claimed they knew something about it and ask for more details. Better not to. Better not to learn the facts that might give substance to the terrible rumours.

And then he would hear another rumour.

And then another.

And then the news was brought by travellers, those who had been visiting Wales, carrying the story like a package, unwrapping the parcel carefully and exposing the terrible contents. Other Welshmen, who had been visiting the Old Country, hearing the story directly from some of the families, those who supported the King. The tales corresponding, the rumours turning into facts.

Rhisiart himself had been on the field at Naseby, yes; but he did not see that part of the battle.

He was in the middle of the attack, where their horses were striking live bodies. The Church of God was calling on them to protect and support that freedom and that Gospel which Divine Providence had given them, and their swords were not to spare the enemies of God and their Religion, those who took the side of the Antichrist. The rush of the red horse. They had been hiding, shooting, choosing their targets carefully, before fetching their horses and galloping out of that hiding place. Hundreds upon hundreds of them on horseback. Colonel Okey and Colonel Powel's dragoons, rushing upon the ranks of the enemy infantry. He knew that there were Welshmen there somewhere, having come to Naseby in the King's army. Rhys Thomas' Regiment of Foot. Sir John Owen's men. His fellow countrymen. Kinsmen. Friends from earlier times. There were plenty of Welshmen fighting on the side of the enemy at Naseby, but mercifully they were not in the same part of the field when Parliament's dragoons rushed from their hiding place behind the trees. The frenetic charge, horses galloping wildly over the uneven ground, and then the fighting, the sounds of metal and flesh meeting, shots, terrified whinnying and diabolical screaming all whirling together in the Babel of battle, deafening him. Rhisiart right in the middle of it, in the midst of the enemy foot-soldiers, his horse turning and turning again, the Royalists trying hopelessly and aimlessly to flee, like chickens with a fox among them. His arm working hard, swinging up and swinging down, up and down, his sword resounding sharply, the blade finding arms, finding necks, finding head after head after head. And then his horse stumbled, lurched to the side, and went down, Rhisiart too falling to the ground. That was all he saw of the battle at Naseby.

He did not see the final actions of the battle. Did not witness that horrific ending.

The Royalist ranks had been broken, and their soldiers were in flight. Parliament's vanguard galloped after them, Cromwell's own cavalry eager to crush the enemy to the end. On they went, on and on, racing from the field and reaching the Royalist camp, chasing after spoil: wagons, tents and packs, the mobile supplies. And there, in the middle of the camp, washing clothes and cooking food, were the women. Camp followers, women of doubtful morals who travelled along behind the army of the King, servants of the soldiers who had taken the side of the Antichrist. Camp followers. Whores who serviced the enemy.

They were Irishwomen, or so Rhisiart heard at first. Of course. Irishwomen. Weren't the papist Irish supporting the King? Weren't the corrupt powers of the Pope battling against them, here on English soil?

They were wild women, wielding knives, threatening to castrate them, trying to kill them. And screaming at Parliament's soldiers in a foreign language, a corrupt language. Irish. The language of a barbaric people.

And Cromwell's soldiers, the vanguard of the Saints, were in the heat of battle and grabbing victory for themselves. These were papists, those who had taken the side of the Antichrist. Irish. And anyway, they were whores. Camp followers. Unclean sinners. And there they were, inhuman creatures, shouting at soldiers of the Saints in a barbaric tongue. And they were armed, refusing to surrender, threatening them with their knives.

About a hundred of them.

They were no different from the enemy soldiers, the forces of the Antichrist.

And so they were slain. Yes, Cromwell's soldiers rushed upon them, the Army of the Saints doing the work that they had taken the field to do. Swords rang out, raining down slaughter, killing nearly a hundred of the women there, the camp followers. But mercy was shown too. Those who tried to flee were seized, those who had not tried to resist with knives in their hands. Mercy was shown to them: their faces were mutilated, leaving scars to show that they were sinners – unclean whores – but letting them live, a few of them.

But they weren't whores. He doesn't believe it makes any difference, no difference at all now, but that's the truth of it. They were not whores.

They were women, married women following their husbands to the war, to cook and wash for them. To try to maintain some semblance of family life, far from home and in a time of war. An occasional lover possibly – someone betrothed, compelled to follow her soon-to-be bridegroom to the war before having chance to get to the church. And perhaps a daughter following her father, her mother staying at home to tend to younger brothers and sisters, the eldest daughter travelling with the army wagons, living in the camp with other girls and women. Keeping up the appearance of family life, cooking and washing, participating in Sunday service and singing at night.

They weren't Irish either. He doesn't think it makes any difference now – he sees no difference between a life and a life. But they weren't Irish. They were Welsh.

Welsh women and girls, having followed their husbands and their lovers and their fathers. Having followed the men led by Rhys Thomas and Sir John Owen. Women of the camp of the King's Welsh forces, having travelled far from Wales, having followed their men all the way to the field at Naseby. And there they were, the Welsh women, busy cooking for their men, knives in their hands, cutting meat or chopping onions, raising their heads every now and then to listen to the sounds of the battle in the distance, talking among themselves, trying to imagine what was happening. And the sounds coming closer and closer; and before they knew it, the Parliamentarian cavalry was on top of them, rushing through the camp. Some stood, screaming, knife in hand. Others cursing, probably, threatening God's vengeance on the devils racing towards them. But most of them were praying, calling on the invaders to have mercy, begging the soldiers to show mercy towards them. Mercy. Screaming and praying and begging in Welsh.

Rhisiart says that he has often spent a dark hour questioning himself, searching the bottom of his heart, asking what he would have done if he were English and convinced that the women were Irish. Would he have stopped and sheathed his sword if he thought they were papists, sinners, unclean foreigners having come to England to take the side of the Antichrist? After all, he went to Ireland. He was on the streets of Drogheda and saw the debris of war on the shores at Wexford. He didn't kill any woman or any child, did not hang any priest or nun. But he knew that many of his fellow soldiers had. Soldiers who talked with him at night, ate with him, prayed with him. Brothers, soldiers in the same army, and that army a True Church assembled to do the good work of God on this earth. What would he have done, in his youth, in the fiery grip of his faith, in the madness of battle? What?

He says he spent long hours imagining the lives of the women of Naseby. Each of them having made the difficult decision to leave home, because she couldn't face letting her man go off to war without something of the comfort of his family. A lover who could not bear her betrothed leaving, terrified that he would be killed on the battlefield before their marriage, without her having the opportunity to spend just a little more time with him. The eldest daughter, sixteen or seventeen years old, telling her mother, no, you stay at home with the other children. Saying, yes, I know my own mind: I will go, I will go with father and follow the war. Girls and women with names like Lowri, Sioned and Gwen. Names like Elisabeth and Alys. Travelling many miles, but finding a way to enjoy camp life, forming a new community, a Welsh-speaking society that travelled from place to place, following the army. Taking pride in their own strength, taking pride in the work they did to support their men. Playing their part in the war to bring down the evil rebels, those who had risen up against their rightful, anointed King and the Church, the only true Church. Praying together in Welsh each morning and singing together in Welsh at night. Enjoying whatever time they could snatch in the company of their husband or beloved or father. Enjoying the friendship and goodwill of the travelling community they had created. Travelling from place to place, following the King's army. And the road bringing them in the end to the edges of the field at Naseby.

–5–

End of February 1657

The heat of the fire and the ringing of the hammer on the anvil: he can lose himself in this present.

He likes feeling the sweat on his body and the slight pain in his muscles: the fruit of his work, as much as the tools he's forming, after hard hours of good, honest labour. He's a creator, one who brings new things into the world. The hissing of the hot iron in the water is a voice, one that foretells the coming, a cry between pleasure and pain that bears witness to the birth. Here he is creating.

He enjoys the company too; working together, taking pride in each other, the friendly competition; the flames of the fire reflecting on the bald head of Griffith John Griffith, and Ifan always ready with his praise and his admiration. The two men are discussing shoeing, describing the craft to Ifan, the way the iron becomes one with the living horse.

Not one of them can remain idle; there's more than enough work for the three smiths. Many tools that have become badly broken and need to be repaired before receiving a new edge. Two shovels and three axes have broken completely: there's no choice but to melt down the iron and create new tools. Form, beat and create.

When Rhisiart feels frustration piling up inside him, when he realizes that his mind is wandering into the bog of his confusion, he picks up his hammer and beats it all out of him, folding the questions that gather silently on his tongue into the hot iron. He's forming, he's creating; he's losing himself in the heat of the forge and this present.

* * *

There's a peculiar feeling inside him. He has woken with it every morning and goes to sleep in the grip of that feeling every night. He succeeded in crossing a bridge and closing a gap, yes, and the nature of his life here has been different since then. He's still waiting, waiting to get answers and explanation, but the nature of the waiting is different.

He has laid bare all of his history to Rebecca, the single room in her small house a place of communion that none but those two share. When they're sitting in front of the fire, the door closed against the long night of winter, he tells it all to her. Every bit of his history. Past beliefs. Shattered dreams. Wounds that maim the soul. Guilt. He describes the paths of one who chose to lose himself in his work and trample the garden underfoot rather than open his eyes and walk in the light of day.

He becomes introspective, mingling his explanations and his confession with questions that arise as he voices them.

When did my journey begin?

Was it when the ship sank during the tempest, dragging its burden of living souls down to the deep, and I alone escaping, reaching these desolate shores with the breath of life in me?

Was it when I agreed to go on that voyage, accepting a commission even though I knew that it was folly? Folly that I wouldn't come back from whole except by accident, like the one moth in a hundred which makes it through the candle flame.

One in a hundred, the rest burnt to ashes, a sacrifice to the foolishness that drove them into the flame.

Or did all my troubles begin the moment I came into this afflicted world?

For her part, Rebecca says that she's also going to reveal everything to him. They have crossed a bridge and closed a gap, and there is nothing but trust between them. She promises that she will tell it all, explain the depth of her concern and the basis of her fears. But he has to wait: she's praying for strength and waiting for the right time to come. She knows it will. She promises. She will tell him, will tell him before the baby comes into the world. But not yet. Not yet.

Richard Morgan Jones has been very ill for many days. He sleeps most of the time, according to what Rhisiart hears from Catherin Huws. He certainly does not have enough strength to talk. He hears Joshua, the oldest of the Mansel children, asking Jeremiah Huws. Yes, it's true, answers the Minister's son. My mother says it's so. The Doctor is dying.

Rhisiart goes to listen to Pyrs Huws in the house of worship regularly. He sits on one of the back benches, the bodies of close to sixty people warming the large room. Although the sermon is different each time, familiar words punctuate all of them.

Preordination.

Election.

Rejection.

True judgement, faultless judgement.

The elect and the damned, some born to life and others to death.

The voice of Pyrs Huws echoes, his scarecrow body moving in the pulpit above the candles, throwing a web of shadows that dance on the wall behind him.

And the same pattern after the meeting winds to an end: he turns to help Rebecca rise, as she is far into her pregnancy. He walks her home, leading her carefully along the icy paths, past snowdrifts that lurk everywhere, like huge animals sleeping under white blankets. Then the two sit in front of the fire, Rhisiart asking the same question and she giving the same answer. I will, I promise; but not yet.

Only once has the subject of the office of Deacon been raised. Rhosier Wyn came to fetch him from the smithy, asking him to come to his house. Although Rhisiart had visited Pyrs and Catherin Huws' home and spent many hours in Richard Morgan Jones' room, this was the first time he had ventured across the threshold of the Elder's house. It was exactly like the houses of the other ministers, except that there was less furniture in the main room. Pyrs Huws was there already, waiting for them. There were but two chairs beside the small table, and so Rhosier Wyn sat on a small chest.

'Thanks for coming to us, Rhisiart Dewi.' Pyrs Huws spoke quietly and slowly, weighing each syllable on his tongue, fingers searching for rough bits of red hair on his chin and his cheeks. 'Elder Rhosier Wyn and I have been discussing the Doctor's situation, and I think it's only right to inform you about what we've been considering.'

'That's so, yes, and I confess it openly.' The thin lips of Rhosier Wyn were drawn into a slight scowl, his hands fidgeting awkwardly on the table, as if he were searching for a button or a penny he had lost in the shadows. 'I have to confess, you see, Rhisiart Dewi, that I am not of the same opinion as Pyrs Huws in this matter. I see no advantage at all in bringing you into all of this today. Wait. That's what I want to do. Wait and see.'

'But the Elder has agreed with my request.' Pyrs Huws looked at Rhisiart out of the corner of his eye, as if he was trying to gauge the nature of his response to this important situation. 'The Elder is responsible for church discipline, as you know, and I respect his judgement greatly. But I am a minister too, and my conscience compels me to speak, especially in light of Doctor Jones' illness.'

And so Rhisiart witnessed the disagreement between the two ministers, the Preacher and the Elder, one saying they ought to respect the wishes of the Doctor to make Rhisiart Dewi Deacon and the other saying they ought to reconsider and wait. Pyrs Huws spoke carefully, weighing and measuring each word. But words flowed swiftly from Rhosier Wyn's tongue, the statements and the answers sounding as if he had already thought them through, his voice rising to a high pitch as he repeated them passionately.

'But he's not in his right mind, is he? I'm sorry to have to say that, but it's true. It doesn't pay for us to ignore the plain truth: Doctor Jones is not in his right mind.' His thin lips turned down into a grimace or open into an insincere smile, revealing his small, gapped teeth. 'He's a man gripped by illness, a weak man. He's not in his right mind. We must wait for him to get better. Let us wait, that's the only answer in this quandary. Wait until he gets better. Wait for him to be healthy again. And then ask him what he has in mind.'

'But you know very well, Rhosier Wyn, that he's not likely to get better.' The voice of Pyrs Huws was unusually sharp, his eyes fastened on his fellow minister. 'He's on his deathbed. That's what Catherin says. She says that he's suffering the kind of illness that takes the old from this world. We cannot wait, Rhosier Wyn. We have to decide now. We have to act on the Doctor's wishes before he departs from this life so that everyone in New Jerusalem knows that it is his wish. So that everyone can see that we, the three ministers left, agree on this matter.'

'But we don't agree, Pyrs Huws,' Rhosier Wyn cried shrilly, throwing his hands into the air. 'And I don't believe it's proper for the two of us to share all this with a man who does not intend to remain here in New Jerusalem. It's not right.' He put his hands back on the table, folding them in an attitude of prayer. He smiled at Rhisiart and said more quietly, 'Forgive me, Rhisiart Dewi, I have to speak out. That is what has been given to me, you see. It's not easy shouldering the burden of responsibility, but that's what has been given to me. And I'm thinking of you, too. You've said you do not intend to stay. That's as good as admitting that you yourself do not see any sense in Doctor Jones' request, isn't it? You said, yes, that you do not understand why he has asked such a thing of you? It wouldn't be right to allow you to speak, to have an influence on the decision, would it?'

'But we have to ask him nevertheless, Rhosier Wyn. Out of respect for Doctor Jones. And out of respect for him too, having dragged him into our dilemma like this.' The Preacher looked at Rhisiart, his eyes urgently enquiring. 'What do you say to all of this? Do you believe that Divine Providence has led you to this crossroads among us?'

Rhisiart didn't answer him properly, just murmured a few disconnected words, excusing himself and trying to hide his perplexity. The Doctor's request was so unexpected and so unlikely. Perhaps he agreed with Rhosier Wyn. Why would the leader of their community ask him to join, when he disagreed so openly with him on a number of theological points? Why ask a man who wasn't keen to commune fully with their church to take up the office of Deacon, one of the four ministers, the pillars of their society? Besides, he was bound by a promise. He had come here all the way from London to New Jerusalem at another's request, and he intended to keep that promise. He would have to leave when the spring thaw came. He would have to return. He apologized to the Preacher, feeling a wrench inside himself as he realized that his rejection meant that he was settling the argument in favour of Elder Rhosier Wyn.

'Alright, Rhisiart Dewi,' Pyrs Huws said before he left. 'But I think somehow that your mind and your heart have not turned absolutely in that direction yet. We'll have to wait, then, but I believe that we have not discussed this for the last time.'

But the subject has not been raised again, and Rhisiart has not spoken directly with Pyrs Huws in the meantime, only listened to him preaching.

He has another conversation with Rhosier Wyn. When he is halfway between the smithy and the gates, an axe over his shoulder, going off to cut wood with Ifan, the Elder comes shuffling after him, calling to him.

'Come, Rhisiart Dewi, come. The Doctor is asking for you.'

There is a small group gathered in the main room of the house – Catherin Huws, her husband Pyrs Huws, and Evan Evans, leader of the Militia. The three of them waiting for Rhisiart and Rhosier Wyn.

'Alright, Evan Evans, you can go now,' says Pyrs Huws quietly. 'We don't need your help here any longer.'

Rhisiart stares, watching the man leave, half intending to ask what exactly has brought everyone together in this way, but then Catherin Huws is there beside him, saying, 'Come, come to him straight away,' and leading him through the door to the bedroom.

She stays in the bedroom with the two men after closing the door behind them. She nods to Rhisiart to sit in the empty chair beside the bed, and then goes to stand beside the small fireplace.

'Good day to you, Rhisiart Dewi.' The Doctor's voice is a low rasping in his throat, and every breath comes as if with great effort. 'I am pleased to see you again.'

His hands are still, folded over his chest on top of the blanket, and his red, watery eyes half closed.

'I'm here.' Rhisiart doesn't continue: he is there to listen.

'I hope you haven't forgotten my request, Rhisiart. And I want to say something else to you.'

He falls silent, the effort too much for him. Rhisiart says nothing. He doesn't try to encourage him to speak, just sits there quietly. The old man has closed his eyes, and Rhisiart assumes he is sleeping, the slight motion of his chest under his hands the only sign that he is alive. And then he opens his eyes again and stares unseeing at the ceiling.

'I haven't finished explaining.' He pauses again, fighting for breath. 'We were talking about signs. Do you remember?'

'Yes, I remember.'

'So many of the others are searching for signs.' He closes his eyes again, but his voice comes a little stronger, as if the effort he is making to try to see is helping him to find his breath and the words. 'They're searching for signs, signs that would prove that their church is a true church, that the invisible church has gathered here among us.'

'I remember.'

'I too have searched for signs, Rhisiart. Yes. In Cardiff. In Llanfaches. In places in England. Searching and searching.'

'I know. You've told me. I remember.'

'And have failed. And after my looking… and searching… and failing… came the… understanding… to me. That I had to create that Church myself. Came the realization that I shouldn't search for signs, but for knowledge.'

'Knowledge?'

'Knowledge, Rhisiart Dewi.' He swallows and opens his eyes

again, looking at Rhisiart, though Rhisiart is not certain he can see him.

'Knowing... my knowing... that the truth is in my heart already... if only... I would listen to it. Know it. And act on it.'

The news comes two days later. Rhisiart is in the smithy, vying with Griffith John Griffith and his son, seeing who can make the sharpest nail without breaking the thin strip of iron. Jeremiah Huws and Joshua Mansel arrive, along with some of the younger village children walking the customary respectful distance behind them, going from door to door, sharing the news.

'Doctor Jones has died.'

He lies for two days in his house, in a coffin made by the carpenter Rowland Williams. A number of men and older children are busy during that time shovelling snow, clearing it, readying the path all the way from the gates to the cemetery. Big Owen, the giant of the militia, is opening the grave, using an axe to cut through the hard, frozen ground, other men relieving him when he tires. It is more like hewing rock than digging a hole, one of them says. Hard work, unforgiving. Two shovels and three axes break, and a number of other shovels and axes are blunted or dulled by the work.

There are three sermons on the day of the burial. First, a long sermon in the house of worship; the coffin lying on a bench in front of the pulpit, Pyrs Huws' voice shaking with emotion, tears running down his cheeks into his untidy red beard. Paying tribute to him, the Moses who led them to a distant land, the one who showed them the way, like a father leading his children, teaching them lovingly and tenderly.

And then, when everyone has formed themselves into a procession, Rhosier Wyn and Pyrs Huws stand on the wooden platform that faces the well on the other side of the path. The two ministers, Elder and Preacher, and the third, the Doctor, unseen in his coffin, lying on the platform between them. Pyrs Huws delivers a short sermon, reminding them that this last journey is of no importance, that it all has been settled already, that God through His divine decree has already decided the fate of every man. After that, Rhosier Wyn speaks, reminding the congregation of the faith that brought each one of them to this place in the middle of the dark wilderness of America. Reminding them that thirty-one sailed across, that some have died and others have been born. That some have journeyed from other settlements to join them, increasing the Church, and that all of it began years ago when Richard Morgan Jones decided that there was no hope of establishing a true church in the Old Country.

The crowd forms itself into a procession again, four of the militia carrying the coffin, together with the two ministers. Owen Williams has to bend slightly because he is so tall – taller even than Pyrs Huws – in order to keep the coffin level at all times. On they go, through the open gates, under the south tower, everyone following except the two Englishmen, Benjamin Cotton and David Newton, who are on duty at the time, walking the walls and guarding. The procession proceeds along the path that has been cleared of snow, around the wall in a half circle, to the cemetery. The ground around the grave has been cleared too, so the old people and the frail ones can stand without getting their feet wet. And there at the graveside Pyrs Huws delivers his third sermon of the day: a simple one, not much more than a prayer of thanks. Owen Williams and Evan Evans step forward, shovels in their hands, to move the mound of dirt back into the hole and close the grave forever.

Rhisiart waits in the cemetery, studying the wooden memorials that rise yellow and brown from the white snow. The smaller ones are hidden completely except for narrow strips, like slats of wood lying on the snow, and others, the biggest ones, stand tall, a layer of snow atop each one like a white hat. Rhisiart walks slowly through the snowdrifts, reading the names. Williams. Huws. Edwards. Owen. And then he finds the grave he was searching for. Miles Egerton. The tail end of the procession has disappeared by now, the congregation making its way back to the gates to seek refuge in the warmth of their homes. But one other has stayed behind. A big man who has quietly followed Rhisiart. Owen Williams, standing like a bear beside him in the snow, studying the same piece of wood.

'It's not a day to hide anything, Rhisiart Dewi. Not a day to tell lies.' The man's breath rises as steam in the cold. He is holding a spade in one of his hands. 'I know, you see. I know you are asking. Wanting to know.'

Rhisiart turns slowly, waiting for him to finish. The big man's eyes are staring at the wooden memorial, his voice sounding tired, like one who needs to do one last little task before seeking his bed and getting the sleep he so richly deserves after a long, hard day's work.

'Divine Providence has brought us to his grave today, and I know what is right. I do. It is not a day to tell lies. Evan Evans shot him. It was all a plan, you see. Say that we were going hunting, searching for deer tracks. Easily believed, you know? So easy. Evan called to him. Asked him to turn around. Face his fate. The look on Miles Egerton's face… not understanding. Stunned. And Evan shot him on the spot. It took him a while to die. Lying there in the snow. Middle of winter. A day like today. Not quite as much snow, maybe, but enough. Lying there, the snow red with his blood. The stunned look on his face, his eyes questioning.'

Owen's voice breaks, and he puts his hand to his mouth, coughs, shakes his head slightly and starts talking again.

'Evan wanted me to kill him. Choke him or break his neck. Finish him. But I couldn't. Only stand there, looking at his blood running into the snow, his eyes not believing, his mouth moving but nothing coming out of it. Nothing. He died in the end. There, lying in the snow in the forest.' He turned and looked into Rhisiart's eyes. 'Some people know. Probably quite a few. I have seen it in their eyes. The truth. They know. The Englishman had been troublesome, you see. That was no secret. He was the subject of talk. Everyone asking, what shall we do with him? Everyone enquiring, what will happen? Does he have influence there on the coast? In Strawberry Bank? In Salem? In Boston? Will they listen to him when he leaves and says that there is a blight on the people of New Jerusalem? Will he heap abuse on us? Censure us? Will he give us a bad name? These questions were on everyone's lips, Rhisiart Dewi. You have to believe that. Everyone was worried, though no one discussed it openly.'

'Thank you, Owen. Thank you for your honesty. Can I ask you one other question?'

'Yes. I have nothing to hide today. It's not a day to tell lies.'

'Good. Can I ask then… whose idea was it to kill Miles Egerton? Evan Evans'?'

'No. It was the Elder's idea. He is responsible for church discipline, you see. Evan Evans listens to him.'

'And you listen to Evan Evans.'

'That's how it is.'

Rhisiart understands: a soldier doing his duty, one who is serving God's Church.

Another question lurks on the tip of his tongue: Owen Williams, did they ask you to kill me? Is that why you are here now? But he examines the face of the big man carefully and sees no sign of danger there. Not today, he thinks.

The two walk back along the path around the wall to the gates, Rhisiart making sure that the big man is always a step or two in front of him, just in case.

* * *

He's enjoying the warmth of the fire and the weight of the hammer in his hand, the striking and ringing on the anvil – sweet music to his ears. He can't walk around on pins and needles every minute of every day, can't live in fear. He has to regroup and forget for a while, clear his mind, and so he's losing himself in this reassuring work. He works in a familiar way, moving like that young apprentice in Edward Wiliam's smithy in Wrexham. He's a creator, someone who's shaping the world.

And when a concern assails him, like a pressure rising from his belly to his throat, he focuses harder on the work. He pounds that frustration and his questions and his fears into the hot iron. He knows things cannot go on for long like this, but for the time being he loses himself in the warmth of the forge and the work before him.

–6–

Middle of March 1657

The big thaw comes. The ice that has been growing into crystal daggers on the eaves of the houses falls piece by piece as it warms, each one falling with a sharp crack and crash, and the snow that has been gathering in heavy blankets on the roofs slides to a wet end in the slush on the ground. Mud is underfoot everywhere within the walls, apart from the few shady spots beside the walls where those snowdrifts that are left lie hidden, the once-white snow now showing the filth of winter's long months. A season of thaw – a dirty season, an untidy season.

Many of the men and youths are already busy turning the soil, preparing for the planting that will come soon. It can freeze again, they all say, and snow could come as late as the middle of April, but we have to do this hard work now. The day of planting will come before long, and we have to turn the earth and wake the land.

One day, Joshua Mansel runs back through the gates, out of breath. There are Indians in the woods, there are! Huw Jones had left the field and wandered into the shadows of the trees to urinate. And that's where he saw the Indians. No, not the Wampanoag. Wild ones, faces painted red. Three or four. Yes, there on the edges of the fields. Why have the watchmen on the walls not seen them? Don't know; there they are, hiding in the shadows of the trees. There was excitement, action, men mustering and searching the area, and then discussion, but the natives have vanished by the time a company of armed men reaches the place.

This is the only excitement, the only event that interrupts the routine as winter slowly yields its last territory to the spring, and the earth is prepared to receive seed in the sowing season.

* * *

She thanks him for coming. Thanks him for the fresh water and the firewood. The days are lengthening, and so it's not dark when he arrives at her doorstep now. It's a lovely evening, sweet smells in the air, the breeze a foretaste of May. He would like to go for a walk through the fields and under the trees, make the most of this lovely day. It might get cold again tomorrow; it's possible that they won't have another day like this for a month or two. But Rebecca is heavy with child, so it's out of the question.

And so they are here again, sitting with each other in front of the fire, as always.

'The time has come, Rhisiart.'

He looks at her, alarmed, trying to uncover the meaning of her words. Is she saying that the baby is on the way tonight? Should he go and ask for help from Catherin Huws and some of the other women?

'It's time for me to say… to keep my promise to you.'

She breathes deeply and leans back a bit in her chair, stretching her feet closer to the fire. She puts her hands on her swollen belly, her fingers knitted together.

'I told you I would tell you before the baby arrives. And I woke this morning knowing that I had to keep that promise. I woke today knowing that today would be the day.'

The day of the thaw and of the revelation.

And she clarifies it all, explaining very precisely what happens when one of New Jerusalem's women gives birth.

When the newborn is about a month old, they hold a special

prayer service. Not in the house of worship, but on the wooden platform, in the open air. There's a sermon on the same text every time, summarizing the beliefs they cannot deny, and the other ministers say a word, explaining the custom they have gathered together to observe that day. All of it deeply rooted in the basic doctrines.

Some are born to eternal life and others to death and damnation.

God has already decided every single person's fate.

Not everybody is created equal; some have been preordained to eternal life and others to eternal damnation. Some are elected and others are rejected, all of it determined before birth. Some are born to life and others to death. All this we know, the members of the True Church of New Jerusalem know all of this.

Rowland Williams the carpenter prepares the house of worship a day ahead of time. He brings three long ladders that he keeps at his house and fetches the long ladder from the smithy. He brings other pieces of wood, pieces that are kept safe from year to year, and fixes them in the proper place on the roof. And there it is, to be seen from afar, like a wooden chimney stack atop the house of worship: the scales.

And then everyone walks slowly from the platform to the bottom of the ladders, the mother holding her baby, and the ministers leading the procession. The four ministers climb the four ladders, the baby wrapped in a blanket and bound safely to the bosom of one of them. Upon reaching the top of the roof, they unwrap the baby and place it on the scales.

And they pray, the ministers at the top of the ladders and the congregation down on the ground. They ask God to reveal His judgement, that which He decided beforehand, that which He decided in his own long eternal time before the birth of that child.

And then the scales will tip. Sometimes immediately, after the ministers take their hands from the baby and the scales. At other times it takes a while, everyone praying fervently, their tears choking their words. But sooner or later, they tip. The scales tip and the baby falls, one way or the other.

It falls back into the arms of the ministers: a baby born to life, God having shown that this child is amongst the elect.

Or it falls the other way, down the other side of the roof: rejected, one who was born to death.

The True Church, the Invisible Church, in perfect union with this earthly church. No need to search for signs to try to see who is amongst the elect. They take comfort in that knowledge, the knowledge that God has chosen and so has revealed his judgement to His elect, if only they ask in prayer. If only they know this truth, accept it and act on it. It's a perfect church, pure, each one having been born to eternal life. Those who came originally were shown to be so by Divine Providence, and those born after are shown for what they are in this way. Such a church is entirely righteous, for it knows that it is here to do the good work of God on earth.

The room is getting cold and the darkness of midnight is a curtain across their eyes. He has not risen to put wood on the fire, hasn't moved. He has sat here, motionless, finding it difficult to breathe as he weighs what he is hearing, Rebecca's voice speaking softly but clearly beside him, explaining it all. And so the fire has died right down, the last few flames surrendering to the ashes.

Rhisiart can see only a shadow in the chair next to him. She has fallen silent, finished her account and is resting for a moment before he finds his tongue. His mouth is dry and it feels like an enormous effort to speak.

'How many… how many… of them…?' The last little piece of wood has fallen as mere embers into the ash, making a sound like air leaving an old man's lungs, the sound of a last breath. 'How many… children have died like that? On the roof?'

'Not one yet. Every one has fallen back from the scales into the arms of the minister. Every one since the beginning.'

'When was that? The beginning? When you first came here?'

'A year after setting the foundations. A year after building the walls of New Jerusalem. The truth had been revealed to Doctor Jones, that's what he said. He had seen that every one of us had been born to be a member of the true church of the elect. But he knew at the same time that it would be necessary to examine the newcomers in order to see whether they too were among the elect. As you know, some other Welshmen came, those from the second boat. Some others came up from Salem or Plymouth or Boston. And sometimes English people. Ben Cotton and David Newton were the last to come here and be accepted. The ministers pray, they examine, and the truth is revealed to them. That's what they say.'

'Who was the last to be rejected in this manner?'

'Can't you see that?'

'Miles Egerton.'

'Yes, he was the last. Only those who stay are examined. It's not the same with those who come to visit for a while, like the Praying Indians who come twice a year.'

No one outside New Jerusalem knows the extent of their faith and the strength of their commitment to the doctrines.

'And the children who are born here are… examined in a different way.'

'On the scales.'

'The scales…'

'Yes.'

'And none has fallen yet? And so been killed?'

'No. None has ever died. Richard Bach, son of John Williams, grandson of Rowland Williams the carpenter, was the last, and he's now three years old. Old Edward Jones was too weak to climb the ladder. Evan Evans had to go up in his place.'

'Edward Jones the Deacon?'

'That's him. He died shortly after that.'

Rhisiart stands then, looking for some small woodchips and larger pieces to rekindle the fire from the embers. Rebecca waits for him to finish and sit down again before she continues. 'Richard Bach was the last. Three years ago. Dorcas Mansel before that. She's four. And before Dorcas, her sister Tabitha. About five years ago.'

'And every single baby has fallen the right way?'

'Yes, every one. Fallen back into their arms. Fallen into life.'

She makes an effort to stand, and Rhisiart rises to help her. She takes his hands in hers, her palm hot and sweaty.

'We have to go, Rhisiart. Before that day. You have to go with us, with me and the baby. I don't want to… to face it, especially now. Without Doctor Jones. Without Deacon Edward Jones. Who will be doing it? I could not put my baby into Rhosier Wyn's hands. I couldn't. I've lost faith in all of it.'

He stands there for a while, trying to get her to sit down again, but she is too upset.

She's still standing, tightening her grip on his hands, imploring him. Rhisiart says he can't see the way ahead clearly or easily. The journey is difficult, even for a man; he can't imagine taking her and a tiny newborn baby. The rivers and streams will be swollen with water from the thaw, and the snow could return, they say, as late as the middle of April. Would the Wampanoag be coming, the Christian Indians who come every spring? Would they come before the birth of the baby, before the day? They could go with them. It would be safer, be a help on the journey.

But no one can say. It depends on the weather, on the rivers, on the ice and snow in the mountains. It depends on the progress of the thaw. No one can say when the first visit of the Wampanoag will be.

'What shall we do, Rhisiart? What shall I do?'

'Wait for a while, Rebecca. There's no choice tonight but to wait. I'll have to think of something. And I will think of something. Take comfort in that.'

* * *

He tries to walk back quietly, but the ground is wet and the mud squelches noisily under his feet. It's a dark, moonless night and the shadows cast by the wall are long, and darker than the night itself. He walks quickly past Hannah Siôn's house, working his way through that area between the houses on the circle road and the wall, the space where there is but an occasional house set here and there, outside the usual order of the plan.

It has got cold but the smells of spring are in the air. The smell of earth newly turned. The smell of buds and blossoms. The smell of food.

He hears some kind of sound, quite quiet but fairly far away.

There, between the houses: someone walking along the circle road. Yes, there it is: the sound of footsteps. He's standing still so he can peer into the shadows: yes, the shape of a man there, walking. Only for a moment, and then he moves out of view behind one of the houses.

Another few minutes and Rhisiart is in the storehouse, getting ready to spread his blanket on the hard wooden floor and prepare for the struggle to come, knowing that it won't be easy for him to steal a bit of sleep before dawn. But a moment after lying down he's sitting up again. He looks around the room. Stares at the few things he owns.

They're gone. When? Does he remember seeing them today,

this morning? Does he remember seeing them yesterday? When was the last time he noticed? When? But they are gone – his weapons. His musket and his sword. Someone has taken them.

–7–

End of April 1657

He wakes to the singing of the birds: a chorus of flutes flitting and chirping, musical instruments of the forest announcing that another spring morning has arrived.

He stands and stretches, shaking the bonds of sleep from his limbs and massaging his right shoulder, which he has been lying on for too long on the hard floor. He relieves himself in the chamber pot in the corner of the room. He eats the piece of dry bread left for him last night and drinks fresh water from the bucket. Puts on his breeches, boots and stockings.

And then he begins to walk. This is his morning routine, pacing back and forth across the small room, walking from wall to wall in eight steps and then turning and walking back. Eight steps and he's facing the wall, eight more steps and he's facing another wall, next to the little fireplace. Back and forth, back and forth. One of the mysteries of the senses: this room looks smaller now that it's empty. Although the goods that used to fill most of the little storehouse left less room for him to move between the chests and the casks, all those contents gave meaning to the room. It was full, and that fact made the room seem bigger. That it could contain so much. But this empty room, the only room in this small building, is small. And he paces back and forth, measuring and remeasuring this smallness.

* * *

He had considered fleeing. Leaving. What other choice did he have? Leaving with Rebecca, going right then. But she could not travel. It was difficult for her to walk from her house to the house of worship; she would not be able to go far past the gates. Waiting was the only choice – stay, and wait till he could come up with a plan. It would not be easy travelling afterwards, even after the baby came. The rivers would be flooding and the paths slippery, and the unsettled weather liable to turn in the blink of an eye. But the iron fist of fear had taken a tight hold around his heart, preventing him from calming down and thinking properly. And so he had been considering fleeing, however impossible and hopeless it was.

He walked in the shadows in those days, knowing that eyes were always watching him. Rhosier Wyn's. Evan Evans' too, when he was not walking the walls. He believed he saw a different kind of look in Pyrs Huws' eyes at times. A wondering look. A question. Rhisiart couldn't concentrate on his work. He was not able to hammer his fears into the hot iron, and Griffith John Griffith and his son Ifan noticed that Rhisiart's heart was not in the smithy. The axe turned in his hands once when he was chopping wood; it sprang from the tree at an angle, missing his leg by a hair. He felt weak, as if all his body's energy was being sapped by his thoughts, those thoughts turning in endless circles, completely failing to find answers.

He tried to talk to Griffith John Griffith and Ifan. Tried to explain that he knows all the secrets without fearing them, without setting them against him. The smith pulled the iron from the fire and handed it to his son.

'Ifan, take a walk after you douse that. Take a walk to the cemetery and decide if it's time to make a new memorial for your mother's grave.'

After the youth left the smithy, Griffith John Griffith stood there, wiping his bald head with a cloth.

'There you are, Rhisiart. It's difficult to keep secrets within the walls of New Jerusalem. Alright, then. What will you do now? Remain with us? Join the church? Or go back across the sea to your Colonel Powel? There's enough work here for another smith. We need two strong hands here, remember. You've settled in here. You have friends here.'

'But how could I remain here, knowing what I know?'

'You think I'm a halfwit, not so smart, do you, Rhisiart Dewi? Standing here, talking like I've been talking since you came to the smithy the first time. Asking you to consider staying, saying you ought to become a member of the church and make New Jerusalem your home. Your stand there looking at me, thinking I'm a halfwit, going on like this, and you knowing what you know. All the secrets of New Jerusalem.'

'No, I don't, Griffith… I don't think you're a –'

'You do. But I don't believe you understand fully. They are not secrets, you see. That's the thing. They're not. It's only that we have to be vigilant, keep them from people on the outside. Before understanding their nature… before understanding their hearts. But they are not secrets. It's all based firmly on the teachings. It goes back to the doctrines of Calvin, that's what the Doctor said, and the doctrines, the teachings of Calvin, are based firmly on the Word of God.'

'They are not, Griffith. They are not. They are inventions… ideas shaped and created by men. Things that have been created by men. Like the iron we work with here in your smithy. Things created by men for men's purposes. That's what they are. Nothing more. Calvin was a man. His teachings are the creations of a man. And Richard Morgan Jones was a man.'

'But I am a member of this church, Rhisiart Dewi. You don't understand. I have been living my life according to the doctrines since before I came here. Ever since I first heard Doctor Jones preaching in Wales.'

'He was Richard Morgan Jones at that time. Before he made himself Doctor.'

'Don't say anything bad about him. You have no right to question things you don't fully understand. You're not a member of our church. You don't understand.'

'But I do understand, Griffith. I understand how it is to be a member of a church and believe that that church is the one right one, one that has been assembled to do the work of the Lord on this earth. I understand that.'

The smith stood there before him, taking the wet cloth and wringing it out, staring at Rhisiart, studying him, as if he were trying to wring meaning from him.

'Listen, Griffith... I do understand... I have lived... have believed. I lived and worked in a smithy like this one. Happy years, as I learned to do good, honest work with my two hands. During those years my heart was opened. Imagine, Griffith, me an apprentice to a smith, and hearing Walter Cradoc preaching for the first time. Feeling my heart open, feeling that I understood the truth of the Word fully for the first time in my life, even though I'd been raised in a godly family.'

'I saw Walter Cradoc in Llanfaches.' The small eyes of the smith are still on him, his voice reflective. 'A number of us had gone there, you see.'

'I know, Griffith. Richard Morgan Jones told me everything.'

'But Doctor Jones didn't find that church appropriate. He saw that we had to create our own church.'

'But you heard Walter Cradoc preaching. It couldn't have been so different from Doctor Jones at that time. You must have heard the same voice I heard. We have lived very similar lives in one sense, Griffith. I understand what's in your heart. Believe me.'

'How can you understand, Rhisiart Dewi? I was here with the first company. I helped set the foundations of New Jerusalem... building the walls with the strength in my arms. The three of us came here. Ifan was a small child at the time. Sarah, my wife, Ifan's mother, died here. She's buried here, in New Jerusalem's cemetery. You don't belong to this place, Rhisiart Dewi. It's not easy for you to understand.'

'But I do understand, Griffith, I do.' Rhisart took a step nearer the smith, looked him in the eye, swallowed before speaking again. 'I too am a widower. My wife is buried in a grave on the outskirts of London. And our child with her. In a grave whose location I do not know. I was away. I was not with her... at the time. I was away... in the army... serving.'

'I'm sorry to hear that, Rhisiart Dewi, but... it doesn't change a thing. You don't belong to this place. You don't understand.'

Rhisiart had to turn away from him, had to move. He paced around the smithy like a cat in a cage. He moved around as if he was searching for answers. He took the hammer from the anvil and hefted it in his restive hands. Then he stopped and turned back to the smith, holding the hammer tightly to his chest like a parent embracing a baby.

'Alright, Griffith. But you have to understand one thing: Doctor Jones himself believed that I belong to this place. He asked me to stay and join your church. And more than that, he asked me to become Deacon.'

'A minister?' He stepped closer to Rhisiart, putting the hand that held the wet cloth out and resting it on the anvil.

'Yes, one of the ministers. One of the four ministers... the Deacon.'

The two men stood like that for a good while, one's eyes searching the other's, and Rhisiart thinking: he's always saying that his sight is going; what does he see in my eyes now? Does he see my soul there? Then he spoke again.

'You know better than I what the office of Deacon is.'

'Yes, I do know.'

'Tell me then.'

'The Deacon is the paragon of Christian charity.'

'Yes, that's what I learned when I first came here. That's what Elder Rhosier Wyn told me during my first days here. The Doctor protects the purity of beliefs and the consistency of doctrine. Then Pyrs Huws, the Preacher, the Minister, is responsible for holding the regular services. The Elder is responsible for church discipline. And the Deacon is the model of Christian benevolence.'

'That's right. But we haven't had a Deacon since old Edward Jones died.'

'But Doctor Jones asked me to become Deacon. It didn't make sense to me at the time. I'll be honest with you, Griffith. I had argued with him. Richard Morgan Jones. All the hours I spent in his company. Listening to him, discussing, but arguing. But he asked me to come back. Again and again, asking me to come back, and listening to my arguments… my doubts. I couldn't understand it, asking me… not only to join your church, but helping to lead it. And besides that, he had heard some of my history which must work against that idea. Knew that I had been a soldier. Knew that I was one who had ignored the commandment, "Thou shalt not kill".'

'As part of your work, serving. In the Army of the Saints.'

'That's what I thought. But the commandment is still the same, isn't it? Thou shalt not kill. I wasn't a man who was accustomed to showing mercy. I was not, if anything… a paragon of Christian charity. So why choose me? Why ask me, of all people, to be Deacon? I couldn't understand his request… I couldn't make head or tail of his offer, for many reasons. But I think I understand his intention now.'

'Do you?'

'I do. He knew that I… had lived the life… had *believed*… had *done*. And he knew that I now doubt many of the things I used to believe in. And he saw value in that.' Rhisiart reached out and put the hammer carefully on the anvil, next to Griffith John Griffith's hand. 'And I now believe that he wanted someone here who would be able to change things. Someone like me.'

The smith looked long at him before turning and beginning to tend to the fire. Rhisiart spoke to his back.

'I'm not lying, Griffith. You know that. You know me. I am not a man who tells lies.' He turned to leave, but stopped. 'Ask Minister Pyrs Huws. Ask the Preacher. He knows. Ask him.'

But the smith did not turn to him, and Rhisiart didn't know if his words had reached him.

Days and nights passed. Rhisiart continued trying to comfort, to reassure Rebecca, promising that he would come up with a plan, saying that he would have the answers when the time came. He knew that someone had been shadowing him at night, when he walked back to the storehouse from Rebecca's house, just as he knew that there were eyes on him every minute of the day.

And then one day, Rhosier Wyn and some of the village men came and said they were going to move the goods from the storehouse. Two of the large houses for the ministers were now empty; it had been decided to empty out the storehouse for Rhisiart. Griffith John Griffith and Ifan came to help, and Rhisiart worked at it too, moving all the goods, chest by chest, cask by cask, basket by basket.

'There's nothing we need more here,' exclaimed the big smith after putting down a heavy cask on the floor of the Deacon's house. 'Horses. That's what's needed. We have to prepare the land without horses, have to plough without horses, and have to move our heavy burdens without horses.'

He gave Rhisiart a friendly slap on the back with his strong hand. 'And I long sometimes for the horseshoe, Rhisiart Dewi. I do, I long for it. The only thing I haven't made in the smithy since I came here. A horseshoe.'

He continued to talk about shoeing horses all the way back to the storehouse, laughing quietly under his breath and teasing Rhisiart. 'I could still bend a shoe better than you, I'm sure, even if I haven't made one for years.'

He stopped laughing when they reached the storehouse. Rhosier Wyn was there awaiting them, standing in front of a row of armed men. Four of the militia – the giant Owen Williams, Huw Jones, David Newton, and Evan Evans leading them. A sword hanging from the belt of each one and muskets in their hands. And there beside them, some of the other village men. Rhisiart knew the names of every one of them. Rowland Williams the carpenter, his son John – a man who never missed the chance to volunteer – and the carpenter's son-in-law, David. Tomos Mansel was there too. Although John Williams had armed himself like men of the militia, the others were holding everyday work implements – pitchfork, axe and hammer.

Rhisiart took a step back, his eyes scanning all the faces, looking at the weapons.

'It has been decided, Rhisiart Dewi.' Rhosier Wyn, his voice shrill, his arms flailing in the air, the only one of the group not holding a weapon of any kind. 'You have been sentenced to prison, until we can find out the truth of the affairs that are before us.'

Rhisiart then remembered that he was not alone – that he had friends – and he turned to seek help from them. And there they stood, Griffith John Griffith and his son, Ifan.

'I'm sorry, Rhisiart Dewi.' The big smith shifted his weight from one foot to the other, his hands hanging at his sides, his fingers restive. 'I'm truly sorry, but if it's been decided, there's nothing for it but to wait and see. Best to submit, and accept the law.' He raised his hands and his shoulders a bit, as if trying to measure something invisible in the air in front of him. 'But I have faith in you. You'll come out of it fine, I'm sure. But you have to accept how things are done.'

From inside the empty storehouse Rhisiart could hear the work going on outside, the hammer blows echoing loudly as if he was a small insect inside a drum which was being beaten hard. Boom, boom, boom.

The carpenter Rowland Williams must have been busy nailing the shutters closed. Boom, boom, boom. Using nails made by Rhisiart himself, of course. Boom, boom, boom. More hammering, as if another kind of wood were being nailed across the shutters, just in case. And then a different kind of sound, some work being done on the door latch, turning the door into the door of a prison cell.

The door is opened once a day, light like a radiant wave flooding into the dark of his cell. Evan Evans is the one who greets him every time, delivering his food and drink for the day and emptying the chamber pot. He is accompanied by at least two armed men, both their muskets aimed at Rhisiart's chest.

And there's the sound of feet always, constantly, day and night. Rhisiart recognizes the rhythm – the pace of a guard, walking. A guard watching the prison. Round and round, around the building, walking in a circle all day and all night, the sounds of his steps a counterpoint to those of the sentries on the walls. The rhythms are meaningful, the sounds of feet hitting the ground or the wood defining the plan and beating out the measure of how it is meant to be.

* * *

And Rhisiart is measuring his wooden cell. Eight paces to the wall. Turn. Eight paces back to the fireplace. He walks slowly, thoughtfully, hoping a light will come, searching for answers with every step.

The room is completely empty except for his blanket and his pack. There's nothing in that but the few things he still has from his journey. His old clothing, the tattered remains he was wearing when he came ashore, the clothing that Malian and Asômi had turned into a new costume by sewing on patches of soft hide and decorating them with the excellence of their stitching. Gwilym Rowlant, the portly merchant in Portsmouth, the Welshman of Strawberry Bank, made him change those clothes. There's the mark of an Indian's hand on that stitching. Don't try to tell me otherwise. People will talk, Rhisiart. You shouldn't draw attention to yourself like that. Doesn't pay, my boy. And the thin pamphlet wrapped in soft material. His *awikhigan*, his map. Fine lines winding around, indicating mountains and lakes. Names and symbols. A guide.

And a few other things they have allowed him. A wooden bucket to hold clean water. A chamber pot – unfired earthenware, the work of one of the village women. A brown, wooden bowl to hold the food that is given to him every day.

There is not one piece of iron in the room. Nothing one could use to break the wood and open the shutters on the windows. Nothing but a bucket and a bowl that one could hold as a weapon when the door is opened, with two men aiming muskets at his chest.

He walks back and forth, his feet measuring and remeasuring. Eight paces to the wall and eight paces back.

–8–

Middle of May 1657

He walks slowly. Despite the circumstances, he's enjoying having something other than the wooden floor of his prison underfoot and feeling the sun on his face again. Step by step, first treading on earth and then hearing the crunch of the gravel of the circle road under his feet.

He has seen processions of the sort many times. The grave and studied motion, armed men guarding and making a show of it. A journey that led to judgement and punishment, the journey itself a ritual, the purposeful procession, a show and a lesson for observers. A blasphemous soldier being punished for breaking the rules of the Army of the Saints, being marched slowly to the middle of the camp where he would be the subject of a moral lesson for the others. Yes, he had witnessed this sort of procession before.

But he's not wearing shackles: that's one thing that Griffith John Griffith and his son have never made in their smithy. Nor have they bound his hands with rope: what could he possibly do, one man against an entire community?

All of the men of the militia walk with him. Other men must be walking the walls at the moment – a couple of young farmers who have volunteered for service. Evan Evans is leading them, his sword hanging from his belt. Two of them walk with their swords unsheathed, resting ritually on their shoulders, one on each side of Rhisiart. The giant Owen Williams and the Englishman David Newton. Behind them are the three others: Huw Jones, Benjamin Cotton and Tomos Bach, the youth who is not yet a man; each of these three with a musket over his shoulder. They're trying to march like soldiers, but Rhisiart notices that they are out of step. They are men who have never learned to march to the accompaniment of a drum, did not train under a sergeant, a professional soldier. But they're trying their best to make a show of the procession, demonstrating what worldly force New Jerusalem can muster.

They move on, walking around the circle, the ordinary houses on their left and the house of worship and ministers' houses to their right. Something catches Rhisiart's eye, some change. He turns to study the scene better. There are four ladders leaning against the house of worship and something sitting on the roof, something like a low wooden chimney.

They walk slowly and soberly, approaching the crossroads where the circle road meets the path that leads to the gates. They turn, Owen Williams trying to hold back his pace to make sure that he doesn't get ahead of the others, but it's difficult for the big man, and he has to walk awkwardly, half pausing and dragging one foot every now and again in order to keep the line fairly straight. On then, along the path, the south tower rising in front of them. Rhisiart looks up briefly, notes the shape of a man standing at the top of the tower, a musket in his hand. Who? One of the volunteers. Maybe John Williams, that young man eager to do militia duty every chance he gets.

But Rhisiart has to lower his eyes to the crowd. There, on the other side of the path, filling the space between the well and the wooden platform, are close to sixty people. The entire population of New Jerusalem, except for the volunteers guarding the walls, and the three standing on the platform itself. The two ministers, Pyrs Huws and Rhosier Wyn. And in the middle, between the two men, Rebecca Roberts. But although there are three standing there above the crowd, there are four living souls on the platform: Rebecca is holding her baby in her arms.

* * *

Feet had been a measure of time to him, the beat of his own feet on the wooden floor of his prison and the sound of the feet of the guards circling the storehouse outside. He called through the shutters that had been nailed tight over the windows, struck the door with his fist, crying out. Listen! Hello! Who's there? Evan Evans? Tomos? Huw Jones? Owen Williams? Answer me! Who's there? He tried tirelessly to get attention, make the guards answer him. Hello? Who's there? Tell me, what are the charges that have been brought against me? I have a right to know. Answer me!

And once, one night, a week or so after he was first imprisoned, an answer came. An uncertain voice, the voice of one not accustomed to talking very much. Rhisiart could imagine him standing there, his weapon in his hand, like the way he had stood there in the cemetery in the snow, the shovel in his hand. That was the only time he had heard Owen Williams say more than an occasional word. It was the only time he had had a conversation with the big, silent man.

'Be quiet, Rhisiart Dewi.' Though he was giving an order, his voice was not uncaring. 'Why are you shouting like that? No one will come to talk to you.'

'But you are talking to me, Owen. You are here.'

Silence again. No sound but the footfalls on the ground on the other side of the wall, and the guard walking his beat around the small prison.

Rhisiart stayed beside the window, waiting for the slow beat of feet to come nearer, and then called out again, pressing his mouth close to the wooden shutter.

'Owen? Owen! I have a right to know. It's not right to keep

anything from me now. It's not a time to tell lies, is it? How have I come to this crossroads?'

Rhisiart thought that Owen had paused for a minute, had waited there on the other side of the closed shutter, listening. But then he heard the sound of his heavy feet again, walking slowly away from the window, continuing with his careful movement, going around the little building step by step.

Rhisiart knocked on the window shutters once with his fist, hard, the blow echoing through the empty room. And again, hard, hammering. He flattened his hands and leaned against the shutters, pressing his forehead against the cold, hard wood. Thinking, considering what he could do to arouse mercy and get a response. And just then feet coming closer again, the cycle having been completed and the guard walking back to the same place outside the covered window. And the voice speaking, as quietly as possible but loud enough for Rhisiart to hear.

'I am not ignoring you, Rhisiart Dewi. It is not fair. You have a right to know.'

And then he summarized the charges that had been brought against Rhisiart. Using abusive language against the church. True, that was not an offence that he could be punished for, if he was not a member of the church. He could be exiled from the community, compelled to leave. But he had been accused of another offence, a serious one that he would have to answer.

'What, Owen? Tell me!'

'Unchasteness, Rhisiart Dewi. With the widow Rebecca Roberts. Elder Rhosier Wyn has accused you of having an indecent relationship outside of marriage. And he has called Evan Evans as witness to support his accusation.'

'How?'

'The two have seen you. Spending the night in her house. Often, they say. Word has gone about, and some others are saying that they too have noticed your relationship. Some are saying that you're the father of her baby.'

'They're lying, Owen!' He pounded the wood again, hard, bruising his hands. 'Lies, Owen! You know that! Look in your heart! Owen?

But the feet had moved on, and Owen did not answer him again that night.

There wasn't much to break up the days, only waking, eating a bit of flavourless food, drinking water, and pacing back and forth in his cell. Sometimes he would open his pack, using the scant light filtering through the chinks in the sealed shutters to study the fine lines and the words on his *awikhigan*, the map his friends had made for him. And sometimes he would finger his old clothing, admiring the stitches used to make new clothes from his old rags, beautiful handiwork by his friends.

Otherwise, the only thing that broke the monotony of his days was when the door was opened, once a day, and light flooded in, blinding him. Evan Evans taking the empty bowl and his bucket and giving him another bowl, full of food, and a bucket with fresh water spilling over its sides. And Rhisiart handing his chamber pot to him in exchange for an empty one, for use that day and that night. Other men were always there, two of them, each with a musket at the ready. Sometimes, Owen Williams was one of them. Once, before the leader of the militia shut the door and locked it, Rhisiart stood there, shielding his eyes from the sun and searching the face of the big man, but Owen lowered his eyes, avoiding Rhisiart's gaze and looking instead at Rhisiart's chest, the same spot where he was aiming his musket. And then the same old routine again. The guard's feet making a circle around the building, Rhisiart's feet striking the wooden floor inside, back and forth, back and forth.

'Pssst!'

One night, with the sound of fine rain pattering on the roof, a voice called through the window shutters. 'Pssst! Rhisiart Dewi? Are you awake?'

'I am, Owen. I'm here.'

'I've got something to tell you. Some news. You've got a right… a right to know.'

He was quiet for a while, the light whisper of the rain on the roof the only sound, and Rhisiart worried that the big man had changed his mind, had decided not to share this news. But then he spoke again, his voice murmuring, only a touch louder than the whisper of rain.

'They are considering bringing another charge against you.'

'What, Owen?'

'They've been here, you see. Yesterday. Stayed the night. They left this morning. The Praying Indians. And Samuel Appleton was with them. The minister.'

'Yes? How is…'

'Shush! Listen, Rhisiart Dewi. They had news. A rumour, to tell the truth. A story working its way from Strawberry Bank to Salem and on to the villages of the Wampanoag. From village to village. Travelling, as tales do.'

'Yes?'

'A strange story, you see. About a man. A man who had come out of the forest, a white man dressed like a wild Indian. And a black cat with him. He remained there for a while, but no one understood his mission very well. And then he went back into the forest. He vanished.'

Silence again, the rain whispering on the roof, like fingers lightly scratching the wood.

'Rhosier Wyn says that you were that man. And he says that it's possible that you are a witch.' A witch from the shadows of the forest, the paths of the dark children of Satan. 'He says he thinks that you were sent here to bewitch us. To get us to turn from the path we've been following since we came here.'

'That's a lie too, Owen.' He speaks softly, his voice as quiet as the other man's. 'You know that, Owen. A lie. Like the other accusations.'

'Not for me to say, Rhisiart Dewi. But you've got a right to know. Pray. Look into your soul. You have nothing to fear if you're telling the truth. So pray. And sleep for now.'

Owen Williams only addressed him through the walls of his prison once more after that. Just once, two days later. Speaking softly on the other side of the closed shutters, saying, 'Listen, Rhisiart Dewi. Listen, I've got more news. Rebecca Roberts has had her baby. Catherin Huws says she's a very healthy little girl.'

And then, today, early in the morning, just after Rhisiart had woken from a restless sleep to the singing of birds, the door opened slightly, a patch of light flowing across the wood floor, and the voice of Evan Evans called out.

'Today's the day. You'll be standing trial before midday.'

And the door slammed shut again.

No more food or a fresh bucket, but Rhisiart had a piece of bread and dried venison left over in his bowl and the previous bucket of water was still half full. And so after eating he took off his shirt and threw it on the floor next to his breeches and his stockings, cupped his hands and threw water on his face and washed. He drank and then lifted the bucket and poured the rest of the water over his head. He hadn't had a knife for a very long time, and his hair and beard had grown long. He shook his head, ran his fingers through his long, wet hair. Then he looked at the filthy clothes that lay in a small, untidy pile beside the blanket that served as his bed. They had begun to smell some time ago, and the cloth felt unwholesome on his skin. He kicked the pile away, walked over to his small pack, opened it, and took out his old clothes.

* * *

The crowd is opening up, people moving to one side or the other, allowing the procession to continue down the path, and then from the path to the platform. They're walking slowly, trying to march, and the giant Owen Williams falters every now and then, compelled to pause and drag his feet a little so as not to disturb the other men's rhythm.

Rhisiart is familiar with every single face in this crowd, although fear or hatred is causing some of them to look like different people today. He can remember the names of almost all of them. Huw Jones the farmer – not Huw Jones of the militia, who is walking behind him holding a musket, but the ploughman. His wife Abigail, their son Moses and their daughter Sabatha. The carpenter Rowland Williams and his wife Margaret. Their eldest daughter Margaret and her husband John Jones. Their son – their only child – Samuel. Jane, second daughter of Rowland and Margaret Williams, her husband David Davies and their daughter Marged. Anna, wife of John Williams, the carpenter's son, and their little son Richard – John himself must have volunteered to guard the walls. He never missed an opportunity to do militia work. Rachel Morgan and Sarah Williams, both childless widows, advanced in years. Robert and Anna Miles, a young married couple. Hannah Siôn, leaning on the arm of Ruth, eldest of Tomos and Esther Mansel's daughters. And the rest of the Mansels – Joshua, Dafydd, Sarah, Rachel, Tabitha and Dorcas, standing in a row alongside the path next to their parents. All of them quiet, all eyes on the slow procession. Faces he used to see every day. Some people he has come to know quite well. Occasionally, one he thought he knew very well. And then, at the edge, far from the path and the platform, the smith, Griffith John Griffith and his apprentice and son Ifan.

All eyes are on him. Everyone is staring at this strange man who is walking under the watchful eye of the militia. He's a mythical creature, the phantom of their imagination. His face pale, the face of one who has not seen the sun for a long time. A mane of untidy brown hair streaked with grey and his face half covered by an unruly beard, his clothing a combination of the world he's been living in and the wild world from which he arrived, not unlike civilized clothing but revealing the handiwork of the uncivilized inhabitants of the forest. He's a dangerous alien creature, and yet they know him. He speaks the same language as they, has learned their names and their secrets. Has been living here among them, almost as one of them. But yet here he is, transformed into his true self. A wild man of the forest, one who has travelled in the shadows with the dark children of the Evil One. Here he is, having corrupted one of them, a woman who had been living a godly life. Here he is, come to accept judgement and punishment.

Evan Evans leads them to the steps at the side of the platform, and he ascends them slowly, ritually, his sword hanging from his belt, his head held high. Owen Williams, his sword still on his shoulder, steps forward, since he cannot walk side by side with Rhisiart and David Newton, but they re-form their little line when they reach the platform. And then the other three come: Huw Jones, Benjamin Cotton, and Tomos Bach, each with his musket. Rhosier Wyn looks at him from the corner of his eye, and then joins Pyrs Huws on the other side of Rebecca, and Evan Evans arranges his men, bringing Rhisiart and his guards to the front of the platform. Owen stands between him and Rebecca on one side, with David Newton on the other side. Behind them are the three musketeers and their captain, Evan Evans.

'Let us pray for guidance.'

Pyrs Huws, projecting his voice from the platform, addressing the crowd stretching out before him. The men remove their hats and everyone in the crowd, even the smallest child, closes his eyes and bows his head. Rhisiart, his eyes wide open, is searching the crowd. From the heads of the Mansels, father, mother and the seven children, to the head of Hannah Siôn, each one bowed in prayer. From head to head, almost sixty of them altogether, and there, at the back, the bald head of Griffith John Griffith catching the sun, gleaming. Rhisiart turns his head slightly to the right, then to the left, noting the exact distance of Owen Williams and David Newton from him. He is about to turn to look at Evan Evans and the others, but the prayer comes to an end. He straightens, holds his head high. The warm May wind plays with his long hair a little, lifting locks from his shoulders, then letting them down again. 'Amen' rolls like a wave through the crowd, and they all lift their heads, the men putting their hats back on again.

'Brothers and sisters, we have come here to…'

The voice of Rhosier Wyn, loud and shrill, dying on the wind. Those standing further away take a step or two closer to the platform, pushing in to hear the Elder better. He goes on, describing in detail the accusations against the two and explaining the system. He says that this man and this widow woman have been accused of wantonness, of having an indecent relationship that is not acceptable outside the blessed seal of marriage. Public flogging is the punishment. Also, and much more serious, this man has been accused of consorting with the Devil and his servants; he is accused of acting on behalf of Satan, having been sent here to bewitch our people and lead them astray. The punishment of those who are guilty of such a thing is death, without delay. The jury has met to try these two persons and the verdict will now be revealed.

'We will continue, afterwards, to test the child who was born recently to Rebecca Roberts. We will test exactly as is our custom, and we will see whether the child was born to eternal life or was born to death.' He's carrying on at length and in detail, enjoying turning over every word on his tongue. He draws the crowd's attention to the serious nature of the day, the fact that there are three cases to test: one against the two adults, another against the man, and the matter of election in the baby.

The wind is rising, beginning to blow across the walls of New Jerusalem, raising dust from the ground and swirling between the buildings. It's difficult to hear the thin voice of the little Elder, and the crowd is pressing tighter, moving closer still to the platform. He goes on and on, detailing the nature of these three cases, suggesting that there is a connection, possibly, between the three, the alleged indecent relationship between the man and this woman, the baby who was born to her recently, and the work of Satan, who is planning the downfall of New Jerusalem, intending to claim this small island of light for the darkness of the wilderness again. He summarizes the essential points of their laws and the nature of their court. He says that the jury has met and that their judgement has been recorded. It is not a secular court, he emphasizes, but an ecclesiastical court. The address of Rhosier Wyn comes to an end with 'So be it' and 'Amen,' the high voice of the little man carried away on the wind that's busy rising.

Pyrs Huws summons Rebecca, then, saying that she has a right to speak, as she is a full member of the church. Speak before God and His Church, don't try to build a defence. The judgement has been decided by the church jury already, according to their custom; this is an opportunity to bare her soul to them before the Lord, before hearing that judgement.

Rhisiart can hear her clearing her throat, preparing to speak. He turns his head, peering, trying to see past the big body of Owen Williams, and by bending forward a little it's possible to see her. He can only see a small parcel, the blanket wrapped around the baby, but he knows that it's a little girl. Rebecca is holding her tight to her chest. She speaks loudly, her voice sounding more like one who is overwhelmed by weariness than one who is gripped by fear.

'I have only a few words that I want to say. You all know me, every one of you. You know me well. And you know that I'm telling the truth when I say that there isn't the least bit of fact in these accusations. I am not going to stand here, my innocent child in my arms, and argue, because I don't want to give that much credence to these lies. It's not fitting for me to try to argue against such untruths. Only to say that they are terrible lies, and ask you to believe me.'

The wind is getting up ever stronger, whipping through the crowd. Here and there a man lifts a hand to hold his hat firmly on his head and another removes his hat to keep it from flying away. A woman or girl holds her white cap on her head with both hands, fearing that the wind is stronger than the strings tied under her chin. Rhisiart lifts his head a little, standing straight, expecting the minister to call on him to say a word. But Rebecca has decided to speak again. She shouts, raising her voice above whistling of the wind.

'But I want to say one more thing. Before you try to take my child to the scales on top of the roof. I am asking you, mothers, and you, fathers, who have allowed the four ministers to take your tiny newborn children up to that despicable test. And I'm asking you to search your hearts and ask yourselves: were you seriously perfectly content to give up your baby, your children, to that horrible fate? I'm asking you, would you have accepted this system if no one else in New Jerusalem had expected you to accept it? And I'll tell you something else: Rhisiart Dewi is right in one thing. He says that these doctrines are the creations of humans, of men. The idea that one baby has been born to life and another to death, and that God has decided it all before their birth, is man-made, the creation of man. That doctrine is made by man, not by God. And a creation of man is that horrible ritual… the terrible test we have been observing here in New Jerusalem for years.'

'That's enough, Rebecca Roberts.'

He can't see Rhosier Wyn, and he's not attempting to move in order to see the little man, who's standing somewhere at the far end of the platform.

'Did you hear Minister Pyrs Huws? This is not a chance to make up excuses, but an opportunity to speak openly in the presence of God and His Church. A time to lay bare the soul and confess. We have not come here to judge and examine the essentials of our church. We have not come here to…'

'But that is what I want to do, Rhosier Wyn. That's what I want to do. Because it's high time for us to do just that. You mothers and fathers, I ask you again. A number of you have given your children into the hands of the ministers, the four of them. But Deacon Edward Jones has been in the ground for several years. And now the Doctor too has been buried. How many of you will be willing to give your baby into the hands of these two men? How many of you will be content to put the life of your child in the hands of Rhosier Wyn? How many of…'

'That's enough!' The Elder's voice is screeching, tearing through the wind and drowning Rebecca's voice. 'Be quiet, woman, or I'll have to ask Evan Evans to shut your mouth.'

'I want to speak. I want to say something now.' Another voice, from a different direction. Heads in the crowd turn towards it, and there she is, Hannah Siôn, the old widow, leaning on the arm of one of the Mansels. Her voice breaks every now and then, but she's calling out loudly enough for everyone to hear her. She says she knows that there is no basis to the accusations that have been brought against Rebecca and Rhisiart. Says that the young widow has been sharing her secrets with her for years, and Hannah Siôn knows that she was pregnant with the baby of her late husband, Robert Roberts, before this man arrived in New Jerusalem. She also says that she knows everyone in the village, everyone, and she insists that there is no one here who is more honest and upright than Rebecca Roberts.

'And I want to say one more thing before I stop, Rhosier Wyn. There is truth in what Rebecca Roberts says. The mothers of New Jerusalem have had to shoulder a particularly heavy burden. Yes, and the fathers too. And it's high time that we examine the doctrines of our church anew. Who can say that there is not truth in what Rebecca Roberts is saying? Who can say that Rhisiart Dewi is not right?'

'And here's another thing!' A deep voice, shouting from the back of the crowd. Griffith John Griffith, his hat in his hand, his bald head easily seen from the platform. 'Doctor Jones listened to Rhisiart Dewi. He asked him to become Deacon.'

Whispers rising through the crowd.

'It's true. Ask Minister Pyrs Huws. He knows.'

'Brothers and sisters, be quiet!' Rhosier Wyn is leaning his big belly against the railing of the platform, rising as high as possible on the tips of his toes and gesticulating wildly. 'Be quiet! We have not come here to discuss, but to hear judgement! We have met, I and Minister Pyrs Huws and seven other men of New Jerusalem, to form a court according to our church rules. And…'

'And what about me? I have a right to speak also!' Rhisiart is shouting, his words aimed at the pot-bellied little man, though his eyes are looking out at the crowd in front of him. 'I must have the opportunity to speak in self-defence too, and I…'

'No, you don't, Rhisiart Dewi! No, you don't! You are not a member of this church, and you are here at our pleasure only, and considering the nature of the charges that have been brought against you, I do not intend to let you charm these good people with your words.'

'Let him speak!' The voice of Griffith John Griffith.

'Yes, let him speak!' Another voice beside him – Ifan, standing there beside his father.

'Be quiet! Or I will have to bring charge against you too, for misbehaving in a church meeting.'

There's the sound of feet striking wood, and Rhisiart notices that other people are mounting the stairs to the platform. He turns to look. There are a number of men filing along the back of the platform. He looks to the other side and sees that they're forming a line there, behind Elder Rhosier Wyn and Pyrs Huws. Seven of them. He can see some of their faces – the carpenter Rowland Williams is there, yes, he and his two sons-in-law. The crowd has fallen silent again in the presence of the jury.

'Here we are, the seven who joined Minister Pyrs Huws and me at dawn today to pass judgement. And this is our verdict.'

The wind, like the crowd, has quietened, but the men who had removed their hats haven't put them on again. Rather, the others too have bared their heads.

'The jury was not unanimous. It was not unanimous in one of the charges that were heard by the court. And I have to note here publicly, according to our custom, that one of the ministers, namely Pyrs Huws, insists on finding them not guilty of the two charges. But though we are not in complete agreement, and though the voice of one minister is against the majority, the majority prevailed, namely eight in the first charge, seven in the second...'

And so the two have been found guilty.

Rhisiart had been preparing his words, shaping them as carefully as possible in his mind, ready to cast them from his tongue and win the hearts of the crowd. But he doesn't get to speak, only gets to go with Rebecca to receive their public flogging for their alleged sin. And then go, according to his sentence, to be put to death. Not to be murdered covertly in the forest like Miles Egerton, but to be killed openly according to the verdict of this church jury. Killing him here, in daylight, in the middle of New Jerusalem. And then the ministers will carry on with their ritual, taking Rebecca's little girl to the top of the ladder and putting her on the scales, and no one lifting a hand to stop them. Rhisiart himself will be dead, having failed to keep his promise to her. He had prepared his words that morning, had chosen them carefully and rehearsed them, but he doesn't get to use them. He considers stepping forward and shouting something before they gag him, plead with the jury and the crowd, not deliver a long, eloquent speech, just a short, sharp outburst. The words of that old Quaker, maybe – what authority gives you the power to persecute me like this?

But he knows that he has no words that can save him. He knows in his heart that he doesn't have a single word that can save *them*.

'Let us pray.' Pyrs Huws is leading them, concluding the proceedings from the platform. All in the crowd close their eyes and bow their heads, all but the smith and his son Ifan, and some small children who can't take their eyes from this great drama. He knows that all those on the platform are doing the same thing, each one bowing his head and closing his eyes. The have to; they're here, before the rest of the church, the models of godliness, following the prayer of their Minister. Each one of them will have bowed his head and closed his eyes, searching for the signs of grace in his own heart.

Rhisiart spins around, stepping back at the same time. Evan Evans looks up, startled, like one awakened from sleep by a sound, but it's too late. Rhisiart has taken his sword from the scabbard at his belt with his right hand and hits him hard in the jaw with his other fist. He doesn't wait to see if the man has fallen or not; he has only seconds to act. He doesn't fear the men with swords, even Owen Williams, but he has only a split second to strike down the musketeers before they have a chance to shoot.

One small, quick step and the front of his sword is sinking into Ben Cotton, into that soft spot just under his chest bone. The musket falls from his hands and hits the floor with a crack and he opens his eyes, looking stunned for a moment before he falls.

Rhisiart moves before the dead body can hit the floor. He's next to Huw Jones, his left hand seizing the man's musket and his right hand taking the sword to the man's neck, the blood gushing from the ugly gash in his throat and his breath rasping, failing to reach his lungs.

And then there is Tomos Bach, the lad not yet eighteen years old. Rhisiart strikes him hard in the face with the hilt of his sword, not out of mercy but from necessity, since he is standing too close to him to be able to draw his right hand far enough back to reach him with the blade. It's enough of a blow to floor the lad, his musket falling from his arms as he stumbles to his knees, his hands trying to hold back the blood that's flowing from his nose.

Confusion and turmoil, the crowd surging, voices shouting and calling out, but Rhisiart is not fully conscious of what's happening away from the platform. Owen Williams and David Newton are facing him, holding their swords awkwardly, and Evan Evans too is busy, taking up the weapon of one of the dead men.

The work is easy. He leaps to the side, strikes, and his weapon sinks into the belly of Evan Evans. Steps away and turns on David Newton, strikes again, twice, his blade reaching the man's neck, just under the chin. Owen strikes awkwardly with his sword, as if he's aiming at a piece of motionless wood with an axe. And the big man moves slowly. He ought to disarm him; the quiet giant doesn't deserve this end. But Rhisiart's muscles are moving more quickly than his mind. He steps aside and thrusts, his blade slicing through Owen's ribs. The militia man falls slowly, first to one knee and then to the other. Today is not a day to hide anything, Owen, not a day to tell lies: it's all in the open today.

Rhisiart turns to face the closest enemies, the other men standing there on the platform – the two ministers, the carpenter Rowland Williams, and the rest of the jury. But not one of the nine has moved to lift a weapon to challenge him. Some have retreated from the platform, jumping over the railing and melting into the riotous crowd. The others, Rhosier Wyn among them, are pressed against the railing, their eyes wide, staring at him, this wild man, his long wild hair falling to his shoulders and blood dripping from the blade of the sword he holds. Pyrs Huws steps aside, and there's not a hint of fear in his eyes. He stands there, straight and quiet, watching God's judgement here before him on the platform of punishment of New Jerusalem. And there next to him is Rebecca, holding her baby tight to her chest, her eyes challenging the crowd. He remembers that there is another one, and he turns quickly to look at him, but Tomos Bach is not fighting. He stands there, his nose broken, blood reddening the lower half of his face, his eyes wild, searching for an escape but failing to move.

Bam!

A shot.

A guard on top of the south tower has fired. John Williams, no doubt, the eldest son of the carpenter, the first to volunteer, eagerly doing the work of the militia.

Rhisiart is facing Tomos, his back to the gates and the tower, but he knows immediately that a shot has been fired.

A wound, a hit, pain in his back.

He's expecting it, the thought rushing quickly through his mind. Yes, so it is. So it is, I die here, in the heat of the sun, in May.

But it's an imagined wound, an instinctive response of his flesh to that possible death, the one that has failed to take him from this life today.

Tomos Bach staggers back, and then takes a step forward again, trying to regain his footing, his hands going to the spot of blood that's spreading across his shirt, failing to comprehend why the blood coming out of his nose is turning up here, failing to understand what hit him so hard in the chest. For some reason, Rhisiart wants to step aside; he wants to drop his sword and hold the youth in his arms. But Tomos falls before he can act, and Rhisiart turns back to the crowd. The house of worship is not far, and there are weapons there, in the chests under the windows; he can't let a single person reach that last stronghold.

But he sees that no further action is needed. It's all over. Griffith John Griffith and Ifan stand beside the platform, holding the axes they had brought from the smithy, glaring about threateningly, ready to move. There's a challenging look in the eyes of some of the men, but they have been surrounded by others – their wives, their mothers, their children – who block their way and keep them out of the action. Ruth Mansel grabs her father's arm and the old widow Hannah Siôn is hanging onto his other arm with all her strength, and Esther Mansel, his wife, is standing in front of him, spitting words into his face. The man lowers his eyes and his body slumps, the fight gone out of him.

Rhisiart sees other, similar little dramas here and there in the crowd. The church is divided, one half keeping the other from acting. Gradually the crowd falls silent, the agitated men yielding and accepting order.

–ΔΩ–

The company walks slowly under the south tower, making their way quietly through the gates. They walk pensively, each step taking them in the direction of another future.

There are seven of them. Anna and Robert Miles, the young married couple, expecting their first child before the end of the coming winter.

Griffith John Griffith and his son. They have set up a new memorial on the grave of Ifan's mother, the first stone one in the cemetery, and now they are leaving. The smith will see a horse again before his eyes fail and he wants to teach his son to shoe, show him the way to set the nails tenderly into the hoof of a living animal.

Rebecca holds her baby daughter. She will be baptized in a church after they reach the end of their journey, but she has been named already. Ffydd – that's her name, but her mother accepts the fact that the English will call her Faith.

And Rhisiart Dafydd, enjoying the feel of a May breeze playing in his long hair, and lifting his face a little towards the sun. His mind is also on the thin booklet that he's carefully rewrapped and put in the pack on his back – the *awikhigan*, the map that will lead them through the mountains and along the rivers to the shores of this free and open land.

They walk on, leaving the walls of New Jerusalem behind, moving towards the comfort of the forest's shadows.

Epilogues

1658

Oliver Cromwell is dead from the fever. His son Richard has succeeded him as Lord Protector, but the leading men of Parliament don't trust him and there are whispers in the corridors. The army is restless, arguments ripping apart the ranks, and thousands of soldiers asking: what man has the authority to command us, what earthly authority is higher than that of the Army of the Saints? Not far from Cheapside there is a narrow street next to an alehouse, a courtyard and stables behind the largest house on that street. There, on the cobbles of the courtyard, in the shadows of the high walls, John Powel and two of his soldiers are burning papers. The old Colonel knows that the tide is turning and he's leaving before he gets caught in the flood. He's burning his papers, his secrets feeding the flames and rising in ashes on the London breeze. He holds one piece of paper in his hand, a letter he received recently, all the way from America. He stands there next to the bonfire, reading the words once again, then he smiles and commends the letter to the flames' embrace.

1659

Morgan Llwyd too is in the grip of the fever. Preacher, writer, visionary – he has laboured for many years and strived to follow the proper path, but his earthly journey is nearly over. He's been living between sleep and wakefulness over these last days, dreaming on his deathbed, his mind meandering through the bog of his memories. He's thinking about his old friend John ap John, who left his flock to join those who would come to be called Quakers. He smiles, remembering his friend chastising him gently before leaving Wrexham, urging him to listen to the voice in his own heart. The window of his bedroom is open at his own request, even though his servant believes that it invites unhealthy air. A dove comes to roost on the window sill, and he thinks he sees a small drop of blood on its light grey breast feathers. He tries to look closer, but the bird has flown off. He closes his eyes, accepting that it was his imagination. He sinks quietly into sleep and doesn't wake again.

1660

Gwilym Rowlant shifts slightly, the chair creaking under his weight. It's not the heat from the fire that makes his cheeks so rosy, but the warmth of the company. His life is comfortable, his business flourishing and the town he takes such pride in is growing, but nothing pleases him more than this simple evening with the opportunity to chat leisurely in his native tongue. He goes through his usual antics, teasing and admonishing playfully. He tells Rebecca that she ought to marry again. She smiles good-naturedly and says she doesn't need a husband and that she's terribly grateful for what family she has in this world. Gwilym Rowlant smiles, the familiar words warming his heart. He tells her then that she should not have to work with the midwife, and reminds her that he has sufficient means to support her. She thanks him, and says firmly that she doesn't want an idle life. The old merchant smiles again, admiring her industry and her determination. The little girl sits on the floor between the two chairs, stroking the old black tomcat sleeping in front of the fire. She's three years old and this is her world, the only life she remembers. Gwilym Rowlant teases her about the animal, saying that it's a wondrous creature that came ashore from the depths of the ocean. The girl smiles indulgently at the old man and reminds him that cats do not like the water. Gwilym Rowlant chuckles quietly and brings his long clay pipe to his lips. He draws deeply on it, the smoke curling slowly around his head.

1661

The monarchy has been restored and Charles II is on the throne. It has been decided that the dead should be punished. They dig up the body of Oliver Cromwell and hang him, as if they were executing a living person. The body becomes an attraction, a wonder. They hang him in chains on one of the streets of Tyburn and let the public come to poke fun at his bones. They cut off what's left of his head and stick it on a pole outside Westminster. There it remains for years. Those who have stood under this *memento mori* insist that they have heard a voice, whispering like a breeze rustling dead leaves. It's difficult to hear it above the clamour and bustle of the streets of London, but they have heard it. Worldly things are not important, sisters – the skull presses close behind the face of every one of us.

1675

New England is at war. Native forces are fighting the British, following a man the English call King Philip. He's not a king but he is a skilful leader, and his real name, his Algonquian name, is Metacom. A number of nations join in this battle against the English – those Wampanoag who have not become Christians, the Narragansett, the Nipmuck, and the Pocumtuck. And further to the north another nation joins the effort, a people the English call Abenaki – the Wôbanakiak, the people who live in the Land of the Dawn. The war lasts for over a year, and by its end thousands of the British will have died and half of their towns and villages will have disappeared.

1676

The natives come to New Jerusalem in the spring. Not the Christian Wampanoag, the Praying Indians who have been visiting the settlement regularly for years, but people who have not accepted the white man's ways. They're Wôbanakiak forces, warriors of the Land of the Dawn, having come to sweep the darkness from their lands. They will leave nothing but ashes behind them, a big black circle smouldering in a clearing in the forest. A name is forgotten that will never be recorded on any map.

1695

There's a smithy in a small village in Pennsylvania, by a riverbank in the district of the Welsh Tract. The smith has been there for years, but he's still surprisingly strong in spite of his age. His hair is white and his greying beard is long and unkempt, and the village children whisper tales about him to each other. He's a wild man, one who came here from the forest years ago, before the woods were cut down to make fields. He's half Welsh, half bear, and half Indian. Yes, there are three halves in him, not two; he's an otherworldly creature, there's more to him than you find in an ordinary man. Today he's working on a large piece. He has two apprentices, and he needs them both, each using tongs to hold one end of the heavy piece in place on the anvil. A ploughshare, to be finished before the farmers head for the fields that spring. Although he's old enough to be grandfather to the youths, it is he who does the hammering. His hammer sings on the anvil, and his mind is singing too. He sings quietly, to himself, and the apprentices can't hear him. But the ploughshare hears; he's folding the secret words into the hot iron, and he knows they will go into the warm earth when the ploughshare cuts its first furrow.

1721

The lad has been climbing up to the loft in the stable. His father says that the building was a smithy in the old days. Yes, the building is old, one of those that was not burned during the wars, one of the oldest ones in this part of Wrexham. The lad has spent hours here, following his curiosity and searching every inch of the building. Although the shadows are long in the loft, the slates are loose and there are holes in the roof, with enough afternoon light streaming in for him to see. He finds a small stone in the wall that's loose, and when he pulls it out, he sees a parcel inside: several layers of material, the last soaked in oil to prevent rust, protecting the bits of iron inside. He studies them, examines them. There are several nails. Little ones. Test pieces made by a smith's apprentice in the distant past. And there are other small items. One is in the shape of a spoon – a little iron spoon, amazingly fine. He begins to rewrap the treasures, deciding to keep them there in the wall, a secret that no one but he knows about, but the little spoon slips out of his hand. It lands on the wooden floor of the loft and bounces once, the iron singing a clear, high note, leaving words hanging like crystal in the air: *If this were fine enough, I'd give it to you, Elisabeth.*

Author's notes and acknowledgements

Patrick K Ford brought this book into being. His enthusiasm for the original Welsh novel, his commitment to producing this English translation of it, and his generosity in including me in the process are great gifts which I will never be able to repay. The many conversations we have had about the book during recent years have made me see my own story in new ways. It is his story now as well, and I cannot thank him enough for embracing it and making it his own.

I would like to thank the Welsh Books Council for supporting both the Welsh and the English versions of this novel. Similarly, I am extremely grateful to Y Lolfa for publishing both *Y Fro Dywyll* and *Dark Territory*. The Commissioning Editor, Lefi Gruffudd, has been a source of encouragement and support since I first started working with Y Lolfa. Carolyn Hodges edited this book with great care; both Patrick K Ford and I are indebted to her for her attention to detail, her great energy, and her ability to get inside the story.

Ac yn olaf, hoffwn ddiolch i'r rhai pwysicaf am eu cefnogaeth gyson – Judith, Megan a Luned.

Jerry Hunter
October 2017

Also from Y Lolfa:

£8.95

y Lolfa

The Shadow of

Nanteos

JANE BLANK

£8.99

Secret Shelter
ROB GITTINS
'Impressive, hard-hitting, well-plotted
and superbly written.'
Crime Review
y Lolfa

Dark Territory is just one of a whole range of publications from Y Lolfa. For a full list of books currently in print, send now for your free copy of our new full-colour catalogue. Or simply surf into our website

www.ylolfa.com

for secure on-line ordering.

TALYBONT CEREDIGION CYMRU SY24 5HE
e-mail ylolfa@ylolfa.com
website www.ylolfa.com
phone (01970) 832 304
fax 832 782